D0397534

WITHDRAWN

SCIENCE FICTION MCD
McDonald, Ian, 1960-
Brasyl

1-08

DURANGO PUBLIC LIBRARY
DURANGO, COLORADO 81301

BRASYL

ALSO BY IAN McDONALD

RIVER OF GODS

IAN McDONALD
BRASYL

an imprint of **Prometheus Books**
Amherst, NY

Published 2007 by Pyr®, an imprint of Prometheus Books

Brasyl. Copyright © 2007 by Ian McDonald. All rights reserved. No part of this publication may be reproduced, stored in a retrieval system, or transmitted in any form or by any means, digital, electronic, mechanical, photocopying, recording, or otherwise, or conveyed via the Internet or a Web site without prior written permission of the publisher, except in the case of brief quotations embodied in critical articles and reviews.

Inquiries should be addressed to
Pyr
59 John Glenn Drive
Amherst, New York 14228–2197
VOICE: 716–691–0133, ext. 207
FAX: 716–564–2711
WWW.PYRSF.COM

11 10 09 08 07   5 4 3 2 1

Library of Congress Cataloging-in-Publication Data

McDonald, Ian, 1960–
    Brasyl : a novel / by Ian McDonald.
        p. cm.
    ISBN 978–1–59102–543–6 (alk. paper)
    1. Brazil—Fiction. I. Title.

PR6063.C38B73 2007
823'.914—dc22

2007001563

Printed in the United States on acid-free paper

CONTENTS

This one, finally, for Enid

OUR
LADY
OF
PRODUCTION
VALUES

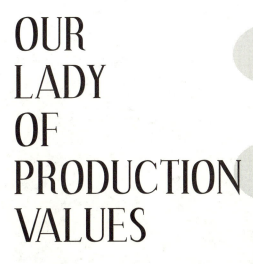

MAY 17–19, 2006

Marcelina watched them take the car on Rua Sacopã. It was a C-Class Mercedes, a drug dealer's car, done up to the tits by the Pimp My Ride: Brasileiro
design crew with wheel trim and tail and blue lighting that ran up and down
the subframe. Subwoofers the size of suitcases. The design boys had done a
good job; it looked a fistful more than the four thousand reis Marcelina had
paid at the city car pound.

One time they passed it: three guys in basketball shorts and vests and
caps. The first time the looking time. A second time, this time the checking
time, pretending to be interested in the trim and the rosary and Flamengo
key-fob hanging from the mirror (sweet touch) and was it CD multichanger
or a hardpoint for MP3?

Go, my sons, you know you want it, thought Marcelina in the back of the chase car in a driveway two hundred meters up hill. It's all there for you, I made it that way, how can you resist?

The third time, that is the taking time. They gave it ten minutes' safety, ten minutes in which Marcelina sat over the monitor fearing would they come back would someone else get there first? No, here they were swinging down the hill, big pretty boys long-limbed and loose, and they were good, very good. She hardly saw them try the door, but there was no mistaking the look of surprise on their faces when it swung open. Yes, it is unlocked. And yes, the keys are in it. And they were in: door closed, engine started, lights on.

"We're on!" Marcelina Hoffman shouted to her driver and was immediately flung against the monitor as the SUV took off. God and Mary they were hard on it, screaming the engine as they ripped out onto the Avenida Epitácio Pessoa. "All cars all cars!" Marcelina shouted into her talkback as the Cherokee swayed into the traffic. "We have a lift we have a lift! Heading north for the Rebouças Tunnel." She poked the driver, an AP who had confessed a love for car rallying, hard in the shoulder. "Keep him in sight, but don't scare him." The monitor was blank. She banged it. "What is wrong with this thing?" The screen filled with pictures, feed from the Mercedes' lipstick-cams. "I need real-time time-code up on this." *Don't let them find the cameras*, Marcelina prayed to Nossa Senhora da Valiosa Producão, her divine patroness. Three guys, the one in the black and gold driving, the one in the Nike vest, and the one with no shirt at all and a patchy little knot of wiry hair right between his nipples. Sirens dopplered past; Marcelina looked up from her monitor to see a police car turn across four lanes of traffic on the lagoon avenue and accelerate past her. "Get me audio."

João-Batista the soundman waggled his head like an Indian, the gesture made the more cartoonish by his headphones. He fiddled with the mixer slung around his neck and gave a tentative thumbs-up. Marcelina had rehearsed this—rehearsed this and rehearsed this and rehearsed this—and now she could not remember a single word. João-Batista looked at her: *Go on, it's your show.*

"You like this car? You like it?" She was shrieking like a shoutygirl-presenter. João-Batista looking pityingly at her. On the car cams the boys looked as if a bomb had gone off under their *Knight Rider* LEDS. *Don't bail, Lady Lady Lady, don't bail.* "It's yours! It's your big star prize. It's all right, you're on a TV game show!"

"It's a shit old Merc with a cheap pimp from graphics," Souza the driver muttered. "And they know that."

Marcelina knocked off the talkback.

"Are you the director here? Are you? Are you? It'll do for the pilot."

The SUV veered abruptly, sending Marcelina reeling across the backseat. Tires squealed. God she loved this.

"They decided against the tunnel. They're taking a trip to Jardim Botânica instead."

Marcelina glanced at the satnav. The police cars were orange flags, their careful formation across Rio's Zona Sul breaking up and reordering as the chase car refused to drive into their trap. *That's what it's about*, Marcelina said to herself. *That's what makes it great TV.* Back on the talkback again.

"You're on *Getaway*. It's a new reality show for Canal Quatro, and you're on it! Hey, you're going to be big stars!" That got them looking at each other. Attention culture. It never failed to seduce the vain Carioca. Best reality show participants on the planet, cariocas. "That car is yours, absolutely, guaranteed, *legal*. All you have to do is not get arrested by the cops for half an hour, and we've told them you're out there. You want to play?" That might even do for the strapline: *Getaway: You Want to Play?*

Nike vest boy's mouth was moving.

"I need audio out," Marcelina shouted. João-Batista turned another knob. Baile funk shook the SUV.

"I said, for this heap of shit?" Nike vest shouted over the booty beat. Souza took another corner at tire-shredding speed. The orange flags of the police were flocking together, route by route cutting off possible escape. For the first time Marcelina believed she might have a program here. She thumbed the talkback off. "Where are we going?"

"It could be Rocinha or up through Tijuca on the Estrada Dona Casto-rina." The SUV slid across another junction, scattering jugglers, their balls cascading around them, and windshield-washers with buckets and squeegees. "No, it's Rocinha."

"Are we getting anything usable?" Marcelina asked João-Batista. He shook his head. She had never had a soundman who wasn't a laconic bastard, and that went for soundwomen too.

"Hey hey hey, could you turn the music down a little?"

DJ Furação's baile beat dropped to thumbs-up levels from João-Batista.

"What's your name?" Marcelina shouted at Nike vest.

"You think I'm going to tell you, in a stolen car with half Zona Sul up my ass? This is entrapment."

"We have to call you something," Marcelina wheedled.

"Well, Canal Quatro, you can call me Malhação, and this América"—the driver took his hands off the wheel and waved—"and O Clono." Chest-hair pushed his mouth up to the driver's headrest minicam in the classic MTV rock-shot.

"Is this going to be like *Bus 174*?" he asked.

"Do you want to end up like the guy on *Bus 174*?" Souza murmured. "If they try and take that into Rocinha, it'll make *Bus 174* look like a First Communion party."

"Am I going to be like a big celebrity then?" O Clono asked, still kissing the camera.

"You'll be in *Contigo.* We know people there, we can set something up."

"Can I get to meet Gisele Bundchen?"

"We can get you on a shoot with Gisele Bundchen, all of you, and the car. Getaway stars and their cars."

"I like that Ana Beatriz Barros," América said.

"Hear that? Gisele Bundchen!" O Clono had his head between the seats, bellowing in Malhação's ear.

"Man, there is going to be no Gisele Bundchen, or Ana Beatriz Barros," Malhação said. "This is TV; they'll say anything to keep the show going. Hey Canal Quatro, what happens if we get caught? We didn't ask to be in this show."

"You took the car."

"You wanted us to take the car. You left the doors open and the keys in."

"Ethics is good," João-Batista said. "We don't get a lot of ethics in reality TV."

Sirens on all sides, growing closer, coming into phase. Police cars knifed past on each side, a blast, a blur of sound and flashing light. Marcelina felt her heart kick in her chest, that moment of beauty when it all works together, perfect, automatic, divine. Souza slid the SUV into top gear as he accelerated past the shuttered-up construction gear where the new favela wall was going up.

"And it's not Rocinha," Souza said, pulling out past a tanker-train. "What else is down there? Vila Canoas, maybe. Whoa."

Marcelina looked up from her monitor, where she was already planning her edit. Something in Souza's voice.

"You're scaring me, man."

"They just threw a three-sixty right across the road."

"Where are they?"

"Coming right at us."

"Hey, Canal Quatro." Malhação was grinning into the sun-visor cam. He had very good, white big teeth. "I think there's a flaw in your format. You see, there's no motivation for me to risk jail just for a shit secondhand Merc. On the other hand, something with a bit of retail potential . . ."

The Mercedes came sliding across the central strip, shedding graphics' loving pimp job all over the highway. Souza stood on the antilocks. The SUV stopped a spit from the Mercedes. Malhação, América, and O Clono were already out, guns held sideways in that way that had become fashionable since *City of God*.

"Out out out out out." Marcelina and crew piled onto the road, traffic blaring past.

"I need the hard drive. If I haven't got the hard drive I haven't got a show, at least leave me that."

América was already behind the wheel.

"This is sweet," he declared.

"Okay, take it," Malhação said, handing monitor and terabyte LaCie to Marcelina.

"You know, you kinda have hair like Gisele Bundchen," O Clono called from the rear seat. "But curlier, and you're a lot smaller."

Engine cries, tires smoked, América handbraked the SUV around Marcelina and burned out west. Seconds later police cars flashed.

"Now that," said João-Batista, "is what I call great TV."

The Black Plumed Bird smoked in the edit suite. Marcelina hated that. She hated most things about the Black Plumed Bird, starting with the 1950s clothes she wore unironically in defiance of trend and fashion (there is no fashion without personal style, querida) and that nevertheless looked fantastic, from the real nylon stockings, with seams—never pantyhose, bad bad thrush—to the Coco Chanel jacket. If she could have worn sunglasses and a headscarf in the edit suite, she would have. She hated a woman so manifestly confident in her mode, and so correct in it. She hated that the Black Plumed Bird could exist on a diet of import vodka and Hollywood cigarettes, had never been seen taking a single stroke of exercise and yet would have emerged from an all-night edit radiating Grace Kelly charm and not skull-fucked on full-sugar guaraná. Most of all she hated that, for all her studious retro and grace, the Black Plumed Bird had graduated from media school one year ahead of Marcelina Hoffman and was her senior commissioning editor. Marcelina had bored so many researchers and development producers over Friday cocktails at Café Barbosa about the stunts and deviations the Black Plumed Bird had pulled to get head of Factual Entertainment at Canal Quatro that they could recite them now like Mass. *She didn't know the mike was still live and the guys in the scanner heard her say . . .* (All together) *Fuck me till I fart . . .*

"The soundtrack is a key USP; we're going for Grand Theft Auto/Eighties retro. That's that English new romantic band who did that song about Rio but the video was shot in Sri Lanka."

"I thought that one was 'Save a Prayer,'" said Leandro, moving a terracotta ashtray with an inverted flowerpot for a lid toward the Black Plumed Bird. He was the only editor in the building not to have banned Marcelina from his suite and was considered as imperturbable as the Dalai Lama, even after an all-nighter "'Rio' was shot in Rio. Stands to reason."

"Are you like some ninja master of early eighties English new romantic music?" Marcelina sniped. "Were you even born in 1984?"

"I think you'll find that particular Duran Duran track was 1982," the Black Plumed Bird said, carefully stubbing her cigarette out in the proffered ashtray and replacing the lid. "And the video was shot in Antigua, actually. Marcelina, what happened to the crew car?"

"The police found it stripped to the subframe on the edge of Mangueira. The insurance will cover it. But it shows it works; I mean, the format needs a little tweaking, but the premise is strong. It's good TV."

The Black Plumed Bird lit another cigarette. Marcelina fretted around the door to the edit suite. *Give me it give me it give it just give me the series.*

"It is good TV. I'm interested in this." That was as good as you ever got from the Black Plumed Bird. Marcelina's heart misfired, but that was likely the stimulants. Come down slowly, all say, and then a normal night's bed; that, in her experience, was the best descent path out of an all-nighter. Of course if it was a commission, she might just go straight down to Café Barbosa, bang on Augusto's door with the special Masonic Knock, and spend the rest of the day on the champagne watching roller boys with peachlike asses blade past. "It's clever and it's sharp and it hits all our demographics, but it's not going to happen." The Black Plumed Bird held up a lace-gloved hand to forestall Marcelina's protests. "We can't do it." She tapped at the wireless control pad and called up the Quatro news channel. Ausiria Menendes was on the morning shift. Heitor would probably call her midday for a little lunch hour. The scuttling fears and anxieties of a middle-aged news anchor were the very un-thing she needed this day. A fragment seemed to have fallen out of her brain onto the screen: Police cars pulled in around a vehicle on the side of a big highway. *São Paulo*, said the caption. Cut to a helicopter shot of military cruisers and riot-control vehicles parked up outside the gate of Guarulhos Main Penitentiary. Smoke spiraled up from inside the compound; figures occupied the half-stripped roof with a bedsheet banner, words sprayed in red.

"The PCC has declared war with the police," said the Black Plumed Bird. "There are at least a dozen cops dead already. They've got hostages in the jail. Benfica will start next and then . . . No, we can't do it."

Marcelina hung by the door, blinking softly as the television screen receded into a tiny jiggling mote at the end of a long, dim tunnel buzzing with cans of Kuat and amphetamines, Leandro and the Black Plumed Bird strange limousines playing bumper-tag with her. She heard her voice say, as if from a fold-back speaker, "We're supposed to be edgy and noisy."

"There's edgy and noisy and there's not getting our broadcast license renewed." The Black Plumed Bird stood up, dusted cigarette ash from her lovely gloves. "Sorry, Marcelina." Her nylon-hosed calves brushed electrically as she opened the edit suite door. The light was blinding, the Black Plumed Bird an amorphous umbra in the center of the radiance, as if she had stepped into the heart of the sun.

"It'll blow over, it always does. . . ." But Marcelina had contravened her own law: Never protest never question never plead. You must love it enough to make it but not so much you cannot let it fall. Her chosen genre—factual entertainment—had a hit rate of a bends-inducing 2 percent, and she had grown the skin, she had learned the kung-fu: never trust it until the ink was on the contract, and even then the scheduler giveth and the scheduler taketh away. But each knock-back robbed of a little energy and impetus, like stopping a supertanker by kicking footballs at it. She could not remember when she had last loved it.

Leandro was closing down the pilot and archiving the edit-decision list.

"Don't want to rush you, but I've got Lisandra in on *Lunch-Hour Plastic Surgery.*"

Marcelina scooped up her files and hard drive and thought that it might be very very good to cry. Not here, never here, not in front of Lisandra.

"Oh, hey, Marcelina, say, sorry about *Getaway.* You know, that's such bad timing. . . ."

Lisandra settled herself into Marcelina's chair and set her shot-logs and water bottle precisely on the desk. Leandro clicked up bins.

"Isn't that always the business?"

"You know, you take it so philosophically. If it was me, I'd probably just go and get really really drunk somewhere."

Well, that was an option, but now that you've mentioned it, I would sooner wear shit for lipstick than get wrecked at Café Barbosa.

Marcelina imagined slowly pouring the acid from an uncapped car battery onto Lisandra's face, drawing Jackson Pollock drip-patterns over her ice-cream peach-soft skin. *Lunch-Hour Plastic Surgery* this, bitch.

Gunga spoke the rhythm, the bass chug, the pulse of the city and the mountain. Médio was the chatterer, the loose and cheeky gossip of the street and the bar, the celebrity news. Violinha was the singer, high over bass and rhythm, hymn over all, dropping onto the rhythm of gunga and médio then cartwheeling away, like the spirit of capoeira itself, into rhythmic flights and plays, feints and improvisations, shaking its ass all over the place.

Marcelina stood barefoot in a circle of music, chest heaving, arm upheld. Sweat ran copiously from her chin and elbow onto the floor. Tricks there, deceivings to be used in the play of the roda. She beckoned with her upraised hand, suitably insolent. Her opponent danced in the ginga, ready to attack and be attacked, every sense open. To so insolently summon an opponent to the dance had jeito, was malicioso.

É, I went walking, the capoeiristas chanted.

In the cool morning
I met Great São Bento
Playing cards with the Dog.

The roda clapped in counterpoint to the urgent, ringing rhythms of the berimbaus. So seemingly unsubtle an instrument, the berimbau, its origins as a war-bow apparent in the curve of the wooden verga, the taut cord. So homespun: a gourd, a piece of wire from the inside of a car tire, a bottle cap pressed against the string, a stick to beat it with, and only two notes in its round belly. A favela instrument. When she began to play capoeira, Marcelina had scorned the berimbau; she was here for the fight, secondarily for the dance aspect of the jogo; but there is no dance without music, and as she learned the sequences, she had come to appreciate their twanging, slangy voices, then to understand the rhythmic subtleties that lay within a trio of instruments that spoke only six notes. Mestre Ginga never tired of telling her she would never attain the corda vermelha if she neglected the berimbau. Capoeira was more than fighting. Marcelina had ordered a médio from the Fundação Mestre Bimba in Salvador, the spiritual home of the classical Capoeira Angola. It lay beside her sofa unopened in its padded instrument bag. For Marcelina in her red-and-white striped Capris and crop top, this day with her defeat at work lying still like sick in her throat, fighting was very good indeed.

Mestre Bimba, Mestre Nestor,
Mestres Ezequiel and Canjiquinha
These are the world-famous men
Who taught us how to play and sing, the roda chanted, ringed three deep inside the humid, verdant concrete quadrangle painted with Umbanda saints and legendary mestres of history caught in leaps of kung-fu-wire-ballet grace. Again Marcelina beckoned, smiling. The rhythm had dropped from the fighting São Bento Grande to the canto de entrada, a formality of the Angolan School Mestre Ginga retained for his own Senzala Carioca, praising famous and lost mestres. Jair stepped across the roda and locked his upraised hand with Marcelina's. Face-to-face they stepped slowly, formal as a foro, around the circle of hands and voices and beating berimbaus. He was a cocky boy with ten years on Marcelina, tall and black and good-looking, if in an obvious and preening way, poised, assured to a point of cockiness. He didn't fight women and whites. White people moved like trees, like truckloads of pigs on the way to the abattoir. Women were incapable of ever understanding malicia. It was a guy thing. Little white women with German names and German skins were most ridiculous of all. They shouldn't even waste their time trying to play capoeira.

This little white German woman had surprised him twice already, the first with a lyrical S-dobrado that began with a feint kick from the floor— only ever hands and feet to touch the earth—that wheeled into a single-hand-stand and a sweeping blow from the right leg that Jair evaded by dropping into an immediate defensive negativa, arm raised to defend the face. Marcelina had easily foreseen and evaded his meia lua sweeping kick. É! É! the spectators had chanted. The second time they had gasped and clapped aloud as she dived into a meia lua pulada, the hand-spin kick that was Rio-Senzala's great gift to the game of capoeira. She had caught Mestre Ginga in her peripheral vision; he squatted with his carved stick like an old Angolan king, his face stone. Old bastard. Nothing she did ever impressed him. *You're not Yoda.* Then a chapeu-de-couro had come wheeling in, Jair wholly airborne, and Marcelina barely dropped back into a queda de quarto, hands and feet planted on the dance floor, watching the fighting foot sweep over her face.

At first capoeira had been another wave on the zeitgeist upon which

Marcelina Hoffman surfed, driven by the perpetual, vampiric hunger for fresh cool. At Canal Quatro lunch was for losers, unless spent in a valid pursuit. For a while power walking had been the thing, Marcelina the first to venture out onto the searing Praia de Botafogo in the shoes, the spandex, the spider-eye shade and pedometer to tick off those iconic ten thousand footsteps. Within a week her few friends and many rivals were out on the streets, and then she had heard over the traffic the twang of berimbaus, the cheerful clatter of the agogô, the chanting from the green spaces of Flamengo Park. The next day she was with them, clapping in her Germanic, loira-girl way while wiry guys with their shirts off wheeled and reeled and kicked in the roda. It was a simple recruitment demonstration by Mestre Ginga for his school, but for Marcelina it was the New Cool Thing. For a season it ruled; every other pitch at the weekly sessions was capoeira-related, and then the Next Cool Thing blew in from the bay. By then Marcelina had donated the spandex and so-last-season shades to a charity store, given the pedometer to Mrs. Costa from downstairs, who was haunted by a fear that her husband was a somnambulist who walked the streets kilometer after kilometer at night, stealing little things, bought herself the classic rig of red-striped Capri pants and stretchy little top, and was taxiing twice a week up the hairpin road up the breast of Corcovado, upon which Christ himself stood, an erect nipple, to Mestre Ginga's Silvestre fundação. She was a convert to the battle-dance. Cool would come around again; it always did.

Hands locked, the capoeiristas circled. A damp night, clouds hung low over the Tijuca. The warm humidity held and amplified smells; the fruity, blousy sickliness of the bougainvilleas that overhung the fundação's fighting yard, the rank smokiness of the oil from the lamps that defined the roda, the honey-salt sweetness of the sweat that ran down Marcelina's upraised arm, the fecund, nurturing sourness of her armpit. She released her grip and sprang back from Jair. In a breath the berimbaus and agogô leaped into São Bento Grande; in the same breath Marcelina dropped to a squat, grabbed the cuffs of Jair's skull-and-crossbone-patterned pants, stood up, and sent him onto his back.

The roda roared with delight; the berimbau players drew mocking laughter from their strings. Mestre Ginga suppressed a smile. Boca de calça; a move so simple, so silly that you would never think it could work, but that was the only way it did work. And now, the finishing blow. Marcelina held out her hand. When the hand is offered, the game is over. But Jair came out of his defensive negativa in an armada spin-kick. Marcelina ducked under Jair's bare foot easily and, while he was still off-balance, stepped under his guard and roundly boxed both ears in a clapping double galopante. Jair went down with a bellow, the laughter stopped, the berimbaus fell silent. A bird croaked; Mestre Ginga was not any kind of smiling now. Again Marcelina extended the hand. Jair shook his head, picked himself up, walked out of the roda shaking his head.

Mestre Ginga was waiting in the yellow streetlight as Marcelina waited for her taxi. Some drive, some are driven in this life. Low-bowing tree branches and scrambling ficus cast a fractured, shifting light on him as he leaned on his stick. The patúa amulets he wore around his neck to defeat spirits swung.

You're not fucking Yoda, Marcelina thought. *Or Gandalf the Grey.*

"That was good. I liked that. The boca de calça, that's a real malandro's move." Mestre Ginga's voice was an eighty-a-day nicotine rasp. As far as Marcelina knew, he had never smoked, never done maconha let alone anything more powdery, and drank only on saints' days and national holidays. Nodules on the vocal cords was the prevailing theory; whatever the biology, it was very *Karate Kid*. "I thought maybe, maybe, at last you might be learning something about real jeito, and then . . ."

"I apologized to him, he's cool about it. His ears'll be ringing for a day or two, but he was the one wouldn't end it. I offered, he refused. Like you say, the street has no rules."

As she come up dancing out of her defensive crouch, she had seen not Jair's face but the Black Plumed Bird in all her grace and makeup, and her fists had at once known what they needed to do: the box on the ears, the most humiliating attack in the jogo. A slap on the face, doubled.

"You were angry. Angry is stupid. Don't I teach you that? The laughing man can always beat the angry man because the angry man is stupid, acts from his anger, not his malicia."

"Yeah yeah whatever," Marcelina said throwing her kit bag into the back of the taxi. She had hoped that the dance-fight would burn away the anger, turn it, as in Mestre Ginga's homespun Zen, into the mocking laughter of the true malandro, carefree, loved by a world that looked after him like a mother. The music, the chants, the sly jig-step of the preparatory ginga had only driven it deeper until it pierced a dark reservoir of rage: anger so old, so buried it had transformed into a black, volatile oil. There were years of anger down there. Anger at family of course, at her mother delicately, respectably turning herself into a drunk in her Leblon apartment; at her sisters and their husbands and their babies. Anger at friends who were rivals and sycophants she kept in line-of-sight. But mostly anger at herself, that at thirty-four she had walked too far down a road, in such special shoes, to be able to return. "I can't see children compensating for the career gain I stand to make." The family Hoffman had been gathered in the Leopold Restaurant for her mother's sixtieth birthday, and she, twenty-three, fresh into Canal Quatro as a junior researcher, dazzled by the lights, the cameras, the action. Marcelina could still hear her voice over the table, the beer, the assurance: a declaration of war on her married older sisters, their men, the eggs in their ovaries.

"I don't want to go the Copa," she ordered, cellular out, thumb dancing its own ginga over the text keys. "Take me to Rua Tabatingüera."

"Good," the driver said. "The Copa's crawling with cops and militaries. It's really kicking off down at Morro do Pavão."

It was not the first weekly briefing she had attended hungover. Canal Quatro's boardroom—the communication-facilitating sofas and low coffee tables, the curving glass wall and the bold and blue of Botafogo with the smog low over Niteroí across the bay—thudded to an über-deep bass line. In keeping with the station's policy of freshness and kidulthood, the board-room's walls were giant photomurals of Star Wars collectibles. Marcelina felt Boba Fett oppressing her. She would be all right as long as she didn't have to say anything; as long as Lisandra did not work out by her bitch-queen spider-sense that Marcelina was coming from two-thirds of a bottle of Gray Goose, and then much much cold Bavaria from Heitor's chiller. Another day, another chemical romance.

She did wish she could stop crying every time she went to Heitor's.

Genre heads, commissioners, execs, and line producers. The Black Plumed Bird in shades and headscarf as if she'd just stepped windswept and sun-kissed off the back of a Moto Guzzi. Rosa the scheduler put the overnights up on the projector. Minimalist leather sofas creaked as bodies sagged into them. Rede Globo's new telenovela *Nu Brasil* had averaged 40 percent audience share over its four sampling periods, critically 44 percent in the eighteen-to-thirty-four grouping. Canal Quatro's *Ninja School* in the same timeslot had taken 8.5, skewing heavily toward the intended male audience, but a full point and a half behind SBT's *Beauty School Drop-Outs* and equal to the peak segment for Globo Sport. And Adriano Russo was coming in now for a quick word.

Canal Quatro's director of programming took care to look as if he had just parked his surfboard at reception, but he still had his own reserved chair at the end of the runway of glass tables, and nicely manicured hands busy busy with folders and Blackberries.

"First of all, IMHO, in this room are the most creative, imaginative, hardworking, and hard-playing people I have ever met. NQA." The etiquette was to nod along with Adriano's chat-room-speak, even when he used English acronyms or, as was commonly believed, made them up. "We've had a bad night; okay, let's not have a bad season." He straightened the folder on the glass table. "NTK senior production and genre heads only. I've come into information about Rede Globo's winter schedule." Even the Black Plumed Bird was jolted. "PDFs have been e-mailed to you, but the linchpin of the season is a new telenovela. Before you begin groaning about boring unimaginative programming, I'll give you a couple of details. It's called *A World Somewhere*, it's written by Alejandro and Cosquim, but USP: it marks the return of Ana Paula Arósio. She's playing against Rodrigo Santoro. They've got them both back in Brazil, and on television. The whole thing was shot on a secret closed set in Brasilia, which is why no one heard a word about it. The big press launch is next Wednesday. The first ep TXs on June fifteenth; we need something big, noisy, look-at-me. Water-cooler TV, rude and edgy, 'How dare those Canal Quatro bastards' the usual sort of thing. We want the television reviewers' EPOOTH."

Eyes Popping Out of Their Heads, Marcelina surmised through the thud thud of too much morning. This was not a show to play against the telenovela. Anything that tried to take on Ana Paulo Arósio and Rodrigo Santoro would go down with ten bullets in its head. But Globo was calculating that *A World Somewhere* would generate a huge inheritance audience inert in front of the television and ripe for whatever came after, almost certainly, in Marcelina's experience, a cheap and cheerful ". . . *Revealed*" puff-doc with lots of behind-the-scenes and actor interviews, teasers but no actual plot spoilers. That was the audience Adriano Russo wanted to steal. For the first time in months arousal flickered at the base of Marcelina Hoffman's heart. Her hangover evaporated in a puff of adrenaline. Blond ambition. Blond promotion. The commissioning merry-go-round between the main networks was spinning again. Factual entertainment would prance round again. Her own little glass cubicle. People would have to knock to come in. Her own PA. She could drops hints for things like Blackberries or pink Razrs and they would appear on her desk in the morning through the tech-fairy. The first thing a new commissioning editor does is decommission all her enemies' shows. She fantasized shooting down all Lisandra's proposals at the Friday Blue Sky sessions. She could get that apartment in Leblon, maybe even a beach view. That would please her mother. She could cease temporizing with her lunchtime shots of Botox and declare full plastic assault on those thirty-something anxiety lines. Thank you, Our Lady of Production.

"We have six weeks to turn it round. Pitches to genre heads on Blue Sky Friday." Adriano Russo squared his papers and stood up. "Thank you all."

Bye Adriano thanks Adriano see you Friday Adriano hugs Adriano.

"BTW," he flicked back from the boardroom door. "Even though we haven't. IMBWR it's World Cup year."

Thanks Adriano legal Adriano we'll remember that Adriano.

Boba Fett still held Marcelina menacingly under his gun, but Yoda seemed to be smiling.

SEPTEMBER 22, 2032

The ball hangs motionless at the top of its arc. It frames Cidade de Luz, fifty hillside streets, its head adorned with the thorny crown of the favela, at its knees the rodovia heat-crazy with windows and wing mirrors. Beyond the highway the gated enclaves begin: red-roofed, blue-pooled, green-shaded. Through the sun-shiver the endless towers of São Paulo recede into half-believed spirits of architecture, their summits orbited by advertisements. Helicopters itch and fidget between rooftop landing pads; there are people up there who have never touched the ground. But higher still are the Angels of Perpetual Surveillance. On any clear-sky day you may catch them, a flicker on the very edge of vision, like stray cells floating in the jelly of the eye, as they turn in their orbits and their vast, gossamer wings catch the light. Sixteen sky-drones, frail as prayers, circle constantly on the borders of the troposphere. Like angels, the robot planes fly endlessly; they need, and can, never touch the ground again; like angels, they see into the hearts and intentions of man. They monitor and track the two billion arfids—radio frequency identity chips—seeded through the cars, clothes, consumer electronics, cash, and cards of the City of Saint Paul's twenty-two million inhabitants. Twenty kilometers above the Angels of Perpetual Surveillance, balloons the size of city blocks maneuver in the tropopause, holding position over their ground data-transfer stations. Exabits of information chatter between them, the seamless weave of communication that clothes not just Brasil but the planet. Higher still, beyond all sense and thought, and global positioning satellites tumble along their prescribed orbits, tracking movements down to a single footstep, logging every transaction, every real and centavo. Highest of all, God on his stool, looking on Brasil and its three hundred million souls, nostalgic for the days when his was the only omniscience.

All for an instant, frozen by the parabola of a World Cup 2030 soccer ball. And the ball falls. It drops onto the right foot of a girl in a tight little pair of spandex shorts with her name across her ass: *Milena*, yellow on green. She holds the ball on the flat upper surface of her Nike Raptor, then flips it up into the air again. The girl spins round to volley the ball from her left foot, spins under it and traps it on her chest. She wears her name there too, blue on the sun-gold of the belly-cropped futebol shirt. *Castro*. Blue and green and gold.

"She could be a bit bigger up top," Edson Jesus Oliveira de Freitas says, sucking morning through his teeth. "But at least she's blonde. I mean, she is blonde?"

"What are you saying? This is my cousin." Two-Fags is a scraggy enxofradawith no style and less jeito, and if that girl out there turning pirouettes under the looping ball in her hot pants and belly-top is his cousin, then Edson is not the sixth son of a sixth son. They sit on folding military sling chairs at the edge of the futsal court, a dog-turd-infested concrete bunker in the overlooked space behind the Assembly of God. Milena Castro, Keepie-Uppie Queen of Cidade de Luz, heads the ball now one two three four five six seven. All good girls they go to heaven. Especially back of the Assembly of God. The ball makes a fine plasticy thwack against her upturned forehead. Seventeen eighteen nineteen twenty. Like the rich and the angels, the ball never touches the ground.

"How long can she keep it up for?"

"As long as you like."

Heading and smiling. A grin and wink in Edson's direction and Milena volleys the ball from knee to knee. She wears knee socks, in patriotic colors. Knee socks work for Edson.

"I'll take her on." Edson almost sees the reis tumble in Two-Fags' eyes, like something from the cartoon channel. "Come round my office; we'll talk." It's a shotgun shack at the side of Dona Hortense's house that smells of dog piss and mold, but it's where De Freitas Global Talent does its business. Milena Keepie-Uppie Queen spins, strikes a pose, and the ball drops right sweet into the crook of her arm. "I'm impressed with what I see." Her lily skin isn't even moist with sweat. "I think you have talent. Unfortunately, talent isn't enough these days. This is where I can help. You need a USP. You know what that is? Unique Selling Point. So, the pants are cute, but they have to go."

"Ey! This is my cousin you're talking about," shouts Two-Fags. Edson ignores him. Local kids are arriving by threes and fours at the futsal court, bouncing their small, heavy ball impatiently.

"Futebol is a thong thing. At some point you will need a boob job as well. It doesn't affect the act, anything like that?"

The Keepie-Uppie Queen shakes her head. The futsal boys are staring at her. *Get used to it*, Edson thinks. It will be forty thousand of them watching you at halftime at the Parque São Jorge keeping it up up up.

"Good good good. Now, what I will do is try you on one of the Série C teams first. Atlético Sorocaba, Rio Branco, something like that. Build you up, get you a rep. Then we move on. But first of all, you have to come round to my office and make it all official."

Marcelina nods matter-of-factly, slips on a silky Timão blouson, and pulls up team color legwarmers. At least she understands business, unlike Two-Fags, who is so dense Edson wonders how he made it to twenty-eight. But he is onto something with this one. De Freitas Global Talent's first major signing—not counting the women's foot-volley team and Petty Cash the pod-warrior, who were just practice. Edson slaps the military chairs just so, and they umbrella down into slender canes a man can sling across his back. Clever stuff, this new smart plastic. Two-Fags has his arm around the Keepie-Uppie Queen's bare waist in a way that is not seemly for any blood relative. Pay him a finder's fee and slip him out the back door.

"I'll be in after nine!" Edson shouts after Two-Fags and Milena. The futsal kids push past, eager for their territory, stringing up their net, slipping off their Havaianas.

An ugly face flashes in the middle of Edson's Chillibean I-shades: Gerson, fifth son of a sixth son and less favored in every way than Edson. Edson dabs a finger to the frame to take the call.

"Hey, unfortunate brother, I have to tell you, I just signed the sweetest deal. . . ."

Edson can name a thousand stupidities Gerson has committed, but today he has excelled himself. The reason he's calling is because he has forty minutes before Brooklin Bandeira's private seguranças track him down and kill him.

A shower of cards coins keys tampons lippy makeup compact mag from an upturned handbag. Coins and keys bounce on the pavement, tampons roll and blow on the hot wind. The gossip mag—handbag-sized edition—falls like a broken-backed bird. The compact hits the concrete edge-on and explodes into clamshells, pressed powder, pad, mirror. The mirror wheels a little way.

Gerson João Oliveira de Freitas jumped the girl blindside of the enclave security systems. He picked her up outside Hugo Boss on Avenida Paulista: tailed the taxi back to Mummy and Daddy's lower-middle-class enclave of colonial-style pseudo-fazendas with cool cool pools, tucked away behind the Vila Mariana Cemetery. *Take her as she's fiddling with her bags.* He pulled the strip on the one-shot plastic gun. She just needed one look. Gerson tipped out the bag, threw away the gun—it began to decompose immediately—spun the little moto on its back wheel. In and out before she could even scream.

His back wheel shatters the mirror as he guns the engine. Bad luck for someone. He pulls the bandana with which he had covered his face down over his neck. Even a glimpse of one is a stop'n'search offense these days. Antisocial clothing. Her I-shades, her watch, her shirt, the taxi; some eye somewhere will have photographed him. He has the moto's license plates in his backpack. When he gets to the chipperia, they'll go back on. Twenty seconds with a screwdriver. The cards will already be blank. The key codes change every eight hours. The coin-tokens are worth less than the plastic they're pressed from. Makeup, tampons, girlie mags are not for a man. But the street value of a new season 2032 Giorelli Habbajabba (which is beyond *must have* into *by any means necessary*) is three thousand réis. For a bag. Yes. Prize hooked over his arm, Gerson accelerates down the on-ramp into the great howl of Avenida Dr. Francisco Mesquita.

Senhora Ana Luisa Montenegro de Coelho taps her big ochre I-shades and sends an assalto report and photo through to Austral Insurance and Security. Bandana over face. For sure. No plates. Of course. But ten kilometers over São Paulo an Angel of Perpetual Surveillance turns on the back-loop of its eternal holding pattern and logs a stolen handbag. From the snow of ever-moving arfid signatures it identifies and locates the radio frequency identification chips that uniquely tagged the Anton Giorelli Habbajabba handbag recently registered to Senhora Ana Luisa Montenegro de Coelho. It calls up its neural-net map of São Paulo's two thousand square kilometers and twenty-two million souls; searches through every burb, bairro, downtown, favela, mall, alley, park, soccer stadium, racetrack, and highway; and finds it swinging purple-and-pinkly from the elbow of Gerson João Oliveira de Freitas, hunched over the handlebars of his hand-me-down moped, buzzing like a neon through the home-run along Ibirapuera. A contract goes out. Automated bid systems in the dozen private security companies that can reach the target on budget submit tenders. Fifteen seconds later a contract is issued from Austral Insurance to Brooklin Bandeira Securities. It's a well-established medium-size company that's been losing recently to younger, meaner, more vicious competitors. After comprehensive retraining and financial restructuring, it's back, with a new attitude.

This for a bag? With purple and pink flowers? Ana Luisa Montenegro de Coelho can have another one before sunset. But there's a crackdown on. There's always a crackdown on somewhere: tough on crime, tough on the perpetrators of crime. Usually around the time for insurance policy renewal. Brooklin Bandeira Securities has a corporate reputation to restore, and its seguranças are dangerously bored watching O Globo Futebol 1. In the garage two Suzukis rev up. The riders fix location on their helmet HUDs. The pillion riders check weapons and buckle on. Game on.

In the gutter outside Ana Luisa's nice little enclave, the discarded one-shot gun turns to black, putrid liquid and drips from the rungs of the grating into the sewer. Over the next few days delirious, poisoned rats will stagger and die across the lawns of Vila Mariana, causing short-lived consternation among the residents.

Edson touches the first two fingers of his left hand gently to his temple in a gesture he has evolved to show his older brother how exasperated he is with him, even when Gerson cannot see him. He sighs.

"What is it you're trying to tell me? They can't blank the arfid?"

"It's some new thing they call an NP-chip."

Gerson had been sipping coffee and enjoying the good sweet morning rolls, still warm from the oven, at Hamilcar and Mr. Smiles' Chipperia. It was parked round the back of a bakery, which meant good sweet morning rolls and pão de queijo for the chipperia's clients while they made stolen things disappear from the sight of the Angels of Perpetual Surveillance. Hamilcar and Mr. Smiles worked out of a thirdhand campervan so full of computers they lived outside in tents and awnings. As all trails ended at the chipperia, mobility was paramount. As Gerson understood it, it was all timing. It took ten minutes average, twenty minutes tops to erase an arfid; the closest the seguranças could get in that time was a five-kilometer circle of confusion, and it would blow their budget to search that large area. Most turned around and headed home as soon as they lost the signal from the arfid.

"How much are you looking for that bag?" Hamilcar was half reading the paper, half peeling the flakes of eczema from his cracked feet.

"Three thousand reis."

"No, I mean seriously."

"That's what they're going for. You cannot get these bags for love nor money nor bribery. I'm telling you."

"Give you eight hundred, and that's including what you owe us for the dechipping."

"Two thousand five."

Hamilcar grimaced as he tore a particularly salty piece of dead white skin a little too far, baring raw flesh.

"You are a man of no education. I was thinking maybe my girlfriend might like it as a present—she likes that sort of thing, all the names and that. Not at that price, though."

Then the door had opened. Mr. Smiles stepped out of the stinky camper. He was an IT graduate from the University of São Paulo, the hacker of the outfit. He was a big skinny Cabo Verde with a great and well-tended Afro and dentition that made him look as if he was always smiling. The smile did not sit naturally with the pump-action shotgun in his hand.

"Hey hey hey . . ." cried Gerson, spluttering flakes of sweet roll.

"Gerson, nothing personal, but you have thirty seconds to get on your bike and depart."

"What what what?" Gerson said, catching the Habbajabba as Mr. Smiles lobbed it to him.

"It's NP-chipped. I can't touch that."

"NP what? What shit? You're the scientist; you should know about these things."

"I'm an information technologist, majoring in database design. This is quantum physics. Get a physicist. Or just go to the river and throw the thing away. You choose, but I'm not facing off with the Brooklin Bandeirantes. And I will shoot you."

And that was when Gerson called his smart kid brother. And Edson says, "Go and throw the thing in a river."

"It's three thousand réis."

"Brother, it's a handbag."

"I need the money."

"Do you owe someone again? Jesus and Mary . . ."

Edson shoos kids away from his bike. It's a Yam X-Cross 250 dirt bike, green and yellow, like a parrot, like a futebol shirt, and Edson loves it beyond everything except his mother and his business plan. It is all jeito, and you can ride it straight up a wall. "Let me talk to Smiles."

"Okay," says Mr. Smiles after Edson explains that he really can't let his dumb brother get killed even over a woman's handbag. "I think you're all dead, but you could try the quantumeiros."

"Who are these? What-eiros?"

"Quantumeiros. You know, those new quantum computers? No? Codes you can't break? They can. They're the physicists. I can give you their code; they move around even more than we do. Careful with them, though. Weird shit happens round these people."

A map of the São Caetano rodovia network appears on Edson's Chillibeans; a license plate is flagged, heading north on R118. Edson wonders how many chippers and crackers and quantumeiros are nomadic on the highways of great Sampa at any instant.

"I shall try them."

"What did Gerson ever do he should have a brother like you?" says Mr. Smiles. "All the same, I wouldn't hang around too long."

The Yamaha starts to Edson's thumbprint. He slips a concentration enhancer from his travel pack, pops it, and as they world sharpens and clarifies around him, rides slow through the alleys back of the crente church. He doesn't want mud splashes from the lingering night's rain on his white flares.

The brothers de Freitas meet twenty-three minutes later on the on-ramp at Intersection 7. Twenty-three minutes for the Brooklin Bandeira to close in, to narrow the circle of possibility down to machine-pistol range. Edson's been checking his custom-fit rearview cameras for oil-slick-black segurança hunting bikes. He could get away from them on the Yam, take it places their big bulky machines could not, but not Gerson, flogging the alco engine on that shitty little putt-putt. Edson can hardly believe he once rode that thing. Gantry cameras read his license plate; hurtling satellites debit his account. They don't make it easy for legitimate men of business.

And there it is, looming out of the traffic, the barquentine of the quantumeiros: a big forty-tonner standing at a steady hundred in the outside lane. The cab is pimped with Fleshbeck Crew—style cherubim and a battery of airhorns on the roof chromed and sweet as the trumpets of archangels. *Cook/Chill Meal Solutions*, says the trail. Fine cover. No cop is ever going to stop and search bad cuisine. Edson weaves Gerson into the truck's slipstream. A touch on the I-shades calls up the address Mr. Smiles gave him. The truck flashes its hazard lights in acknowledgment and sways into the slow lane, drops to seventy sixty fifty forty. The back shutter rolls up, a middle-aged guy in a Black Metal muscle top swings from a chain and manages to smoke at the same time. He beckons them close, closer. The loading ramp extends, lowers. Steel hits road. Sparks shower around the brothers Oliveira. Black Metal beckons them again: *Come on, come on, on the ramp.* Sparks peel away round Edson as he lines up the run. He's a businessman, not a stunt-rider. Edson edges forward: the concentration pill gives him micro-accelerations and relative velocities. Wheel on wheel off wheel on wheel off, wheel on; then Edson throttles hard, surges forward, and brakes and declutches simultaneously.

Smoking metalhead applauds.

Thirty seconds later Gerson skids to a halt on the platform, pale and shaking. Edson tries to imagine what the commuters on the São Caetano rodovia make of a male with a pink handbag around his neck driving onto the back of a moving truck. Probably reckons it's the telenovelas and are looking round for the flittercams: *Hey! We're on* A World Somewhere, *we really are!*

Death Metal raises the ramp and pulls the shutter down with a clatter. Recessed mood-lights flood on. Edson feels his eyes widen behind his wrap-around I-shades. The rear of the container is docking space; the forward two-thirds is split-level business accommodation. The lower floor—reception—is Karma Café kitsch, all shag rugs, leather beanbags, inflatable chairs, and zebra-skin sofas on spindly legs. There a battery of rollscreens tuned to sports and news channels, a complex coffee engine with attendant barista and low-laid bossa nova. Upstairs is the office, a transparent cube of plastic, harshly neon-lit to the downbeat downlighting of the club below. The cube is stacked ceiling-high with server farms, wiring alleys, and tanks conspicuously marked *liquid nitrogen*. Edson makes out a figure moving among the racked boxes, a glimpse of swinging red hair. Heaven and clubland are connected by a spiral staircase of glowing blue plastic.

A floppy-haired queen in a good suit and shiny shirt unfolds from a sofa. He has pointy pirate shoes, immaculately polished.

"So this is the handbag?" The bicha turns it over in his hands. "I suppose it was going to happen sooner or later as quantum technology gets cheaper. It would have been a lot simpler just to have thrown it away."

"My brother can make money out of this."

The truck accelerates; the seguranças have a fix on the arfid and are running them out of road.

"We can certainly blank this for you. It's not the most up-to-date model. Fia."

You can fall in love with someone for their shoes. These are gold jacaré-skin wedge heels, strappy at the ankle. They descend the top turn of the spiral staircase. Above them, slim ankles, good calves not too full, Capri-cut tapered pant-bottoms with a little dart in the side and white piping running up to a matching jacaré belt. The pants belong to a black jumpsuit, confrontationally retro in its cut, shoulder pads, trim and kitschy tit-zips. All this detail gleams in Edson's edged perception. Then the head descends from the suite upstairs. Third-generation Japonesa cheekbones and nose—she's had the eyes done, round *anime* doe-eyes. Hair that super-silky straightness that all aspire to but only the Japanese have the DNA to achieve. Bobbed so severely it might have been measured with a spirit level. Red is the color again, this year. She wears top-marque Blu Mann I-shades pushed up on it.

"Good bag," she comments.

Edson opens his mouth and nothing comes out. It's not love. It's not even lust. The closest emotion to it he can recognize is *glamour*. If he had a religious cell in his body, he might know it as worship, in that word's oldest, truest sense: *worth-ship*. She fascinates him. She is all the things he hopes to be. He wants to orbit in her gravity, circle her thrilling world and thrilling clothes and thrilling friends and thrilling places to go and do and be and see. She takes the jeito he thinks he has earned and spreads it all over the road behind her like a mashed cat. She makes him feel like favela scum. That's all right. Compared to her he is, he is.

"They're about two minutes out," chides the bicha.

"You want to give me that bag?"

"Um, can I watch?"

"There's nothing to see. You'll be disappointed."

"I don't think I will. I'd like to see."

"You will. Everybody is."

"About a minute and a half," says bicha-boy. Gerson is having a cafezinho. She lets him carry the bag upstairs.

"Fia? Fia what?"

There's barely space for the two swivel chairs among the technology. The cubicle is swagged with enough cable to rig a suspension bridge.

"Kishida." She says it fast, with Japanese emphases though her accent is pure Paulistana. Fia sets the Giorelli on an illuminated white plastic tray under a set of micromanipulator arms. She sweeps her Blu Manns down over her face. Her hands dance in air; the robot arms gavotte over the handbag, seeking the arfid chip. Edson sees ghosts and circuitry in increasing magnifications flicker across Fia's shades.

"I know this tune, I really like it. Do you like baile?" Edson says, twitching his muscles to the house beat. "There's a gafieira on Friday; I've a client doing a set."

"Could you just shut up for thirty seconds while I try and do some work?"

The arms locate and lock. Icons appear on Fia's glasses: her pupils dance across the display, issuing commands. Edson finds his attention hooked by a glowing object beneath the glass surface of the desk. He cups his hands around his face and presses it to the desktop. The glass is cool enough for his breath to dew. Far below, seemingly farther than the architecture of the trailer allows—below the floor of the lab, below the club lounge, below the truck chassis and the surface of the road—is a shifting, morphing glow.

"What's that?" He lowers his brow until it touches the cool glass.

"Reality," says Fia. "Quantum dots in superposition. The light is vacuum fluctuation photons leaking through from some of the parallel states in which the computation is being made."

"Ah, you're the physicist," Edson says, and bites his tongue: is it the pill that is making this muscle that has never let him down before speak only stupid? She looks at him as if he has shit on her glass desktop. She reaches across Edson to hit a key. The robot probes move in a fraction of a hair, then withdraw to their standby position.

"Okay, that's it. Safe and anonymous."

"What, you mean, that quick?"

"I told you you would be disappointed."

"But nothing happened."

"I ran through possible combinations in ten to the eight hundred universes. That's not exactly nothing."

"Of course," says Edson unconvincingly.

"There's always an answer out there somewhere."

Edson has heard a little about this—he makes it his business to know something about everything that occupies adjacent niches to him in the twilight economy—and he has seen with his own eyes now what it can achieve, but it still feels like witchcraft to him. Quantum dots in superwhateverpositions. Ten to the eight hundred universes. That is not reality. Reality is Brooklin Bandeiras running back to the office, out of funding and out of quarry. Reality is people stupid enough to pay three thousand reis for a handbag, and people stupid enough to steal one. Reality is the necessity of getting with this magnetic, strict creature.

"If you say," says Edson. If she thinks he is ignorant, he might as well put it to work. "But you could explain it to me over lunch."

"I'd rather you just paid me now."

Down in the lounge, he throws the bag to Gerson while the bicha in the suit prints out an invoice. A movement distracts Edson, someone/thing among the quantum computers above. Impossible. No one could get past them on the neon staircase. *Weird shit happens around them*, Mr. Smiles had warned.

"We'd prefer cash," the bicha says. Whatever preferred payment option, it's impossible.

"Don't be owing us," advises the Black Metalista. Edson's money-sense cues him that he is the wealth behind the operation.

"I'll take the bag," says Fia. Edson snatches it away from his brother.

"So, gafieira?" he chances as the truck pulls into a safe stop and the shutter clatters up. "José's Garage, Cidade de Luz."

"Don't push it," says Fia quantumeira, but Edson can see deep down, at the quantum level, she's a baile queen.

JUNE 19, 1732

The mule went mad on the cobbled pier of the Cidade Baixa. The insanity fell on it in an instant, one moment doggedly hauling the laden wagon with the tenacity of its breed, the next shying in its traces, ears back, teeth bared, braying. It tore free from the barefoot slave who had been steering it half-asleep, such was the stolid placidity of the mule, from the engenho to the dock where the low, slow carracks rolled on the swell of the Bahia de Todos os Santos, fat with sugar and Vila Rica gold. The slave snatched for the bridle; the mule shied away from the hand, eyes rolling. The mule reared, kicked. The wagon rocked, spilling white pillows of sugar that split on the cobbles. The dockside whores, come down for the arrival of *Cristo Redentor* in Salvador harbor—a ship from Portugal, a navy ship—flew with cries and oaths. Soldiers in the buff and crimson of the imperial infantry under the command of a sword-carrying Teniente ran from the customhouse. The mule leaped and plunged; the slave danced around before it, trying to seize the lead rope, but the cry had already gone out across the harbor: *The rage the rage.*

"Help me!" the slave cried. A hoof caught the carter a glancing blow; he reeled across the quay, blood starting from his smashed jaw. The mule bucked and plunged, trying to twist off the heavy cart. Yellow foam burst from its mouth. Its chest heaved, sweat stained its hide. Cries, shrieks from the ladies in their headscarves and petticoats. Slaves left their rail carts, their master and mistresses, encircled the insane mule, arms outstretched. The soldiers unshouldered their muskets. Eyes wide, the mule reared again and launched into a full gallop along the pier. Slaves and soldiers fled.

"The priest! For the love of God, Father!" the Teniente shouted.

Father Luis Quinn looked up from where he had been supervising the unshipping of his small trunk of possessions from *Cristo Redentor.* The mule and leaping cart bore down upon him like a blazing war chariot from the Fianna legends. Luis Quinn threw his arms up. He was a big man, larger and more imposing yet in the simple black robe of his order, a piece of night fallen into day. The mule leaped straight up into the air in its traces, came down foursquare, and stopped dead, head bowed.

Every sailor, every officer, every soldier, every slave, every whore in her bright jollyboat, stopped to stare at Luis Quinn. Slowly he lowered his arms and stepped toward the twitching, foaming beast, clicking and shushing under his breath all the words for horses he knew in both his natal tongues, Portuguese and Irish.

"I advise you not to approach the creature, Father," the Teniente called, a pale, European face among the caboclo faces of the Salvador Auxiliaries. "We will shoot the beast and burn its body; that way the rage will not spread."

"Hush, hush there," Luis Quinn said as reached out for the rope halter. He could see the infantry forming a line, taking aim. His fingers closed around the rope. With a cry more like a human scream than any right sound of a beast the mule reared, flashing out with its steel-shod hooves. Quinn twisted out of the path of the killing hoof; then the mule leaped. For a moment it seemed suspended; then mule and wagon plunged into the green water of the bay. Whore-boats scattered. Luis Quinn saw the mule's head fight out of the chop, eyes wild with the knowledge of its certain destruction, the cream foam at its mouth now bloodstained. The weight of the cart pulled it under. Luis Quinn saw its knees kicking against the dragging green water; then it was lost. Empty sugar sacks rose to the surface one by one as their contents dissolved like white, night-blooming water flowers.

"Ah, the creature the creature." It had been but an animal, but Luis Quinn nevertheless murmured a prayer. The Teniente, now at Quinn's side, crossed himself.

"You are all right, Father."

"I am unharmed." Quinn noticed all across the dock the soldiers, the slaves, even the strumpets, make the same blessing. He did not doubt it was as much for his habit as the sudden fatal madness of the mule. Thus had it been on the slow, calm-bound, scurvy-racked voyage of *Cristo Redentor* from the bar of the Tagus: mutterings, scratchings, charms, and prayers. A priest, a black Jesuit, aboard. No luck upon this ship. "I heard mention of a rage."

"A madness of horses first, latterly of all beasts of burden, God between us and evil." The Teniente signaled for one of his troopers to bear the father's trunk. As the young officer escorted him toward the Custom House, Quinn opened his senses to this place in which he had so freshly landed. He noted with a start that there was not one horse. No animal at all on this great stone apron beneath the sheer bluff of the Cidade Alta. No beast on the steep ladeira that wound up the steep cliff between low and high Salvador. Human muscle alone powered this city. The cobbled paths and quays teemed with slaves pushing laden barrows and gurneys on iron rails, bent under sacks slung from brow straps, carefully negotiating sedan chairs through the thronging black and red bodies and fat white sacks of king sugar. "As with all afflictions, rumors run wild," the Teniente continued. The soldier, a ragged mameluco in half uniform of frock coat and loose duck breeches, unshod like a slave, followed six paces behind. "The rage is a thing of the índios from out of the deep forest; it is the work of the Dutch or the Spanish; it is a punishment from God. Not last week angels were seen in Pelourinho, battling with knives of light, three nights in succession. It is attested to by some of the best in Salvador."

"We have not heard of this in Coimbra."

"There is much in Brazil never reaches the ears of Portugal." The Teniente halted short of the bustling portico of the Custom House. "Ah. As I feared. It is always so when a ship's arrival corresponds with the sailing of the sugar fleet. The Custom House is the most hopeless jam; I cannot see you getting clear for hours. As a crown officer, I am empowered to authorize your permissions of entry to the colony."

"For a small consideration," said Luis Quinn.

"A trifling impost, that's all."

"I am under the direct authority of the Provincial of Brazil." Luis Quinn retained the bones of his birth-accent; a linguist, a speaker in tongues, he was well aware of the advantage its air of the uncanny lent him. A big man, hands like spades, softly spoken as big men so often are.

"Indeed, Father, but Brazil is not like other places. You will find that little happens here without inducement."

Brazil is not like other places. So many had said that to him, from Father James his spiritual director, even as he ordered him on the task most difficult, to this cocky puppy of a soldiereen in his wig and three-cornered hat gay with feathers.

"I do not think it would suit my cloth to be seen enjoying preferment over others. No, I shall wait my turn in the Custom House, Teniente. Sure when God made time He made plenty of it." The officer bowed, but his mouth was sour. He took his bearer with him.

I ask only that I might be given a task most difficult. In the studies and libraries of the College at Coimbra, Luis Quinn's request, made every year on the day of the patron of his native Ireland to his spiritual director, had sounded rich in zeal and honesty. Candlelight, cloisters work such deceptions. Every year for five years the same reply: *When the need and the man meet.* This year, Father James, the mathematics instructor to the missionaries to China where that art commanded special admiration, had said, *My room, after compline.*

"Brazil."

"Brazil, yes. Where all the sin in the world has washed up. A request from the provincial of the College at Salvador for an admonitory."

"To what purpose?"

"Our own provincial says only that he requires an admonitory from outside the colony." Then, with a wry smile: "That seems to me to imply a task most difficult."

Luis Quinn drew again in his memory Father James, a short laconic Ulsterman with his province's flinty accent and humor. A fellow refugee from the penal laws swept down the sea-lanes to Portugal.

Luis Quinn hefted his small sea chest and joined the noisy crowd at the arcade. The ship had seemed like a prison, yet the world felt too expansive, the horizon too close, the sky too distant, the colors too bright and people too brash and clamorous. The sailors and the captains, the feitores and the senhores de engenhos moved away from him, touching their miraculous medals, bowing a nod: *Go through there, Father; after you, Father.*

Beyond the interminable questions and inspections and opening and resealings of the Customs House were the carriers, squatting around their feitor, a fat caboclo with ripped stockings and high-heeled shoes.

"Father Father, a carry a carry." The slave was an índio, bow back and bow legs, yet his muscles were like bands of iron. He wore a brow strap that hung to beneath his shoulder blades. A pair of rope stirrups dangled around his neck. He knelt on the cobbles before a worn wooden mounting block.

"Get up get up," Quinn cried in Tupi lingua geral. "This is the harness of a horse."

"Yes yes a horse, your horse," the slave answered in Portuguese, eyeing warily his foreman. "The only horse not mad or dead, mad or dead. I am strong, Your Holiness."

"Up up," Luis Quinn commanded in Tupi. "I will not have any man for my beast of burden." He turned on the feitor; the man's face paled at the righteous rage in Quinn's gaunt face. "What manner of vile, luxurious creature are you? Here, what's your price for your man to guide me to the Jesuit Colégio?" The caboclo named a sum that even with the smell of the sea still on his cheeks, Luis Quinn knew for usury. He imagined his big fist striking into the middle of the greasy man's round face. Breath shuddering in his lungs, Quinn fought the anger down. He threw a handful of small coppers. The caboclo dived to snatch them up. The slave made to lift Luis Quinn's chest. "Leave it. All I require from you is guidance."

Carriers, each with a passenger clinging to his back, jogged past as Luis Quinn toiled up the zigzagging ladeira. A group of sailors released from *Cristo Redentor* held a race, kicking their mounts with their heels, pricking their buttocks with their knives to goad them into speed. They called greetings to Father Quinn as they passed; amicable now that he was off their ship onto his God's element.

"Animals!" he raged at them. "Beasts on the backs of men! Down with you!"

Shamed and no little intimidated by the big man's righteous rage, the sailors slipped from their mounts. As Quinn strode up through the white-clad carriers and gauze-shrouded chairs, riders climbed down from their straining mounts and toiled with him up through the heat. He heard their murmurs: *Black priest, fiery Vieira has returned.*

Before the steps of the Jesuit basilica, Father Luis set down his small pack. He reached inside the pocket of his robe for a wooden cylinder, rounded at one end, the other stopped with cork. This he drew and removed from it a cigar. He ran it briefly under his nose. The first since Madeira. Luis Quinn held the fragrant leaf out to the slave.

"This you can do. Find me a fire for this."

The slave took the cigar, bowed, and scuttled off across the thronged square. Luis Quinn observed that he moved crabwise; half crippled by his habitual labor. From individual to general, particular to universal. A slave society. In such a society what is meant is never said, what is said never meant. Secrets, subtleties, subterfuges—he must expect nothing open or direct in this New World. Truth there will be—truth there must be, but disguised. So like the ship, where resentments and attachments alike must be hidden; alluded to by codes and rituals of behavior so that every word holds both its conventional meaning and its opposite and which is to be taken is entirely dependent on a hundred subtle social clues. Daily bread to a linguist who had learned the lingua geral in a single ocean crossing, or even to a priest, skilled in the deceptions of the human heart.

Faces black, brown, coffee. Few white. No women, save for a few slaves in wrapped fabric headdresses. The white women, the Portuguese, were nowhere to be seen. Then he saw a subtle movement behind a carved wood grille at an upper window, shadow within shadow. The mistresses were sequestered in their great houses, veiled behind the curtains of the sedan chairs, less free than their slaves. The men's world of the street, the women's world of the house. Casa and rua. Ways of home and ways of world. Hidden and public.

The slave returned, smoldering cigar in hand. With pure God-granted delight Luis Quinn drew on the leaf and felt the rich, spicy smoke curl down inside him.

Alleluias echoed from the host of trumpets and psalteries that flocked and perched around the roof beams. Luis Quinn walked at the rear of the choir. The recessional was a piece unfamiliar to him, accompanied by a consort of viols, theorbos, and a metronome bass drum, pagan almost to his European sense, unsettling in harmony and discord; yet the steady beat was a memory of the dance tunes of his childhood, harpers and fluters by the fire in the hall, fingers bright in the light. Spiritual and at the same time profane. Like this frenetic carbuncle of rococo: masters and patrons lifted on the twisted, crudely carved bodies of their slaves to turn hearts and hands and faces to the saints. And God, his Christ, his descending dove? Crouching, cowed among the colonels and donatories, the trade feitores and senhores de engenhos in the host of their wives and children and wealth: carved and painted negro slaves cutting cane; ships, the proud banners of exploring bandeiras; cattle; slaves coffled together by wire of purest gold threaded through their earlobes. New panels were being installed, old ones updated with new triumphs. The west end of the church was a wall of bamboo scaffolds and canvas sheeting.

"I noticed that you seemed moved during the Avé." Provincial João Alves de Magalhães removed his stole and pressed it perfunctorily to his lips before handing it to his altar boy, an oily-skinned youth, son of a feitor of the elite Misericordia lay order. "Are you a man much affected by music?"

"I recognize in it a reflection of divine perfection." Luis Quinn raised his arms for his attendants to remove his lace surplice. "Much like mathematics in that respect. Like number, music is a thing entirely of itself, that makes no representation of any reality."

"And yet the physical motions of objects, the very act of navigation of that ship on which you came in, find their most accurate descriptions in mathematics."

Altar boys carried Father de Magalhães' heavy, gold-worked cope to the fan-shaped press. In Coimbra such display would have been considered affectation, even worldliness. Sober black and white was all the uniform the soldiers of Christ Militant required.

"Or is it that these physical effects are the gross manifestations of an underlying mathematical truth?"

"Hah! Coimbra sends me a Platonist!" Father de Magalhães laughed. "But I am pleased you enjoyed the choir; our Mestre de Capela's liturgical pieces are performed as far afield as Potosí. He studied with the late Zipoli in the Parana missions. Striking, isn't it? That combination of índio voices for the higher parts and negroes for the tenor and bass. An uncanny sound." He washed his hands in the spout from a gold ewer and let an índio servant towel them dry. Father de Magalhães clapped Luis Quinn on the back. "Now, small coffee in the cloister before supper while I instruct you."

The walled garden behind the college was returning the heat of the day to the evening, the air thick with the strangely stimulating damps and musks of heavy foliaged plants. Birds and bats dashed through the gloaming. What divine law is it, Luis Quinn wondered, that where the birds are fantastical in color and plumage their song offends the ear, yet at home the dowdy blackbird could wring the heart? In the time it took the boy to bring coffee the sky had changed from purple-streaked aquamarine to star-flecked indigo. On the ship the swift sunset of the tropics had been ameliorated by the breadth of the horizon; in this walled, private place night seemed to drop like a banner. The boy lit lanterns. Stars fallen to earth. His face was uncannily beautiful. Father de Magalhães dismissed him with a wave of his hand, stirred two spoons of sugar into his coffee, sipped, winced, and held his hand to his jaw.

"I sometimes think God needs no other hell than an eternity of toothache. Tell me, Father Quinn, what do you make of this Brazil?"

"Father, I only stepped off the ship this afternoon. I can hardly have an opinion."

"You can be in a place five minutes and be entitled to an opinion. Commence by telling me what you have seen."

From childhood Luis Quinn had been able to vividly recall scenes in his memory and mentally walk through them, re-creating the finest details—the color of a dress, the position of a bottle on a table, a bird in a tree—by the strength of his visual memory. In his mind he left the soft, lush college garden and traced in reverse the short walk from the Colégio across the Praça de Sé winding down the thronged ladeira to the harbor, back along the jetty to the ship warping in to land. The image that faced him at every turn was of the mule's face, eyes wide, nostrils bursting bubbles, going down into the green water of the Bay.

"I saw a mad mule destroy itself in the harbor," he said simply.

"The plague, yes. Insanity comes on them as sudden as a colic, and if they do not run themselves to death then they wreak such insane destruction that they must be destroyed there and then."

"It is a universal plague?"

"It seems so. Already it is spreading to draft-oxen. You have heard our latest fantasy as to its origin? Dueling angels in Pelourinho?"

"And I also saw men in horses' harness. These are not unconnected, I think."

"The letter from Coimbra said you were a perceptive man, Father. I heard someone caused a commotion on the ladeira. Of course, since the time of Father Antonio Vieira we have maintained a consistent moral position regarding slavery. However, of late we find that position challenged."

Luis Quinn sipped his coffee, rapidly achieving equilibrium with the general environment. An unrelenting climate; no release in the dark of the night. A cigar would be a fine thing. After months of enforced chastity aboard *Cristo Redentor*, he found his appetite for smoke had returned redoubled. The beginning of attachment, of indiscipline?

"I am not quite certain what you mean, Father."

"The Society is little loved in Brazil. We are seen to be meddlers, do-gooders. We offend against a natural order of races: the white, the black, the red. We have the ear of the Conselho Ultramarino still; but Silva Nunes continues his attacks in the heart of the viceroyalty, and general society—in particular the property holders—mistrusts us. There will be a new treaty soon between Portugal and Spain, a repartition of Brazil. The Amazon frontier is Portuguese almost by default. When it comes, the destruction of our reduciones along the valley of the Paraná will be nothing compared to what the entradas will unleash on the Amazonian aldeias. Our enemies are already seeking proofs against us."

"Have they cause?"

"They have. Father Quinn, in the name of Our Lord Jesus Christ, I task you with this mission: to proceed with all haste by ship to Belém do Pará, then by the Amazon to São José Tarumás on the Rio Negro where, as an admonitory of the Society, you will locate Father Diego Gonçalves and restore him to the discipline of the Order."

"What is the nature of Father Diego's offense?"

"I fear that a fine strong priest's zeal has led him into great transgression. Tell me, Father Luis, since you landed how many people have told you that Brazil is not like anywhere else?"

"Only a few dozen, it seems. And more while I was still on the ship."

"Well, I shall not add to their number, but I will say that the Rio Negro is not like anywhere else in Brazil. Beyond São José Tarumás they say there is no faith, law, or royalty. But there is Father Diego Gonçalves. Reports are few and far between, and those there are are more legend than truth: monstrous vanities involving the labor and resources of entire aldeias, an empire claimed in the name of God and of his Order over a thousand miles of the Rio Negro. The Lord's vineyard is rich and ready there, but my reports suggest that he reaps more than the souls of the red men."

Father Luis said, "I know that as little as a fallen crucifix may be grounds for Just War against a native village. I had thought it entirely a trick of the Franciscans."

"If Father Diego Gonçalves' transgressive soul has fallen into vanity and barbarism—and I pray Jesus and His Mother it is not—then you must act immediately. Word cannot be permitted to return to the Reconçavo; it could be the splitting-wedge our enemies need to destroy our order. I have drafted letters patent investing you with full executive authority. It is important that you understand this, Father; full power of admonition."

"Father, you cannot . . ."

A rectangle of yellow light suddenly appeared in the indigo-on-indigo, insect-loud wall. A shadow filled it, spilled across the flagged court, became a face.

"Fathers, the visitor for the admonitory."

The first shadow gave way to a second, taller, more flamboyantly outlined in hat and wig, coat and sword. Provincial de Magalhães said under his breath, "As if God did not ask enough, Caesar now requires his percentage."

Luis Quinn smelled the man's perfume and the sweat it scant concealed, read his mild swagger and faint stoop, and knew him for a government man before the tall, still flames of the lanterns disclosed his face. The visitor made leg.

"Your service, Fathers. José Bonafacio da Nóbrega. I represent His Excellency the viceroy. Please, no introduction. Father Quinn, I was of course informed the instant of your arrival in Salvador; a high-ranking officer of the church will always attract our attention." He flicked out the tails of his coat, adjusted his sword, and seated himself at the table, legs crossed at the ankle. "The Society of Jesus, in this country at least, has long attracted the favor of the crown. You are the confessors of viceroys and fidalgos. However, the Third Order of St. Francis claims the support of our captains and senhores de engenhos, as reflected in the ornateness of their churches." He held the basket hilt of his sword as he jerked, laughing silently at his own humor. Luis Quinn thought, *Wear your graces and weary sophistications like your fine coat and sharply folded hat, but you are nothing but a legman, a runner. I have seen a dozen of you among the quintas of Porto, English spies tasked to scent out priests waiting to be smuggled back into Ireland.*

Father de Magalhães raised a hand to summon fresh coffee. Nóbrega waved him down. "No coffee if you please, Father. I find it disturbs my sleep. I much prefer this of an evening." He took a small, flat silver case from his sleeve and set it on the table. Within were small balls of rolled leaf, each the size of the tip of the smallest finger. Never taking his eyes from Luis Quinn, Nóbrega produced two limes from a handkerchief with a prestidigitatorial flourish, quartered them with a pocket knife, and squeezed a single segment over three herb-balls. One he lifted daintily and placed on his tongue, the other he presented to Father de Magalhães on the silver lid. The third he offered to Luis Quinn.

"I am unfamiliar with this . . . refreshment."

"Oh, it's the most marvelous stuff. Acculico, the Spaniards call it. The feitores ship it across the Pantanal from Characas. The mines at Cuiabá simply couldn't function without it. Sharpens the mind most wonderfully, enlarges the faculties, fills body and soul with energy and well-being. Too good for slaves."

"And excellently potent against the toothache," Father de Magalhães added. "I do believe it could benefit meditation on all-night vigils and stations."

"Totally the wrong climate for it here, alas," said da Nóbrega.

"Thank you, but I will keep my old European ways," Luis Quinn said, taking out a cigar. The boy brought fire. Quinn drew hard, releasing slow spirals of smoke into the star-soft night. "Senhor da Nóbrega, what do you require from me?"

"Yours is reputed to be a learned order, a scientific order."

"It's my particular call to be a linguist, but mathematics and the natural philosophies are widely studied at Coimbra."

"In the city of Belém do Pará is a madman who intends to take the measure of the world with a pendulum." Nóbrega leaned toward Luis Quinn, his manner animated, his eyes wide.

"I believe this may be connected with a heretical English theory of gravitation," said Luis Quinn, marking the influence of the acculico on Nóbrega's body and personality. "The Society teaches the Cartesian theory of vortices, which is a complete physical explanation. As I understand it, the English theory is purely mathematical."

"As you say, Father. This man—this mad scientist—is a Dr. Robert Falcon, a geographer, from the French Academy of Sciences in Paris."

"I understood that Brazil was closed to foreigners, save those in the regular orders. Such as myself, by birth an English subject, if not by inclination."

"His Excellency finds his presence expedient. He arrived with his brother, one Jean-Baptiste, a self-taught mathematician who was inordinately proud of some device he had invented to take all the drudgery out of weaving. I say that's what slaves are for—it gives them something to do—but that is your French petty intelligentsia. Jean-Baptiste was repatriated with the bloody flux six weeks ago, but Robert Falcon remains. He is in some desperate race with fellow academicians to precisely measure the circumference of the globe. It seems, like everything else in this modern world, there is profound disagreement on the shape of our terrestrial sphere—or rather, not quite sphere. You still have salt water behind your ears, so you will have a keen appreciation of just how imprecise an art navigation at sea is, and Portugal is a maritime, mercantile empire. We have received informations that the rival expedition, which is to measure the globe by mensuration and trigonometry, has been granted leave of access by Spain to its viceroyalty of Peru and will shortly embark for Cartagena. Dr. Falcon has been cooling his heels in Belém do Pará for five months already."

"Senhor, with respect, what do you require of me?"

Nóbrega dressed and savored a second acculico. Its effect was almost instantaneous: Quinn wondered if Nóbrega might be habituated to this benign, stimulating herb.

"For the most precise measurements, Dr. Falcon must conduct his experiment on the line of the equator. He has picked a spot five hundred miles above São José Tarumás on the Rio Negro as the most favorable, where what he calls 'continental influences' are in equilibrium."

"I understand. I might travel with him."

"The other way around, Father. He might travel with you. The wrath of the crown is properly turned to the Dutch pirates and adventurers, but the memory of Duguay-Trouin and his pirates strutting around Rio like gamecocks is all too fresh. Has the father-provincial apprised you of the political situation on the Amazon?"

"I understand it is in a state of renegotiation."

"France has long held ambitions in South America far beyond that plague-hole in the Guianas. An uncertain transfer of territory could hand them their opportunity to annex everything north of the Amazon-Solimões. They could have aldeias fortified, tribes armed with modern weaponry before we could even get a fleet to Belém."

"You suspect Dr. Falcon is an agent," Luis Quinn said.

"Versailles would have been insane not to have asked him."

Magalhães spoke now. "I require you merely to observe and record. I have already alluded to your particular sensory acuity, and your facility at languages. . . ."

"Was I chosen as an admonitory or a spy?"

"Our duty is of course to the greater glory of God," de Magalhães said.

"Of course, Father." Luis Quinn dipped his head. New light fell on the table and the fat-leaved, aromatic shrubs: woman slaves brought baskets to dress the dinner table set up in the cool of the cloister. Candles sparked to life; covered silver dishes were laid on the cloth.

"Excellent," cried Nóbrega leaping up from his seat, rubbing his hands. "That coca-stuff is all very fine, but it makes you damnable hungry."

A flurry, a whistle of wings in the night above Luis Quinn's head. Dark shapes dived on folded, curved wings to perch along the tiled eave of the private garden. Light caught hooked beaks, round cunning eyes, a raised, agile claw. Parrots, thought Luis Quinn. *A task most difficult, by God's grace.*

OUR
LADY
OF
SPANDEX

May 24, 2006

Marcelina loved that minuscule, precise moment when the needle entered her face. It was silver; it was pure. It was the violence that healed, the violation that brought perfection. There was no pain, never any pain, only a sense of the most delicate of penetrations, like a mosquito exquisitely sipping blood, a precision piece of human technology slipping between the gross tissues and cells of her flesh. She could see the needle out of the corner of her eye; in the foreshortened reality of the ultra-close-up it was like the stem of a steel flower. The latex-gloved hand that held the syringe was as vast as the creating hand of God: Marcelina had watched it swim across her field of vision, seeking its spot, so close, so thrillingly, dangerously close to her naked eyeball. And then the gentle stab. Always she closed her eyes as the fingers applied pressure to the plunger. She wanted to feel the poison entering her flesh, imagine it whipping the bloated, slack, lazy cells into panic, the washes of immune response chemicals as they realized they were under toxic attack; the blessed inflammation, the swelling of the wrinkled, lined skin into smoothness, tightness, beauty, youth.

Marcelina Hoffman was well on her way to becoming a Botox junkie.

Such a simple treat; the beauty salon was on the same block as Canal Quatro. Marcelina had pioneered the lunch-hour face lift to such an extent that Lisandra had appropriated it as the premise for an entire series. Whore. But the joy began in the lobby with Luesa the receptionist in her high-collared white dress saying "Good afternoon, Senhora Hoffman," and the smell of the beautiful chemicals and the scented candles, the lightness and brightness of the frosted glass panels and the bare wood floor and the cream-on-white cotton wall hangings, the New Age music that she scorned any-where else (Tropicalismo hippy-shit) but here told her, "You're wonderful, you're special, you're robed in light, the universe loves you, all you have to do is reach out your hand and take anything you desire."

Eyes closed, lying flat on the reclining chair, she felt her work-weary crow's-feet smoothed away, the young, energizing tautness of her skin. Two years before she had been in New York on the *Real Sex in the City* production and had been struck by how the ianqui women styled themselves out of per-sonal empowerment and not, as a carioca would have done, because it was her duty before a scrutinizing, judgmental city. An alien creed: thousand-dollar shoes but no pedicure. But she had brought back one mantra among her shopping bags, an enlightenment she had stolen from a Jennifer Aniston cos-metics ad. She whispered it to herself now, in the warm, jasmine-and-vetiver-scented sanctuary as the botulin toxins diffused through her skin.

Because I'm worth it.

"Oh, I love the World Cup." Dona Bebel visited twice a week. Mondays the dry cleaning: dusting, vacuuming, putting things away. Thursdays the wet cleaning: bathroom and toilet, dishes and the laundry Marcelina strewed across her bedroom until by Wednesday evening she could not see the floor. She was a round woman in the indefinable late-fifties, early-sixties; hair heaved back into a headache-inducing bun; eternally in leggings, baggy T-shirts, and Havaianas; and Marcelina treasured her beyond pearls gold cocaine commissions.

"Querida, she comes twice a week, does your disgusting pants, and it's still all there when she leaves?" Vitor was an old gay man, a former participant in a daytime makeover show Marcelina had produced, who lived a handful of streets from her decrepit apartment block with its back hard to the sheer rocks of the morro. An old and unrepentant Copa-ista, he took tea in the same café in the same evening hour every day to watch his bairro pass by. Marcelina had taken to meeting him once a week for doces and bitching as part of her extensive alt dot family, all bound to her in different degrees of gratitude or sycophancy. "Whatever she asks, you pay her."

After a succession of Skinny Marias who had thieved all around them as if it were an additional social security levy and hid warrens of dust bunnies under the bed, Marcelina had been reluctant to take on another cleaner from Pavão. But price was price—the favela tucked away like an infolded navel into the hills behind Arpoador was that that unspeakable elephant of cheap labor upon which the Copa depended. She left the glasses twinkling like diamonds, the whites blinding, and when she discovered what it was that Marcelina did for her money, pitched a program idea: "You should do a show where you go and clean up people's houses while they're out at work. I'd watch that. Nothing people like better than looking at someone else's filth."

Filthy Pigs had on-screen screamfests, fights, camera-smashings; destroyed friendships of years; opened generational rifts children against parents; ruined relationships; wrecked marriages; and provoked at least one shooting. Audiences watched through their fingers, faintly murmuring, "No, no." Raimundo Sifuentes had thundered upon it in the review pages of *O Globo* as "the real filthy pigs are at Canal Quatro." It was Marcelina's first water-cooler show.

Over three years many of Marcelina's best commissions had come from Dona Bebel. *Kitsch and Bitch*, which had brought Vitor to prominence and turned his small store of immaculate twentieth-century kitschery into a must-shop destination featured in in-flight magazines, had come from a comment as Dona Bebel slung the washing over the line in Marcelina's precious roof garden that she always knew which men she cleaned for were gay because they had always had 1950s plastic around the place.

Guilt and remorse were as alien to Marcelina as a nun's habit, but she honorably put a sliver of her bonus into Dona Bebel's weekly envelope for every commission she won. She never asked what Dona Bebel thought when she saw her casual aside up in sixteen-by-nine with full graphics. She did not even know if Dona Bebel watched Canal Quatro. She was right off its demographic.

"Oooh, World Cup." Marcelina's whites went round in the washing machine on Wets Thursday. The apartment's bare, tiled floors smelled of bleach and pine. "They're going to put a big screen up down at the Gatinha Bar. I'm going to watch them all. Brazil versus Italy in the final, I say. I'd put money on it. This time we'll beat them. They may have the best defense in Europe, but our Magic Quadrilateral will go through them like a knife. I think a program about the World Cup would be a very good idea—I'd watch it. But if you want controversial, you have to go for the Fateful Final."

"The what?" Marcelina said over the twelve hundred rev spin cycle gearing up.

For the first time Dona Bebel was taken aback.

"You mean, you don't know about the Fateful Final? Every true Brazilian should have July sixteenth 1950 engraved on her heart. This wasn't a soccer match. This was our Hiroshima. I don't exaggerate. After the Fateful Final, nothing was the same again."

"Tell me," said Marcelina, settling down on top of the upturned plastic laundry basket.

Well, I was a very little girl at the time and we didn't have a television, no one did, but . . ."

This is not history. This is legend. We built the Maracanã for the 1950 World Cup—then, as it is now, the greatest stadium in the world—and in front of two hundred thousand people, we were going to show the world the beauty and the poetry of Brazilian futebol. A war had ended, a new world had risen from its ashes; this was the World Cup of the Future in the Nation of the Future.

This was the team: it was as great as any Seleção, as great even as the squad of 1970, but you won't see it listed on the statue outside the Maracanã. Coach: Flávio Costa. Front to back: Chico, Jair da Rosa Pinto, Ademir, Zizinho, Friaça; Bigode, Danilo, Bauer; Juvenal, Augusto; Barbosa. Five three two. Beautiful. Moaçir Barbosa: you hear much more about him. Now, in 1950 the system was different from the way it is now; it was a group system all the way to the final.

My father was working then on a bridge and had money, so he bought a radio just for the World Cup. He wired it into the streetlight. It was the only radio on the street, so everyone came around to listen. You could not move in our good room for people come for the game.

We kicked off the World Championships on the twenty-fourth of June against Mexico. Bam! Down they went. Four-nil. Next! Switzerland. Here we had a bit of a wobble—but that's the best time to have a wobble, early on. A draw, two all. Now we had to beat Yugoslavia to qualify for the finals group. There can be only one from each group. We played it at the new Maracanã and we won: two nil. We're through to the final group!

In the final group are Sweden, Spain, and Uruguay, the Sky-blue Celestes.

Now we have to put the radio in the window, because we couldn't fit all the people who wanted to listen into the house. My father set it on an oil drum, and people lined up all the way down the hill.

Game one, we crush Sweden seven-one. Game two, Spain, six-one. Nothing—nothing—can stop Brazil. This will be one of the greatest Seleçãos in history. The only thing that stands between us and glory is tiny Uruguay. Rio expects, the nation expects, the world expects we will raise the Jules Rimet in the most beautiful stadium in the world in the most beautiful city in the world. *O Mundo* even prints pictures of the team in the early editions with the headline: *These Are the World Champions!*

On July sixteenth one-tenth of Rio is inside that oval. A tenth of the entire city, yes. The rest of the nation is listening on the radio: everyone remembers exactly where they were when the referee blew for kickoff. The first half is goalless. But in the twenty-eighth minute something very strange happens: Uruguay's captain, Obdulio Varela, hits Bigode, and it's like macumba. Everyone knows the energy in the stadium has changed; you could even feel it through the radio. The axé was no longer with Brazil. But then one minute into the second half, Friaça sees the angle . . . shoots. Gooool do Brasil! One-nil, one-nil, one-nil, one-nil. Everyone is dancing and singing in the house and every other house and all the way down the street onto the Copa. Then in the sixty-eighth minute, Gigghia for Uruguay picks up that macumba and runs with the ball. He's past Bigode on the right wing, crosses. Schiaffino's on the end of it and puts it past Barbosa. God himself could not have stopped that shot.

But we can still win. We've come back from worse than this. We're Brazil. Then, at 4:33, all the clocks stop. Once again Gigghia beats Bigode. He's into the box. But this time he doesn't cross. He's close on the post, but he takes the shot. Barbosa doesn't think anyone could get in from that angle. He moves too slow, too late. The ball's in the back of the net. *Goal to Uruguay*, says Luis Mendes on the radio, and then, as if he can't believe what he said, he says it again: *Goal to Uruguay.* And again, six times he says it. It's true. Uruguay two, Brazil one. There's not a sound in the stadium, not a sound in our house or on the street, not in the whole of Pavão, not in the whole of Rio. Gigghia always said, only three people ever silenced the Maracanã with one movement: Frank Sinatra, the pope, and him.

Then the final whistle went and Uruguay lifted the World Cup, and still there wasn't a sound. My father couldn't work for a week. A man up the hill threw himself in front of a bus; he couldn't stand it. Rio froze over. The whole nation went into shock. We've never recovered from it. Maybe we expected too much; maybe the politicians talked it up until it wasn't just a game of soccer, it was Brazil itself. People who were there in the Maracanã, do you know what they call themselves? "Survivors." That's right. But the real pain wasn't that we lost the World Cup; it was the realization that maybe we weren't as great as we believed we were. Even up in our shack on the Morro de Pavão, listening on a radio wired into the streetlight with an oil drum for an amplifier, we still thought we were part of a great future. Maybe now we weren't the nation of the future, that everyone admired and envied, maybe we were just another South American banana republic strutting around all puffed out like a gamecock in gold braid and plumes that nobody really took seriously. The Frenchman de Gaulle once said, "Brazil is not a serious country": after the Fateful Final, we believed him.

Of course we looked for scapegoats. We always do. Barbosa, he was the hated one. He was our last line of defense, the nation was depending on him, he let Brazil down, and Brazil was never going to let him forget it. He only played again once for the Seleção; then he gave up the game, gave up all his friends from the game, dropped out of society, and eventually disappeared completely. Brazil has given him fifty years of hell; you don't even get that for murder.

"So it's a trial format," Marcelina Hoffman said. This Blue Sky Friday the pitching session took place in Adriano's conference room, a glass cube with the titles of Canal Quatro's biggest and noisiest hits etched into an equatorial strip. There were a couple of Marcelina's among them. Toys and fresh new puzzles were strewn deliberately around the floor to encourage creativity. Last week it was Brain Gym for the PSP; this week, books of paper marked and precreased for Rude Origami. The Sauna, as its nickname around Rua Muniz Barreto implied, was notorious for its atrocious air-conditioning, but the sweat Marcelina felt beading down her sides was not greenhouse heat. Roda sweat: this glass room was as much a martial arts arena as any capoeira roda. It would take all her jeito, all her malicia, to dance down her enemies. Aid me, Nossa Senhora da Valiosa Producão.

"We track him down, haul him in, and put him on trial before the people of Brazil. We present evidence, for and against—he gets a fair trial. As fair as we want it to be. Maybe get a real judge to preside. Or Pelé. Then the viewers decide whether to forgive him or not."

Glass tables in a glass room; arranged in a quadrilateral. Community-facilitating and democratic, except that Adriano and the Black Plumed Bird, so very very Audrey Hepburn today, sat on the side of the quadra farthest from the sun. Lisandra and her pitch team were to Marcelina's right; the über-bosses on her left. Keep your enemies in your peripheral vision but never be seen looking; that is foolishness. Directly across the square from her was Arlindo Pernambucano from Entertainment; too too old to be creaming and shrieking over celebrity mags and general girliness but who, nonetheless, had a phenomenal hit-rate. But he was out of this jogo. It was Lisandra and Marcelina in the roda.

"What happens if he's guilty?" Adriano asked.

"We make him apologize on live TV."

Adriano winced. But that's all right; that's the cringe-TV wince, the car-crash/guilty-pleasure wince. Embarrassment TV. He was liking it.

"And is he still alive?"

"I ran a check through public records," said Celso, Marcelina's boy researcher and newest member of her alt dot family. He was intimidatingly sharp, nakedly ambitious, was always at his desk before Marcelina arrived and there after she left. She had no doubt that someday he would reach for Marcelina's crown but not this day; not when the joy—the old heat of the idea that burned out of nowhere perfect and complete as if it had *Made in Heaven* stamped on the base, the joy she thought she had lost forever and might now only glimpse in Botafogo sunrises and the glow and laughter of the streets of Copa from her roof garden—glowed in her ovaries. *I'm back*, she thought.

"We could make the search for him part of the program," Adriano said. *He's making suggestions*, Marcelina observed. *He's taking ownership of it.* She might get this. She might get this.

"He must be a very old man by now," the Black Plumed Bird said.

"Eighty-five," said Celso at once.

"It's an interesting idea, but is it Canal Quatro to hold an old man up to ridicule and humiliation? Is this just pelourinho by television?"

Yes, Marcelina wanted to scream. Nothing is more Canal Quatro than the whipping post, the pillory, the branding iron. It's what we love most, the suffering of others, the freak show. Give us torment and madness, give us public dissections and disgust, give us girls taking their clothes off. We are a prurient, beastly species. They knew it in the eighteenth century; they knew the joy of public disgrace. If there were public executions, Canal Quatro would run them prime time and rule the ratings.

"It's a chance for us to get closure on something that still festers, fifty years on. We've won since, but not when it really mattered, on our own soil, in our own stadium, in front of our own people."

Adriano nodded. Lisandra had folded a page from her origami book into two red rabbits, fucking. She jiggled them in the edge of Marcelina's vision.

"No, I like this," the director of programming announced. "It's edgy, noisy, divisive—we'd run an SMS guilty/innocent vote. It's absolutely Canal Quatro. IPTRB."

It presses the right buttons, Marcelina guessed.

"List shows have always performed well for us," the Black Plumed Bird said, inclining her head a degree toward Lisandra. "All-Time Greatest Seleção would get people talking." Celso had folded a sheet from his book into a green penis, which he slowly erected in Lisandra's direction.

"No, thank you all," Adriano said, pushing himself back a fraction from the glass table. Anticipation cracked around the room like indoor lightning. "I knew you'd do it. Okay, IRTAMD."

I'm Ready to Announce My Decision.

"The universe has ten to the one hundred and twenty calculations left to perform," said Heitor, feet on his desk in his corner office, gazing out at the traffic headed beach-ward and the rectangle of gold and blue on blue at its end, like a flag of jubilee. "Then it all stops and everything ends and it's dark and cold and it goes on expanding forever until everything is infinitely far apart from everything else. You know, I am sure I'm developing a wheat allergy."

"You could say, 'Well done, Marcelina, congratulations, Marcelina, killer pitch, Marcelina, I'll take you out and buy you champagne at the Café Barbosa, Marcelina.'"

The newsroom was accustomed to Marcelina Hoffman bursting out of scruffy, bitchy Popular Factual into their clean, focused atmosphere of serious journalism like a cracked exhaust muffler, striding thunder-faced between the rows of hotdesks to Heitor's little sanctum where he contemplated his role as the bringer of bad tidings to millions and the futility of the news media in general. The door would close, the rants would start, the stringers would put their heads down or look up holidays online. So when she came in grinning as if she had done six lines off a toilet seat, small tits pushed out and golden curls bouncing, the newsroomers were momentarily flustered. No yells from Heitor's office. Everyone in the building, let alone the eighth floor, knew they were occasionally fucking; the mystery was why. A few understood that a relationship can be born out of a necessity not to have sex with anyone who needed to have sex with you. They kept the insight to themselves. They feared they would have to play that card themselves someday.

"Fully funded development and a complete proposal in two weeks moving to a commission green light before the end of the month. Am I fucking hot or what?"

Heitor took his feet off his desk and turned toward Marcelina, seemingly filling two-thirds of his office, capoeira queen, haloed in success.

"Well done, Marcelina."

He did not hug her to his big, bear body in its gray suit. It was not that kind of relationship.

"What are your shifts like this afternoon?" Café Barbosa: always a sign somewhere. Thank you, Our Lady of Production Values.

"Early evening bulletin and the main seven o'clock."

Heitor the depressive newsreader was a media joke far beyond Canal Quatro, but Marcelina knew that his sweet, contemplative melancholy was not caused by the constant rain of sensationalist, violent, celebrity-obsessed news that blew through his life, but because he felt responsible for it. He was Death invited to a nation's TV dinners. Marcelina, in contrast, was quite happy to pursue a career of insignificant triviality.

"Here's what going to happen. I have an appointment with a needle. I go to the Café Barbosa with my team, my alt dot family and anyone else who wants to buy me a beer. You come round, we go on to Lapa. We go back to yours. I fuck the ass off you. But first, I need you to help me."

"I thought there'd be a price."

"The commission's dependent on finding Barbosa. Do you know how I might go about that?"

"Well, I don't. . . ."

"But you know someone who might." The standard joke of journalists and lawyers.

"Try this guy." Heitor inscribed a pink Post-it. "He can be a bit hard to find, but he knows Rio like no one else. Try catching him on Flamengo Beach, early."

"How early?"

"Whatever you call early, earlier than that. He says it's the beach's best time." Heitor turned away and grimaced as e-mail flurried into his in-box. "It's bread, definitely. I'm going to give it up. You should read this." A hard-back book lay prone, praying on the desk. Heitor read aggressively, trying to find in printed pages ideas he might weave into an excuse for this mad world he found himself presenting twice a day. He pressed a book a week on Marcelina, who passed them on unread to Dona Bebel. Reading text was so static, so last century. "It's about information theory, which is the latest theory of everything. It says the universe is just one huge quantum computer, and we are all programs running on it. I find that very comforting, don't you?"

"Try and make it, Heitor. You need a lot of beer and hot hot sex."

He lifted a hand, absorbed with the incoming world.

Her car was not waiting outside on Rua Muniz Barreto. Marcelina looked up, Marcelina looked down, then went into reception.

"Did you call my taxi?"

"Called, came, went," said Robson on the door, who was a glorious creature, tall, killer cheekbones, swimmer's muscles, so black he glowed, and regularly voted Most Lickable in the Christmas Awards. Marcelina could not believe he was natural.

"What do you mean, went?"

"You tell me. You went off in it."

"I went off in the taxi? I only just got here now."

Robson looked at his hands in that way that people do when confronted by the publicly insane.

"Well, you came out of the elevator and said just what you said to me there now, 'Did you call my taxi?' And I said, yes, there it is outside, and you got in it and drove off."

"I think that one of us is on very strong drugs." It could be her. This could all be a guaraná and speed flashback from the all-nighter. The pressure is off, you get the result of results, and your brain geysers like Mentos in Diet Coke.

"Well, I know what I saw." The people who voted Robson Most Lickable had never spoken to him when riled, when a tone of camp petulance entered his voice.

"What was I wearing?" Marcelina said. Time was ticking. "Aw, fuck it, I'll walk."

Mysteries could wait. She had an appointment with the thin steel needle of love.

"Black suit," Robson called after her. "You were in a black suit, and killer shoes."

SEPTEMBER 25, 2032

Hot hot hot in skinny-heel knee boots, high-thigh polo neck body, and a cutie little black biker's jacket cut bolero style, Efrim stalks the gafieira. Cidade de Luz is bouncing. This is a wedding gafieira, and they're the best. The open end of José's Garage is now the sound stage; the speakers hauled up on engine-tackles. A kid DJ wearing the national flag like Superman's cape spins crowd-pleasers. A rollscreen displays a shifting constellation of patterned lights, the arfids of the gafieira tracked through the Angels of Perpetual Surveillance and displayed as a flock of beauty. Kid DJ sticks his fingers in the air, gets a small roar, claps his hands and holds them aloft, gets a big roar. Senhors, senhoras . . . Her entrance is lost in the dazzle of swinging lights and the opening drum-rush of "Pocotocopo," this year's big hit, but the audience sees the silver soccer ball lob into the air, freckled with glitterspots. Milena Castro, Keepie-Uppie Queen, volleys her ball across the stage and back; head tits ass and knees. A smile with every bounce. The V of her thong bears the blue lozenge and green globe of Brasil. Ordem e Progresso. She turns her back to the crowd, shakes her booty. There's a ragged cheer.

Good girl, thinks Efrim. She's the first of his two acts on tonight, in his other incarnation as MD of De Freitas Global Talent. But tonight he is in party mode, fabulous in huge afro wig and golden-glow body-blush with a tab of TalkTalk from Streets, his supplier of neurological enhancements, down him so he can say anything to anyone: absolutely flawless. The girls stare as Efrim stalks by, bag swinging. They're meant to. Everyone is meant to. Tonight Efrim/Edson—a lad of parts—is hunting.

"Hey, Efrim!" Big Steak is over by the bar, one arm holding up a caipi, the other curled around fiancée, Serena. He owns a half share in the gym with Emerson, Edson's brother number one. "Are you enjoying it?" From his ebullience and sway, Big Steak's been loving the hospitality of his own gafieira. Serena Most Serene frowns at Edson. She has glasses but is too vain to wear them. Big Steak's engagement present to her is a lasering in a proper Avenida Paulista surgery. "Looking foxy." Efrim curtseys. Serena checks his fab thighs. "So you finally got yourself a good act. How long can she keep it up?"

"Longer than you," says Efrim, gabby on the TalkTalk and striking the kind of pose you can only get with spike-heel boots and a monster Afro. Serena Most Serene creases over. Big Steak waves him away and someone is beckoning him over from beside the gas tanks, *Hey Edson, get on over here.* It's Turkey-Feet with a posse of Penas, that old gang of Edson's, at the back of the garage where they're storing the knockoff vodka.

It had never really been a gang in the sense of honor and guns and ending up dead on a soft verge; more a group of guys who hung together, stealing the odd designer valuable, dealing the occasional dice of maconha or illicit download, here a little vehicle lifting, there some community policing, all as The Man up in the favela permitted. It had gone that way, for the younger ones saw no other road out of Cidade de Luz than walking up into the favela and taking the scarifications of a soldado of the drug lord. By then the old Penas were moving on, moving out, marrying, getting children, getting jobs, getting lazy and fat. Edson inevitably followed his older brothers into the Penas, but he had understood at once that it would ultimately be an obstacle to his ambitions. Edson subtly loosened the ties that bound him to the gang, flying farther and freer as his separate identities developed until, like a rare comet, he drifted in shaking his gaudy tail only for parties, gafieiras, weddings, and funerals, a fortunate portent. He was his own gang now.

"It's Efrim, honey."

"Efrim Efrim, you got to see this."

It catches the scatter-light on its curves like a knife, it fits the fist like a knife, it smells like a knife—but Efrim can see a shiver along the edge of the blade, like a thing there and not there, like a blade made from dreams. This is much more than a knife.

"Where did you get this?"

"Bought it from some guy from Itaquera, says he got it from the military. Here, want a go?" Turkey-Feet waves the knife at Efrim.

"I'm not touching that thing."

Turkey-Feet masks his rejection by making three sharp passes, blade whistling. Cutting air. Efrim smells electricity.

"Look at this. This is cool."

Turkey-Feet squats, sets a brick on the oily ground. With the delicacy of a dealer measuring doses on a scale, he rests the handle on the ground, sets the edge of the blade against the brick. The knife blade swings down through the brick as if it were liquid. Turkey-Feet quickly props a cigarette packet under the hilt. The blade continues its downward arc through José's Garage floor until it starts to slide, to pierce, sliding into the concrete until its hilt finds purchase.

Q-blade. Yes, Efrim has heard of these. No one knows where they come from: the army, the US military, the Chinese, the CIA, but since they started appearing in funk-bars as the weapon of preference, everyone knows what they do. Cut through anything. Edge so sharp it cuts right down to the atoms. From his sessions with Mr. Peach, Edson knows its sharper than that. Edged down to the quantum level. Break one—and the only thing that will break a Q-blade is another Q-blade—and the shard will fall through solid rock all the way to the center of the earth.

"Is that not the coolest thing?"

"That is a thing of death, honey." He can feel it from the blade, like sunburn. Streets' pirate empathics have a fresh little synesthetic edge.

José's Garage quakes as Kid DJ starts up a new set. Efrim leaves the Penas playing finger-and-knife games with the Q-blade. *You will never get out of Cidade de Luz that way.* It is time for De Freitas Global Talent's other act to make its debut.

"Senhors senhoras, pod-wars! Pod-wars! Pod-wars!" the DJ bellows, his voice reverbing into a feedback screech. "Round one! Remixado João B versus PJ Suleimannnnnnn! There can be! Only! One! Let the wars begin!"

A wall of cheering as the contenders bounce onto the soundstage. Petty Cash will face whichever of these two wins the crowd's hearts, hands, and feet. Efrim positions himself by the churrasco stand to check out the competition.

"Foxy, Efrim," says Regina the churrasco queen. Efrim grins. He loves the attention on the special occasions when he trots out in his travesti aspect. He lifts the bamboo skewer of fatty, blackened beef to his glossed lips. PJ Suleiman takes João B so easily it is embarrassing: the kid's got no beats, takes everything down to this vaqueiro guitar riff he thinks is funky but to the audience sounds like the theme from a gaucho telenovela. They pelt him off with empty caipiroshka cups.

Senhors, senhoras, Petty Petty Petty Caaaaaash!

Petty Cash had been the perfect alibi—quiet, no gang connections, deeply deeply devoted to the beats trilling out of his headphones. In Total Surveillance Sampa even the most respectable man of business needs an alibi to swap identities with sometime: many were the afternoons Edson had gone about Cidade de Luz and even up to the favela with Petty Cash's identity loaded on his I-shades while Petty Cash sat missing beats as Edson Jesus Oliveira de Freitas. Then one day Edson, as he switched identities back, actually listened to the choons dancing across Petty Cash's I-shades, and for the first time the words crossed his lips: *I might be able to do something with that.* On that tin-roofed verandah De Freitas Global Talent was born. Now the world will see him shake mass booty.

Straight up Petty Cash catches PJ Suleiman's hip-swaying samba paulistano, hauls a mangue bass out of his sample array, and brings in a beat that has the bass drivers bowing and booming in their cabs. The crowd reels back all at once, whoa! Then in midbeat everyone is up in the air, coming down on the counterpoint, and the bloco is bouncing. Suleiman tries something clever clever with a classic black-metal guitar solo and an old drum-bass rinse, and it's itchy and scratchy but you can't dance to that. Petty Cash takes the guitar solo, rips off the bass section and bolts on funk in industrial quantities: an old gringo bass line from another century and a so-fresh-they-haven't-taken-the-plastic-off pau-rhythm. Efrim can see the track lines on Petty Cash's I-shades as his eyeballs sample and mix in real time. The audience are living it loving it slapping it sucking it: no question who wins this face-off.

Then God says, *Tonight, Efrim/Edson/everyone else you ever were or might be, I smile down from beyond satellite and balloons and Angels of Perpetual Surveillance on you.*

Her. At the bar with a caipiroshka in a plastic cup in her hand and a gang of girlfriends. Pink jacaré boots (what is this she has with endangering the cayman population?) and a little silver snake-scale A-line so short it skims her panties but moves magnificently, heavily, richly. Korr I-shades that go halfway around her head. Space-baby. Her hair is pink tonight. Pink and silver: perfect match for the seasonal must-have Giorelli Habbajabba bag on her arm. She came.

PJ de Peeeeepoooooo! Kid DJ announces the next challenger as Efrim moves through the crowd toward the bar.

"Efrim Efrim Efrim!" The cries in his ear are like pistol shots. When Edson was in the Penas, Treats followed him like a dog around a bitch. Treats's eyes and manic insistence betray a load of drugs. "Trampo's dead, man. He's dead!"

Trampo is—was—a dirty little favelado stupid enough to want to look mean who presumably took Edson's place as the sunshine in Treats's life when Edson walked out of the gang. Some are born with bullet marks on their bodies, like stigmata. Even in semirespectable Cidade de Luz murder is the most common death for young males. You properly come of age if you make thirty.

"They cut him in half, man; they fucking cut him in half. They left him at the side of the rodovia. There was the sign cut into the road."

It would be a slope-sided rectangle with a domed top, a stylized garbage can. *Take out the trash.* Cut with one of those same weapons that the Penas played with so casually in the back of José's Garage. That's how everyone knows the Q-blade. It's the real star on what has for the last six seasons been São Paulo's top-rated TV show. No network could sanction a reality program where José Publics compete to join the resident team of bandeirantes to hunt down street hoods. But this is the time of total media, of universal content provision, wiki-vision. A bespoke pirate production house casts it pay-per-view to twelve million pairs of I-shades. Reformers, evangelical Christians, liberation priests, campaigning lawyers, and socialists demand something be done, we know where these people are, close them down out of great São Paulo. The police turn a blind eye. Someone has to take out the trash. Efrim would never filthy his retinas with such a thing, but he admires their business plan. And now they've come to Cidade de Luz. This is not a conversation for now. Frightening people at a wedding gafieira, and Efrim on the hunt. She is still there, at the impromptu bar made from trestle tables borrowed from the parish center. The priest has more sense than to come to see what is being done with his tables; but the crentes, with their infallible noses for the unsaved, are handing out hell-is-scary-and-real tracts, all of which have been trodden underfoot into alcohol-soaked papier-mâché. Women scoop caipiroshkas into plastic glasses from washing-up basins. Two guys in muscle tops pound limes in big wooden mortars. Get rid of this fool quick. Efrim rolls a little foil-wrapped ball of maconha out of his bag.

"Here, querida, for you, have this." The kid is wasted already, but Edson wants him so far away that he can't scare anyone else. How rude. "Go on, it's yours, run on there."

Senhors, Senhoras, PJ Raul Glor—ee—aaaaaah! G-g-g-gloriiiia! Another win for Petty Cash.

"Hooo honeys!" Efrim cruises in, hips waggling samba-time, looking their style up and down, down and up. "My, what shocking bad shoes." Fia and her girlfriends whoop and cheer. Efrim lets the TalkTalk roll, swaggers up and down in a mock military inspection of each in turn. "Honey, has no one told you pterodactyl toes are no no no? Oh my sweet Jesus and Mary. Pink and orange? Efrim shall pray for you, for only Our Lady of Killer Shooz can save you now. Now you, you need a workout. Make an effort. Efrim is the one has to look at you. Telenovela arms, darling. Yours sag like an old priest's dick. And as for you, honey, the only thing can save you is plastic. I'll have a little whip round. I know a couple of cheap guys—don't we all wish?" He stops in front of Fia. The Habbajabba is crooked over her arm, comfortable as a sleeping cat. *You don't know who I am. But I know who you are.* Efrim loves the anonymity of the mask.

"But for you, I do some travesti magic. You don't believe me? We all have the magic, the power, all us girls. You give me that bag and I will tell you magic things." Laughing at the damn effrontery of Efrim, Fia hands over the Habbajabba. Efrim rubs his hands all over it, sniffs it, licks it. "Ah now: this bag says to me that it was given to you, not bought with money. A man gave this to you: wait, the bag tells me he is a businessman, he is a man with contacts and connections and people." Efrim puts the bag up to his ear, pouts, eyes wide in mock shock. "The bag says the man gave it to you because you did him a big favor. You saved his dumb-ass brother from the seguranças."

Efrim has been carefully steering Fia away from her girlfriends. They think it is funny—they wave, they kissy-kiss—and she is willing to be steered on this gafieira night. Edson holds the bag up and whispers to it, nods his head, rolls his big big eyes.

"The bag says, the man of business still owes you. After all, it was his brother, and he may be useless but he is still worth more than a bag. Even this bag."

Fia laughs. It is like falling coins bouncing from a sidewalk.

"And how does this big businessman want to treat me?"

"He is about to do a deal on an Arabic lanchonete. Their kibes just slay you. He would like you to be the first to try what will surely be Sampa's hottest food franchise and make him a rich rich man with an apartment on Ilhabela."

That has always been Edson's great dream: a house by the sea. Someday, before he is too middle-aged lazy to enjoy it, he will have a place down on Ilhabela where he can wake every morning and see the ocean. He will never visit it until it is built, but when it is he will arrive by night so all he can sense is the sound and the ocean will be the first thing he sees when he wakes. Santos is half an hour away by the fast train, but Edson has never seen the sea.

"Flowers are cheaper. And prettier," says Fia.

"Flowers are already dead."

"The bag told you all this?"

"With a little travesti magic."

"I think you've worked enough magic tonight, whatever your name is."

Efrim's heart jumps.

"Tonight, I am Efrim."

"So what other little secrets have you got, Efrim/Edson or whoever else you are?"

Only one, says Edson/Efrim to himself, *and not even my mother knows that.* He flounces, shaking his big Afro wig, because Efrim can get away with it.

"Well, you made the gafieira, so now I think you have to do the kibes. The bag says."

"Do you remember what I said last time?"

"'Don't push it.'"

He can see Fia run through all the reasons why she should say no again and dismiss them. It is only lunch. A call comes through on the peripheral vision of her Korrs. Her face changes. Efrim can hear a tinny, trebly man's voice cut through the seismic bass of the pod-battles. He wants to stab that man. Fia opaques her I-shades, concealing her caller's image. Her mouth sets hard. Frown lines. This is not a good call. She glances around to two men standing on the edge of the gafieira. She touches his hand.

"I got to go."

"Hey hey honey, don't leave me now. What about that little lanchonete?"

She turns back before the crowd can take her away, touches her Korrs. A com address flicks up on Efrim's I-shades.

"You be careful, now. There are killers out there."

"I know," she calls. "Oh, I know."

Gone.

Dona Hortense at her Book of Weeping knows it. The dead and the abandoned and the ill and the down-in-heart and dispossessed and debt-haggard and wives of feckless husbands and mothers of careless children she remembers in her book know it. Useless Gerson, back home now and swinging his afternoons away in his brother's hammock, knows it. All the living brothers know it, including number four son Milson out with the Brasilian UN peacekeeping force in Haiti. Décio, who shaves Edson under the araça tree in his black leather chair, smooth and soft as a vagina, knows it. His broker knows it, his dealer knows it, the brothers who maintain his Yam know it, the kids who play futsal behind the Assembly of God, all his old irmãos from the Penas know it, all his alibis and his alibis' alibis know it.

Edson's in love.

The only one who doesn't know it is Mr. Peach. And, dressed as Miracle Boy, Edson is trying to find a way of telling him.

It's a slow crime day in Great São Paulo, so Captain Superb and Miracle Boy just lie on their bed in the fazenda. Miracle Boy smokes maconha; exhaling small, miraculous smoke rings up to the ceiling. His cape and mask hang on the knob of the carved, heavy mahogany bed. He keeps his boots on. Captain Superb likes that.

Sometimes it's hero and villain. Sometimes it's villain and hero. Sometimes, like today, it's hero and hero. The superman and sidekick. Miracle Boy's spandex costume is split green and yellow, head to toe. The left side, the yellow side, is emblazoned with a wraparound knee-to-chin blue six. Big six, little six. Sextinho. He's been that nickname to Mr. Peach—sorry, Captain Superb—half his life. This particular costume is cut a little cheap and digs into his ass crack. Miracle Boy has the mother of camel-toes.

Miracle Boy's glad it's hero on hero. Hero/villain–villain/hero tends to involve more bondage. There's a lot of old slave-days stuff down in the basements of this fazenda, including an iron slave-mask for gagging unruly peças that scares him. The house is full of old stuff that Mr. Peach keeps giving to Edson, but he'll never have anyone to pass it on to. Edson could make more online, but he prefers his cash quick and secretive and vends through the guy at the Cidade de Luz Credit Union. De Freitas Global Talent is built on Alvaranga antiques.

In this scenario, it's the gym and a lot of mutual appreciation in front of the mirrors. He passes the spliff to Captain Superb, who takes a little tentative puff through his mask, leaks aromatic smoke through his nostril-holes. Captain Superb is in titanium and black: boots, pants, belt, gloves, full-head mask. Even afterward, in the chill, he likes to wear the mask. Seen, not seen. Lying on his back his belly doesn't show. Edson doesn't mind the belly as much as Mr. Peach thinks he does. He loves the old fuck.

"Hey hero."

"What?"

"What do you know about quantum computing?"

"Why are you asking?"

Hero passes spliff back to boy wonder.

"I was talking to someone."

"You were talking to someone about quantum computing?"

"It was business. Don't give me a hard time. So: how does it work?"

Captain Superb's civilian aspect is Mr. Peach, a semiretired professor of theoretical physics at the University of São Paulo, last heir of the former coffee fazenda of Alvaranga, superhero fetishist and Edson Jesus Oliveira de Freitas's mentor and afternoon delight.

"Well, do you remember when I told you about shadows and frogs?"

Edson/Sextinho wriggles in his costume and presses up against Mr. Peach. Ever since the first tentative, apologetic fumble—Mr. Peach much less comfortable than teenage, cocky Sextinho—every session has been paid for with a story. Like a superhero, Edson feels he can fly, high and vertiginous, on what physics tells him about the real.

The story of the shadows and the frogs is one of the best, simple yet confusing, moving from the mundane to the extraordinary, weird yet of profound importance. Edson is not sure he has worked out all the philosophical and emotional implications of it yet. He suspects no one can. Like all the best stories, it starts with a blindingly obvious question: what is light made of? Not so simple a question, not answerable by the simple razor of chopping it finer and finer until you reached fundamental units that could not be split any further (though Edson had learned, in his superhero sessions, that even that was correct; the fundaments had fundaments, and even those might be made up of vibrating strings like guitars, though Mr. Peach did not hold with that interpretation of reality). For what fundamental units of light—photons— were seemed to differ depending on what you did with them. Fire a single photon at certain metals and they would kick out debris, like when Edson would watch his older brothers practice on the road signs with the airgun. Fire one through two tiny, tiny slits, and they do something very different. It makes a pattern of shadows, dark and bright lines, like two sets of waves on a puddle meeting. How can a single photon go through both slits? One thing cannot be two things at the same time. Physics, Mr. Peach always says, is about physical reality. So what is the photon: wave or particle? This is the question at the heart of quantum physics, and any answer to it means that physical reality is very very different from what we think it is. Mr. Peach's answer is that when the single photon goes through, the real photon goes through one slit but a ghost photon goes through the other slit at the same time and interferes with it. In fact, for every real photon that goes through, a trillion ghosts go with it, most of them so wide of the mark they never interfere with the this-worldly original. Of course Edson wanted to know what was so special about photons that they had ghosts. To which Mr. Peach said, *Nothing.* In physics the laws apply everywhere, so if photons have ghosts, so does every other particle (and these they had covered in Physics 101, years before) and everything made from those particles. A trillion ghost Sextinhos. A trillion ghost fazenda Alvarangas, a trillion ghost Brasils and ghost worlds and ghost suns. Ghost everythings. And there is a word for a physical system of *everything*, and that is a *universe*. A trillion and more, vastly more, universes, as real to their Sextinhos and Mr. Peaches, their Miracle Boys and Captain Superbs, as this. To which Edson thought, head frying, *Maybe somewhere I never took the peach from the bag the driver offered when he didn't have any change for the thirteen-year-old car-minder.* Physical reality is all these ghost universes stacked beside each other: the multiverse and—on the very smallest, briefest, weakest scales—the doors between the universes open. Edson's still thinking about that; more real to him now he's obsessed with a girl who works in ten to the eight hundred universes. But what about the frogs?

Oh, that's easy, Mr. Peach had said. A frog's eyes are so sensitive it can see a single photon of light.

"Frogs see on the quantum level; they can see into the multiverse," says Miracle Boy as Captain Superb moves his gloved hands over the firm curve of his ass. "That's why they sit around with their eyes wide."

"So what's the sudden interest in quantum computation?" asks Captain Superb. The slatted light beaming through the shutters fades. The room goes dark. A gust of wind rocks the hanging flower baskets on the verandah. Sudden rain rattles on the roof tiles. "You've met someone, haven't you? You bitch! Who is she, go on, tell me!" Captain Superb sits up, fingers raised to tickle Miracle Boy into submission. There is no bitch or bitterness in his voice. It's not that kind of affair; it's not that kind of city. Here you can lead many lives, be many selves. Mr. Peach has seen many half-heartbreaks pass through Sextinho's life, but none ever touch what they have in the fazenda up on the hill. There are whole provinces of Edson's life he barely knows, many he suspects he never will.

"Just tell me, and maybe then I might tell you," Miracle Boy says, springing out from beneath the tormenting fingers, the stub on the maconha in his hand. Someday Edson hopes to graduate from being something Boy to something Man, or even Captain something.

"Okay. Come on back to bed, but you tell me, right?" He cups his hands over Miracle Boy's semierect cock and begins the story.

Says Captain Superb, there are two classes of computations: the doable and the budget-busters. Time is money in computing as in any enterprise, so you need to know how long it's going to take to do your computation: *now*, or longer than the universe has left to run. A surprising number of everyday problems fall into that latter category and are called NP problems. The most common problem is factorizing prime numbers.

Miracle Boy says, "I know about prime numbers. They're the magic numbers from which all the others are built. Like the chemical elements for mathematics."

"That's a good analogy, Sextinho," says Captain Superb. "It's easy and quick to multiply two prime numbers—doesn't really matter how big, even up to a hundred thousand digits—together. What's not so easy is to take that number apart again—what we call factorization. There are a number of mathematical tricks you can pull to eliminate some obvious no-contenders, but at some point you still have to divide your original number by every odd number until you find a result that divides evenly. If you add a single extra digit to your original number, it triples the amount of time a computer needs to run through all the calculations. A two-hundred-and-fifty-digit number would take our fastest conventional computers over ten million years. That's why very large primes are code-makers' best friends. It's easy to take two-thousand-digit primes as your keys that unlock your arfid chip and multiply them together. But to take that million-digit product down into its prime factors, there literally isn't enough time left in the universe for a single computer to crank out that sum. But quantum computers can crack a problem like that in milliseconds. But what if you divided a number that would take ten billion years to factor up into chunks and farmed them out to other computers?

"Ten computers, it would only take a billion years to solve. A million computers, a thousand years. Ten million computers would be a hundred years; a hundred million . . .

"There is at least that number of processors in São Paulo. But with modern crypto, you're looking at computation runs at least ten billion times that. There aren't enough computers in the world. In fact, if every atom of the Earth was a tiny nanocomputer, there still wouldn't be enough."

"But there are ghost universes," Miracle Boy says. The rain lashes hard on the roof, then eases. The eaves drip. Sun breaks through the shutter slats.

"Correct. At the smallest level, the quantum level, the universe—all the universes of the multiverse—display what we call coherence. In a sense, what seem like separate particles in the other universes are all the same particle, just different aspects of it. Information about them, about the state they're in, is shared between them. And where you have information, you have computing."

"She'd said ten to the eight hundred universes. There was this glowing thing, they had to keep it cold." He thinks about the frogs that can see into quantum worlds.

"That sounds like a high-temperature Bose-Einstein condensate, a state of matter in one uniform quantum state. An array like that could do computations in, let me see, ten to the hundred thousand universes. That's a lot for a handbag. It's approaching what we'd call a general-purpose quantum computer. Most quantum computers are what we call special purpose—they're algorithm crackers for encryption. But a general-purpose QC is a much more powerful and dangerous beast."

"What could you do with one?"

"What couldn't you do? One thing that immediately springs to mind is that no secret over three years old is safe. Certainly the Pentagon, the White House, the CIA, and the FBI are open for business. But the big picture is rendering, what we would call a universal simulator, one that can get down to that level. What's the difference between the real weather, and the rendering?"

Miracle Boy tried to imagine a hurricane that blows between worlds. He shivers. He says, "Do you think she might be in danger?"

Captain Superb shrugs in his spandex suit.

"Isn't everyone these days? Everyone's presumed to be guilty of something. Hell, they can cut you up just for a television show. But the gringos and the government guard their quantum technology very carefully; if she's using an unlicensed machine, someone will be interested. Even at São Paulo U the quantum cores were so heavily monitored you had to have a security officer with you. You've got yourself a scary girlfriend, Sextinho. So who is she, this Quantum Girl?"

"She's called Fia Kishida."

And it is as if Captain Superb has been struck by a White Event and been turned into a real superhero, for he flies off the bed. Miracle Boy sees him clearly suspended in midair. Captain Superb leans over Miracle Boy, spandex puffing and sucking around his mouth. He fumbles for the zips, pulls it down, shakes his graying, wavy hair out.

"What did you say? Fia Kishida? Fia Kishida?"

July 22, 1732

"So you're the swordsman," the bishop of Grão Pará said as Luis Quinn touched his lips to the proffered ring. "Younger than I'd expected. And bigger. Most of the swordsmen I've met were small things, scrawny chickens of things. Effete. But then many big men are light on their feet, I've found."

"The sword belongs to another life, Your Grace." Luis Quinn regained his feet and stood, hands folded in submission. Bishop Vasco da Mascarenhas's chamber was dark, furnished in heavily carved woods from the Tocantins, deep reds and blacks. The ornate putti and seraphs had African mouths and noses, índio eyes and cheekbones. The heat was oppression, the light beyond the drawn shutters painful.

"Yours is a military order, is it not? Of course I cannot compel you, but it would be no bad thing for your society to be seen to be . . . muscular. Brazil respects power and little else. There are fellows here aplenty—big idle lumps, up from the captaincies to make their fortunes—who fancy themselves a rip with the blade. Yes, the very thing: I shall arrange a sport."

"Your Grace, I have foresworn—"

"Of course you have, of course. Wooden swords, a good poke in the arse, that sort of thing. It would be good to show those arrogant turkey cocks a thing or two. Teach them a little respect for Church authority and keep them away from the índio girls. We get little enough novelty here, as you might imagine." The bishop rose from his ornate chair. Wood scraped heavily over stone. "Are you a man for the sport, Father? I tell you, there is a great game they have here, the índios brought it, played with a ball of blown latex, though the blacks have the best skill at it. It's all in the feet; you're allowed to use the head as well, but not the hands, never the hands. You steer it to the enemy's goal purely by foot. A splendid sight. You'll come with me to the cloister garden; the heat is intolerable indoors this time of the day."

Bishop Vasco was a big man and not at all light on his feet. He sweated luxuriously as he ambled around the shaded garden. Decorative panels of hand-painted blue-on-white Portuguese tiles depicted allegories of the theological virtues. A fountain trickled in the center of the worn limestone flags, a sound as fragile and deep as years. Birds peered and whooped from the eaves.

"I wish they had sent you to me, Quinn. Sometimes I wish Belém were a dog, that I might shake it by the throat. Carnality and lust, I tell you, carnality and lust. Lust for gold; not merely the Vila Rica gold, but the red gold and the black gold, especially in this time of plague and madness. You know what I speak of. Oh, for a dozen—half a dozen—stout mission fathers: even just one examiner from the Holy Office! That would set them about their ears. I have heard about your railing at the porters of the Cidade Baixa. That is exactly the type of thing we need here, Quinn, exactly. A tedious enough passage, I take it?"

"Contrary winds and currents, Your Grace, but I am no sailor. I spent the time in prayer and preparation."

"Yes yes, my captains say it is faster and easier to sail to the Island of

Madeira and then Belém than the uncertain seas off Pernambuco. Pray, what is it the Society requires so urgently it must have an admonitory sent from Coimbra? I am aware of the Frenchman—how could one not be, fluttering around the promenade like a butterfly with his fripperies and gewgaws."

"Your Grace, it is a matter of some delicacy within our Society."

Bishop Vasco stopped in his tracks, face red with more than afternoon heat. He rapped his stick on the stones. Birds flew up in a clatter from the curved eave-tiles. Faces appeared in dark doorways.

"Wretched Jesuitical . . . It's that Gonçalves, isn't it? Don't answer; I wouldn't make a liar of you. Keep your Jesuitical secrets. I have my own informations." He ducked his head; sweat flew from his long, curled wig. "Forgive me, Father Quinn. The heat makes me intemperate, aye, and this country. Understand this one thing: Brazil is not as other places. Even in this city the Society of Jesus, the Franciscans, and the Carmelites are in the scantest of communions with each other over the status; high on the Amazon, it is naked rivalry. The Holy Church is little more than an engine fed with the souls of the red man—and his flesh also. What's this, what's this?" A secretary bowed into the bishop's path and knelt, offering up a leather tray of documents. "Hah. My attention is required. Well, Father Quinn, I shall send with instructions for that diversion I mentioned. I may even risk a little wager myself. I very much look forward to seeing you in action."

The bishop mimed a sword-lunge with his stick as Luis Quinn bowed, then, before objection could be mouthed, hobbled heavily after his white-robed secretary into the sweating shadows of the chapter.

The Ver-o-Peso roared with laughter as the red-faced youth in the torn shirt went reeling across the cobbles from the boot-shove to his arse. Red laughter, black laughter from the roped-off wagons and drays on the city side of the wide dock where ships and rafts from the high Amazon and Tocantins moored four deep. White laughter from the chairs and temporary stands set up on barrel and planking. From the street and the steps and all around Luis Quinn, the laughter of males. From the wooden balconies on the macaw-colored façades of the feitores' houses and inns, immodestly open to heat and regard, the laughter of women. Luis Quinn stood victorious before the stone slave block. The young pretender had been dragged away by his friends to the jeers and fruit of slaves; a fat, arrogant son of a jumped-up cane-grower with pretensions to gentry, humiliated in two plays, spanked around the quadrangle like a carnival fool by the flat of Luis Quinn's mock sword, jipping and whining before the convulsed audience. Then, the final boot: *Out of my sight.* Luis Quinn took in the faces, the wide, delighted faces. Many skins, many colors, but the open mouths were all the same: red, hungry. Looking up he saw eyes above fluttering fans and beaded veils. Luis Quinn strode around the ring, arms held high, receiving the praise of the people of Belém do Pará.

"Some men wear their sins on their faces," said Bishop Vasco, lolling in his chair, sweating freely despite the fringed canopy shading him from the molten sun and the work of two boy-slaves with feather fans.

"The women?" said the royal judge Rafael Pires de Campos. A noble-brother of the Misericordia banished to a pestilential backwater, he was keen on any sport that might break the monotony of striving feitores. It was widely known in Grão Pará that Pires de Campos financed the bishop's foray into private mercantilism, and that the Episcopal fleet had suffered repeated and expensive drubbings from Dutch pirates whirling down from Curaçao.

"No, the pride, man, the pride. Yes, I am quite sure that our admonitory there was quite the blade before he took his first Exercises. And that's another fifty escudos. How did you ever imagine that fat bumpkin could beat the Jesuit? Cash or offset?"

"Stroke it from the tally. Where is he from, the Jesuit? His accent is exceedingly rare."

"Ireland."

"Where is that? I don't know of any country with that name."

Bishop Vasco explained the geography and briefly the country's repressive heretical laws. Pires de Campos pursed his lips, shook his head.

"I am little wiser, Your Grace. But I do think it is a good thing your Jesuit there is leaving Belém soon. Cloth or no cloth, there are a few would cheerfully have him pistoled in his bed."

Quinn washed his face and sweat-caked hair in glinting handfuls of water from a street seller's cask. The sport was over; the people would have to wait for the next auction from the block. The crowd stirred, dusted itself, reached to close its shutters, its brief corporate life dispersed when a movement at the port end of the market sent a ripple of turning heads around the rope ring. Applause swelled to full-throated cheering as a slight, slender man entered the ring. His dress was formal to the edge of foppishness, European, overrefined for Brazil. Eccentrically, he wore green-tinted circular eyeglasses, a source of comment and hilarity among the spectators. The man bowed elaborately.

"Father Luis Quinn?"

Quinn dipped his head. Water mingled with sweat dripping from his face; he stood in the arena, and under the terrible noon sun he realized how it had drawn the old hot joy high in him, like a tide, heat calling to blood heat. *Cease now.* But he could never walk away from a challenge from God or from a man.

"Your service, Father. I am Dr. Robert Francois St. Honore Falcon, a geographer and geometer of the French Academy of Sciences in Paris and guest of this colony. I understand you have some facility with a sword. I myself trained with Master of Defense Teillagory himself in Paris and very much relish the opportunity to try my skill against yours."

"Very well, monsieur," Luis Quinn said in French. "It is especially pleasing to fight someone who can pronounce my name correctly. I trust you have no issue with being beaten by a priest."

The crowd hooted its appreciation.

"Do not think your collar will protect you," Falcon said, passing cane, hat, wig, and heavy coat to his slave, retaining his curious, soul-screening glasses. "I come from a family of notorious freethinkers."

Luis Quinn raised his wooden stave in salute. Falcon picked up the discarded baton and returned the courtesy. Each man folded his free hand into the small of his back and began to circle. The Ver-o-Peso fell silent as if struck by an angel.

"Another fifty on the Jesuit," Bishop Vasco said.

"Really? I think this Frenchman may yet surprise him." Pires de Campos delicately dabbed his perspiring face with a scented handkerchief. "See?" The encircling faces let out a great gasp and cheer as Quinn made a mistimed lunge that Falcon deftly sidestepped; Falcon rapped the priest across the back as he stumbled past. Quinn shook his head, smiled to himself, recovered. The two men resumed their circles in the afternoon heat.

"Your man has been seeing off rapscallions all morning. The Frenchman is fresh as a nosegay," Pires de Campos commented, then found his fist clenched around his kerchief, throat tight to yell as Falcon made a series of dazzling feints that drove Luis Quinn across the ring before launching a flying *fleche* that had even breathless Vasco out of his chair. Tension turned to wonder to a thunder of amazement as Quinn threw himself back, under and away from the spearing staff. Both men fell heavily to the cobbles and rolled, Luis Quinn first to his feet. The tip of Quinn's stick struck a point from the back of Falcon's stockinged calf.

"That would not count in Paris," Falcon said, rolling into his stance and dancing away from Quinn.

"As you can see, we are not in Paris," said Quinn, and, laughing joyously, insanely, launched a flurry of cuts that drove Falcon back to the edge of the water.

"Even for a Jesuit, that is subtle," cried Falcon, catching Quinn's blade and turning it away. As space opened between the two combatants, the little Frenchman leaped and kicked the priest in the chest. Quinn reeled back toward the center of the ring. The Ver-o-Peso was a circle of roaring voices.

"Teillagory never taught that," Quinn answered. The two men faced each other once more in the *garde*. Action upon action, lunge and parry, circle and feint. The barbs and witticisms of the swordsmen devolved into grunts and gasps. Bishop Vasco's knuckles were white as he gripped the golden knurled head of his cane. The cheers of the spectators softened into mute absorption. A true battle was being fought here. Luis Quinn circled in front of the dapper, dancing Frenchman. The rage flickered like far summer lightning, haunting clouds. Luis Quinn pushed it down, pushed it away. He flicked sweat from the matted tips of his hair. Tired, so bull-tired, and every second the sun drew the strength from him; but he could not let this little man beat him before these slaves and petty masters. Again the old rage called, the old friend, the strength from beyond comprehension, from beyond right and wrong. *I will come. I have never failed you.* All the sun of the square was gathered up and burning in his tight, nauseous belly. Luis Quinn saw himself bearing down on this prancing fencer, with one stroke snapping his ridiculous stick, driving him down, punching the tip of his wooden sword through his rib cage and out through his back, organs impaled and beating.

Luis Quinn snapped upright, eyes wide, nostrils flared. He unfolded his left hand from the *garde* position and let it fall. He lifted his sword to his face, touched his nose in salute, and threw the stick to the cobbles. Falcon hesitated. *Behind that green glass, what do your eyes read?* Luis Quinn thought. Falcon nodded, harrumphed through his nose, then swept his own sword into the salute and threw it down beside Quinn's.

Whistles and jeers swelled into a thunder of disapproval. Fruit began to fall and burst fragrantly on the sun-heated cobbles. In the edge of his eye Luis Quinn saw Bishop Vasco's slaves hasten him away on his litter. Some of his household remained, arguing strenuously with the retainers of a fidalgo in pale blue. *You set me a test and I beat it*, Luis Quinn thought. *Brazil respects only power, but power is nothing without control.*

Falcon gave a courtly bow. "So, Father, I look forward to our voyage together. We have much to explore."

The pelt of derision falling around the duelist grew thin and failed as the spectators drifted away, the order of the enslaved day restored. The tropical fruits, crusting in the sun, began to smell nauseatingly and drew flies. One by one the ladies of the Pelourinho closed up their gelosias.

Dona Maria da Maia da Garna looked again from the lemon to the orange.

"So tell me again how a piece of clock can tell us whether the world is pointed or flattened? Once more and I am sure I shall have it."

Dr. Falcon sighed and again set the little lead bob swinging in its gimbals. The dona persisted out of politeness to her educated guest; the other women had long since abandoned the demonstration and turned to their own small talk, which, though they saw each other daily, never seemed to stale. Five months Falcon had itched in social isolation in his rotting, rack-rented casa by the ocean docks, daily applying to bureaucrats and magistrates for a permission here, a docket there, only to be sent away with a demand for supporting applications, informations, and affidavits. Now the advent of a Jesuit had swept away all obstacles; the permits and letters of comfort arrived by special messenger that day, and the doors on polite society, barred so firmly, swung open. He suspected that as a geographer, a scientist, he was far less extraordinary a beast than as a Frenchman with a facility for the art of defense.

Dona Maria had indeed hoped for an after-dinner sport; a preto Bahian slave who knew the foot-fighting dance was ready and a space cleared in the sugar warehouse to try the thing. Thus far the only martial skill the Frenchman had demonstrated was a few Lyonnais wharf-side tricks with fish knives that anyone might learn down by the Atlantic dock. Instead she was watching a pendulum swinging tick-tock-tick-tock while he held a lemon in his right hand and an orange in his left.

"The attractive force—the gravitational force—that acts upon the pendulum is directly proportional to its distance from the center of gravity that attracts it—in this instance the center of our Earth. My pendulum—your clock mechanism is too crude to display the variation, alas—will thus vibrate faster if it is closer to the center of the Earth, slower if it is farther away."

João the foot servant stood solid as death by the dining-room door, wearing the same stern face that he had when Dr. Falcon had darted swift as a lizard around all the casa grande's clocks, lifting his uncouth green glasses to leer into their faces. His eyebrows had lifted a wrinkle as Dr. Falcon opened the case of the German long-case, the master's prize and time-keeper for all the escapements of the house, and deftly unhooked the pendulum mechanism.

"In this way, we have a sensitive means of determining the exact shape of our globe, whether prolate like this lemon—greater across its polar axis than its equatorial—or oblate, like this orange, bulging at its girth." A titter from down the table, Dona de Teffé, much gone on wine.

Dr. Falcon acknowledged the dona with a nod. His lips had barely touched his glass; wine did poorly in this morbid heat, and it was wretched Portuguese stuff. But it was pleasant, uncommon pleasant, to dine in the company of women. Unheard-of at home; not even in Cayenne were such liberties taken. As everyone insisted on reminding him, the Amazon was another country, where affairs of commerce kept the senhores and the Portuguese merchants from their city houses months at a time.

"Yes yes. Forgive me, Doctor—I must be very stupid—this is all fine and mathematical and scientific, I have no doubt, but what it does not explain to me is what holds it up."

"Holds what up?" Falcon peered over his rounds of green glass, perplexed.

"The lemon. Or the orange. Now I can easily see how it is we whirl around the sun, how this gravitational force of yours tethers us to it; it is no different from the bolas our vaqueiros use on our fazenda. But what I cannot understand is what holds it all up, what keeps us from plummeting endlessly through the void."

Falcon set down the fruit. A breath of small exasperation left his lips.

"Madam, nothing holds it up. Nothing needs to hold it up. Gravity draws us to the center of the Earth, as it draws our Earth to the center of the sun, but at the same time, the sun is drawn—infinitesimally, yes, but drawn nonetheless—to the center of our Earth. Everything attracts everything else; everything is in motion, all together."

"I must confess I find the old way much simpler and more satisfying." The dona skillfully quartered and peeled the orange with a sharp little curved knife. "The mind naturally rebels against a round Earth with everything drawn to the dark, infernal center. It is not only against nature, it is un-Christian; surely if we are attracted to anything, it should be upwards, to heaven, our hope and home?"

Falcon bit back the riposte. This was not the Paris Academy, nor even the Lunar Society meeting in some bourgeois salon. He contented himself to watch the sensuous deftness with which she slipped a lith of naked orange between her reddened lips. *And you presume to call heaven your hope and home?* Dona da Maia da Garna turned with relief from lemons and hell to the conversation at the far end of the table. Her chaperone, a tall preto woman with an eye patch, once handsome, now run to fat, leaned forward from her position behind the dona's seat to study the pendulum. Falcon saw her press her thumb against her wrist to measure it against her pulse. Even in undeclared house arrest, Falcon had been close enough to Belém society to understand the meaning of the eye patch. Jealous wives often revenged themselves on their husbands' slave lovers by blinding them with scissors.

"Forgive me, Father, I missed what you were saying there?" Dona Maria said to Luis Quinn.

Even in his priestly black, Quinn was a massive presence, drawing all attention and conversation as if he himself exerted a human gravitation. He held Dona da Maia da Garna's gaze steadily, with none of the simpering humility of the religious that so incensed Falcon. The dona herself did not flinch from his look. *Like a man*, Falcon observed.

"I was merely relating one of the interesting linguistic characteristics of my native language—that is Irish," Quinn said. "In Irish we have no words for *yes* or *no*. If you are asked a question, all you can do is confirm or deny the questioner. Thus, in reply to the question 'Are you going to Galway?' the answer 'I am indeed going.'"

"That must make conversation very trying," the dona said.

"Not at all," Quinn answered. "It just makes it very hard for an Irishman to say no to you." Women's laughter chimed around the table. Falcon felt a needle-prick of envy at Quinn's casual flirtatiousness. To those who use it least it is given greatest. He had always relished the company of women and thought himself adept in it, a sharp conversationalist and silver wit, but Quinn captivated the table, leaning to their conversations, listening, making each one feel the sole recipient of his attention. *The skill of a linguist, or a libertine?* Falcon thought. Now Quinn was enchanting all with a rolling, rhythmic monologue that he said was a great poem in his native tongue.

"And is it a love poem?" asked the dona.

"What other kind is worth reciting, madam?" Applause now. Falcon idly stabbed his discarded and forgotten lemon with the paring knife. He interjected, "But my dear Father Luis, to not be able to say yes or no, does that not demonstrate a direct linkage between language and thought? The word is the thought itself, and conversely, what cannot be said cannot be thought."

The conversation died; the guests wore puzzled frowns. Father Quinn tapped a forefinger on the table and leaned forward.

"My colleague the doctor makes an interesting point here. One of the fascinations of the Amazon—to a linguist like myself, I suspect, rather than general society—is its richness of tongues. I understand there are Indians among the far-flung tributaries who have no word for the color blue, or for any relation outside son and daughter, or for past or present. It would be a pleasantly diverting conversation to speculate on how that affects their perceptions of the world. If they cannot say blue, can they see blue?"

"Or indeed, the effect upon their spiritual faculties," Falcon replied. "If you have no concept of a past or a future, what meaning does the doctrine of original sin then hold? Could they even entertain the concept of future promise, a life of the world to come? No heaven, no hell, just the eternal present? But then is that not eternity; a place beyond time? Do they already live in heaven, in sinless innocence? Perhaps ignorance truly is bliss."

Several of the ladies were fanning themselves, uncomfortable at the baiting radical-talk at their table. No one alive could remember the Holy Office's visit to Recife, but the trauma of the *autos-da-fé* in the Praça there was still sharp enough in folk memory for the Bishop Vasco's jeremiads against the vices of Belém to alarm. The hostess said decorously, "I have heard that there are peças fresh arrived from someplace so backward that they can only express one idea at a time. It seems that each sentence is but a single thought. We can understand their tongue, with some difficulty, but they can never understand ours. It is as Dr. Falcon conjectured: if you cannot say it, you cannot think it. Who ever thought of descending these creatures? Quite useless for work."

Dr. Falcon was poised to reply again, but the house steward Anuncão entered, rattled a small wooden clapper to attract the party's attention, and announced that the musical piece would follow with coffee.

"Oh, I had quite forgotten!" the dona said, clapping her hands in delight. "Father, dear Father, you will so much enjoy this. The most charming little creature, truly the voice of an angel." The chaperones poured coffee from silver pots, wiping drips from the cups with soft cotton cloths. Anuncão led in a tiny índio child, thin as want, dressed in a rough white shift. Falcon was unable to tell if it was boy or girl. The child knelt and kissed the stone flagging. "Picked it up for nothing at the Port House Tavern auction. Poor thing was hours from death. Obviously from some reducione raid: only the Jesuits, your pardon, Father, train the voice so. Go on, child."

The child stood arms at side, a distant animal look in its eyes. The voice when it came was so small, so distant, it hardly seemed to issue from the open mouth but from a hidden place beyond Earth and heaven. Falcon had given his wig to the house slaves early on account of the dreadful close heat and now felt the close-shaved nape of his neck prickle. The little voice climbed to a pure, spearing perfection: an Avé, but not by any composer known to Falcon; its rhythms were skewed, its time signature shifting and mercurial, its inner implied harmonies disquieting, discordant. Yet Falcon felt the tears run freely down his face. When he glanced up the table, he saw that Quinn was similarly moved. The women of Belém were stone, unmoving stone. The eyes of the chaperones, each behind her lady, were averted from the white race. Despite the dona's declaration, this was not the voice of an angel. This came from a deeper, older place; this was the voice of the far forest, the deep river, the voice a child might find if it had followed those waters down to the slave markets of Belém do Pará.

While the child sang, João removed the pendulum from before Dr. Falcon and, heels clicking on stone, went to replace it in the belly of his master's clock.

OUR
LADY
OF
TRASH

MAY 25–28, 2006

The Last of the Real Cariocas sent the weighted line looping out into the pink light of Guanabara Bay. It was the Hour of Yemanja. The sun was still beneath the hills on the far side of the bay, the light that pink only seen in travel shots of Rio, the ones in which a skinny boy in Bermudas turns somersaults on the beach. Lights still burned along Flamengo Park, and the curve of Botafogo, a surf-line of brilliants around the feet of the morros. Headlights moved across the Niteroi Bridge. The red-eye shift moved like a carnaval procession out on to the strip at Santos Dumont Airport, the aircraft delicate, long-legged like hunting spiders in the shimmering light. The Brotherhood of Dawn Fishers was stalking silhouettes, elegant as cranes as they flicked and cast, the broadenings and heavinesses of age and middle age erased against the sunrise. Their soft voices carried far on the peach-perfect, intoxicating air, yet the grosser thunder of the jets powering up one by one into their takeoff runs was pressed down and muted. Marcelina found her own voice dropping to a whisper. Police sirens among the hills, the linger of tire smoke on the air added to the sense of the sacramental. Marcelina had not been so close to spirituality since she had made *UFO-Hunt* down in Válo de Amanheçer outside Brasília. The pink turned to lilac to Marian blue as the sun rose.

"I know a hundred World Cup Stories." Raimundo Soares watched his weight drop into the glowing water. He claimed to be the last professional carioca; sometime journalist, sometime writer with a good book about the new bossa nova, a better book about Ronaldo Fenômeno, and a so-so guide to how to be a professional carioca on his backlist. A little fishing early with the brothers, a little cafezinho when the heat got up, a few hundred words on the laptop, the rest of the afternoon he'd spend in a café, watching ass on its way to the beach, or strolling around his city, remembering it, memorizing it. In the evening, receptions, parties, openings, his many lovers: a late sleep and up again at fish-jump. He claimed to have worn nothing but surf-Ts and Bermuda shorts for twenty years, even to his own mother's funeral. He was the loafer, the malandro who doesn't have to try too hard, carioca of cariocas: they should make him a Living Treasure. "This is true. David Beckham comes to Rio; he's going to play at the Maracanã for a benefit for Pelé. He's the guest of the CBF, so he's got the wife, the kids; everything. They put him up at the Copa Palace, nothing's too much trouble for Senhor Becks; presidential suite, private limo, the lot. Anyway, one evening he goes out for a little kick-about on the beach and these hoods jump him. Guns and everything, one two three, into the car and he's gone. Lifted. Right under his guards' noses. So there's Beckham in the back with these malandros with the gold-plated guns thinking, Oh sweet Jesus, I am dead. Posh is a widow and Brooklyn and Romeo will grow up never knowing their father. Anyway, they take him up into Rocinha, up the Estrada da Gávea, and then from that on to a smaller road, and from that onto an even smaller road until it's so steep and narrow the car can't go any farther. So they bundle him out and take him up the ladeira at gunpoint and anytime anyone sticks so much as a nostril out of their house, the hoods pull an Uzi on them; up and up and up, right up to the top of the favela, and they take him into this tiny little concrete room right under the tree line and there's Bem-Te-Vi, the big drug lord. This was back before they shot him. And he stands there, and he looks at Beckham this way, and he looks at Beckham that way; he looks at Beckham every way, like he's looking at a car, and then he makes a sign and in comes this guy with a big sack. Beckham thinks, Jesus and Mary, what's going on here? Then Bem-Te-Vi stands beside him and they pull out the World Cup, the original Jules Rimet, solid gold and everything, right out of the sack. Bem-Te-Vi takes one side, Beckham takes the other, and this guy gets out a digital camera, says, 'Smile, Mr. Beckham.' Click! Flash! And then Bem-Te-Vi turns to Becks and shakes his hand and says, 'Thank you very much, Mr. Beckham, it's been a real honor. . . . Oh, by the way . . . if anyone *ever* finds out about this . . .'"

Raimundo Soares slapped his thigh and rolled on his little fishing stool. He was a squat, broad-featured man, his bare arms powerfully muscled, his hair black by artifice rather than nature, Marcelina suspected. The Dawn Fishers smiled and nodded. They had heard his hundred stories hundreds of times; they were litany now.

"Now that's a great film."

"Heitor Serra said you might be able to help me with a program idea." Marcelina sat in the just-cool sand, knees pulled up to her chest. Raimundo Soares was right: this was the beach's best time. She imagined herself joining the shameless old sag-titted men in their Speedos and Havaianas, chest hair grizzled white, and the chestnut-skinned, blonde-streaked women, of a certain age but still in full makeup, all sauntering down for their morning sun sea and swim. No better, truer way to start the day.

A sweet idea, but her world was a tapestry of sweet ideas, most of which had no legs. Coffee and cigarette in the roof garden watching them all dandering back from the sea, leaving patters of drips on the sidewalks of the Copacabana. The TV professional habitually overidentifies with the subject. On *UFO-Hunt* she'd wanted to run off and live in a yurt selling patúa amulets to seekers.

"So how is the man? Still convinced life's brutal, stupid, and meaningless?"

Marcelina thought of how she had left Heitor; tiptoeing around his death-rattle snores, dressing by the lights from the lagoa that shone through the balcony window of the Rua Tabatingüera apartment. He liked her to walk around naked in front of that window, in stocking and boots or the sheer bodysuit he had bought her, that she didn't want to say cut the booty off her. And she enjoyed the anonymous exhibitionism of it. The nearest neighbors were a kilometer away across the lagoon. Most balconies fringing the Lagoa Rodrigo de Freitas bore tripods and telescopes: let them take their eyefuls. She would never meet them. Heitor was excited by the voyeurism of being voyeured: the watchers would never know that the apartment in which that short loira woman paraded around like a puta belonged to the man who daily told them of riots and robberies, tsunamis and suicide bombings.

He had rolled over heavily with a growl, then woke. He had made it the Café Barbosa. There had been beer for Celso and the rest of her development team, Agnetta and Cibele; vodka and guaraná for Marcelina; and vodka martinis for Heitor. They hadn't gone dancing, and she hadn't fucked the ass off him.

"Where are you going what the hell time is it?"

"I'm going to the beach," Marcelina said. The buzz of the guaraná glowed through the vodka murk like stormlight. "Like you said, it's best early. Give me a call later or something."

Like soldiers and flight crew, newsmen have the ability to seize any opportunity for sleep. By the time Marcelina reached the front door Heitor was emitting that strange, gasping rattle that at any time might break into words or cries. The short hallway was where he kept his library. Shelves would have reduced the space to a squeeze too tight for a big man in a shiny suit, so the books—random titles like *Keys to the Universe, The Long Tail and the New Economy, The Fluminense Year Book 2002, The Denial of Death*—were stacked up title on title into towers, some wedged against the ceiling, others tottering as Marcelina tiptoed past. One particularly heavy door-slam, perhaps after a bad news day, they would all come down and crush him beneath their massed eruditions.

"And over much much too soon," Marcelina said. "Heitor said you might be able to help me find Moaçir Barbosa."

The Brotherhood of Dawn Fishers went quiet over their reels.

"Maybe you should just tell me what the idea is," Raimundo Soares said.

"We think it's high time he was forgiven for the Fateful Final," Marcelina lied.

"There's a fair few people would disagree with you still, but I think it's years overdue. There'd be a lot of interest in a program about the Maracanaço, still. Of course, I was too young to properly remember it, but there are a lot of people still remember that night in July and a whole lot more who still believe the legend. There's a journo down in Arpoador, João Luiz, my generation, he got a print of the original film and recut it so it looks like the ball hits the post, then cut in footage from another game of Bigode clearing it. There's a guy younger than you made a short movie a couple of years back about this futebol journalist—I think he was based on me—who goes back in time to try and change the Fateful Final, but whatever he does, the ball still goes past Barbosa into the back of the net. I even heard this guy talking on some science show on the Discovery Channel or something like that about that quantum theory and how there are all these parallel universes all around us. The metaphor he used was that there are hundreds, thousands of universes out there where Brazil won the Fateful Final. Still didn't understand it, but I thought it was a nice allegory. There's a great story about Barbosa: it's a few years after the Maracanaço, before it got to him and he drifted away. He gets a few friends from the old team around—all the black players, you know what I mean—for a barbecue. There's a lot of beer and talk about soccer and then someone notices that the wood in the barbecue is flaring up and sputtering and giving off this smell, like burning paint. So he looks closer, and it is burning paint. There's a bit of wood still unburned, and its covered in white paint. Barbosa's only chopped up the goalposts from the Maracanã and used them for firewood."

"Is it true?" Marcelina slipped off her shoes and buried her feet in the cool sand, feeling the silky grains run between her toes.

"Does it matter?"

"Do you know where he is?"

"Barbosa? No. He disappeared completely about ten, fifteen years ago. He might even be dead. People still claim to see him in shopping malls, like Elvis Presley. He's an old man; he's been an old man for fifty years. If I thought you were going to do some hatchet job on poor old Barbosa, I wouldn't give you the time of day. The poor bastard's suffered enough. But this . . ."

"No, we wouldn't do anything like that," Marcelina lied for the second time.

"Even Zizinho's dead now. . . . There's one left who might know. Feijão. The Bean."

"Who's he, a player or something?"

"You really don't know anything about this, do you? Feijão was the physiotherapist, the assistant physiotherapist. He was still in training, his dad was on the CBD, as it was then before it became the CBF, and got him a job on the team. Basically all he did was keep the sponges wet in the bucket, but he was like a lucky mascot to the team; they used to ruffle his hair before they went down to the tunnel. Lot of good he was. He ended up team physio with Fluminense and then opened a little health club. He sold it and retired about five years ago; I met him while I was researching the Ronaldo book and the Society of Sports Journalists. Did you know I ended up in court in a libel case over the length of Ronaldo's dick?"

He's right, murmured the irmãos of the rod.

"The judge found for me, of course. If anyone would know, Feijão would. He's over in Niteroi now; this is his number." Raimundo Soares took a little elastic-bound reporter's notebook from the hip pocket of his Bermudas and scrawled down a number with a stub of pencil. "Tell him I sent you. That way he might talk to you."

"Thank you, Mr. Soares."

"Hey, you'll need someone to present it; who better than one of Brazil's best writers and the last professional carioca?"

That's him, chorused the fisher kings. *He's the malandro.*

"I'll mention it to the commissioner," Marcelina said, her third lie. No cock crowed, but the float on Raimundo's line bobbed under.

"Hey, look at that!" He pushed his tractor hat up on his head and bent to his reel. When Marcelina looked back, from the shaded green of Flamengo Park, the Brotherhood of Dawn Fishers were unhooking the catch and returning it to the sea. Fish from Guanabara Bay were tainted, but it pleased Marcelina to imagine the old men offering it in honor to Yemanja.

She could hear the electric organ from the bay where the taxi dropped her: Aquerela do Brasil; samba-exaltação rhythm, heavy on the lower manual, wafting down over the balconies, among the satellite dishes and water tanks. Her mother's favorite. She found her step quickening to the rhythm as she nodded past Malvina on the concierge's desk. The music swirled down the stairwell. Malvina was smiling. When Dona Marisa played organ, the whole building smiled. Even the music in the elevator was unable to defeat Dona Marisa on the manuals as her chords and chachachas boomed around the winch drums and speeding counterweights.

Every child thinks her childhood is normal. Wasn't everyone's mother Marisa Pinzón the Organ Queen of the Beija-Flor? Queen Marisa's most lustrous days, when she ruled the land beyond midnight, Venus arising from the Art Deco shell of the Beija-Flor Club Wurlitzer, were already fading when Marcelina was born. Her two older sisters shared increasingly bitter and resentful memories of grandmothers and tias, cigarette girls and gay cleaners sent to babysit while their mother, swathed in satin and rhinestones, diamante tiara on her brow, gilded shoe tapping out the rhythm, played rumbas and pagodes and foros to the discreet little silver tables. There were photographs of her with Tom Jobim, flirting with Chico Buarque, duetting with Liberace. Marcelina had only the unfocused memory of staring up at a glitterball turning on the ceiling, dazzled by the endless carnival of lights.

She had no memories whatsoever of her father. She had been a primitive streak when Martim Hoffman put on his suit and took his leather briefcase and went out to do business in Petropolis and never returned. For years she had thought Liberace was her dad.

Marcelina shivered with pleasure as the elevator door opened to a sweeping glissando up the keys. Her mother played less and less frequently since the arthritis that would surely turn her knuckles into Brazil nuts had been diagnosed. She hesitated before ringing the bell, enjoying the music. Her alt dot family would have mocked, but it's always different when it's your mother. She pressed the button. The music stopped in midbar.

"You don't call, you don't visit . . ."

"I'm here now. And I sent you an SMS."

"Only because I sent you one first."

The hugged, they kissed.

"You're looking tight again," Marcelina's mother said, holding her daughter at arm's length to scrutinize her face. "Have you been on the Botox again? Give me his number."

"You should get a chain on that door. Anyone could be in here, they'd just brush you aside."

"You lecture me about security, still living in that dirty, nasty old Copa? Look, I've found you this nice little two-bed apartment down on Rua Carlos Góls; it's only two blocks from me. I got the agent to print out the details. Don't go without them."

The organ stood by the open French windows, lights glowing. The table had been set on the little balcony; Marcelina squeezed into her plastic patio chair. It was safest to look at the horizon. Golden surfer boys played there on the ever-breaking wave. She could never look at surfers without a painful sense of another life she could have lived. Dona Marisa brought stacked plates of doces: lemon cake, toothachey peanut squares from Minas Gerais, little honey wafers. Coffee in a pot, and an afternoon vodka for the hostess. Her third, Marcelina judged from the empties on the organ and the arm of the sofa.

"So what is it you have to tell me?"

"No no no, let's have your news first. Me, I live up here fifteen floors above contradiction and excitement." She offered the Minas Gerais peanut cookies. Marcelina opted for the honey wafers as the least deadly to her daily calorific intake.

"Well, I've got a commission."

Her mother clasped her hands to her chest. Unlike every other mother of whom she had heard at Canal Quatro, Marisa Pinzón understood completely what her daughter did for a living. Marcelina was her true heiress; Gloria and Iracema disappointed in their successful marriages and expensively clad families. Mundanity as the ultimate teenage rebellion. In Marcelina's informal casual name-droppings, professional brushes with stellar celebrity, and occasional affairs with a smart man on a pale blue screen who told the country terrible things every night was the lingering perfume of an age when the Queen of the Keyboard ruled from the Copa Palace to Barra. Time for men and babies when you are older while the stars are low enough for you to still touch and magic works yet.

Marcelina could never deflate her mother's flight over the thousand lights of Ipanema with her aching doubt that her sisters had made the right choice, that she had sold her eggs for edginess and a two-second producer's credit. Marcelina explained the premise. Her mother sipped her clinking vodka and scowled.

"Barbosa, that bad black man."

"Don't tell me you remember the Fateful Final?"

"Every carioca remembers what they were doing at the Maracanaço. I was having a stupidly giddy affair with Dean Martin's lawyer. Dino gave five shows in the Copa Palace. He deserves what you do to him, he made us a laughingstock."

"What? Who?"

"Barbosa. Evil man."

Dona Marisa was Marcelina's infallible one-woman focus group. She drained her vodka.

"Querida, would you get me another one?" Marcelina quartered lemon and spooned ice into the glass. Her mother called, "I'm going to have a little feijoada."

"What's the occasion?"

Dona Marisa was the kind of cook who used excellence at just one dish to absolve her of every other culinary wrong. A sous-chef in the Café Pitú had given her his recipe for feijoada ten years ago when she was freshly moved to Leblon and she had produced this prodigy on the closest Saturday to every family high-day since.

"Iracema is pregnant again."

Marcelina felt her grip tighten on the pestle as she carefully pounded the ice.

"Twins."

A crack, a crash. The bottom of the glass lay on the floor in ice, lime, and reeking vodka, punched out by an overheavy blow from the marble pestle.

"Sorry about that. My hand slipped."

"Never mind never mind I drink too many anyway. The ruin of many a good women, drinking at home. But twins! What do you think of that? We've never had twins in our branch of the family. Now Patrícia and that lot down in Florianopolis, they dropped doubles all over the place, as alike as beans in a pod."

"Play something for me. You never play these days."

"Oh, no one wants to hear me. It's old, that kind of stuff I play."

"Not to me it's not. Go on. It was lovely hearing you when I was coming up; I could hear you right down in the car park."

"Oh dear oh no what will everyone think?"

You know full well, Queen of the Fifteenth Floor, Marcelina thought. *Like me they've seen you playing on your balcony in your tiara and pearl earrings. You make them smile.*

"Oh, you talked me into it." Dona Marisa straightened herself on the bench, ran her feet up and down the bass pedals like an athlete warming up for high hurdles. Marcelina watched her fingers fly like hummingbirds over the tabs and rhythm buttons. Then she caressed the red power switch with a flick of her nails, and "Desafinado" swelled out like angels bursting from the heavenly spaces between the apartment towers of Leblon.

Liberace winked at her from the top of the sideboard.

Feijão the Bean wore a packet of American cigarettes tucked into the top of a pair of Speedos. Speedos, a pair of Havaianas, and his own hide, tanned to soft suede. He padded, restless and edgy as a wasp, about his luxuriant verandah, settling on a wooden bench here, the tiled lip of a plant bed there, a folding table there. He was thin as a whip and comfortable with his body; she was nevertheless thankful that he was devoid of all body hair. The very thought of the gray, wire-haired chests of sixty-something men gave her cold horrors.

"Raimundo Soares. So how is that old bastard?"

"Doing a lot of fishing these days."

Feijão poured herbal tea from a Japanese pot. It smelled of macerated forest.

"That's the right answer. He called me, you know. He said you don't know anything but you're all right. I get a lot of media sniffing round after Barbosa—oh, you're not the first by any means. I tell them he's gone, he's dead. I haven't heard of him in ten years. Which is about right. But you've done it the right way."

Our Lady of Production Values, whom Marcelina pictured as the Blessed Virgin crossed with a many-armed Hindu deity—those arms holding cameras, sound booms, budgets, schedules—smiled from within her time-code halo. Feijão tapped a cigarette out of his pouch, an oddly sexual gesture.

"They all ended up here over the years, the black men of 1950. They'll try and tell you that there's no racism in Brazil; that's shit. After the Maracanaço, the blame fell heaviest on the black players; it always does. Juvenal, Bigode. Even Master Ziza himself, God be kind to him. Most of all, Barbosa. Niteroi is not Rio. That bay can be as wide as you want it."

Feijão's mezzanine-level apartment faced a view that only selling a successful business can afford. His walled patio was long and narrow, humid and riotous with flowering shrubs and vines tumbling over the walls. Jacarandas and a tumbling hibiscus framed Rio across the bay. Marcelina had reached around the planet in pursuit of the glittery and schlocky but had never been across the stilt-walking bridge to Niteroi. The Marvelous City seemed smaller, meaner, less certain; Niteroi the mirror to Rio's preening narcissism.

Feijão sipped his tea.

"Great for the immune system. Raimundo Soares will tell you a hundred wonderful tales, but he's full of shit. There's only one of them true: fifteen years ago Barbosa went into a shop to buy some coffee and the woman beside him at the till turned around and shouted to all the customers, 'Look! That's the man who made all Brazil weep.' I know that because I was there. After he retired he came to my gym because he wanted to stay in shape and because he knew me from the old days. Little by little he lost touch with all the others from 1950, but never me. Then he found religion."

"What, like the Assembly of God?" It had become fashionable for sportsmen to turn crente, to thank the Lord Jesus for goals and medals and records they would previously have ascribed to saints and Mary.

"You didn't listen." Feijão ground out his cigarette butt under the sole of his Havaiana, immediately drew another. "I said found religion, not found God."

In response to the cigarette, Marcelina drew her PDA.

"An umbanda terreiro?" The blacks were finding lily-white Jesus; the whites were finding Afro-Brazilian orixás. So Rio.

"You could try listening instead of rushing in with questions. The Barquinha de Santo Daime."

Marcelina held her breath. The Cursed Barbosa a convert to the Green Saint. The ratings would go into orbit.

"So Barbosa's still alive."

"Did I say that? You're getting ahead of me again. He walked out of his apartment three years ago and no one has seen hide nor hair of him since, not even me."

"But this Daime Church would know. . . . I can find them." Marcelina opened Google on her PDA. Feijão reached across the table and covered the screen with his hand.

"No no no. You don't go rushing in like that. Barbosa has been in hell for longer than you've been alive, girl. There are few enough he trusted; you're only sitting here in my garden because Raimundo Soares trusts you. I will talk to the Barquinha. I know the bença there. Then I will call you. But I tell you this, if you try and go around me, I will know."

The thin, sun-beaten man drained his herbal tea and stubbed his cigarette fiercely out in the porcelain bowl.

It was in the taxi as it arced back over the long, slender bowstring of the Niteroi Bridge that Marcelina, Googling images, realized she recognized the sacred vine. *Psychotria viridis*: it glossy oval leaves and clusters of red berries had set off Feijão's view over the Marvelous City.

Aleijadão was riding an A-frame bicycle up the center of the Glass Menagerie, weaving in and out of the boxes of tapes and slumping pillars of celebrity magazines on wheels the size of industrial castors. He wobbled twice around Marcelina.

"What is that thing you're on?"

"Do you like it? It's the future of commuting."

"On Rio's hills? You want to try a tunnel at rush hour on that?"

"No, but it's kind of cool. Folds up to the size of a laptop." Aleijadão tried to throw and turn and almost came into the printer recycle box. His job was office monkey in the long, open-plan development office known as the Glass Menagerie. "Steering's a bit tricky and it doesn't half cut the ass off you. It's the latest thing from that English guy, the one who invented the computer."

Always: the latest thing.

"Alan Turing? He's—"

"No, some other guy. Invented those things on wheels you sat in and pedaled: daleks? Hawking? Something like that?"

Days there were when Canal Quatro's playfulness, its willingness to face into the breaking wave of the contemporary and ride it, thrilled and braced Marcelina; then there were the others when Canal Quatro's relentless hunger for the new, for novelty, oppressed her, a shit-storm of plastic trivia; and knowingness and irony became grim and joyless.

Marcelina's workplace Alt dot family looked up from their glass cubicles at the entrance of their über-boss. So much she could read from their lunches: at their desks, of course. Celso lifting sushi with the delicacy and deftness of professional rehearsal in private. Agnetta, as ever so completely dressed for the moment she had been known to have new shoes delivered to the office in order to wear them home that evening, chewed morosely on a diet lunch-replacement bar snack. Cibelle, the only one Marcelina respected in addition to fearing, picked apart a homemade bauru. She had been bringing them in every day. Homemade was the new sushi, she said. Cibelle understood how the trick was done, how to add your own little ripple to the crest of the hip and watch the chaotic mathematics of storms and power laws magnify it into a fashion wave. Already half of Lisandra's production group were making their own lunches. *Clever girl, but I know you.*

"Oh my God, is this some thing like we're all going to have to do now, change clothes at lunchtime?" Agnetta flapped.

"What are you talking about?"

"Like, when you were in just now you were in the suit and now you're in the Capri pants."

Marcelina shook her head. Eighty percent of what Agnetta said to her was incomprehensible.

"Any calls for me?"

"Same answer as five minutes ago," Celso said, mixing wasabi.

Marcelina held her hands out in a shrug of bafflement.

"What is this, National Freak Marcelina Hoffman Day?"

Then she saw Adriano break from his creative huddle with Lisandra and the Black Plumed Bird to beckon her with a lift of the finger, a raise of the eyebrows.

"That was a very funny e-mail. Someday someone will make a program like that and the ratings will be through the roof, but I don't think it is Canal Quatro. In fact, if I thought you were seriously proposing a series where members of the public hunt down and assassinate favelados like some kind of *Running Man* show, I MBATC."

Might Be a Tad Concerned.

"Ah, well, yeah . . ." Marcelina spluttered.

"In future, IMBAGI to pitch ideas through the regular creative channels."

She returned blazing like a failed space-launch to her luv-cluster. Lunches were set down in a flash.

"I don't know whose idea of a joke that was, but nothing ever, ever goes out of this production team unless it's cleared by me. Ever."

"We always do that, boss."

She turned on her laptop.

"Well, someone sent a hoax e-mail to Adriano, and it wasn't me."

"It was," said Agnetta faintly. "You did it. I saw you."

The chattering, ringing, beeping tunnel of the Glass Menagerie suddenly turned on end and Marcelina felt herself falling through desks and workstations and heaps of paper toward a final shattering on the great window become a floor.

"Imagine I'm very very stupid and haven't the faintest idea what you're talking about."

"About five, six minutes ago you came in, said hello, logged onto your laptop, and fired off an e-mail," said Celso. Cibelle sat back in her chair, arms folded.

"But my laptop is biometric locked." Standard security in a world where ideas were currency.

"Well, it's open now," Celso said.

Marcelina went to the screen. The login icon spun in the taskbar. She opened the in-house e-mail system.

To: Adriano@canalquatro.br

From: capoeiraqueen@canalquatro.br

Subject: Take Out the Trash . . .

The glass tube of the development office revolved around her, Marcelina a shiny ort in a kaleidoscope of flying madnesses.

She had drunk the tea.

The Green Saint was the saint of visions and illusions.

Feijão had the sacred vine growing in his garden.

The Barquinha of Santo Daime was a church of hallucinations.

She had drunk the tea. There was no other rational explanation.

Marcelina closed the program and touched her thumb to the log-out pad.

OCTOBER 12, 2032

A trip to the market. A trip into the biodiesel smog beneath the unfinished rodovia intersection of Todos os Santos, the missing buckle of the cincture of highways that binds the city of Saint Paul. A trip to the printer, to buy new shoes.

The taxi drops Edson and Fia at the edge of Our Lady of Trash. It's not that the drivers won't go inside—and they won't no matter how high you tip them—it's that they can't. Todos os Santos, like hell, is arranged in concentric rings. Unlike hell, it ascends: the summit of the great waste mountain at its heart can just be glimpsed over the roofs of the slapped-together stores and manufactories, the pylons and com towers and transmission lines. The outermost zone is a carousel of motion where cabs, buses, moto-taxis, private cars drop and pick up their rides. Trucks plow through the gyre of traffic, blaring tunes on their multiple digital horns. Priests celebrate Mass under the forest of big umbrellas that is Todos os Santos's rodoviaria, along rows of neatly spread tarpaulins piled with pyramids of green oranges and greener limes, shocks of lettuce and pak choi, red tomatoes and green peppers, past palisades of sugar cane waiting for the hand-mill and past the chugging, sweet steam of cachaça stills. The first circle of Todos os Santos is the vegetable market. Every hour of every day motorbike drays, cycle carts, pickups, refrigerator vans bring produce in from the city gardens. There is never a time where there are not buyers pressing in around the farmers as they unload boxes and sacks onto the spread ground-sheets, the clip-together plastic stalls, the rent-paying shops with shelving and cool cabinets. By night the buying and selling continues unabated by a million low-energy neons and, for those who can't afford biodiesel generators, lantern light; and for those whose profit margin would be damaged even by that, stolen electricity.

"My mum does this," Fia says. "She has a little urban farm, a couple of backlots, and she hires half a dozen rooftops. She wouldn't come here, though; she specializes in designer brassicas for the Japanese restaurant market. She's boring. It's beautiful."

She's secretive; she takes it slow. Edson hasn't gotten to kiss her yet, let alone sex. Over kibes in that little Arab lanchonete he had promised (and they had not disappointed—Yellow Dog lanches would soon be added to the De Freitas Global Talent portfolio) Edson had thrilled her with his telenovela of family: *The Sons of Dona Hortense.* Emer the bricklayer who bought a share in a gym with the money he brought down from the tower cranes of São Paulo; Ander the dead this eight years gone, cut down up in the favela; Denil the builder of fine planes for mighty Embraer; Mil the soldier boy in a violent and foreign land, remembered every night in Dona Hortense's Book of Weeping that no high-velocity round might seek out his blue beret; Ger the aspirant malandro if he could do a decent day's work; and Ed the man of business and affairs and talent management and many faces who would one day buy this lanchonete, turn it into an empire, and retire to his place by the ocean to watch the sun rise out of the sea. The Brothers Oliveira: on festivals and public holidays the house was so full of testosterone that Dona Hortense would send them all out into the street to play soccer; anything to work off the male aggression.

Fia had applauded but turned away his question about her family. Edson supposes there's only so much you can say when you are a secret quantumista.

Now they've been out together ten times and she's taking him to Our Lady of Trash to buy a pair of shoes and telling him finally about her family.

"And my dad runs a stable of accountancy ware, but what he really likes best are the pieces he writes for this cheesy New Age feed in Brasilia. He's got this idea of fusing Mahayana Buddhism with umbanda Paulistana—as if Brazil doesn't have enough religions already. My kid brother Yoshi is on a gap-year—he's surfing his way around the world. All the girls think he's fantastic. And I grew up in a little house with black balconies and red roof in Liberdade like six generation of Kishidas before me. We had a swimming pool and I had dolls and a pink bike with candy-stripe ribbons on the handlebars. See? I told you it was boring."

"Do they know what you do?" Edson asks as Fia hauls him by the hand through the temporary alleys between trucks and buses.

"I tell them I'm freelancing. It's not a lie. I don't like to lie to them."

Edson knows the date is a test. Our Lady of Trash rules a landscape of superstition and street legend. Whispers of night visions; strange juxtapositions of this city with other, illusory landscapes; angels, visitations, UFOs, ghosts, orixás. Some, they say, have received strange great gifts: the power of prophecy, the talent to discern truth, the ability to work the weather. Some have been lost entirely, wandering away and never returning to their homes and families, though relatives may sometimes glimpse them among the trash towers, close yet far away, as if trapped in a maze of mirrors. It changes you, they say. You see farther; you see things as they really are.

Edson's damned if he's going to let Todos os Santos scare him. But it surely is a place to move with confidence and smarts, and so he has dressed for authority and jeito in a white suit and ruffle-fronted shirt. Fia's shopping outfit consists of slinky boots, goldie-looking shorts with button-down pockets, calf-length shimmer coat, and Habbajabba bag.

"Hey!"

Edson almost dislocates her shoulder as he yanks her to a stop. She turns, cartoon eyes wide, to open her hot little temper on him and sees the garbage truck sway to a stop blasting all fifteen horns at her. The driver crosses himself. Trucks pile up behind him, a garbage jam. There is one direct road into the heart of Todos os Santos, and it belongs to the huge municipal caminhãos da lixo, laboring through dust and biodiesel reek. Their multiple wheel sets deeply rut the red dirt road; under rain it turns to mud and the trucks lumber and lurch axle-deep, like dinosaurs. The track leads to the only completed on-ramp of the unfinished intersection; from it they wend higher, like some kid's Hot Wheel toy-car set, up the curving roadways until they reach the edge of the drop, reverse, lights flashing and warnings yelling, to evacuate their bellies onto the ever-growing trash mountain of Todos os Santos.

"Saved your life," says Edson. Fia holds his eyes for three seconds. That's enough to signal a kiss. But Edson hesitates. The moment is lost. She lets slip his hand and heads up into the second circle. This is the district of the ware shops, the copywrong vendors, the black pharmers. Your child has tuberculosis, flu, malaria? HIV? Here's a pill for your ill, at noncorporation prices. You can't get yourself up in the morning, your husband just wants to sit and watch telenovelas all day, your children won't go to school and are eating the walls? We can give you something for that. It's been how long since you last had an erection? Oh my man, I feel for you. Here. And it will make you come buckets. You really like this track this movie this installment of *BangBang!* or *A World Somewhere* but you can't keep up the rental payments and don't want to lose it at the end of the month? We strip it, you keep it. Entertainment is for life not for hire. You want, you need, the futebol feeds but you can't afford the payments? We have a chip for every need. You are a man of debts, mistresses, crimes; seguranças police priests lawyers lovers wives after you? Here are eyes, here are fingerprints, here are names and faces and alibis and doppelgängers and ghosts and people who never lived. We can wash you purer than the crentes' Jesus. And among them, a spray-bombed pink door to a tottering upstairs office and a hand-rollered pichacão sign slung on a self-adhesive peg: *Atom Shop Is Open.*

It wasn't always sex and spandex. Today Mr. Peach was making Edson a moqueca. *You need feeding up, Sextinho; you don't look after yourself. Wasting away*

like a love-struck fool. Superhero costumes were hung up in the Bat-wardrobe. Mr. Peach was dressed now in dreadful shorts and a beach shirt. Edson in his sharp-creased whites said, "I still can't believe you knew her at São Paulo U."

Onions slid into the pan with a hiss. It was an old family recipe, a slave dish from the coffee estate days. Captains and masters were the Alvarangas, but they faded and failed until only one remains of the name. Edson has an enduring fantasy that Mr. Peach makes him son and heir of *fazenda* Alvaranga.

"Why so surprised? It's a big multiverse and a small world, even smaller in quantum computing. I was an adviser on her doctoral dissertation in computational and information physics. Her thesis was that all mind is a multiversal quantum computer and therefore a fundamental element of reality, and also linked across universes by quantum entanglement. I always enjoyed sessions with her; she was one of my top students. Scarily bright. We'd argue the toss—she had a foul temper. Great arguer. Have you discovered that yet? Her theory was that the multiverse is a massively multiply parallel quantum computer and therefore a mindlike state. I'd argue that was metaphysics at best, religion at worst: whatever way you looked at it you ended up back at the strong anthropic principle, and that's another word for solipsism. There's nothing special about us. Given enough universes, something like us is bound to occur, many times over."

A rich tang of garlic, then the astringent perfume of peppers.

"I'm not surprised she's working with the quantumeiros—I couldn't see anything in academia or even research giving her that adrenaline rush, but I can't say I'm delighted."

Crayfish now, fresh from the pond-farm up on the hill under the wind turbines. The power farms with their rotors and golden fields of rape crept down on the Fazenda Alvaranga while the housing projects crept up; street by overbright street and Mr. Peach gave his heritage away to Edson table-lamp by painting by vase. It is as if he wants the Alvarangas to be gone, wants to disappear completely. Mr. Peach slides a serving straight from the pan onto a plate; drops a little chopped coriander on top, green on yellow. A patriotic dish.

"But the real question is: have you fucked her yet?"

"I thought we'd agreed that we could see whoever we liked, that it didn't matter." Knowing that Mr. Peach had a wide circle of friends straight and gay, none of whom he would ever dress up in Lycra and cape.

"It doesn't matter until it's one of my ex-students."

Edson had been uncomfortable with Mr. Peach's former relationship with Fia since the Captain Superb/Miracle Boy session. They had been through Captain Truth/Domino Boy, Bondage Man/Pony-Lad and Lord Lycra/Spandex Kid, and Edson still feels as if he is sharing her.

"Well, she may be super-bright, but I bet you didn't know she watches *A World Somewhere*. Addicted to the thing. She'll download it and we could be having a beer or eating something or even at a club and if she doesn't like the music, I'll see her watching it on her I-shades."

"She always was like that."

Edson pushed his plate away from him.

"I'm not hungry."

"Yes you are. You're always hungry. Does your mother not feed you?"

"My mother loves me. You don't talk about my mother like that."

They're having a fight over a woman. Edson can't believe it. They're letting a girl come between them. And Mr. Peach has taught Edson much more than postcoital physics. He has educated him in other disciplines: shaving and how to buy and drink wine and shake cocktails; dressing for style not fashion; ten ways to knot a tie; etiquette and how to talk to people to make them appreciate and remember you and call you back and what women expect and like and what men like and expect and how to be respectful but still get your own way in a hierarchical society.

Once when he was very small, a man hung around outside the house and Edson asked Dona Hortense if he was his father. *Why bless the child, no.* The days when men would come round to play cards and drink were gone, but Edson remembers the heat of that embarrassment in his cheeks.

Edson glances over at Mr. Peach, the tanned skin, the wiry gray hair sprouting from his shirt collar, the thin legs rattling in the baggy shorts. *You are the father I never knew, the father I suck off.*

"Just eat it," says Mr. Peach. "For me. I like making you things."

Edson suspects that Mr. Peach may not have set the worlds of quantum physics ablaze, but in one area he excels. He's a great cook of old slave food.

In Atom Shop Edson hunts for kissable moments. As she brushes between him and the big 3-D polymer printers, as she leans over to squirt the design from her I-shades into the renderer, as he bends with her to study the holographic image of the noo shooz on the screen. A touch, a whisper, the scent of her perfume and honey-sweat and fabric conditioner but never contact.

"Good bag," says the girl on the reception, who has eyes the size of mangoes and a cloud-catching look from the fumes. The place smells strongly of plastics, like glue-sniffers' paradise. "This original?" Fia hands it to her. She holds it up to the light, turns it this way that way, squinting, peering. Atom Shop prints print necklaces, hats, earrings, formal masks, body armor, watches, costume shades, I-clothing, anything you can weave from smart polymers. Top-marque handbags. "Looks like it. We couldn't print at that resolution."

"I know," says Fia clutching her bag back to her. "But you can do me these shoes." She touches her I-shades and loads the pattern onto Atom Shop's house system. Edson does not doubt it's stolen. Bad thing to get shot for; copywrong violation on a pair of top-marque shoes. The girl loads up the cartridges, closes the transparent cover. Lights blink on, mostly yellow. The print heads rear like striking snakes, then bend to their furious business, molecule by molecule, millimeter by millimeter, building the soles and heel-tips of a pair of Manolo slingbacks.

It will take about an hour for the shoes to print, so Fia leads Edson up into the third circle of Todos os Santos, the circle of the vendors. Recycled reconditioned reengineered reimagined are the straplines here. Car parts, washing machine engines, lathes taps and dies, entertainment equipment, jerry-built white goods, custom mopeds, domestic and civil robots, surveillance systems, computers and memory, I-shades and guns—all constructed from the flow of parts that comes down the spiral from the next circle in, the circle of the dismantlers.

Circuit boards cook on coal griddles, release their lead solder like fat from pig-meat. Mercury baths grab gold from plated plugs and sockets. Homemade stills vaporize the liquid metal, depositing the heavy treasure.

Two boys stir a stream of sand-sized processors into a plastic vat of reagent, dissolving the carbon nanotubes from their matrix. Two eight-year-olds sitting cross-legged on a soy bean sack test plastic from the heap beside them by heating it over a cigarette lighter and sniffing the fumes. Younger children rush handcarts of e-junk down from the central dump. This is the circle of the slaves, sold into debt indenture by parents crushed by 5,000 percent interest. The drones pause only to pick and scratch at their skins. The loudest sound is coughing. Wrecked neurology and heavy metal poisoning are endemic. Few here are out of teenage; few live so long. Those who make it do so with ruined health. Edson chokes on a waft of acid. All around him is a sense of heat, a sense of defilement. The air is sick with fumes. He folds a handkerchief over his mouth. Fia marches blithely ahead, untouched, untouchable, stepping over the rivulets of diseased cadmium yellow, toward the heart of Todos os Santos.

Edson did not think it was just shoes that brought her here.

Supply-side economics built Nossa Senhora da Lixão from a tiny chip. The shady, dry understory of the interchange had been a fine place to set up businesses processing e-waste; out of the way and unseen. In those days the catadores pushed their handcarts ten kays along the highway verges to the old municipal dump at São Bernardo do Campo. The first driver to take a jeitinho to drop his load at the unfinished intersection had started the slow glacier of trash that over twenty years of accumulation made Todos os Santos the premier midden of the Southern Hemisphere. The population of a small town scavenges the slopes of the tech-trash mountain. By night it is extravagantly beautiful as twenty thousand torches and oil-lanterns bob and play across the ridges and valleys. Todos os Santos is big enough to have a geography: the Forest of Fake Plastic Trees, where wet ripped bags hang like Spanish moss from every spar and protrusion. The Vale of Swarf, where the metal industries dump their coils and spirals of lathe trim. The Ridge of Lost Refrigerators, where kids with disinfectant-soaked handkerchiefs over their faces siphon off CFCs into empty plastic Coke bottles slung like bandoliers around their shoulders. Above them, the peaks: Mount Microsoft and the Apple Hills; unsteady ziggurats of processor cubes and interfacers. Pickers crack them open with hammers and pry bars and deftly unscrew the components. A truck disgorges a load of terminally last-season I-shades, falling like dying bats. The catadores rush over the slippery, treacherous garbage. The fermenting trash raises the ambient air temperature three degrees. Evaporating moisture and volatiles linger in the peculiar dead spot in the wind patterns caused by the interchange: Our Lady of Trash is a true urban jungle: steamy, poisonous, diseased, wet. The scavengers wear plastic fertilizer sacks as rain capes as they work their way over the steaming rubbish in a perpetual warm drizzle, extricating a circuit board here, a washing machine motor there, and throwing them into the baskets on their backs. Their children—second-generation catadores—are the sorters and runners, grading the emptied baskets by type and then running them down on handcarts to Circle Three.

Among the dashing barrows, Fia stops, turns, lays a hand on Edson's chest.

"I've got to go on now."

Edson walks into her hand. "What?" He sounds dumb. That is bad.

"Ed, you know there's our stuff, and then there's my stuff. This is my stuff. I'll meet you back at Atom Shop."

A dozen protests occur to Edson. He keeps them: the best sound clinging. The worst are whining.

"Toys for me," Fia says. She takes Edson's face in her hands, kisses him hard, full on the mouth, with tongue and saliva. But he's still not going to let her see him walk away, so he hangs back as she picks her way up the trash-scree in her impractical boots, coat hood pulled up against the sour drizzle, climbing up into the Quantum Valley.

Every guy thinks he wants a Mystery Girl, but what men really want is all the bases covered and no gaps in the record. Mr. Peach has one end of the story of Fia Kishida, Edson the other, but the two halves don't match. There is too much unexplained between her walking out of São Paulo U and turning up in the back of a Cook/Chill Meal Solutions trailer. Edson's done some discreet research—he is an insatiable busybody. Cook/Chill Meal Solutions Company is a brand name legally registered with the Department of Trade. His intuition was right; it's all owned by Metal Guy, Floyd. He made a fist of money with *Preto* and *Morte*-Metal, sourcing those little pre- and post-gig peccadilloes that Black/Death Metal bands demand, like crack cocaine, cheerleaders, American whiskey, lapsed nuns, live goats, automatic weapons and light mortars, Chinese girls in latex, and applications to be contestants on *Take Out the Trash.* He invested his money and tips in a little business venture: Cook/Chill Meal Solutions. The driver is Aristides, ex of the Goias-São Paulo alco-tanker run. The bicha who runs cover twelve layers deep reinforced by a strategy of spread-bribery is Titifreak. And Fia to operate the array of four reconditioned quantum cores, hacking NP computations. Edson's problem, and the reason he waits until she is out of sight before following her path toward a steaming ridge of LCD screens, is that if he can find that out in six discreet inquiries, who else has?

It is inevitable as death that Q-waste should find its way to the great gehenna of Todos os Santos. It is the weirdness leaking like CFCs from so much quantum technology piled in one place that gives Nossa Senhora de Lixão her myths and legends. Quantum technology is licensed; use is government monitored, and stern controls are in place over manufacture and disposal. But trash has its own morality and gravity. One plastic casing is very much like another; get it out of here, we're filling up with this stuff, send it south. Once a few months the catadores will unearth an operational Q-array. On those holy days word flashes across the city like lightning, like scandal. Tenders come in from as far as Rio, Belo Horizonte, Curitiba. Fia is here to inspect a fresh lot.

A turn-up on Edson's white flares tears on a jagged edge. Almost he curses, but to swear is undignified. The basket-people in ragged shorts and flip-flops ignore him. Edson squats low up just beneath the skyline, peeps between shattered angular plastic frames. Down in the valley Fia talks with the two males who summoned her at the gafieira. A bulky cylinder stands on an upturned crate between them. Fia crouches, examining the cylinder with her I-shades, turning her head quizzical as a parrot. Slightly behind them is a figure Edson does not recognize, a tall chisel-featured man with his hair scraped back into a greasy ponytail. Incongruously, he is dressed as a priest. These quantumeiros do all the geek looks. He says something Edson cannot hear, but Fia looks up and shakes her head. The man speaks again; again Fia shakes her head: *no.* She looks frightened now. As Edson stands up he feels a whisper across his back. His jacket falls forward around him. Its two severed halves slide down his arms to flop over his hands. He stares, dumb, miracle-struck, then turns.

Bicha-boy Titifreak does a martial-arts thing, drawing a pattern of glowing blue in the air with the Q-blade. He holds it still, perfectly horizontal. He looks at Edson under his floppy fringe, over the blade, then snaps it down to its magnetic sheath. The air smells wounded, ozonic.

"You favelados really don't have any manners, do you?"

Edson shifts on his feet, surly, stupid stupid stupid with his disfigured white leather jacket hanging around him.

"She told you not to go but you just had to, didn't you? Look, there's nothing special about you. There's been dozens before you. She likes boys of a certain type, but she is out of your class. It doesn't mean anything. Did you think it did? This is business and you can't even begin to imagine what we're doing here and, frankly, ignorance is bliss. Really. Look, you think they give these away in packets of Ruffles?" He flips back his jacket to reveal the blade. "So you're going now. And you're not going to come back. Leave her alone. You are Sorocaba playing against São Paulo. You won't see her again. Go on. Go; I will cut you."

Edson's face is hot with rage, and humiliation sings in his ears. He shrugs off the halves of his jacket. Whatever is in the pockets can stay. He will not bow to pick them up.

"Bicha!" he shouts as he tries to maintain dignity descending the treacherous scree of tech-trash. The knifeman shrugs.

"Give my head peace, favelado."

On the third day Gerson comes to his kid brother, sixth son of a sixth son, and stands over him, rocking and raging in the hammock beside his office. His calls have fallen into dead air. It's that puta of a bicha blocking him, he's sure of that. Three days, stomping round the house; kicking over Dona Hortense's little piles of farofa and cubes of cake offered to the Lady; getting nothing done; earning no money.

"You're in my light."

"You know, if you were half the man you claimed you were, you'd be right over there, Q-blade or no Q-blade."

And Edson thinks, *He's right.* And *Fuck it fuck it fuck it.* And *It's a sorry state when Gerson is right.* Thirty minutes later, the green-and-yellow scrambler bursts out of the alley behind Dona Hortense's. But they're not Edson's sweet thighs straddling it. They're Efrim's; in a short silvery strappy dress like the one Fia wore at the gafieira (not that Efrim would admit playing copycat) soft suede calf boots in pink, and his beautiful big Afro. One final layer of costume: he swapped identities with Petty Cash, his most trusted alibi.

Edson bumps over the debris-strewn approach to the decaying mall where the quantumeiros have parked up the truck. He rounds the collapsed delivery bay. Mothers and kids, escaped debt slaves, a life lower than even the favela, follow him with their eyes. Edson would not leave an empty Coke can there, but the quantumeiros' spooky reputation keeps the street kids away. The vast parking lot is empty. Efrim touches one pink suede boot to the blacktop, spins the bike, accelerates across the weed-strewn parking lot to the highway.

The tail is back to three kilometers, says the traffic report on his Chillibeans, but Efrim slips up the side of the convoy of food trucks up from Santos. He can see the top of the truck over the cars and gridlocked executivo coaches. The roof slants at an odd angle. The police have traffic cones out and are trying to wave vehicles into one lane. There are three cruisers, one ambulance, and a lot of rotating orange lights. Two camera drones circle overhead. Now sick with dread, Efrim duck-waddles the Yam up between the grinding cars. No one will notice another rubber-necker among all the passengers craning out their windows.

The truck lists as if capsized by a sudden melting of the road. The line of the cut starts just above the fender and slices perfectly through cab, engine, and coupling. The driver's side front wheel has a neat spiral of glittering swarf sheared off from it. Efrim knows that if you were to touch that bright metal, it would cut you quicker than any razor. Sharp down to the quantum level. The slash runs the length of the trailer, makes the same strange spiral pattern on the rear wheels before exiting at the rear. The sheared-away material lies some hundred meters down the highway. Oils and hydraulic fluids spread from severed lines.

It would have been like this, Efrim thinks as he paddles his scrambler bike past the wreckage of Cook/Chill Meal Solutions. He would have waited on the verge, like a hitcher. Aristide would have given him the horns: *You're too close to the road, fool.* But he needed to be close; he needed to be at fingertip reach. All he would have to do was flick out the Q-blade and let the truck drive straight down his cut. The pattern of the wheels would be a turning tire intersecting a moving line of incision. A miracle the driver kept it upright. A clean circle is cut into the side of the trailer.

Analyze, script it, play it. Stops it being real. Stops the dreading. Makes that lingering glance at the figure under the plastic sheet just curiosity. Those are not hydraulic fluids. The roadway is black with flies. There are black vultures overhead. Sticking out from the sheet, a hand, palm upturned, imploring the Angels of Perpetual Surveillance. Shirt cuff, silver links, ten centimeters of good jacket. That would be enough to identify Titifreak, let alone the broken blade, severed almost to a stump. He fought, then. No point looking for the rest of the blade. It's on its way down to the center of the Earth.

"Hey, what are you staring at?"

Caught. Efrim throws his hands up in dismay. The cop fixes him with her mirrored visor.

"Go on, get out of here before I lift you for obstructing a police investigation."

"Yes yes yes," Efrim mumbles, ducking his head. For he was staring. Staring at the paramedics in their green and hi-visibility yellow lifting a stretcher into the back of the ambulance. On that stretcher, a body under plastic, but the sheet is too short and the body's feet stick out, feet flopping away from each other; feet in shoes. Efrim recognizes the soles of those shoes. The last time he saw them was in a Todos os Santos print-shop, being woven layer upon layer from smart plastic.

August 22–28, 1732

Fé em Deus
Rio Amazonás: above Pauxi Fort

My dearest Heloise,

Finally, my dear sister, finally, I sail the calm waters of the great Amazon and I find myself in the realm of the mythological. The island of Marajó, which in former times was the habitation of many advanced Indian tribes, is the size of Brittany and Normandy together yet lies easily in the mouth of the river. A flow equal to that of every river in Europe passes out of the river every day. The water, so our Captain Acunha tells us, is sweet up to seventy leagues out to sea. Yet the Amazon drops only fifty toises over its entire length, and its flow is so gentle it may take a leaf a month to drift from the rank, miasmic foothills of the Peruvian Andes to pass beneath the hull of our *Fé em Deus*.

While I languished in Belém at the governor-general's pleasure, not a day passed that I did not see La Condamine and his expedition descending upon the coast in a cloud of sail. But now our vessel beats upstream under the command of her master Acunha, a river trader of surly and aloof disposition, yet I was assured at Belém do Pará that there was none more experienced in the ever-treacherous seasonal patterns of shoals and banks that form and shift in this great stream. What with the manioc and beans, powder and shot required to equip an expedition into the high Amazon—I am assured I can find bearers, guides, and crew in plenty at São José Tarumás—let alone the many cases of scientific equipment, Captain Acunha mutters about the loading of his barque. But we make excellent haste: we have already put the narrows at the Fort of the Pauxis behind us; São José Tarumás lies before us. This far inland from coastal influences the winds are too light and variable and the river too excessively braided to allow us to raise sail, so it is by the power of human muscle we ascend the mighty Amazon, bent to oars, a true classical slave-galley.

Slavery is an alien state to me; those few I have seen in Paris are novelties: as a society we practice the subtler oppressions of seigneury. God forfend that this plague of draft animals should cross to France! Not a day passes that we are not passed by flotillas of tethered rafts laden to the waterline with bound slaves: men, women, children, all red, all naked as innocent Adam and Eve. This is a monstrous traffic. The prices at Belém do Pará are insultingly low; the Indian has not our resistance to diseases, and life on the engenhos is so hard and dispiriting few see more than five years—few desire more than five years. This economy serves the senhores de engenhos well: a slave pays for himself in two cruelly hard sugar harvests; everything after that is profit. In five years the owner has returned double on his investment, so there is no incentive not to work them to death. I am told many Indians simply put an end to themselves rather than face such an existence. Yet the supply of red flesh up the great river is seemingly as endless as its flow of waters: whole nations are being "descended," as the euphemism runs here.

What may I tell you of my traveling companion? For a start, he is more chaperone than traveling companion: I am in no doubt whatsoever that his advent alone secured my permission to travel upriver, the usefulness of my researches to the mercantile Portuguese being balanced against their sensitivities at being tenuous owners of a vast, largely unmapped, and almost wholly undefended territory that our kingdom has historically viewed with envy. No matter, it is the least of incivilities; indeed, it is almost a flattery that they consider me so important a spy that they have placed me under the watchfulness of as extraordinary a man as Father Quinn, SJ.

You know well my scant regard for the religious, but every so often one meets a member in holy orders of such force of personality, such qualities and charisms that one is forced to speculate, what could possibly have moved this man to take his vows? Luis Quinn is surely one of these. Of an Old Catholic family dispossessed of its lands and forced into the port trade by the accession of the House of Orange, he is a great bear of a man—Irish, a race of lumbering, uncouth giants much given to brooding and the taking of slights and offenses—yet in the Ver-o-Peso, when we fought in mock duel, he moved with a grace, an energy and economy that I have never seen in any of his compatriots, and also an unregenerate ferocity that leads me to speculate what may have led him to his vow and habit.

He is an intelligent man. I have never met a Jesuit who was not at worst a pleasant conversationalist, at best a fine intellectual spar. Languages I have always found peculiarly broadening to the mind: to speak is to think; language is culture. Father Quinn speaks his native Irish in two dialects, the western and the northern; Latin and Greek of course; English; Spanish; French; Portuguese; Italian; can get by in Moroccan Arabic and claims to have taught himself the Tupi lingua geral, which is more commonly spoken than Portuguese on these waters, on the crossing from Lisbon. How that rowdy family of voices must shape the interior of a man's skull is a fine speculation.

Last night, in the long and tedious dark that falls so early and swift in these latitudes, I showed him the working model of the Governing Engine. I demonstrated how the chain of cards fed from the hopper and thus governed the lifting patterns of the weft harnesses in the loom. "Thus the most complicated of brocades can be simply rendered as a series of holes or solids in the card: mathematically, substance or absence, ones or nulls. In a sense, an entire weave of cloth can be reduced to a single chain of figures: ones and zeroes." He handled the device and toyed intelligently with the wooden mechanism, observing how the pegs on the riser-heads fell into the holes and held the weft down, while the solid card pressed down on those same pins and caused the harnesses to rise.

"I can see how it might be possible to use such a set of cards to play a program in a musical automaton," he said perspicaciously. "It is a much more flexible system than the pins on musical boxes; one mechanism could play any piece that could be rendered in holes and solids—ones and nulls, as you suggest. One of those new-fashioned fortepianos would be an ideal instrument, being not so far from a loom in its construction. A loom of music, one might say."

I speculated then of other tasks that might benefit from the auto-motivation of the Governing Engine: arithmetical calculation was easily simplified, and Jean-Baptiste, whose touch of genius the punched card was, developed a number of card-sets that could perform mathematical computations as complex as factorization and deriving square roots, notoriously cumbersome and time-consuming.

"I must confess that this thought fills me with intellectual excitement," I said to Quinn as we stood by *Fé em Deus*'s stern rail, taking what cool the evening offered. "If such straightforward arithmetic computations can be reduced to a string of ones and nulls, might not all mathematics be ultimately reducible to the same basic code? The great Newton's laws of motion, his rules for the gravitational forces that order the physical universe, these too may be simply reduced to ones and zeroes, something and nothing. Might this simple machine—given a sufficiently large stack of properly coded cards—be capable of rendering the entire universe itself? A universal governor?"

I shall not soon forget his reply: "Your words come close to blasphemy there, friend." To him, I was reducing the vast created order, and everything in it, to something even less than Newton's dumb mechanism, to a mere string of somethings and nothings. That Earth and the heavens could be governed, in effect, *ex nihilo*—by nulls, by the absence of God—was not lost on this acute man. He said, "Mathematics is the product of the mind, not the mind of mathematics, and all creations of the perfection of God."

I should have understood that he was offering me a space in which to pause, even to withdraw from what he saw as the logical and, to him, heretical consequences of my speculation. But the wide vistas of mental abstraction have always called me on, to run like a horse turned loose after years at the mill; or perhaps the mad, dying horses of Brazil? I asked him to consider the auto-motive fortepiano: the same mechanism that turned digits on the cards into notes could be reversed, encoding the strokes of the keys into marks on a card, to be punched into holes. Thus we could obtain an exact record of a player's performance *at that moment and no other*; in effect, the very thoughts and intents of Mr. Handel or Father Vivaldi preserved forever. This record could be copied many times, as a book is printed, a permanent memory of a performance, not subject to the frailties and imaginings of human memory. A model of part of mind: I surmised that within a very few years of the Governing Engine's general acceptance into the world of industry, ways would be found to record and code other aspects of the human mind.

"Then thank God that our souls are more than mere numbers," Quinn said. He hefted the Governing Engine and for an instant I feared he might fling it into the river. He set it down on the deck as he might a colicky child. "A model of a model of a mind. Your engine, M. Falcon, will make slaves of us all."

And so it is that human intelligence is the slave of doctrine, shackled and sold as utterly as any of the wretches that drift past us on those waterlogged slave rafts. The divine is invoked and there can be no more argument. Damnable Jesuit condescension! The arrogance of his assumption to possess all truth, that no debate need be entered into for I could only be correct insofar as I concurred with his doctrine. We spoke no more that night: we retired to our hammocks, he to banish the mosquitoes with the fumes of the powerful cigars he favors, I to rage and draw up arguments and counterblasts, exposing follies and inanities. It will be fruitless; truth is not ours to discover; it is what is revealed. It angers me to see a man of such gifts and intellectual grasp reduced to the state of child by the dogma of his order.

God keep you and save you, my dear sister, and my affections to Jean-Phillipe and little Bastien, Anette, and Joseph—he must be quite the pup now! Surely Jean-Baptiste must by now have returned to France and is making a recovery from his bloody flux; convey my warmest brotherly affections. Beyond São José Tarumás there will be few, if any, opportunities for communication, so this may be the last letter you receive from me until I complete my experiment. If you should see Marie-Jeanne, the simple imparting of these words would give her comfort and certainty while we are necessarily parted: *My mind is made up, I am decided: yes, I shall, yes. With all my heart.*

With loving affection
Your brother
Robert.

Luis Quinn made his first exercise at dawn. The *Fé em Deus* lay anchored to a cable from the northern bank, a guard against escape though the slaves slept chained to their oars. Rags of mist coiled across the water and clung to the trees that crowded down to the cracked, muddy strand. The river was an ocean, its farther bank invisible through the vapors stirred from its deep-secreted heat. Sound hung close to the surface, pressed low by the layers of warm and cool air; it seemed to come from all sides at once, from immense distances. Luis Quinn found himself holding his breath, holding every creak of joint and pulse of blood still to unpick the weave of voices channeled along the river. The pagan roar of howler monkeys—they no longer terrified him as they had that second night out from Belém when they seemed the infernal host of Babylon—the frogs, the insects, the whoop and scrape of the morning birds, but beyond them . . . splashing? Oars? He strained to hear, but an eddy in the flow of heat and cool swept the faint noise back into the general chorus. Suddenly all other senses were overwhelmed by the smell of deep water, cool and sacred. A joy so intense it was pain made Luis Quinn reach for the rail. He could feel the river run, the world turn beneath him. He was infinitesimal, embedded in glory and unknowing, like a nut in its thick casing on the branch of a great tree. Quinn turned his face to the pearl-gray hidden sun; then pressed his hand to his heart. Sin to worship the creation before the creator. And yet . . . He set his leather-bound book on the rail, undid its lacing, opened the handwritten pages. A joy, a fire of another kind, his painstaking translation of the *Spiritual Exercises* into Irish. The Second Week. Fourth Day. A Meditation on the Two Standards. Loyola, that subtle soldier: the untranslatable pun.

"A glorious morning indeed, Father."

The violent loudness of the voice as Quinn prepared to descend into quiet was like a blow. He lurched against the creaking, unsound rail.

"Forgive me, Father, I did not mean to alarm you."

Falcon stood at the aft of the ship half-shadowed by the awning. He too balanced an open book on the rail, a soft suede-bound sketchbook in which he drew with charcoal.

"Our superior general prescribes dawn as the best time for meditation."

"Your superior general is right. What is today's subject?"

"The Two Standards, of Christ and of Lucifer." At many junctions and embarkations in his life Luis Quinn had returned to the disciplines of the Spiritual Exercises. The packet from Coimbra to Lisbon had been brusque business, he no more than freight. The calm-bound crossing to Salvador was for preparation, for the lingua geral and the writings of the great explorers and missionaries. The slow crawl up the coast to Belém do Pará had been the opportunity to study his follow traveler and subject—this small, fierce man of strangely juxtaposed convictions and doubts and swift, ill-concealed humors. But the river, that province of time as much as distance, unchanging and never the same from breath to breath, was the true embarkation to the celebration of discipline. "We are commanded to envision a vast plain about Jerusalem, and mustered upon it around his banner the armies of our Lord; and in the same work of the mind's eye that other vast plain around Babylon, where around the banner of the deceiver are gathered the forces of Lucifer."

"How do you imagine it, the standard of Lucifer?" *Fé em Deus* was waking; the movements of the crew sending luxurious ripples across the glassy water.

"Golden of course, like a bird, a proud bird of prey with feathers of flame and diamonds for eyes. He was a Lord of Light, Lucifer. Quite quite beautiful and so skillfully made that the diamond eye enchants and seduces everyone who sees it so they think, Yes, yes, I see myself reflected there and I am good. Excellently good. Who would be drawn to it if it did not mirror their vanities and answer their hopes?"

Falcon gave his whole weight to the rail and looked out into the morning, where bands of blue were appearing as the higher mists evaporated. "You have a great gift for visualization, Father. I find that I must augment my memory with material aids." Quinn glanced at the doctor's book. The double-page was covered in a drawing of the visible shore, the line of the trees, the taller tops rising above the general canopy, the jumble of high birds' nests, the zones of the strand: the scrub vegetation—a writhe of black denoted the jacaré in the lee of the bleached fallen branch—the edge-grasses and the cracking reach of the exposed muds and silts. Captain Acunha never tired of saying he had never seen the river so low. The whole was annotated with comments and footnotes in a strange cursive.

"I have no hand for the drawing," Luis Quinn said. "Your writing is unfamiliar to me. Might I ask what language?"

"A code of my own devising," Falcon said. "It's not unknown for scientists to need to keep their notes and observations secure. Ours is a jealous profession."

"Some might see it as the work of a spy."

"Would a spy show you that he writes in code? Look! Oh look!" Quinn's attention darted to where the doctor pointed, leaning intently over the rail. *Yes*, he had been about to say, *if that spy thought that those notebooks would be found later, by stealth or theft.*

A mound in the water, a wheezing spray of mist broke the surface and vanished into spreading ripples. A moment later a second apparition surfaced and submerged in a soft rain of exhalation. The two circles of ripples met and clashed, reinforcing, canceling each other out. Falcon dashed, flapping coat-tails and loosely bound sheaves of paper, along the narrow gunwale to the bowsprit, where he clung, keenly scanning the misty water through his peculiar spectacles. "There! There!" The two humps arced through the water as one a short distance ahead of the ship, blowing out their lungs in a gasp of stale air. "How marvelous, did you see, Quinn, did you see? The beak, a pronounced narrow protrusion, almost a narwhal spear." He dashed excitedly with his coals on the paper, never taking his eyes off the close, hazed horizon. "The boto—the Amazonian river dolphin. I have read . . . Did you see the color? Pink, quite pink. The boto: extraordinary and I think unclassified. To catch one, that would be an achievement indeed: to have the classification *Cetacea Odontoceti falconensis*. I wonder if the captain, the crew, even my own staff might obtain one for taxonomic purposes? My own cetacean . . ."

But Luis Quinn stared still into the pearl opacity that hung across the river. A plane of shadow, a geometry, moving out in the mist upstream of *Fé em Deus*, glimpsed and then lost again. There. There! His flesh shivered in superstitious dread as the dark mass resolved in the mist, like a door opening onto night, and behind it, another rectangle of lesser grayness. What uncanny river-phantasm was this? Silent, utterly silent, without a ripple, floating over water not on it. Luis Quinn opened his mouth to cry out in the same instant the lookout yelled a warning. Captain Acunha on the stern deck whipped glass to eye. Quinn saw his unmagnified eye widen.

"Sweeps! Sweeps!" Acunha roared as the house appeared out of the rippling mist. The coxswain and his mates lashed still-drowsing oarsmen awake with knouts as the floating house spun ponderously on its pontoon and drifted past within a biscuit-toss of the *Fé em Deus*. Behind it was the second object Quinn had glimpsed: another pontoon house, and behind it, appearing out of the fog, a whole village upon the waters, turning slowly on the deep, powerful currents of the stream.

"Larboard sweeps!" Captain Acunha shouted, running along the central decking with a landing hook to the station where the two benches of chained rowers craned over their shoulders to find a roofless wooden house bearing down on them at ramming speed, corner-forward. "On my word fend off. Any one of those putas could sink us. Cleverly now, cleverly . . . Now!" The sweep slaves had pushed their oars as far forward as they could, and on their captain's command hauled back, making gentle, oblique contact with the side of the house pontoon, forcing it slowly, massively, ponderously away from the side of the ship. The captain thrust away with the landing pike, fighting for leverage, his whole weight behind the spike, face trembling with effort. Forward oars passed the runaway house to aft oars; clenched muscles shone wet in the mist. The house grazed past *Fé em Deus*'s stern by a lick of paint and vanished through the downstream horizon.

From the forward deck Luis Quinn watched the houses sail past. A village afloat—a village cast adrift. The latter houses, many of them caught together in duets and trinities by tricks of the current, showed signs of burning: few had roofs; some were charred to the very waterline, stumps and sticks of blackened wood, like shattered teeth. Twenty, thirty, fifty. Six times the sweepers fended off a castaway house, once at the price of a third the larboard side's oars. Not a village. A town. A deserted town, abandoned, slaughtered, taken.

"Hello the village!" Luis Quinn thundered, his deep sea-formed voice carrying across the smooth, unruffled water. And in the lingua geral. "The village, ho there!" No answering hail, no word, not even the bark of a dog or the grunt of a pig. Then a house, burned down almost to waterline, turned in the stream and through the gaping door Quinn saw a dark object, and a pale hand lift. "There's someone there!" he thundered. "There is one yet alive!"

"Raise anchors!" Acunha shouted. Windlass catchpawls rattled over capstans. The anchors rose from the water, gray and slimy with river silt. "Sweeps! Starboard side. On my command." The drum beat; the oars rose and dipped; *Fé em Deus* turned on the steel waters. "All pull."

The slaves strained to their oars. *Fé em Deus* dashed forward, gaining on the house that Quinn had seen. Acunha deftly commanded his sweeps to negotiate the boat through the drifting, turning pontoons.

"Again lads, let's have you."

A final effort and *Fé em Deus* drew alongside. Quinn strained to see; a figure was visible lying on the floor of what, by the fallen statues and charred altar, must have been a church. Acunha's scouts, lithe, agile Pauxis all, leaped aboard with lines and secured house to ship.

Quinn followed Acunha on to the raft. His feet slipped on wet, charred paper as he walked through the collapsed, smoking, still-warm ruin. Acunha and the Pauxis knelt around a delirious woman who clutched the rags of a Carmelite postulant's habit to her like children. A caboclo from the angle of her cheekbones, the fold of her eyes: her face was too direly burned for any other features to identify her. She stared up dumb into the ring of faces that surrounded her, but when Luis Quinn's shadow fell on her she gave a keening shriek that made even Captain Acunha step back.

"What is it, what happened my daughter?" Quinn asked in the lingua geral, kneeling beside her; but she would not answer, could not answer, slapped away his ministering hands, gasping with fear.

"Leave her, Father," Acunha ordered. "Bid Dr. Falcon come over from the ship."

Falcon was helped over the narrow water between the two vessels.

"I'm a geographer, not a physician," he muttered, but yet knelt down beside the sister. "Get back get back, give the woman some air, let her see the light." After a brief examination he drew Quinn and Captain Acunha into his confidence. "She is terribly burned over the major part of her body; I do not know if she inhaled flame, but her breathing is shallow, labored, and heavy with phlegm: at the very least I would say that her lungs have been damaged by smoke. I have seen many a loom fire in Lyon; they can spontaneously combust in cotton duff. I certainly know that it is more often the smoke that kills. But I fear the greatest damage lies here." He held up a pair of botanical tweezers; caught in their tips a tiny white ovoid the size of a grain of rice."

"A botfly egg," Acunha said.

"Indeed sir. Her burns are infested with them; infested, some have already hatched. From that we may deduce that the town was set to the torch not less than three days ago."

"God and Jesus, they will eat her alive." Acunha crossed himself, kissed his two fingers.

"I fear there is very little we can do save make her comfortable and easy. Captain, there is an herbal simple I have seen used in Belém do Pará; acculico it is called, a stimulant herb but with a potency for analgesia. I believe it would ease this woman's suffering."

Captain Acunha dipped his head in acknowledgment.

"The galley master keeps a supply in his sabretache. It puts a wondrous spark in the slaves' stamina."

"Good good. A few balls should suffice. Now, we must move her. Gently, gently." A hammock slung from a bamboo pole negotiated the postulant as tenderly as they could over to *Fé em Deus*, but she still screamed and wept at every jolt and rub of her exposed tissue against the weave of the fabric. The slaves carried her to an awning on the aft deck. Falcon administered the leaf and in time soothed the woman's ravings to a dull, relentless mad burble.

Quinn remained on the boat-church. He knelt to the altar, blessed himself, and lifted one of the charred papers. Music notation: a Mass by Tassara of Salvador. To the greater glory of God. A simple, riverside church; Quinn had passed many such in the floating villages along the varzea, the seasonal flood plain of the river, rising and falling on their pontoons with the waters. They were without exception trading posts, supply depots for river traffic and lines into the vast hinterland; their church a simple wood-and-thatch pontoon, a raised wooden platform for sanctuary, horns and clappers for summoning bells. An altar cloth worked with glowing, fantastical representations of the four Evangelists in braid and plaited feathers lay half burned at the foot of the altar. It would have brought a fine price at any floating market, but the defilers had preferred to burn it, to burn everything.

This was a judgment, Luis Quinn thought.

The altar was strewn with lumps of rain-softened excrement. Quinn swept them away, cleaned the Communion table with the rags of its former covering, choking at the reek of human filth, smoke, and wet ash. He fetched the cross from the midden of half-burned rubbish where it had been flung. It was as intricate and fabulous as the altar cloth; minutely carved and painted panels depicted the Stations of the Cross. Quinn kissed the panel of Christ Crucified at its center, held his lips a lingering moment before setting the cross in its place. He stepped back, dipped his head in a bow, then genuflected and again crossed his breast.

The Fallen Cross. The permit for Just War.

The postulant would not tolerate Quinn's presence until he changed his dress for a white shirt and breeches. "She fears my robe not my face," Quinn commented, setting lights to drive off the mosquitoes. "A Carmelite mission, a poor enough place though they modeled themselves on the Jesuits. Music in church; daub, all that stuff. Who would attack a river mission?"

"Not bandeirantes, never bandeirantes," Captain Acunha said, shaking his head. He was a thickset, squat man, of bad complexion and coarse, greasy hair; thickly bearded; more slavemaster than shipmaster. "They would never descend a raft town."

"These are hungry times for flesh," he said.

Acunha stared at Luis Quinn, eyes dark like a monkey's in his thick facial hair.

"It was the Dutch, Dutch bastards; they've always had their eyes on the northern bank. Weigh there! Weigh anchor, get us moving, we've been too long here." The bluff assertion of command, but Quinn heard a discord of anxiety in his voice. *The Dutch are traders, not slavers.* Three days ago the raiders had struck. The people stolen from this town must have already passed them, anonymous, unremarked, wired together through the ear, or the nose, like animals tamed to the plow.

Calls from the water; the Pauxi scouts had swum over to other burned houses and returned with news that they exchanged with Acunha in short, accented stabs of language like arrows.

Acunha beckoned Quinn to him.

"They have found the bodies of the friars in other houses," he said in a low voice,

"Dead," Quinn said.

"Of course. And . . . bad. Badly used. Used abominably."

"I do not need to hear," Quinn said with heat and power. "They desecrated . . . I went into the church . . . the altar, the filth, human filth . . ."

Falcon joined them.

"She is speaking now."

"Has she any information?" Quinn asked.

"Ravings. Visions. Again and again she returns to a hallucination of angels of judgment, angels of retribution, a host of them, their feet touching the treetops. Gold and silver angels. The friars and irregular sisters went out to meet them. The angels told them they had been judged and found wanting. Then they seared the village with swords of fire. She herself hid beneath the altar when the angels burned the church around her. The rest were gathered up and told they had failed and would be descended into slavery."

"Angels?" Quinn asked.

"Her mind is utterly destroyed."

"And yet I am reminded of a legend from Salvador, of the angels battling in Pelourinho with blades of light. The angels that brought the horse plague."

"And there is your habit. . . ."

"The Society of Jesus has no habit; our attire is nothing other than conventional priestly dress; sober, simple, practical."

A dry, cracking cry came from the awning. Quinn hastened to the Carmelite's side, lifted her head to offer her water from the pewter mug. Falcon watched him gently sponge the ruined face and clean the botfly eggs from the suppurating burns. Pity, rage, sorrow, helplessness—the violence of his emotions, the complexity of their interactions like patterns in a weave, shocked him. *Brazil, you madman?* Orsay at the Academy had exclaimed when Falcon had approached him to fund his expedition. *Greed, vanity, rapacity, brutality, and contempt for life are vices to all the great nations of the world. In Brazil they are right virtues and they practice them with zeal.*

Weary and world-sick, Falcon stepped through the chained bodies pulling at their oars to his hammock reslung in the bow of the ship. The slaves, the ship, the river and its fugitive peoples, its sacked aldeias and vain mission churches, were but gears and windlasses in a vast dark engenho never ceasing, ever grinding, crushing out commerce. Nation building, the enlightened uplift of native peoples, the creation of culture, learning, art, were trash: wealth was the sole arbiter, personal wealth and aggrandizement. No university, not even a printing press in all of Brazil. Knowledge was the preserve of noble, queenly Portugal. Brazil was to keep its back bent to the capstan.

The peças hauled, and *Fé em Deus* crawled along the vast river. Falcon watched Quinn sit with the destroyed woman, at times talking to her, at times reading his Spiritual Exercises with fierce concentration. Falcon tried to sketch in his expedition log his memory of the boat-town. Planes, angles of mist and shadow; meaningless, hieratic. *This is a river of fear,* he wrote. *The refined soul naturally veers from melodrama, but Brazil turns hyperbole into reality. There is a spirit here, lowering, oppressive, dreadful. It saps the heart and the energy as surely as the monstrous heat and humidity, the ceaseless insects, the daily torrential downpours; rain warm as blood that yet chills the bone. I find I can almost believe anything I am told of the Amazon; that the boto is some mermaid-creature that rises from the river at night to take human lovers and father pink-skinned children; of the curupira with his feet turned the wrong way, deceiver of hunters, protector of the forest. On these hot, sleepless nights it is too easy to hear the uakti, vast as a ship, hasting through the night forest, the wind drawing strange music from the many fluted holes throughout its body. And what of the woman-warriors after whom this river was (mis)-named, the Amazons themselves?*

The shadows grew long, the swift dark came down, and *Fé em Deus* resounded with the cries and noises of a ship anchoring for the night. Falcon felt old, thin, and fragile as a stick in a drought, close to his own mortality. The figures in the aft deck, darkest of all, ink on indigo. The palm oil wicks in their terracotta pots drew studies of Quinn's face as he ministered to the dying woman. Falcon knew well the hand gestures, the motions of the lips.

Quinn came forward for a fresh breaker of water and Falcon said softly, "Did you administer extreme unction to that woman?"

Quinn ducked his head. "I did, yes, I did."

The fear that he too was no more than a notch on a belt running through this airless, blood-fueled mill kept Falcon from easy sleep, but as the immense, soft southern stars arced over him, the gentle sway of *Fé em Deus* on the current sent him down into dreams of angels, huge as thunderheads, moving slowly yet irresistibly along the channels and tributaries of the Amazon, their toenails, the size of sails, drawing wakes in the white water.

In the morning the postulant was missing from the ship.

"You were with her; how could this have happened?" Falcon's voice was an accusation.

"I slept," Luis Quinn said simply, mildly. Falcon's temper flared.

"Well where is she, man? She was in your care."

"I fear she went into the river. The acculico was used up. In the madness of her torment she may have made an end of herself."

"But that is desperation, that is a mortal sin."

"I trust in the grace and mercy of Our Lord Jesus Christ."

Falcon looked again at his companion. He wore again his simple, unaffected black habit and skullcap and his face a set of resigned concern, spiritual distance, sorrow, and inevitable loss. *You lie, Jesuit,* Falcon said to himself. *You were complicit; she confessed that final, mortal sin to you and you absolved her. You did not stop her. Did you even help her? From her hammock, to the side, over the rail into the kind water?*

"I bitterly regret my inability to save the sister," Quinn said as if reading Falcon's doubts. "I shall pray for her soul and repose when we reach São José Tarumás and for myself do penance. For now, by your leave, my Spiritual Exercises have been neglected and I must attend to them."

OUR
LADY
WHO
APPEARED

MAY 30–JUNE 4, 2006

The adherents of Santo Daime drove good cars: Scandinavians, Germans, high-end Japanese. They were parked ten deep around the private gym in Recreio dos Bandeirantes. Valets cleaned windows and vacuumed interiors; their fresh wax finishes hugging the yellow parking-lot lights to their streamlines. Private security with berets and their pants tucked into their boots patrolled in pairs, hands resting lightly on light automatic weapons. A woman with her blonde-streaked hair scraped painfully back beneath her green beret inspected Marcelina's letter of introduction three times. Her cap badge carried a crest of a mailed fist clutching crossed lightning bolts. A little excessive, Marcelina thought. She took Marcelina's PDA and cellular.

"No pictures."

127

Her colleague, a shave-skull thug, harassed the taxi driver, checking his license plate against his hackney license, mumbling intimidating nothings into his collar-mike. Marcelina loathed security. They had bounced her out of too many and better gigs than this. But in the scented cool of the parking lot she heard the drums sway on the heavy air and felt the rhythms of the Green Saint begin to move her.

Her letter was again inspected in the lobby by an abiá with a white cloth wound around his head in a loose turban. He was a very young, very pure alva. Marcelina suspected it was so for most of the iâos of the Barquinha do Santo Daime. He had no idea what he was reading.

"This will get you into the terreiro. After that it's up to you; my favors are all used up."

Go somewhere once and you will go there again. For the second time that week Marcelina had arced out over Guanabara Bay to receive herbal tea in Feijão's humid, scented bower. She had let the porcelain Japanese bowl sit untouched on the low plastic table before her. *Did you drug me, did you feed me holy secrets?* But she felt that Feijão might have been close for some time to the Barquinha; some fissure had taken place and he had called in an uncomfortable debt. Such intrigue for a disgraced goalkeeper.

Exu, Lord of the Crossings, stood on either side of the futsal court's double doors; cheap poured concrete effigies of the deity in his malandro aspect: a grinning preto in a white suit and Panama hat and shoes, garishly painted. Marcelina pushed open the doors. The drumming leaped in her face.

Marcelina adored the frenzy of Rio's homebrew religions; at New Year she loved to step out the front door of her apartment block and lose herself in the chaos of two million pressing souls on the Copacabana, throwing flowers into the waves as offerings to the Lady of the Sea. For a week after, the beach stank of the rotting petals cast up on the strand, but Marcelina would swing barefoot through them, sensing through her bare feet the water-memory of madness. The truest religions were the ones that most deeply kissed the irrational, the ecstatic, and in that Santo Daime was less ridiculous than many. The mood in the room was taut, breathless, alien. She knew that the worshipers had been drumming, dancing, spinning since early evening. It would not be long now. She only needed to be there for the third act.

She found a place at the low curving wall of the futsal court among the shuffling, hands-raising devotees. As a dancer in the center of the court spun back to the walls a worshiper, eyes closed, would spiral out to take his place, bare feet rucking up the carefully laid plastic sheeting.

Marcelina knew what that was for.

All the worshipers wore some measure of white; the headcloth as minimum for the abiás, a white shift in what looked to Marcelina like shiny, ugly, static-clingy polyester for the initiates. She would have felt conspicuous but that the worshipers had been spun so far out of themselves by two and a half hours of drum and dance that they would not have noticed Godzilla. Not so conspicuous, though, as an elderly, black ex-goalkeeper. She scanned the room. White meat, whiter even than her carioca-German DNA. She could understand the appeal of the shamanistic, the communal and unconstrained to the white middle classes behind their security fences and surveillance cameras and armed guards. The wilder world, the spirit of the deep forest, within reasonable limits and a twenty-minute commute-time every other Tuesday evening. Her eyebrows rose slightly at a handful of Nationally Recognizable Faces: two telenovela stars and a pop-ette famous for emulating everything Madonna did, but in a Brasileiro way. No wonder beret-girl had lifted her cameras. Marcelina entertained herself by calculating how much *Caras* magazine would pay for shots of the worship's inevitable conclusion.

The urn, covered with a white cloth, stood on a small altar beneath a garden sun canopy over the penalty area. The bateria was behind the goal line: they played as well as white people could be expected. A very spaced girl pounded on a hip-slung bass drum. A tall man with long, graying hair tied in a ponytail and a grayer Santa Claus beard could only be Bença Bento. An environmentalist, Marcelina knew from her research. Went up to protect the Roam and came back having met God. Or whatever Santo Daime believed ordered the universe. The divine. She wondered how many of the high-gloss SUVs parked outside ran on biofuel. Bença Bento was as relaxed as if he were in his own front room, chatting amiably to the bateria's alabé and the Barquinha's ekediss, who all seemed to be postmenopausal women swathed in white, moving unconsciously but stiffly to the drums. In a momentary flash, Marcelina pictured her mother among them, imagined her bossa nova organ doubling with the bateria. Flash again: she momentarily locked eyes with a figure across the barracão. Its head was completely wrapped in white cloth so that only the eyes were exposed. Marcelina could not tell if it was man or woman, but the eyes were at once familiar and disturbing. She looked away; the rhythm changed, the dancers, loose-limbed and drenched with sweat, spun back to the edges of the court. Bença Bento stepped into the pavilion and removed the white cloth from the urn.

The communion was about to begin. The eguns stepped forward with supermarket tubes of disposable plastic cups, cafezinho sized. Not so ecofriendly that, either. *Why are you mocking?* Marcelina asked herself as the women filed past the urn, filling cups. *What do you do up in that walled garden in Silvestre with your songs and your berimbaus that is so very different?*

The music ended. Bença Bento raised his arms.

"In the name of Santo Daime, the Green Saint and Our Lady of the Vegetable Union, draw near, receive with love and unite with the order of the universe."

He looks like Christopher Lee playing Saruman, Marcelina thought, and giggled. Worshipers stepped forward, then broke into a run. Middle-class cariocas mobbed the prim ladies of the egun; reaching, snatching, clawing for their cups of the ayahuasca tea. Marcelina noted that the abiás held back, as did the Head-Wrap Spooky Eyes. Her immediate neighbor, a lanky thirty-something man whose hair was receding patchily and unattractively, returned, eyes wide, pupils shrunk to pinpricks under the hallucinogenic tea. She saw him gag once, then stepped back neatly out of the arc of the projectile vomit that spattered onto the plastic sheeting.

True iâos held that the vomiting, a side effect of the mix of forest vines and shrubs that was the Green Saint, was as valuable in its purging, its purifying, as the hallucinations it whip-cracked across the frontal lobes. Now the bateria beat up again—Marcelina noticed that neither they nor the bença took the Daime—and the worshipers danced and turned, self-absorbed in their hallucinations. Some rolled, spasming on the smeared plastic, the bolar, ridden by sprits from beyond the edge of physical reality. Teenagers in white, boys and girls both, in white turbans and T-shirts knelt with the tranced; they were the ekedis, protecting them from the trampling feet of the worshipers.

Marcelina had done Daime—something as like it as spit—two years ago in a co-pro for the National Geographic Channel: *World's Wackiest Religions*. It sure beat Catholicism. She watched the Madonna wannabe and the two telenovela stars puke ecstatic jets onto the floor. It beat Kaballah too, for that matter. She wondered idly who had the cleaning contract. There was not enough money in Brazil to pay her to clean up hallucinogenic vomit.

She felt watched and looked over her shoulder to see Scary Eyes leave the court. Almost she seized it, demanded, "Hey, what gives?" She shivered. In this futsal court anything could happen: she had already experienced the power of the Daime. She hoped it was the Daime.

She waited until the mass had ended, the worshipers hauled to their feet, their soiled, fouled whites stripped off and stuffed into bin bags and the people sent into the world in peace. *You're going to let them drive in that condition?* she thought. The police of Recreio dos Bandeirantes had more important tasks than hauling in cosmic white folk who could pay the jeitinho anyway: the task of keeping the favelas bottled up. Marcelina stepped over the plastic as the ekedis rolled the foul sheeting into the center of the court. The bateria packed its drums.

"Mr. Bento?"

The bença had heavy wizard's eyebrows, which he flashed in genuine welcome.

"My name's Marcelina Hoffman. I'm a producer with Canal Quatro." She gave the bença a card; he passed it to an egun. "Feijão."

A different eyebrow flash now.

"Ah, yes, of course. He called me to say you would call. I hadn't thought it would be at a mass."

"I'm trying to make a program where we find Moaçir Barbosa and forgive him for the Maracanaço." She almost believed the lie herself now. "Feijão told me that Barbosa had associations with this terreiro. I came along because I hoped I might run into him here."

"You won't find Barbosa here."

Marcelina's hope reeled as if it had taken a meia lua de compasso she had not the malicia to anticipate.

"I'm sorry, Ms. Hoffman, that you've had a wasted journey."

"Feijão said he had been involved with this church some years ago."

"Feijão says too much. As you've probably guessed, Feijão and I do not see eye-to-eye on many things."

Marcelina's investigative senses raced: some scandal between the former Fluminense physio and the leader of a successful, middle-class, and assuredly wealthy Daime church? The feeling of ideas spinning around her like a storm of leaves was an old demon, Saci Pererê with his one leg and red hat and pipe, the imp of perverse and inverse of Nossa Senhora da Valiosa Producão: every time an idea was bounced her mind would race in compensation, leaping, snatching whatever idea came within her grasp to prove to herself that she was still creative, that she still had it.

"Do you know where he might have gone?"

The bença was gray stone.

"At least could you tell me if he's alive or dead?"

"Ms. Hoffman, we're finishing up here."

Teams of ekedis tackled the futsal court with mops and buckets. Marcelina fantasized coercing the information from Bença Bento. *You lie, old man, tell me where he is.* She could probably take the Bucket Brigade, but girls with pants tucked into boots and light automatic weapons were a league apart. Heitor's first rule of television: never get killed for a TV show.

She wasn't beaten.

She could hear the high song in her inner ear of near tears, that she had not heard since the first time she went into the roda full of jizz and jeito and was humiliated in front of the fundação by a sixteen-year-old.

She would find a way around. She would find Barbosa.

Her malicia and the taxi driver's professional jeito jerked at the same moment on Avenida Sernambetiba: her glance over her shoulder; his lingering look in the mirror. There is a sick vertigo when the pattern of traffic resolves into the certainty that you are being followed. Innocence becomes stupidity; every action is potential treachery. You feel those headlights like thumbs at the base of your skull. In the backseat of your cab you have anywhere to go and nowhere to arrive because they will be behind you. You don't look—you daren't look, but you begin to impute character and motivation. Who are you, what do you want, where do you expect me to lead you? You enter an almost telepathic communication, a hunter's empathy: Do you know that I know? If you did, would that be enough to make you peel out and go away?

Marcelina had been followed once before, tailgated in a crew car on the *Love Trials: Test Your Fiancé* shoot by a jealous bride-to-be of one of the contestants. Production security had pulled her in, but Marcelina had shivered for hours afterward, her city suddenly full of eyes. There had been nothing remotely *Miami Vice* about it.

"Can you see who's driving?" Marcelina asked.

"It's a cab," the driver said. She could see his eyes scanning in the rearview mirror. She knew every driver in the Canal Quatro taxi firm by his or her eyes.

"Give me the number. I'll call them and tell them one of their drivers is harassing me."

"He'd get fired."

"And I care?"

"I can't see the number anyway," the driver muttered. "There's someone in the back."

"Man or woman?"

"I am trying to drive this thing as well, you know."

Marcelina was convulsed by a sudden shiver. The boys down in SFX had once turned a wing of the Canal Quatro building into a haunted house for a Halloween party. Her flesh had crawled; she had been seized by inexplicable, disabling anxiety. She had feared what was in the locked storeroom at the end of the corridor. It had all been a clever trick of infrasound, air currents, and subtly distorting perspectives. But this was the pure shudder of irrational dread. In that car was the thing that haunted her, all her sins drawn out of the hills and beaches, the bays and curving avenues of her city and made flesh. In that taxi was the anti-Marcelina, and when they met, they would annihilate each other.

Stop it. You're still flashing back to the herbal tea. Or maybe they put something into the air at the terreiro.

"How far back is he?" she asked the driver.

"About five cars."

"Head up into Rocinha."

The driver drifted across lanes onto the Auto-Estrada Lagoa-Barra. Marcelina risked a glance behind her. The hunting taxi slid out of the traffic onto their tail, still keeping a chaperoned distance of five cars. *You are in your TV show now. This is* Getaway: *ultimate reality television. But I will get you*, Marcelina thought. Rocinha butted with the jarring abruptness of an artificial limb against the million-real apartment towers of São Conrado. The great favela unfolded like a fan of jeweled lights across the rocky saddle between the great city forest of Tijuca and the sheer rock peaks of Pedra Dois Irmãos. The cheek-to-cheek impromptu apartment blocks, some several stories tall, were built to within meters of the mouth of the Gávea Tunnel. The military police had a permanent checkpoint at the flyover by the Largo da Macumba flyover: two armored riot-control vehicles, a half dozen young people in the light chestnut of the military police standing around eating fast food from the bar across the road. Same expressions of boredom and anger she had seen in the parking lot security at the Barquinha; same pants tucked into boots. Much bigger guns.

"Pull in there."

They looked up as one as the cab drew in to the side of the road ahead of the lead APC. Edgy times. They had only just succeeded in pushing the favelados back into their slums. Construction machinery lined the edge of the street, shuttered for the night with galvanized plates over the glass and guarded by private security. Another favela wall. A tall twenty-something male cradled his assault rifle and sauntered toward the cab. Marcelina switched on her camera phone. A photograph would prove it. Here it came. Here it came.

The taxi passed at speed, accelerating into the Gávea tunnel that led under Rocinha to the Zona Sul. In the back, in the back, there . . . The camera phone flashed. In the electric flicker she saw a figure with its head wrapped in a loose turban of white cloth. The man from the terreiro. Marcelina felt a sob of relief burst inside her. You are not mad. The universe is rational. *You've been working too hard, to much pressure too much anxiety, that's all.*

A rap at the window. The militar gestured for her to wind it down.

"Is there a problem here?" He stooped and peered into the taxi.

"No, Officer, no, no problem at all."

"Can I see some ID please?"

It was not quite a smell, but it inhabited the air; not quite a sensation but it pricked like electricity; not quite a change but a disturbance in the domestic order—nothing sensible yet she knew it the moment she opened the door to her apartment. When she was an underpaid and loving-it production runner straight off her Media master's, Marcelina had shared a tatty little apartment by the cemetery with a Fortaleza travesti come to seek his fortune in Rio. He worked night shifts in a Lapa bar and drank Marcelina's beer, ate her food, used her washing powder, watched her cable TV, broke her Japanese tea-set bowl by bowl, and never paid a centavo toward the rent but imagined that his innate colorfulness was ample recompense, blithely disregarding the evidence of his own eyes, that travestis were cheap as beans in Lapa. Marcelina would be returning when he was leaving and thus never caught him in his violations, but she always knew when he had been through her panty drawer. However carefully he covered his crime there was always a sense, a ripple in the aether, a linger of an alien but maddeningly familiar perfume.

She smelled it now in the small tiled lobby of her apartment.

Somebody had been in her home.

It was one of the mysteries of her alt dot family that, though their lives were strewn all over Centro and Zona Sul, they always arrived together and left together. Marcelina received them in her garden. She customarily entertained up on the roof. Adriano himself had been up here for her Stones Party, revolving with the rest of her guests through the corner of the garden with the ocean view to peer through the slot between the buildings at the tiny spider figure prancing and kicking beneath orbit-visible lighting. There, that's Rick. I mean Mick. The roof was her refuge and temple; the roof was air and the lilac and pink evening light; the roof connected her to the ocean by that parallelogram of beach, sea, and sky; the roof was the reason she had bought this ugly, clattery, strange-smelling apartment with its back to the morro as if it had been mugged by the street; and she had been sleeping on the roof for the past three nights.

The apartment was infected.

She had gone straightaway to Gloria the concierge. She had seen nothing. Mangueira samba school could have marched through the lobby of Fonseca apartments in spangles, feathers, and skin with full bateria and she would have chittered away on her cellular.

Celso, Cibelle, Agnetta, Vitor up from his street-watching café, Moises and Tito whom she had met on the *Gay Jungle* (elevator pitch: can eleven gay men marooned in a stilt-house in the middle of the Amazon turn the one straight guy gay?) series and recruited to her alt dot family. Mediaistas and gay men. See who you run to in a crisis. All her guests were welcomed with a spliff. When the real estate agent had opened the rusting roof door, Marcelina had followed him up into a sunlit field of waving maconha. "Is this included in the price?" she'd asked. There was at least ten thousand street-reis of shade-grown Moroccan beneath the water tanks and satellite dishes. Dona Bebel had showed her how to dry it in the airing cupboard. It would take her five years to smoke her way through it.

"I've brought you all here tonight . . ."

Laughs, cheers.

"You know what I mean. You're my urban family, my gay dads. I tell you things I wouldn't tell my own flesh and blood."

Oohings, cooings.

"No seriously seriously, if I can't trust you, who can I trust? And I'd like to think you could trust me as well—not just work stuff. Other stuff." It was coming out wrong; it was coming out as stupid and insincere as the night she tried to tell the guys who'd lifted the *Getaway* car they were on TV. But she had never asked so great a thing from them, never stripped herself so bare and pale.

"I need your help, guys. Some of you have noticed that I've been acting a bit . . . distracted lately. Like I can't seem to remember things I've done, and then I get really paranoid."

No one dared answer.

"I need you to tell me if there's other stuff that maybe I haven't remembered; things I might have done or said."

Alt dot family looked at each other. Feet twisted, lips pursed.

"You walked right past me the other day," Vitor said. His voice tight-ened, grew sharp and confident. "You didn't even look round when I called after you. Mortified, I was. I almost didn't come tonight, you know. I was this close."

"When was this?"

"Oh, I don't know, sometime around my time, you know the time I keep. Tea o'clock."

"I do need to know, Vitor."

"About five, five thirty. It was Wednesday."

Marcelina touched her hands together, an almost-prayer, a particular ges-ture her development team knew well, when she was trying to pin down a part-baked idea.

"Vitor, you have to believe me when I tell you that at that time I was in Niteroi getting a letter of introduction to the Barquinha from Feijão. I can give you his number, you can call him."

"Well, you walked right past me. Cut to the bone, querida; to the bone."

"What direction was I walking?"

"The same as always; from here down to the taxi rank."

Marcelina lifted her explaining hands to her mouth now.

"That wasn't me, Vitor. I wasn't there; I was in Niteroi, believe me."

Everyone had stubbed out their spliffs now.

"Has anyone else experienced anything like this?"

Now Moises shuffled uncomfortably. He was a big fat sixty-something queen who ran a series of mysterious *objet d'arts* emporia; a true old-school carioca, he had an unrelenting if not always accurate wit, but delivered in a voice like velvet-covered razors. Since *Gay Jungle*, Marcelina had been looking for ways to get him his own series.

"Well, you did call me the other night. I thought I was on the *Da Vinci Code*, all those mysterious coded messages and everything."

Marcelina's head reeled. It had nothing to do with secondary maconha.

"When was this?

"Well. I know I'm a night owl, but half past three in the morning."

"Was it on the house phone or the cellular?"

"Oh the cellular, of course. Took me hours to get back to sleep, every-thing buzzing round my head."

"Moises, could you tell me what I said?"

"Oh, weird stuff, honey, weird stuff. Time and the universe and the order we see is not the true order. Are you in some kind of conspiracy thing? How exciting."

"I'm trying to make a TV show about a World Cup goalkeeper, is all." Marcelina sat down on the wall. "Guys, at work, has there been anything else I don't know about?"

"Apart from the e-mail thing, no," Celso answered.

Agnetta said, "But you should know that the Black Plumed Bird has bunged Lisandra a few K to develop her Ultimate Seleção idea." Unraveling, detuning, melting like a wax votive baby offered to a saint.

"Is everything all right?" Cibelle asked.

"There's stuff going on I can't explain," Marcelina said. "All I can say is, if you know me, trust me: if it looks like me but doesn't act like me, it isn't me. I know this makes no sense at all, but it makes even less sense to me. I'm being haunted."

"A ghost?" Tito, her third gay dad, was a specter of a man himself, pale and nocturnal. He knew every spook of old Copacabana personally, greeted them each dawn as he swung back through the streets to his home.

"No, something else. Something that's not dead yet."

"You know, there's a program idea in that," Celso said, but the eyes of her alt dot family were slipping away from hers. For the first time they made their separate farewells and left one by one.

You did not hold me, Marcelina thought. The spirit of maconha waited in the air. In its frame of tenements the sea still held late lilac. The surf was up and the air so still that the ocean-crash carried over the traffic on the Copa and the air smelled like she imagined hummingbirds must: sweet and floral and shimmering with color. A huge pale moon of Yemanja was floating free from the water tanks and aerials. Gunfire cracked in the distance: the little favela of Pavão at the western end of the Copa still tossed and scratched. She remembered a lilac night a lifetime ago; suddenly swept out of her bed by a tall queen from a Disney movie, all swish and swinging diamonds. *Come on, get dressed.* The three Hoffman sisters had sat pressed in round their mother in the back of the cab as it swept along the boulevards, the dark sea booming. *Is it carnaval?* Marcelina had asked when she saw the crowd in front of the floodlit hotel, white and huge as a cliff. *No no,* her mother had replied, *something much more wonderful than that.* She had pushed into the rear of the crowd. Some of the people had glared and then went, *ah!* or *oh!* and bowed from her path; most she shoved past: *Come on girls, come on.* Gloria and Iracema and Marcelina holding hands in a chain until they were at the front of the crowd. She had looked up at men in uniforms and men with cameras and men in evening dress and women even more glamorous than her mother. At her feet was a red carpet. A broad man with graying hair but the bluest eyes has walked up the carpet to flashing cameras and cheers and applause. Marcelina had been afraid of all the noise and the lights and the bodies, but her mother had said, *Cheer! Cheer! Yoo-hoo! Yoo-hoo!* The man had looked over, looked puzzled, then raised a hand, smiled, and walked on down the alley of lights.

In the taxi back she had peeped up the question Gloria and Iracema were too big and shy to ask.

"Mum, who was that?"

"My love, that was Mr. Frank Sinatra."

Her mother's face had shone like the women in St. Martin's on solemn novena.

One moment of silver. The flicker on the screen. Her mother had shown it to her, on the steps of the Copa Palace, in every beautiful old tune she had pumped out of the organ. Marcelina had chased, leaped for it, snatched with her hands until she caught it and held it up, shivering and flowing from form to form, and she had seen in an instant how the trick was done.

She got her mattress and lightweight bag, stripped down to panties and vest in the backscatter of light from the morro.

January 27, 2033

How to weep, in Cidade de Luz.

Every new entry in the book requires Crying Cake. Flour, margarine, sugar, nuts, more sugar—the saints have sweet teeth—and a generous glug of cachaça, which the saints don't mind at all. Bake. Cut into cubes with a knife cleaned in holy water, one cube per invocation. The rest must be left on the cooling tray on top of the front wall, for all the neighborhood. Select a saint. Her I-shades tell Dona Hortense the best for this entry is St. Christina (the Astonishing). She prints an image that she carefully snips out with scissors, pastes onto a matchbook-sized board with other Catholic tat ripped from the parish magazine, and decorates the border with plastic beads and tinsel and shards of broken glass ornament from the Christmas box. The icon is then purified with salt and incense. Divination with the Chinese compass gives the best alignment; then the Book of Weeping is opened before the altar, the name and the need written in felt marker that gives a nice thick line, easy to read in the dim of the barracão, and the whole is dusted with farofa, which is then tipped down the valley of the book into an offertory cone before St. Christina the Astonishing. Thereafter until the weeping stops, the entry, with all the others for that day, will receive a tear.

St. Christina, be true, prayed Dona Hortense. *Astonish me. For my littlest and second-favorite son suffers. He lies in his hammock, and from the flicker of his eyes I can tell he plays games and reads chat on his glasses; the food on his plate goes cold and draws flies; he neglects his deals and contacts and plans: this is a boy of energy and business and determination. I know Gerson—stupid, soft Gerson—slips pills into Edson's Coke and coffee and they steal his energy, sap his will. Get him up get him out get him around his friends and clients for they can help him. Until then, let me launder his clothes and straighten his papers and fetch him coffee and leave him plates of chicken and beans and rice and tell Gerson to stop it with the pills and instead bring some proper money into the house.*

Early in the morning of the day of the Feast of Nossa Senhora Aparecida Dona Hortense finds her littlest and second-favorite son climbing on the house roof. He is in shorts and a sleeveless T and Havaianas, poking at the geometry of white plastic pipes that surround the solar water heater. Cidade de Luz wears its civic bairro status proudly, but the every-man-for-himself plumbing uphill and down alley and the sagging, crazy-crow wiring—you can still plug into the streetlamps—betrays its favela provenance.

"These pipes need replacing." Edson stands hands on hips looking around him. Not at pipes and plumbing, Dona Hortense knows, but at the city, the sky, his world. It's begun.

"I've made kibes," she says.

"I'll be down in three minutes."

That night Dona Hortense turns St. Christina the Astonishing's icon facedown and crumbles her Crying Cake as an offering to the birds.

In the mornings pensioners get special rates at the gym. Edson passes treadmills churning with men in baseball caps and saggy shorts and women in Capri tights and big Ts. Afternoons the soldados of the drug lord come down from Cidade Alta to pump. The Man has negotiated a corporate membership for them. The deal's good, but they have a habit of leaving the weights at max to look macho to the next user. Emerson is out back trying to weld a broken weight machine, squinting through a square of smoked glass at the primal arc.

"Still taking old people's money off them?" asks Edson.

Emerson looks up, smiles, then grins.

"At least I'm making money." Emerson kills the welding gun, slips off his gloves, hugs his brother to him. Little Sixth always was fiercely independent, never needing anyone's permission, but he always brought his plans to Emerson as if for a blessing that Dona Hortense and all her saints could not bestow. There are Skols in cool-jackets in the store refrigerator. Emerson chases receptionist Maria-Maria out of the office—"all she ever does is chat-bots anyway"—and they sit across his battered desk. Pensioners thump and hiss behind the ripple glass.

"So."

"I'll be all right. It's time, isn't it? Everything's time. It's like, I'm back again. Does that make sense? I was away, somewhere, like on holiday in my own house, and now I'm back again and it's like it was spring and now it's summer."

Emerson doesn't say, *It's been three and a half months.* Nor does he say any stupid talk-show shit like, *I don't think I can ever understand what she meant to you.* Emerson recalls how he felt when Anderson was killed. He had been up in the favela working on a newlywed floor on the top of an apartment block. They worked together: bricklayer and electrician, brothers Oliveira. Then the fireworks went up all around like a saint's day. Police. Out on the steep ladeiros The Man's foot soldiers had dumped I-shades, cash cards, arfided valuables—anything that might betray their location to the Angels of Perpetual Surveillance. The police stun drones swarmed in over Cidade Alta like black vultures. Already gunfire was rattling around the intersections where Cidade Alta grew out of Cidade de Luz. Anderson had gone to pick up electrical tape. Anderson had been caught out there. Firing everywhere now. Nowhere to run from it. Nowhere to go but stay on this roof. He'd called Anderson to tell him to get out, get home, get down to Luz, and if you can't get out, get in, anywhere with a door and walls. No answer; the police had shut down the network. Scared now. He'd done a locate on Anderson's I-shades. The seek function was accurate to millimeters. The center of Anderson's I-shades was resting eight centimeters above ground level. That is the height of the bridge of a nose of a head lying sideways on the street. That was how Emerson had found him, in a great dark lake of drying blood. He had looked so startled, so annoyed. The police tried to make him out to be a soldado. Outrage from the Cidade de Luz District Council forced an admission that Anderson had been caught in crossfire trying to find safety. It was as much as anyone could hope for. A platitude to add to the stumbling well-wishes of friends and neighbors. Words were not sufficient, so they resorted to platitudes, trusting that Dona Hortense and her five surviving sons would read the unsayable truth behind them. Sometimes only platitudes are enough.

Edson says, "I need to ask you something."

Emerson has learned to be wary of questions with preludes, but he says, "Go on."

"Was there a video?"

"What do you mean? Like . . ."

"*Take Out the Trash.* Did you see one?"

"I don't watch that kind of thing."

"I know, but—"

"I haven't heard."

"Me neither."

"What are you thinking?"

Again, he hears the shudder in Edson's breath.

"It was a Q-blade, so everyone automatically thinks, *Take Out the Trash*. But what if it wasn't?"

"Go on."

Edson twists his bottle in its plastic sleeve on Emerson's desk.

"The last time I saw her, at Todos os Santos, when the gay guy tried to scare me off, she was talking to some people. One of them was a priest—a white priest. Well, he dressed like a priest, but a lot of white guys have this priest thing. And the night of the gafieira she got called over to some people who were not on the guest list."

"What is it you want to do?"

"I just want to go down and have a look."

"What for?"

"A trash can."

"And if you find it?"

"Then that's the end of it."

"And if you don't?"

"I don't know."

"Let it lie."

"I know, I should. But I don't think I can."

"Then brother, you be very fucking careful."

The old fit people thud and creak.

Edson makes his first pass on the wrong side of the road, then turns through the Ipiranga alco station on the central strip and pulls over onto the verge. He can re-create every slo-mo frame of the massacre scene, but now, here, he cannot find it in all the empty blacktop. No flowers, no Mass cards, no edible blessings. He leaves the Yam and walks up and down the margin, grit-stung by fast trucks. An off-cut of tire here, like a snake's shed skin. A coil of sheared-off steel: street jewelry. He stands where the killer waited, hand out, hitching a lift. Edson extends his arm, draws an imaginary line of division across the blur of vehicles, houses, towers, sky. He feels nothing. This edge-place is too dislocated for anything like memory or grief to attach.

A moto-taxi stops on the opposite verge. A long-haired woman dismounts. The flowing cars frame her like the shutter of a movie camera. The woman walks up and down the verge. She leans forward, hands braced on hips, staring across the highway. Edson jerks upright. The image is branded onto his visual centers. The fall of the hair; the tilt of the cheekbones; the false-innocence of the doe-eyes, the anime eyes. Her.

Their eyes meet across car roofs. Heart stopped, time frozen, space congealed, Edson steps toward her. The blare of horns sends him sprawling across the grit. She is running for the moto-taxi, gesturing the driver to *Go go*.

"Fia!" The highway swallows it. He saw her on this same margin, this spot where he stands. He saw her dead. Face covered. Logos on the soles of her shoes. He saw them take her away from this margin.

The moto-taxi weaves into the traffic. The thrall is broken. Edson snaps off a tracking shot on his Chillibeans. He jumps onto his bike, kicks up the engine. She wears a green leather jacket. Green leather jacket and long long hair streaming. He can find those. He takes a scary scary cut across the central strip and into the fast lane. She's twelve cars ahead of him, shifting lanes. Edson's Yamaha can outrun anything on this highway; dodging between biodiesel trucks on the Santos convoy, he closes the gap. She glances over her shoulder; her hair whips across her face. *It's me, me!* Edson screams into the slipstream. She punches the rider on the back, jerks her thumb forward, then right. The rider bends over the throttles; the bike takes off like a fighter. Edson's right behind it. She told him she never rode pillion. The sudden slowdown almost sends him into the back of a school minibus. One of São Paulo's endemic roadlocks. He's lost her. Edson cruises up the line of stationary traffic. She's not in this line. He walks the scrambler between two cars, so close to the big RAV that the driver yells at him, *Mind the chrome, favelado.* Not in the center lane. Not in the inside lane. Where? He sees green leather accelerating up the off-ramp from the opposite side of the highway. Caught him with his own trick. But he knows where that road leads: Mother of Trash, Todos os Santos.

"Take it." Mr. Peach offers the gun handle first to Sextinho. It's a handsome, cocky piece he keeps in his bedside cabinet, for the night when the indentured biofarm workers above and the housing projects below meet and the world breaks over Fazenda Alvaranga.

"I wouldn't know what to do with it."

"It's easy, I've shown you; this, this, and you're ready. Just take the fucking thing."

He never swears. Mr. Peach never swears. "I'm sorry . . ." He presses hand to head. "It's just you don't know what you're doing. So take the fucking gun."

Edson lifts the bone handle in limp fingers. It's much heavier than he imagined. He understands now what the boys see in these pieces, the sexy metal, the potency. He stashes it away quickly in his bag. Dona Hortense must never find it. It would be a nail in her heart to see her littlest and second-favorite son gone to the gun. Quickly, he says, "You've seen the video, what do you think that was?"

"A ghost," says Mr. Peach.

"I don't believe in ghosts," Edson says.

"I do," says Mr. Peach. "The most real things there are, ghosts. Take the gun, Sextinho, and please, please, querida, look after yourself."

That evening in his hammock Edson takes a fistful of pills and invents a new self: Bisbilhotinho, Little Snoop the private dick. He is polite and quite slow spoken. He plans everything carefully and moves slowly and deliberately so that people will make no mistake about his seriousness. He always leaves himself a clear way out. He deals with killers. Little Snoop is a young personality and has yet to spread wide his wings and flash the colors hidden there, but Edson likes him, can see where Little Snoop might surprise him.

"You're going where?" Petty Cash says as Bisbilhotinho trades identities with him. "Hey, I'm not so sure about this; if you get killed, I'm dead."

"Then you get to inherit my clients," Little Snoop says.

"What clients?" Petty Cash calls after him.

It's a risk, leaving the bike with all its engine parts in place, but he may need to get away fast. He's paid two different kids well to mind it, with more on his return. They'll keep an eye on each other. Todos os Santos at night is a blazing city. Truck headlights dip and veer as they plow the rutted road into the heart of Our Lady of Trash. Garbage fires smolder; kids gather around burning oil drums stirring the flames with broken planks. Churrasceiros tend their small braziers, charcoals red under white, flyaway ash. Boys shoot pool under clip-on neons in tattered lanchonetes. Edson can see the guns tucked in the backs of their baggies, like his own. But it doesn't make him feel safe at all. Heads turn as he works his way up the spiral road. Atom Shop is closed.

The bar is jammed with customers watching soccer on a big screen. Little Snoop orders a Coke and shows the video grab to the barman. Edson has watched the clip so many times it has become a visual prayer: her face turning away from him as the moto-taxi accelerates into the traffic.

"Her parents are worried," he says to the barman.

"I'd be too, if you're looking here," says the bartender, a handsome twenty-something. "No, I don't recall her."

"Do you mind if I pass it around?"

The fans pass the I-shades hand to hand, a cursory look, a purse of the lips, a shake of the head, a small sigh. Some comment that that is a good-looking girl. *Goooooooooooool!* roars the commentator as Little Snoop steps down onto the road. Half the bar leaps to its feet.

Patiently, politely, Little Snoop works up the spiral. As the trash-deliverers and collectors never rest, neither do the workshops and the disassemblers. The kids running handcarts of parts to the grill plates and ovens barely glance at the video. *Have you seen her, have you seen her?* The chippers and smelters bent over in the hissing light of bottled gas shake their heads, irritated at the distraction.

"Her parents, eh?" The woman is big, easy, rolls of fat lapping generously as she sits, one leg outstretched, on the step of the gold refinery. Her wealth is in her teeth, around her neck, on her fingers, the stubby, sweet-smelling cigar she smokes with simple relish. "And they hired you? Son, you're no private detective. But you're not anything else either, so I'll answer your question. Yes. I know this face." Edson's heart kicks inside so hard she must hear it: a meaty knock. "She was selling stuff, tech stuff; gear, good gear. Gear like I've never seen before, like no one had ever seen before. And some jewelry."

"In the last month?"

"In the last twenty-four hours, son."

Beyond the shotgun shacks, the dark trash mountains crawl with stars; LED head-torches and candle lanterns flickering like fireflies. The miasma the dump constantly exudes blue and yellow. It is radiantly beautiful. Weird stuff here by superstition, street legend. Whispers of night visions; strange juxtapositions of this city with other, illusory landscapes; angels, visitations, UFOs, orixás. Ghosts.

"Do you know who bought them?

"Son, there's always someone buying something around here. Some of the usual dealers—you won't catch them here this time of night. They've more sense."

"Do you know if she's staying around here?"

"She'd be a bigger fool than you if she were. I got one set of eyes, son, and a failing memory. Count your blessings."

Descending the spiral Little Snoop calls in at the futebol bar and has a bottle of good import whiskey sent up to bling woman. It's expensive, but that's the way his city works. A favor given, a favor returned. And his Yamaha is intact, untouched, absolutely flawless.

Eleven thirty-eight and Edson's ass feels like a spill of hardened concrete. There's one safe little niche on the hotel roof, but it's small, uncomfortable, and ball-freezingly cold. This is an unglossy neighborhood, forgotten like discarded underwear behind the kanji frontages and Harajuku pinks of the sushi bars and theatrical teppanyaki eateries. Hardpoint sensors and an aerial drone on a three-minute orbit supplement the bored teen with the stupid near-moustache crewing the security barrier. Edson watches the HiLux pickup laden with vegetables drive through the gates into the cul-de-sac. Close behind the scooped red-tile roof the pencil-thin apartment towers rise, crowned in moving ads for beer and telenovelas. He's never been so close to the mythical heart of the city. Praça de Sé is ten blocks away.

She grew up here, Edson thinks. Her life was shaped in this long, bulb-ended street like a vagina. She pedalled that pink kiddie-bike with the streamers from the handlebars around this turning circle. She put up a stall made from garden tools and sheets to sell doces and iced tea to the neighbors. She tongue-kissed her first boyfriend just around that step in the build-line where the segurança couldn't watch her. Her parents are unloading the truck now, boxes bursting with green and dark red so soft you could imagine rolling over in them to sleep.

"Ghosts. Like, the way you mean ghost?" he had said to Mr. Peach, the gun hard against the crack of his ass.

"Go on." There was a way Mr. Peach carried himself—eager, leaning, hands tense—when he expected more than affection and sex from Sextinho.

"There are millions of other Fias out there in other universes, other parts of the multiverse."

"Yes."

"And one of them . . ."

"Go on."

"Has come through."

"That's a nice expression. Come through."

"That's impossible."

"What you think is impossible and what quantum theory says is impossible are very different things. What's impossible is covered by the Heisenberg uncertainty principle and the Pauli exclusion principle. The rest is just shades of probable. Quantum computing relies on what we call a 'superposition': a linkage between the same atom in different states in different universes. An answer comes through from somewhere out in those universes. And sometimes something more than an answer."

To the right. On the roof of the garage. Movement, a figure. Edson's heart thumps so hard it hurts. He needs to hurl. He moves to the low parapet, leans over. He can't make out any detail in this damn yellow light. His hand goes to click up the zoom on his Chillibeans; then the figure sets a can of paint on the parapet. Some kid, a pichaçeiro, leaning over the edge to roller his tag. The heart eases, but the nausea peaks.

On the left. Walking slowly down the street, hood up, hands folded in the front pocket of a weird knitted short hoodie thing, like a street-nun. Skinny gray leggings tucked into fuck-me boots. Boots. Good boots, but who wears boots with leggings? He knows that too-tight walk, those too-short steps. Her face is shadowed by the hood, but the highlights, the glances are identification enough for Edson. Fia/Not Fia. Her hair is longer. But this is Fia. A Fia. Another Fia. She stops to glance down the guarded street. *You were born there too, in that other Liberdade, weren't you? The city, the streets, the houses are the same. What brought you? Curiosity? Proof? What are you feeling? Why are you in this world at all?* The guard stirs in his booth. The Fia turns away, walks on. Edson drops from his surveillance, sits back to the coaming, panting, knees drawn up to thin chest. He has never been so scared, not even when he went up the hill to The Man to get his blessing to open De Freitas Global Talent, not even the night when Cidade Alta exploded around Emerson and Anderson.

You've identified her. Now get off this roost, get down there. Edson falls in thirty meters behind the Fia. The security kid checks him. Edson closes with the Fia. She glances over her shoulder. Twenty paces now. He knows how to do it. It's all there in his head. Then the car stops across the end of the road.

"Fia!"

The car door opens; men step out. Fia turns at the sound of the name no one should speak. Edson pulls the big chrome gun out of the back of his pants. The security guard leaps to his feet. All in a bubble of space-time, beautiful, motionless.

"Fia! To me! Run to me. Fia, I knew you, do you understand? I knew you."

She makes the decision in the instant it takes Edson to bring the gun up two-handed. She flees toward him, a tight-elbowed, flapping girl-run. The two men pelt after her. They are big; they know how to run; their jacket tails flap. Edson snatches Fia's hand, drags her in his wake. He stops dead. Fia slams into him. From the other end of the street comes a third running man, a little flicker of blue light dancing around his right hand where the naked tip of his Q-blade wounds space-time. And the stupid stupid security kid has his gun gripped in both hands like something he's seen in a game and he's shouting, "Don't move! Don't fucking move! Put the gun down! Put the gun down!"

"Don't be stupid, they'll kill us all," Edson shouts. "Run now!" The kid panics, throws away the piece, and flees up the street into the palm-creaking dekasegui gardens. Lights come on behind bamboo blinds as Edson snatches Fia down the side alley where he has parked the Yam. Jesus and all the Saints this is going to be tight. . . . Her arms close around his waist. Start. Start. *Start.* The engine yells into life. Edson steers one-handed down the alleyway, dodging trash cans and junk.

"Take the gun take the gun. Anything you see in front of you, shoot it."

"But . . ."

But he's already flying. The gun crash/flashes twice by the side of his head; he hears shells scream off walls and girderwork. He sees two dark shapes whirl away from him. Gone. But the third man, the man with the knife, blocks the exit from the alley. An arc of blue. He holds the Q-blade level; the bisecting stroke. This is how it was; let them come to you; let their own velocity cut them in half. *Bang bang.* The knifeman anticipates, dives, comes up with the blade ready. Crying with fear, Edson kicks out. The backhand slash shaves rubber swarf from the heel of his Nikes, but the man goes down. Edson guns the throttle and wheelies out into the street. Behind him, the two other killers are up. A whisper of jets: security drones are arriving on-scene and deploying antipersonnel arrays. Sirens close from all sides, but Edson is through them, out into the light and the endless traffic of his Sampa.

The muzzle creeps cold into the hollow behind his ear on Rua Luís Gama.

"There's no bullets in that thing."

He feels Fia's breath warm against the side of his head.

"Are you sure? Did you count them?"

"You're going to shoot me in this traffic?"

She reaches round and locks one hand on the throttle, beside his. "I'll take that risk."

Tetchy. So her. So Fia.

"So who the hell are you."

"Put that thing away and I'll tell. God alone knows how many cameras have seen it."

"Cameras?"

"You really aren't from round here, are you?"

Cold muzzle is replaced by hot whisper: "Yes I am."

"I'm Edson Jesus Oliveira de Freitas."

"That doesn't mean anything. That's just a name. Who are you with? The Order?"

"I don't know what you're talking about."

"Did she know you? My . . . alter?"

"We were, she was my girlfriend."

She says quickly, harshly, "I'm not her. You must know that."

"But you are Fia Kishida."

"Yes. No. I am Fia Kishida. It was you on the rodovia, wasn't it? Where are we going?"

"Somewhere. Safe." Not home. Some things, even more than guns, cannot be explained to Dona Hortense. Emerson can put a couple of mattresses down in the office; that will do until Edson thinks of what to do with a murdered girlfriend's double come through from a parallel São Paulo and being hunted by pistoleiros and Q-blades. He feels Fia's arms tight around his waist as he blurs through the wash of taillights. Behind him in the slipstream she says nothing. She knows where she is. It's always São Paulo.

Her grip tightens as he turns off the highway onto the serpentine road that is the gut of Cidade de Luz. She takes in the moto-taxis, the buses, the grand pillared frontage of the Assembly of God Church like a jerry-built heaven, the swags of power cables and tripping runs of white water pipes clambering up through the houses and walled yards into the glowing, chaotic mass of the high city, the true, unrepentant favela.

The road takes another wind; then Edson hauls on the brakes. There's someone in the road, right under his wheel. The bike skids; the Fia—Fia II, he thinks of her—slides across the oily concrete to hit the high curb. The fool in the road: it's Treats who has dashed out from his usual roost at the Ipiranga station where he hassles drivers into letting him clean their windshields while they fill up.

"Edson Edson Edson, Petty Cash! He's dead, man, they've killed him, came right in."

Edson seizes Treats by the scruff of his too-too-big basketball vest and drags him round the back of the fuel station, out of the light, among the gas cylinders.

"Shut up with my name, you don't know who's listening or looking."

"Petty Cash, they—"

"Shut up. Stay there."

He picks up the beautiful, delicate Yamaha and wheels it over to Fia II. *You have to stop calling her that, like she's a movie.* Fia. But it's not right.

"You all right?" She goes to say something about her torn top, but Edson hasn't time for that. "Keep your hood up, stay out of the cameras, and lock yourself in the women's toilet. There are people here who could recognize you. I will come for you. There's a matter I have to deal with right now."

Edson orders Treats to go round to Dona Hortense and ask for his go-bag.

"She'll know what that means. And show my mother some manners, uneducated boy."

He goes through the alleys and ladeiros beneath the swags of power cable and bougainvillea. Moto-taxis hoot past, pressing him to the walls in the steep narrow lanes. The ambulance is still outside the house. Edson can hear police drones circling overhead. The small crowd has the patient, resting body language of people who have passed from witness to vigil. A man-sized hole has been cut sheer through the gate and part of the wall. It matches another through the door and doorframe. And it is like a storm of dark birds flying out of that hole, flying at Edson's head, blinding him with their wings and claws and beaks, bird after bird after bird, too many too fast, he swipes, slaps at them, but there are always more and they keep coming, wing after wing after wing, and he knows that if he misses, once, he will go down and their claws will be in his back.

"What happened?" Edson asks Mrs. Moraes seated on the side of the road in her shorts and flip-flops, hair still up in foil and her hand frozen to her mouth. Her neighbors stood around her.

"They came on a motorbike. The one on the back, he did that. Jesus love my boy my boy my poor boy, what did he ever to do to anyone?"

Now he sees Old Gear his antique dealer by the ambulance. All Edson's alibis are there in the crowd. They all have the same look: *He died for you.*

What if you get killed? Petty Cash had joked. But he did. That is what the ambulance crews are taking away in their black bag: a body wearing a pair of I-shades that say *Edson Jesus Oliveira de Freitas.* Edson is an unperson now.

There is no place for him in Cidade de Luz. At the Ipiranga station he sees the ambulance pass, lights rotating, sirens hushed. Treats has his go-bag.

"One more thing, Treats. Go back and tell Dona Hortense I'm with the Sisters."

"The Sisters."

"She'll know. Good man." The jeitinho is fully paid. Next time, it will be Edson owes Treats.

The Yamaha heads west through the contrails of light. Edson calls back to Fia on the pillion. "Have you any money?"

"Some cash from selling tech and jewelry and stuff, but I've spent most of it on food and a capsule to stay. Why?"

"I don't have anything. I don't exist. That ambulance that went past, that was me in the back."

She asks no questions as Edson explains his world. Carbon-fiber angels watching the city by day and night, never ceasing, never hasting. Universal arfid tagging and monitoring where the clothes on your back and the shoes on your feet and the toys in your pocket betray you. Total surveillance from rodovia toll cameras to passersby's T-shirts or I-shades snatching casual shots; only the rich and the dead have privacy. Information not owned but rented; date-stamped music and designer logos that must be constantly updated: intellectual property rights enforceable with death but murder pay-per-view prime-time entertainment and pay-per-case policing. Every click of the Chillibeans, every message and call and map, every live Goooool! update, every road toll and every cafezinho generates a cloud of marketing information, a vapor trail across Sampa's information sphere. Alibis, multiple identities, backup selves—it is not safe to be one thing for too long. Speed is life. She will be trying to work how she can exist—must exist—in this world of Order and Progress, with no scan no print no number, a dead girl come back to life. As he is a dead man, driving west through the night traffic.

September 16–17, 1732

Robert Francois St. Honore Falcon: Expedition Log

A wonder a day and I do not doubt we should all live forever! I am comfortably domiciled in the College adjoining the Carmelite Church of Nossa Senhora da Conceição, shaved, in clean linen, and anticipating my first decent dinner in weeks, but my mind returns to the phenomenon I witnessed today at the meeting of the waters.

Captain Acunha, desiring to show a proud Frenchman a marvel of his land, called me to the prow to observe the extraordinary sight of two rivers, one black, one milky white, flowing side by side in the same channel; the black current of the Rio Negro, its confluence still two leagues distant, running parallel to the silty flow of the Solimões. We steered along the line of division—I filled page after page with my sketchings and I saw that, closely observed, the black and the white waters curled around each other like intricate silhouette work; curls within curls within curls of ever-diminishing scale, as I have seen in the pattern of ferns and the leaves of certain trees. I wonder, does it decrease in its self-similarity *ad infinitum?* Am I prejudiced to the macroscopic? Is there an implicit geometry, a mathematical energy in the very small, that cascades up into the greater, an automotive force of self-ordering? I do think that there is a law here, in river flow and in fern and leaf.

Now by contrast I consider São José Tarumás do Rio Negro. A fort, manned by a handful of officers half-mad from malaria and a company of native musketeers; the landings; a government custom office; a court; the trading houses of spice factors; the taverns and their attached caiçara; the huddled rows of whitewashed taipa huts of the settled índios, the praça, the College; the church over all. The Church of Nossa Senhora da Conceição is a gaudy of mannerist fancies and frenetic painted decoration that seemed to rise sheer from the dark water as we drew in to the wharf. It proclaims itself so because it is the last: beyond São José lie the scattered aldeias and far-between reduciones of the Rio Negro and Rio Branco. This sense of the frontier, of the immense psychic pressure of the wilderness beyond, gives São José its peculiar energy. The docks are thronged with canoes and larger river craft; rafts of pau de brasil logs lie marshalled in the river. The market is loud and bright, the traders eager for my business. All is build and bustle; along the river frontage new warehouses are being knocked together, and on the higher ground walled houses, the bright new homes of the merchants, want only for roofs. In every citizen from priest to slave I see an eagerness to get down to business. It would, I believe, make a good and strong regional capital.

Father Luis Quinn's reputation precedes him. The Carmelites welcomed the visiting Jesuit admonitory with a musical progress. Trombas, tambourines, even a portative organ on a litter, and a veritable host of índios in white—men, women, children—sporting headdresses woven from palm fronds, waving same and singing together a glorious cantata that combined European melodies and counterpoints with native rhythms and exuberances. As I dogged along behind Quinn with my baggage train, I found my pace adjusting to the rhythm. Quinn, being a man much moved by music, was delighted, but I wonder how much of his pleasure masked annoyance at being forestalled. Despite the opulence of the friar's welcome, I sensed unease.

Father Quinn received the sacraments; I reconciled myself to Mammon by presenting my travel permits to Capitan de Araujo of the fort and a subsequent prolonged questioning neither unfriendly nor inquisitorial in tone, rather born out of long isolation and a lack of any true novelty. Here I received the first setback to my plans: I was informed that Acunha would be unable to take me onwards up the Rio Negro: new orders from Salvador forbade any armed vessel from proceeding beyond São José for fear of the Dutch pirates, who were once again active in the area and could easily seize such a ship and turn it against this garrison of the Barra. I did not like to comment that the wood, sand, and adobe revetments looked well capable of laughing off *Fé em Deus*'s pop guns, but if I have learned one thing in Brazil, it is never to antagonize local potentates on whose goodwill you depend. The captain concluded by commenting that he had heard that I enjoyed a reputation as a swordsman, and, if time permitted, would welcome a chance to try his skill on the strand before the fort, the traditional dueling ground. I think I shall decline him. He is an amiable enough dunderhead; his denial a frustration, nothing more. There are canoes by the score beneath the pontoon houses in the floating harbor. I shall begin my bargaining tomorrow.

(Addendum)

I am troubled by a scene I glimpsed from my window in the College. Raised voices and a hellish bellowing made me glance out; by the light of torches, a fat ox had been manhandled into the praça before the church, a rope to each hoof, horn, and nostril and men hauling on them, yet scarcely able to control the bellowing, terrified beast. A man stepped forth with a poleax, set himself before the creature, and brought his weapon down between the ox's ears. Seven blows it took before the maddened animal fell and was still. I turned away when the men started to dismember the ox in the praça, but I am certain that it was stricken with the plague, the madness. It has reached São José Tarumás, the last place in the world, it would seem, or is it from here that it originates?

I trust the bloody barbarism does not upset my appetite for the friar's hospitality.

The men fell on them at the landing. Faces hidden behind kerchiefs, the three attackers stepped out from the cover of the pontoon houses on either side of the bobbing gangplank. Flight, evasion, was impossible in so narrow a pass. Quinn had no time to react before the big broad carpenter's mallet swung out of the twilight shadows of the river town and caught him full in the chest. He went down and in the same instant the assailant swung his weapon to bring it down finally on the father's head. Falcon's foot was there to meet the attacker's wrist. Bone cracked; the man gave a shrill, shrieking cry as the weight of the mallet snapped his hand over, broken, useless, agonized. The assailants had miscalculated their attack; the stricture of the plank walks compelled them to attack one man at a time. As Quinn fought to regain presence, the second assailant thrust his wounded colleague out of the way and pulled a pistol. With a cry and a delicate kick, Falcon sent it spinning down the planking. He retrieved it as it skidded toward the water and extinction, drew the muzzle on the second masked man as the assailant raised his foot to stamp down on Quinn's bowed neck.

"Hold off or you die this instant," he commanded. The man glowered at him, shook his head, and pressed forward. Falcon flickered his thumb over the wheel lock. Now the third assassin elbowed his colleague out of the road. He held a naked knife, faced Falcon at breath distance, hands held out in the knife-fighters pose seeming half-supplication.

"I hardly think—"

The man struck. Falcon saw the top finger-length of the pistol fall to the wood. Worked hardwood, steel, and brass had been cut through as cleanly as silk. The man grinned, wove a pass with his knife. Falcon thought he saw blue fire burn in its trace. Falcon threw his hand up to protect his face and, heedless, pulled the trigger. The explosion was like a cannon blast in the strait labyrinth of wooden verandahs and gangways. The ball careered wide, sky-shot, lost. Falcon had never intended it to hit. In the daze and confusion, he struck the knife-man with two short, stabbing punches; Lyon harbor-blows. The blade fell from the assailant's grip, struck the wood, and continued into it as if it were water until the hilt brought a halt. Now Quinn entered the fight, windful and hale. He snatched up the dropped blade. It cut through the planks; the boardwalk cracked and settled beneath him. Quinn drew himself to his full height; his bulk filled the coffin-narrow alley. The wounded mallet-man and the pistoleiro had already fled. The knife-man too scrambled away but in his panic tripped on a board-end and went sprawling on his back. With a bestial roar, Quinn was on top of him; knife slung under-hand, a gutting blow, no Christian stroke.

"Luis. Luis Quinn."

A voice, through the brilliant, lordly rage. For an instant Luis Quinn considered turning and using this blade, this divine, hellish edge on the tiny, whining voice that dared to deny him, imagined it cutting and cutting until there was nothing left but a stain. Then he saw the houses and the doors and windows close around him, felt the thatch stroking his shoulders, the man beneath his blade, the helpless, ridiculous man and the glorious fear in his eyes above the masking kerchief. *In the last instant before you face eternity you still maintain your disguise*, he thought.

"Fly!" Luis Quinn thundered. "Fly!"

The assailant crabbed away, found his feet, fled.

Quinn pushed past the pale, shaken Falcon and descended to the jetty where moments—it seemed an age in the gelid time of fighting he knew so well from the dueling days—before they had been dickering with the canoe feitores. A marveling look at the blade—no shop in Brazil had ever made such a thing—and he flung it with all might out over the heads of the canoe-men into the river. His ribs ached from the effort: had the angelic knife left an arc of blue in its wake, a wound in the air? Now Falcon was at his side.

"My friend, I seem to have outstayed my welcome."

The church was death-dark, lit only by the votives at the feet of the patrons and the red heart of the sanctuary lamp, but Falcon was easily able to find Quinn by following the trail of cigar smoke.

"In France it would be considered a sin most heinous to smoke in a church."

"I see no vice in it." Quinn stood leaning against the pulpit; a vertiginous affair clinging high to the chancel wall like the nest of some forest bird, dizzy with painted putti and allegorical figures. "We honor the cross with our hearts and minds, not our inhalations and exhalations. And do we not drink wine in the most holy of places?"

The stew of the Rio Negro day seemed to roost in the church. Falcon was hot, oppressed, afraid. Twice now he had seen the rage of Luis Quinn.

"Your absence was noted at supper."

"I have a set of exercises to complete before I continue my task."

"I told them as much."

"And did they note the attack at the landing today?"

"They did not."

"Strange that in so contained a town as São José the friar has nothing to say about a deadly assault on a visiting admonitory." Quinn examined the dying coal of his cigar and neatly ground it to extinction on the tiled floor. "There is wrong here so deep, so strongly rooted, that I fear it is beyond my power to destroy it."

"'Destroy,' that is a peculiarly martial word for a man of faith."

"Mine is a martial order. Do you know why I was chosen as admonitory in Coimbra?"

"Because of your facility with languages. And because, forgive me, you have killed a man."

Quinn snapped out a bark of a laugh, flattened and ugly in his uncommon accent.

"I suppose that is not so difficult a surmise. Can you also surmise how I killed that man?"

"The obvious deduction would be in the heat and passion of a satisfaction."

"That would be the obvious deduction. No, I killed him with a pewter drinking tankard. I struck him on the side of the head, and in his helplessness I set upon him and with the same vessel beat the life from his body, and beyond that, until not even his master could recognize him. Do you know who this man was?"

Falcon felt his scalp itch beneath his wig in the stifling heat of the church.

"From your words, a servant. One of your own household?"

"No, a slave in a tavern in Porto. A Brazilian slave, in truth, an indío; recalling now his speech, I would guess a Tupiniquín. The owner had made his fortune in the colony and retired with his household and slaves to the Kingdom. He did not say much to me, only that he had been instructed to refuse me any further drink. So before all my friends, my good drinking and fighting friends, I took up the empty tankard and struck him down. Now, can you guess why I gave myself to the Society of Jesus?"

"Remorse and penance of course, not merely for the murder—let us not bandy words, it was nothing less—but because you were of that exalted class that can murder with impunity."

"All that, yes, but you have missed the heart of it. I said that mine was a martial order: the discipline, friend, the discipline. Because when I murdered that slave—I do not choose to bandy words either—do you know what I felt? Joy. Joy such as I have never known before or since. Those moments when I have taken or administered the Sacrament, when I pray alone and I know I am caught up by the Spirit of Christ, even when the music stirs me to tears: these are not even the faintest echoes of what I felt when I took that life in my hands and tore it out. Nothing, Falcon, nothing compares to it. When I went out, in my fighting days, I merely touched the hem of it. It was a terrible, beautiful joy, Falcon, and so so hard to give up."

"I have seen it," Falcon said weakly. The heat—he could not breathe, the sweat was trickling down the nape of his neck. He removed his wig, clutched it nervously, like a suitor a nosegay.

"You have seen nothing," Quinn said. "You understand nothing. You never can. I asked for a task most difficult; God has granted me my desire, but it is greater and harder than Father James, than anyone in Coimbra, ever imagined. Father Diego Gonçalves of my Society came to this river twelve years ago. His works the apostles themselves might envy; whole nations won for Christ and pacified, the cross for two hundred leagues up the Rio Branco, aldeias and reduciones that were shining beacons of what could be achieved in this bestial land. Peace, plenty, learning, the right knowledge of God and of his Church—every soul could sing, every soul could read and write. Episcopal visitors wrote of the beauty and splendor of these settlements: glorious churches, skilled people who gave their labor freely, not through coercion or slavery. I have read his letters on the ship from Salvador to Belém. Father Diego applied to the provincial for permission to set up a printing press: he was a visionary man, a true prophet. In his petition he included sketches of a place of learning, high on the Rio Branco, a new city—a new Jerusalem, he called it, a university in the forest. I have seen the sketches in the College library at Salvador; it is sinfully ambitious, maniacal in its scale: an entire city in the Amazon. He was refused of course."

"Portugal's colonial policy is very clear; Brazil is a commercial adjunct, nothing more. Continue, pray."

"After that, nothing. Father Diego Gonçalves sailed from this fort seven years ago into the high lands beyond the Rio Branco. Entradas and survivors of lost bandeiras told of monstrous constructions, entire populations enslaved and put to work. An empire within an empire, hacked out of deep forest. Death and blood. When three successive visitors sent from Salvador to ascertain the truth of these rumors failed to return, the Society applied for an admonitory."

"Your mission is to find Father Diego Gonçalves."

"And return him to the discipline of the Order, by any means."

"I fear that I understand your meaning too well, Father."

"I may murder him if necessary. That is your word, isn't it? By rumor alone he has become a liability to the Society. Our presence in Brazil is ever precarious."

"Kill a brother priest."

"My own Society has made me a hypocrite, yet I obey, as any soldier obeys, as any soldier must."

Falcon wiped sweat from his neck with his blouse sleeve. The smell of stale incense was intolerably cloying. His eyes itched.

"Those men who attacked us: do you believe they were Father Diego's men?"

"No; I believe they were in the hire of that same father with whom you dined so well so recently. He is too greasy and well fed to be much of a plotter, our Friar Braga. I questioned him after the Mass; he lies well and habitually. The wealth of the Carmelites has always been founded on the red gold; I suspect their presence is only tolerated here because they descend a steady supply of slaves to the engenhos."

"Do you believe he could be responsible for the destruction of the boat-town?"

"Not even the Carmelites are so compromised. But I am not safe here; you, my friend, enjoy some measure of protection through your crown mission. I am merely a priest, and in this latitude priests have always been dispensable. We leave in the morning, but I will not return to the Colégio, not this night."

"Then I shall watch and wait with you," Falcon declared.

"I would caution against spending too much time in my company. But at the least leave me your sword."

"Gladly," Falcon said as he removed his weapon belt and handed it, buckles ringing, to Quinn. "I could wish that you had not thrown that uncommon knife into the river."

"I had to," Quinn said, lifting the sheath into the sanctuary light to work out its character and feel. "It was a wrong thing. It scared me. Go now; you have been here too long. I shall watch and pray. I so desire prayer: my spirit feels sullied, stained by compromise."

❖

Light on the black water; a million dapple-shards brilliant in the eastering sun that sent a blade of gold along the river. The far bank was limned in light, the shore sand bright yellow; though over a league distant, every detail was pin sharp, every tree in the forest canopy so distinct Falcon could distinguish the very leaves and branches. The pandemoniac bellowing of red howler monkeys came clear and full to his ears. Falcon stood a time at the top of the river steps blinking in the light, shading his eyes with his hand against the vast glare; not even his green eyeglasses could defeat so triumphant a sun. The heat was rising with the morning, the insects few and torpid; he hoped to be out in the deep stream by the time both became intolerable. But this moment was fresh and clean and new-minted, so present that all the terrors and whisperings of the night seemed phantoms, and Falcon wanted to stretch it to its last note.

Quinn was already in his canoe. The Jesuit, a smallpox-scarred índio in mission whites, and an immense, broad black were its entire crew. The remainder of the pirogue was filled with Quinn's manioc and beans. Falcon's much larger fleet rocked on the dazzling ripples: a canoe with awning for the geographer, three for his staff, five for his baggage, a further three for their supplies, all well manned with São José Manao slaves.

"A great grand morning, thanks be to God!" Quinn called out in French. "I cannot wait for the off."

"You travel light," Falcon remarked as he descended the steps. The river had fallen farther in the night; planks had been hastily laid across the already-cracking mud, but there were still a few oozing, sinking footsteps through the mud to the canoe. "Is this the best the fabled Jesuit gold can purchase?"

"Light and fast, please God," Quinn said in Portuguese now. "And sure the paddles of three willing men are worth a whole fleet of pressed slaves."

The black man grinned broadly. Determination set in his face, Falcon picked his way up the rocking canoe to his seat in the center under the cotton awning. He could feel the silent derision of his crew, the more audible laughter of Quinn's small outfit, in the flush of his face. He settled delicately into his wicker seat, the sunshade hiding him from insects and scorn. Falcon raised his handkerchief.

"Away then."

The golden river broke into coins of light as the paddles struck and pulled. Falcon gripped the sides as the bow-water climbed the flanks of the canoe. A moment's fear, then his fleet fell in around him, paddlers slipping into unconscious unison, an arrow formation curving out into the Rio Negro. Quinn's smaller, lighter craft, frail as a leaf on water, surged ahead. Falcon noticed how easily Quinn's massive frame, despite the terrible blow it had sustained so recently, learned the paddle's rhythms. Falcon could not resist the infantile urge to wave his kerchief to him. Quinn returned the acknowledgment with a wide, careless grin.

Time vanished with the rolling stream; when Falcon glanced back around the side of his shade, São José Tarumás had dropped from view behind a turn of the stream so subtle that it had been beneath even his trained regard, so vast that the walls of green seemed to close behind him. Against will and reason, Falcon found the spirit of the river entering him. It manifested itself as stillness, a reluctance to move, to lift any of the instruments he had set in his place to measure the sun and space and time, to engage in any action that might send thought and will rippling out across the black water. The calls of birds and canopy beasts, the splash of river life, the push and drip of the paddles and the hum of the water against the hull, all seemed to him parts of a greater chorale the sum of which was an enormous, cosmological silence. The still spires of smoke from across the green canopy, the riverside settlements, the squat thatched cones of churches, their wooden crosses erect before them, the frequent river traffic that hailed and waved and smiled—all were as far from him as if painted in aquarelle on paper and Falcon were a drip of rain running down the glass. His hands should be measuring, his hands should be sketching, mapping, annotating; his hands gripped the sides of the canoe, river-tranced, hour after hour.

Quinn's hail broke the spell. His pirogue had drawn ahead, hour on hour, until it seemed a mosquito on the surface of the water. Now, where the channel divided into a braid of marshy islets and eyots, he bade his steersman turn across the current and waited in midstream. As he drifted toward Falcon's phalanx, Quinn raised his paddle over his head in his two hands and thrust it into the air three times. On the instant every paddler in Falcon's fleet put up his oar. Impetus lost, the inexorable hand of the Rio Negro took the boats, checked them, turned them, scattered their line of order into chaos.

"Paddle, you oxen!" Falcon roared, and, to Juripari his Manao translator, "Command them to paddle, this instant." The translator remained silent, the paddles unmoving. Falcon struck at the back of a slave kneeling immediately before him. The man received the blow with the stolidity of a buttressed forest tree. Quinn and his crew were stroking swiftly toward the drifting canoes. He hauled in along side the swearing, berating Falcon.

"Apologies, my friend, but this is as far as you travel with me."

"What have you done? What nonsense is this? Some wretched Jesuit plot."

"More that fabled Jesuit gold to which you alluded, Doctor. The Society has never feared the power of lucre, like some others. But you will come no further with me, Dr. Falcon. Ahead lies the Arquipelago das Anavilhanas, which Manoel tells me is a mapless maze of ever-shifting sand bars and lagoons. I have instructed your crew to make camp on an island for five days. In that time I will have so far outstripped your expedition that you will never find me. My friend, it is not safe for you to go with me, and to be truthful, my own mission may lead me to actions that I would not wish witnessed by one outside my Order. Neither was it safe, even for you, to remain in São José Tarumás. But in the Anavilhanas, no one will ever find you." Quinn lifted the Frenchman's sword from the bottom of the pirogue and offered it to him. "This is your weapon, not mine; and if I do not have it, Grace of Our Lady I shall not be tempted to use it." He tossed the sword; Falcon caught it lightly in his two hands. The canoes rocked on the still water, all bound together in the dark current. "Argument is futile, my dear friend, against Jesuit authority, and Jesuit gold." Quinn nodded to his índio pilot; paddles dipped, the pirogue drew away from the helpless Falcon. "I must confess a further crime against you, Doctor, though, as I have returned your sword, it is more in the nature of a trade. Your device, your Governing Engine; in this land it would become a tool of the grossest human subjugation conceivable. Forgive me; I have removed it from your baggage, together with the plans. It is an evil thing."

"Quinn, Quinn!" Falcon shouted. "My engine, my Governing Engine, what did you do with it, you faithless blackrobe?"

"Look for me around the mouth of the Rio Branco," Quinn called back, and the river carried them apart until the pirogue, pitifully small and fragile against the green wall of the várzea, was lost among the narrow mud-choked channels.

Only when the sudden clap of flighting birds or the soft clop of a jumping fish or the sun brilliant in the diamond of a water-bead dropping from paddle-tip summoned him did Father Luis Quinn start from rapture to find that hours had passed in the reverie of the river. He had ceased counting the days since the parting at Anavilhanas; morning followed morning like a chain of pearls, the great dawn chorus of the forest, then the run out into the misty water and the time-devouring stroke of the paddles; the simple sacrament of physical work. No need, no desire for speech. Never in all his disciplines and exercises had Quinn found so easy and complete a submergence of the self into the other. The indolent slide of jacaré into the water; the sudden scatter of capybara as the pirogue entered a marshy furo between river loops, noses and tiny ears held above the surface; the dash of a toucan across the channel, a nestling in its outlandish beak, pursued by the plundered mother. Once—had he imagined, had he truly beheld?—the wide prideful eyes of the solitary jaguar, kneeling warily at a salt lick. Their unthinking, animal actions were of one with the automatic obedience of his muscles to the paddle. In physicality is true subjugation of the self.

On and on and on. As Quinn's spirit went outward into the physical world, as often it was cast backward. Memory became entangled with reality. Luis Quinn knelt not in the waist of a pirogue, a frail shave of bark, but stood at the taff-rail of a Porto carrack beating for the Spanish Gate of Galway under a spring sky of swift, gray-bottomed shower-heavy clouds. Fifteen years and his first return since childhood; he had thought he would barely remember the old language, but as Suibhne the captain led him from warehouse to port-merchants to tavern and the men had greeted him like a sea-divided relative, he found the grammar and idiom, the words and blessings swinging into place like the timbers of a house. Seamus Óg Quinn's son; big strapping lad he grew up to be, grand to see a Quinn back among his old people and lands. Again, recollection: the great hall on the upper floor of the casa in Porto; Pederneiras the tutor taking him by the hand down from the schoolroom on the top floor to this great, light-filled hall lowering with allegories of wealth, and power crowning the merchants and navigators of Porto. As he had peered down through the colonnaded window into the rattling street, Pederneiras had opened a long, narrow shagreen-bound case. Within, bound in baize, the blades. "Go, take one, feel it, adore it." Luis Quinn's hand dropped around the hilt and a thrill burned up his arm, a belly-fire, a hardening and pressing he now knew as sexual, a feeling that twenty years distant, kneeling in supplication, still stirred him physically.

"I see you need no encouragement from me, Senhor Luis," Pederneiras had said, observing the precocious pride in his pupil's breeches. "Now, the *garde*."

Bright metal in his hand once again, the flattened silver of a stout tankard, crushed by repeated blows to the skull of a man. *The master has commanded me to serve you no more.* Still his body remembered that deep, exultant joy. Luis Quinn turned the disciplines of his exercise to expunge the luxurious memory of sin. *Preparatory prayer*: ask of Christ his grace that all intentions, actions, and works may be directed to his greater glory. *First point*: the sin of the angels. Naked they were, and innocent, dwelling in a paradise of bounty and clemency, yet still in their forests and great rivers the Enemy corrupted them. They consumed human flesh, they rejoiced in the meat of their enemies, and so we condemned them as pagan, animal, without soul or spirit, fit only for slavery. In so doing we condemned ourselves. *Second point*: the sin of old Adam. Quinn's memory turned from the battered shell of metal in his fist to the smashed skull on the floor. He heard again the hooting animal howls of his friends cheering him on through the fire of lust and drink. *Third point*: the sin of the soul condemned through mortal vice. Father Diego Gonçalves, what do you know of him? Manoel the pilot, a diligent altar boy, dared say nothing against the Church, but his hunched shoulders and bowed head, as if cowering from the vastness of the Rio Negro, spoke old dread to Luis Quinn. Zemba, a freed slave who since his manumission at Belém had worked his way up the river to the rumors of an El Dorado in the immensity beyond São José Tarumás, a land of future where his history would be forgotten. *The City of God*, he said. *The kingdom of heaven is built there.*

Luis Quinn turned the three sins beneath his contemplation and saw that they were indivisible: the pride of kings, the pride of the spirit, the pride of power. *Now I understand why you sent me, Father James. Conclude the meditation with the Paternoster.* But as the comfortable words formed the river exploded around him, dashing him from contemplation: botos, in their dozens, spearing through the water around the pirogue, curving up through the surface to gasp in air, some bursting free from their element entirely in an ecstatic leap. Quinn's heart leaped in wonder and joy; then, as he followed a flying, twisting boto to the zenith of its arc, to wordless awe. Angels moved over the várzea, striding across the forest canopy, their feet brushing the treetops. Angels carmine and gold, Madonna blue and silver, angels bearing harps and psalteries, drums and maracas, swords and double-curved warbows: the host of heaven. *We strive not against men but against principalities and powers.*

The pirogue shot clear from the narrow gut of the furo to rejoin the main channel, and Quinn involuntarily rose to his feet in wonder. From bank to bank the channel was black with canoes; men perched in the stern driving their bobbing wooden shells onward, women and children in the waist. Some were entirely crewed by grinning, spray-wet children. At the center of the great fleet rose the object of Quinn's awe. A basilica sailed the river. Nave, chancel, apses, buttresses, and clerestory; in every detail a church from the wooden-shingled dome to the crucifix between its two towers. Every inch of the basilica was covered in carved, painted reliefs of the gospels and the catechisms, the martyrdoms of saints and the stoopings of angels; the illumination caught and kindled in the westering light as radiantly as any rose window. Each wooden roof-slat was painted with the representation of a flower. Figures stood on the railed balcony above the porch, tiny as insects. Insect was the image caught in Quinn's reeling mind; the great church seemed to stride across the water on a thousand spindle legs. A second, colder look revealed them to be a forest of sweeps propelling the towering edifice down the channel. The basilica did not move by human muscle alone; the finials of the wall-buttresses had been extended into masts slung with yardage and brown, palm-cloth sail; the towers too bore sprits, stays, and banners. One pennant was figured with Our Lady and child, the other a woman, standing on one foot, her body entwined with forest vines and flowers. Naked red bodies patterned black with genipapo swarmed the ropes and ratlines. Then Luis Quinn's attention rose to the mastheads. Each mast was capped with a titanic carving of an angel: trumpet, harp, lozenge-bladed sword, shield, and castanets. Their faces were those of the people of the canoes: high-cheeked, narrow-eyed, black-haired Rio Negro angels.

Now bells sounded from the basilica. The figures on the balcony moved with sudden activity, and a large canoe was pushed out from the line of mooring poles at the church-ship's bow. Quinn read the inscription over the main portal, though he already knew what it must say: *Ad maioram Dei Gloriam.*

OUR LADY OF THE FLOOD FOREST

JUNE 6–8, 2006

Silver rain woke Marcelina Hoffman. Her face and hair were dewed; her sleeping bag gleamed beneath a mist of fine droplets like the pupa of some extraordinary Luna moth. A ceiling of soft, ragged cloud raced above her face, seemingly low enough to lick. The morros were abruptly amputated, their tops invisible in the mist. Marcelina watched the streaming gray tear around the spines and quills of antennae and aerials that capped the taller apartment towers. She put out her tongue, a taste not a kiss, and let the warm drizzle settle on it. The noises from the street were subdued, baffled; car tires slushy on the wet, greasy blacktop. Gulls sobbed, hovering seen and unseen in the mist; the rain-sodden Copacabana lay beneath their yellow avaricious eyes.

Raucous weather-prophets. Marcelina shivered in her bag; gulls calling had always disturbed her; the voice of the sea calling her out over its horizon: new worlds, new challenges.

Downstairs the apartment felt chill and abandoned. The furniture was cold to the touch, damp and unfamiliar; the clothes in the closets belonged to a previous, fled tenant. The apartment had reverted to its natural smell, that distinctive pheromone of place that had struck Marcelina with almost physical force the moment the agent had opened the door, that she had worked so hard to banish with scented candles and oil burners and coffee and maconha but that crept back, under doors through air-conditioning vents every time she left it for more than a few days. Marcelina made coffee and felt the kitchen watching her. Carpet-treading in your own house.

Her cellular, charging on the worktop, blinked. Message. Received 2:23. The number was familiar but evoked no name or face.

Bip.

A man's voice raged at her. Marcelina almost threw the phone from her. It spun on the bare, almost surgically clean worktop, voice gabbling. Marcelina picked up the phone. Raimundo Soares, furious, more furious than she had thought possible for the Last Real Carioca. She killed the message and called back straightaway.

He recognized her number. Seven hours had not mellowed him; he was furious beyond even a hello good morning how are you?

"Wait wait wait wait, I understand you're angry with me, but what is it you're actually angry about?"

"What do you mean? Don't you play any more stupid games with me. Bloody women you're all the same, tricks and games, oh yes."

"Wait wait wait wait." How many times has she said these words in just seven days? "Pretend I don't know anything, and start at the very beginning." She could never hear those words without recalling her mother's medley of hits from *The Sound of Music*, Samba-ized. Christ on crutches; it was Feijoada Saturday: feijoada and organ, the happy Annunciation of the blessed Iracema. But it was marvelous indeed how the mind reached for the ridiculous, the incongruous in dark and panic.

"Oh no, I'm not to fall for that soft-soap; I know how you reality TV people work. That e-mail; it's all a joke at my expense, isn't it? There's probably a camera over there watching me right now; you've probably even got one in my toilet so you can watch me scratching myself."

"Mr. Soares, what e-mail are you talking about?"

"Don't you mister me, don't you ever mister me. I've heard of these things; people hit the wrong button and the e-mail goes out to someone it's not supposed to; well, I saw it and I know your game. You may have made a fool out of me, but you won't make a fool out of the people of Rio, oh no."

"What was this e-mail?"

"You know, maybe you can sound all innocent, maybe you don't know, seeing as how it was an accident. You wouldn't deliberately have sent me the proposal for your Moaçir Barbosa show, would you?"

The native smell of her kitchen assaulted Marcelina, cloying and dizzying. There was no help in words here. She had done it. She had lied, she had betrayed, she had joyfully schemed to send an old man to the pillory to build her career. Our Lady of Production Values had averted her eyes. But there was mystery still.

"I didn't send that e-mail."

"Look, little girl, I'm no silver surfer, but even I can recognize a return e-mail address. You just think you're so fucking clever, and we're all so old and slow and you can just laugh at us. Well, I still know a few people in this town, you know? You haven't heard the last of this, not by a long long chalk. So you can fuck yourself and all your fucking TV people as well; I wouldn't present your show for a million reis."

"Mr. Soares, Mr. Soares, it's important, what time . . ." Dead line. "What time did I send that e-mail?"

You never were going to present that show, Marcelina raged silently at the dead cellular. She knew it was a mealy little vice, her need to have the last word when her enemy had no possibility of reply. *Not if you were the last fucking carioca on the planet.* But it was bad, worse than she had ever known it. Christ Christ, Christ of Rio, Christ of the Hunchback Mountain with your arms held out the sea, Christ in the fog; help me now. Marcelina glanced at the clock on the microwave, perpetually eight minutes fast. She had just time to get to the office and then out to her mother's.

Robson didn't do Saturdays, and his replacement edgy-but-inclusive public-facing homosexual with the nickname Lampião was new on the desk and asked Marcelina for her ID. She didn't bite him in two. She would have need of him later.

The drizzle had steepened into full rain; streaks turned the Glass Menagerie into a strange tech jungle. The Sent Items folder on her workstation confirmed: proposal for *Barbosa: Trial of the Century* sent to raicariocão @wonderfish.br at 23:32 August fifth. While her alt dot family was singularly failing to comfort her. Proper passwords and logins and everything. Marcelina called up the security page and tabbed the change password button. One by one blobs vanished as she deleted them. New password? Her fingers halted over the keys halfway through *mestreginga*. She knows you. Every thought every reaction every detail and diary entry of your life. She knows you play capoeira. She knows your shoe size dress size playlists how many bottles of beer are in your fridge what kind of batteries you use in the Rabbit. In the streaming gray Marcelina hugged herself, suddenly chilled. *That's it, isn't it? You're in a program within a program; a pilot for an ultimate reality TV show: Make Marcelina Mad. Even now the cameras are swiveling to the direction of some dark control room. They're all in on it: Celso and Cibelle and Agnetta, the Black Plumed Bird, even Adriano. They were never going to make your show; he just agreed at Blue Sky Friday because it's part of the script: the clever clever comedy of a program maker who doesn't realize she's starring in her own show. The Girl Who Haunted Herself. Lisandra. That cow. She'd do it. She'd do anything to make it to CE. She's laughing at you right now up in the gallery with a couple of APs and Leandro the editor.*

It has to be all just a show. Any other theory is madness.

Marcelina pulled a book at random off her shelf, opened at page 113, typed the 113th word into the pulsing box. *Testament*. Good word. One unlikely to be stumbled upon at random in Canal Quatro.

Saturday Boy Lampião was SMSing in a blur of thumbs behind his desk.

"Could you do me a favor?"

His lips pursed in irritation at the interruption to his messaging.

"Well I don't know, I mean what if I got into trouble or something?"

"I know a few people in production."

He rolled his eyes.

"Tell me what you want, then."

"Were you on last night?"

He shook his head.

"I need a look at the security footage."

"What's that?"

"From the cameras." She pointed them out like a trolley-dolly indicating the emergency exits. "It all goes on to a hundred-gig hard drive. Back there." He had been looking in mild panic under his desk. "It's easy enough to download."

"I'm not supposed to let anyone round this side of the desk."

"It's for a show."

"There should be something in writing about this."

"I'll get it for you on Monday."

"I'll get it for you."

"It would be simpler . . ."

He was at the black LaCie drive.

"How much do you want?"

"A couple of hours. Say from ten thirty to twelve thirty."

"I'll burn a DVD."

I'd rather download it onto my PDA, Marcelina was about to say. She bowed in acquiescence. Never underestimate the Brazilian gift for bureaucracy. She watched the rain and the cable cars vanishing into the cloud-cap of the Sugar Loaf. A helicopter buzzed over Dois Irmãos. Not even winter rain could damp down the embers of the recent unrest. *A rich hot magma runs beneath our beautiful streets and avenues; we walk, we jog, we exercise our little dogs on its crust, preening and strutting like we are New York or Paris or London until the hidden order breaks through and the woman who cleans your house, cooks your food, cares for your child; the man who drives your taxi, delivers your flowers, fixes your computer is suddenly your enemy and the fire runs down to the sea.*

Then she thought, *What if a helicopter hit a cable car? Now that's a CNN moment.*

"There you are. What's the show?"

"I'm not supposed to say, but we're all in it."

The clouds clung low to the Dois Irmãos and the long ridge of Tijuca, turning Leblon into a bowl of towers, offered to the sea. Hardy boys in toucan-bright neoprene braved the gray-on-gray breakers. In the dash from cab to elevator lobby Marcelina was drenched and shivering. No swirling glissandos of the Queen of the Beija-Flor today. Moisture was bad for the electronics. The cab driver had bought flowers and a surprisingly good bottle of French wine. Most of Canal Quatro's account drivers were better production assistants than the channel's own wannabes. Bottle in one hand, flowers—with inscribed card—in the other, Marcelina rode the mirrored box, dripping onto the fake marble floor.

She pressed the doorbell. Behind the chime came a fermata, the opposite of an echo, a silence more sensed than heard of conversations abruptly ending. Canal Quatro had made Marcelina experienced in the subtleties of that silent click. Her mother opened.

"Oh, so you decided to come, then." She pulled away as Marcelina went to kiss her.

They were lined up in neat rows on all the available seating space in her mother's cramped living room: Gloria and Iracema on the sofa, babies between them, children at their feet caramelly with the sugared treats on the coffee table; husband one perched on the side of an armchair, husband two on a plastic seat brought in from the balcony and wedged between a floor lamp and the organ. A tall glass of vodka stood on a small side table by her mother's chair. Bubbles rose through the ice cubes, a swizzle stick with a toucan on the end perched against the edge of the glass. A rich smell of the long-simmered meat and the beans filled the little apartment, the mild acridity of the greens, the fresh top note of the sliced orange. Feijoada had always been celebration to Marcelina. The windows were steamed up.

"What is this, a jury of my peers?" Marcelina joked, but the wine felt like a Ronald McDonald mask at a funeral and the flowers the death itself.

"You've got a nerve, I should say," Gloria said. Marcelina heard her mother close the door behind her.

The feijoada was now stifling and sickening.

Iracema slid the card across the table. Twin babies in fuzzy-angel fur-suits ascended to heaven among hummingbirds and little fluffy clouds. *Congratula-*

tions: it's two! Marcelina opened it. . . . *I hope you miscarry and lose them, and if you don't lose them I hope they have Down syndrome* . . . Marcelina snapped the card shut. The room wheeled around her. Her family seemed at once removed to cosmological distances and so close she could taste the film on their teeth.

"You have to know I didn't write this."

"It's your handwriting." Gloria opened the prosecution.

"It looks like it but—"

"Who else knew Iracema was expecting twins?"

Gloria's husband Paulo rose from his perch.

"Come on, kids, let's see how the cooking's getting on."

"I did not write that, why would I write that?"

Gloria flipped the card over.

"Write it out again on the back."

. . . *smug with your perfect kids and perfect husband and you never even suspected that he sees other women. Why do you think he goes to the gym four nights a week . . .*

Stroke for stroke. Loop for loop. Scrawl for scrawl.

"I didn't write this!"

"Keep your voice down," Marcelina's mother hissed. "You've done enough already without the little ones overhearing."

"Why would I want to send something like that?" It was the only question she could ask, but she knew even before she spoke the words it was a fatal one.

"Because you're jealous. You're jealous because we have things you don't." Gloria looked her cold and full, sister to sister, eye to eye. And if she had not done that, Marcelina might have been wise, might have apologized and turned around and walked away. But it was a challenge now, and Marcelina could not to be left without the last word.

"And what could you have that I could possibly be jealous of?"

"Oh, I think we all know that."

"What, your lovely house and your lovely car and your lovely gym membership and lovely medical insurance and lovely lovely kindergarten fees? At least what I have, I earn." *Marcelina stop it. Marcelina shut up.* But she never could. "No, no, I'm not the one has the jealousy issues here. I'm not the one who still can't handle the fact that she wasn't favorite. And that's always been your problem. You're the jealous one; I'm the one having a life."

"Don't you dare, dare try and turn this round on me and make it like I'm to blame. I didn't send that card, and nothing can take away from that."

"Well I didn't either, but I'm not going to try to explain it to you because no one can explain anything to you, you're always so right and sweet and dandy and everything's just perfect."

The hum of voices from the kitchen, bass and piccolo, had fallen silent. You're hearing right, kids. Your aunt's a monster. Don't be expecting any presents until you finish university. I'll pay for your therapy. Iracema was in tears. Husband João-Carlos had moved from his plastic chair to kneel beside her, caressing her wrist. Fragrant, festive feijoada now revolted her: smell was the great imprinter of memory and it was forever changed. *Get out Marcelina, before you slash deeper than any healing.* But she turned back from the door to spew, "Did any of you even stop to think that maybe something wasn't right, that maybe there was more to this than just your blind assumption that that's just Marcelina, isn't it? Have any of you given even one moment's thought that maybe something is very, very wrong? Fuck you, I don't need you, any of you."

She gave the door as good a slam as she could over an over-springy plastic doormat. The elevator doors closed on a two-dimensional strip of her mother flinging open the door, calling, "Marcelina! Marcelina!" Then she turned to a line, to silence.

The wind had come down from the hills and was carrying away the low, weeping clouds, blowing away the tops of the gray waves. Gulls hovered over the spray line, webs outspread, wings tilting a breath here, a feather there to hold them over the wave tops. Handsome boys in cute rubber suits lounged on the sand and waited for the sky to clear. On the black-and-white patterned sidewalk of Avenida Delfim Moreira, Marcelina realized she still had her saturated flowers clutched in her fist. She drew an orchid from the cellophane and launched it at the surfer boys. They laughed and waved. She speared flowers into Leblon's rain-pocked sand until she had no more. Surf's up. That noise was back in her head, the whistle of world's end; tears wrung out of the hollows of her skull.

You said that you said that you said that. But it wasn't me, it wasn't me. Then what was it? A reality television show? At her most cruel, most desperate for shock, Marcelina would never have done anything like that card. The family, you never touch the family. But didn't you do that in *Filthy Pigs?* Friendships ended mothers and daughters sundered, families at war?

At the bridge over the canal that drained the lagoon into the ocean, where Leblon ended and Ipanema began, she chewed the plastic seal off the bottle of wine, pushed the cork in with her thumb, and swigged down hundred-real imported French Margaux. Cyclists and rollerbladers in wet spandex stared as they whirred past, wheels throwing up narrow wakes of rainwater. *Stare at me, stare all you like.* She had downed the entire bottle by Arpoador, sent the empty bottle arcing up into the air to smash among the power walkers. Marcelina peeled the saturated hair back from her face to scowl at the staring faces.

"So? So?"

The brief woo of sirens sent Marcelina down with a wail onto her ass. She sat gaping at the police cruiser as if it had fallen from an angel's purse. A policewoman helped her to her feet. Rain spilled from the peak of her cap onto Marcelina's upturned face.

"You've got your pants tucked into your boots," Marcelina said.

"Come on, now. How much have you had?"

"Only wine officer, only wine."

"You should be ashamed of yourself, in public too. Come on, now."

"I'm a corda vermelha, you know," Marcelina said. "I could make you look very very silly." But the policewoman's grip on Marcelina's elbow was irrefutable. She steered her toward the car. Her partner, a broad-faced mulatinho, shook with laughter.

"I'm glad you think it's funny," Marcelina said as the policewoman pressed her down into the seat. "Oh, I've gotten all your upholstery wet." She tried to wipe away the drips with her sleeve. "Where are you taking me?"

"Home."

Marcelina seized the policewoman's shirt.

"No, don't take me there, I can't go there, she's there."

The policewoman quickly and firmly unhooked Marcelina's fists.

"Well, you're in no condition to be out on the street. Would you rather I took you in?"

"Heitor," Marcelina said. "Take me to Heitor. Heitoooor!"

He thanked the officers patiently, who were genuinely awed to be in the presence a television celebrity and delighted at the prospect of profitable gossip. Marcelina sat on the topmost of the terrace steps, runoff from the morro that rose sheer behind Heitor's apartment block cascading around her.

"This is going to be all over Quem by Monday," Heitor said. There was the discreet exhibitionism of a woman in a sheer playsuit parading under the lenses across the lagoon; that same woman drunk and shrieking on his back steps was quite another thing. "Jesus. Are you going to come in? My car's going to be here in five minutes and I'm going to have to change, this suit is ruined."

"Well boo hoo for your suit," Marcelina shouted to Heitor's rain-soaked shoulders as he stepped through the sliding doors into his bedroom. "It's my fucking life that's over, that's all."

Heitor threw a towel out to her. She wrapped it round her head like Carmen Miranda but got to her feet, glitter pumps careful careful on the treacherous waterfall steps and stumbled into the bedroom. Heitor stood in his shorts and socks, knotting a knitted silk tie Marcelina had brought him back from New York. She stood dripping onto his carpet.

"Do you think it's like axé, that power can go out and take shapes?

Heitor pulled on his pants, checked the propriety of his creases.

"What are you talking about?"

Marcelina staggered out of her shoes as Heitor pulled his on with a tortoiseshell shoehorn. Her Capri-cut jeans followed; she fell back onto the bed as she tried to disengage her feet.

"Like some very strong feelings or stress or wanting something too much can go out of you and gather together and take on a life and body of its own," she said. "Like the umbanda mestres were supposed to be able to tear off part of their souls and make it take the shape of a dog or a monkey."

Marcelina put her arms up and slid off the bed out of her saturated strappy top. Her bra followed. Heitor studied her small, tight-nippled breasts in the full-length mirror. He shrugged on his jacket.

"That's legend. Magic. Superstition. We live in a scientific, entropic universe."

"But suppose suppose suppose . . ." Marcelina said in her tanga. The intercom buzzed. Taxi. Heitor kissed her, circled his thumbs over her nipples.

Marcelina pressed close, tried to slip the tongue. Heitor gently pressed her down to the bed.

"I'll see you in there later. And do try and get some water down you."

"Heitor!"

The rain streaking across the coffin-narrow concrete garden was now stained ochre with eroded soil. Marcelina sat up under the sheet, knees pulled to chin, watching the morro wash between the potted plants and down the steps, shivering at the horror. Sleep was impossible. She scuffed around on Heitor's polished hardwood floor in her bare feet, looking for water. Marcelina slowly bent over and bared her ass to the telescopes across the lagoon. Wipe your lenses, boys and girls. She slapped her backside.

But she had still wished her own sister's twin babies aborted in the womb.

Marcelina flicked on the plasma screen. Noise, chatter, brainpan jabber. Stop you thinking about yourself. And there was Heitor, the remote control camera moving in for a close-up as the title graphics rolled. The headlines tonight. Burning cars, police helicopters, corpses in Bermudas. The walls around the favelas another course of bricks taller. Lula rocked by fresh corruption allegations. Brazil, the nation of the future. Then Marcelina saw Heitor scan the next line on the autocue and his eyes widen. There was the tiniest of pauses. Heitor never did that. Heitor was the old-school public-service commitment to the Truth Well in a jungle of eighteen-to-thirty-four demographics and noisy edginess. Heitor was professional down to the shine of his shoes. All her attention was focused on the screen.

"And Canal Quatro finds itself in the news with the allegations by journalist Raimundo Soares to be published in the *Jornal de Copacabana* tomorrow that it is to make a television program about the Maracanaço. He alleges that he received a confidential e-mail from a Canal Quatro producer that the entertainment program will track down the eighty-five-year-old Moaçir Barbosa, seen by many as being chiefly responsible for the Maracanaço, and publicly humiliate him in a mock trial reality show."

VT insert of Raimundo Soares in surf shirt and shorts on rain-swept Flamengo Beach, his brotherhood nodding over their lines behind him. Cynicism. Lied to. Pillorying an old man. Then Marcelina could not hear anymore because the sound in her eyes in her head in her ears squeezed out into the world.

It was all ended. Our Lady of Production Values had abandoned her.

She pointed the remote and sent Heitor into the dark. Her heartbeat was the loudest sound in the room.

"Who are you?" Marcelina shouted. "Why are you doing this to me? What did I do?"

She fled into the bedroom, emptied her bag onto the bed. There, there, the translucent plastic clamshell. She slid the DVD into the side of Heitor's plasma screen.

Her finger hesitated over the play button.

She had to know. She had to see.

Marcelina wound through Canal Quatro staff slipping out home, a nod and a silent word to Lampião. There went Leandro. Several fast-scans minutes of Lampião dully gaping at a flickering television. How little he moved. Then Marcelina saw the edge of the door revolve across the shot. A figure in a dark suit entered. Marcelina's fingers stumbled over the buttons as she tried to find slo-mo. Back. Back. The drive whined. Again the figure entered. A woman. A woman jogging forward frame by frame in a good suit—dark gray. A woman, short, with a lot of naturally curled bouncing blonde hair. A loira woman. Lampião looked up from his TV and smiled.

Frame by frame, the woman turned to check the location of the camera.

Marcelina hit pause. The only snow that Rio knew blew across the top of the screen.

Her face. She was looking into her own face.

JANUARY 28–29, 2033

After midnight the axé flows strongest through the Igreja of the Sisterhood of the Boa Morte. Taxis and minibuses bring suppliants from all across the northern suburbs: when the saints are tired the walls between the worlds are weak, and the most powerful workings may be dared. Edson tosses a coin to St. Martin, the Christian aspect of Exu, Lord of the Crossroads, Trickster and Rent-boy of the orixás, patron of all malandros.

The Sisters of the Good Death have orbited Edson's life like fairy god-mothers. His grandmother from the northeast had given the Sisterhood her two daughters, Hortense and Marizete, in exchange for the success of her sons in hard, clutching Sampa. But Dona Hortense had loved pirate radio and dancing and boys with fast cars and the madre had released her from her vows (truly, no God regards the vow of a fourteen-year-old as binding). Tia Marizete found peace and purpose in the discipline of a post-Catholic nun and remained and for twenty-five years had brought the Dignified Burial and unofficial social services to the bairros and favelas of north São Paulo. Unlike their mother church in Bahia, the Paulistana daughters did not practice seclusion: their Baiana crinolines and turbans were familiar and welcome sights on the streets as they gave healings, told fortunes, and collected reis in their baskets. Twice a year, at the Lady Days, Tia Marizete would call on her sister and nephews and the entire bairro would land on Dona Hortense's verandah with a variety of small but niggling maladies.

"Does your mother know where you are?" Tia Marizete asks, clearing the guest room of gay abiás ("we've become icons again, Mother help us"). She sets wards of palm and holy cake on the windowsills and door lintels.

"She knows. She's not to come looking for me. Don't let her. I need money. And I may have to stay a while."

"You are welcome as long as you need. But I have a service to conduct. And Edson, remember, this is God's house." Then the drums start so loud he can feel them in his bowels, but they are a comfort; he feels himself slipping down into their rhythm. By the time the tetchy initiate slips a tray of beans and rice and two Cokes through the door he's nodding, exhausted.

The Sisters have always saved him. When he was twelve he had been given a fluky antibiotic that kicked off a massive allergic reaction that left mouth, tongue, lips covered in white-lipped ulcers and drove him fever-mad, hallucinating that a ball at once chokingly small and jaw-wrenchingly huge was being forced endlessly into his mouth. The doctor had rolled his eyes and shaken his head. Biology would take its course. His brothers had carried him on the back of a HiLux to the Sisters, wrapped in sweat-soaked sheets. Tia Marizete had laid him in one of the acolytes' rooms, bathed him with scented and herbal waters, anointed him with sweet oils, scattered prayers and consecrated farofa over him. Three days he had raged along the borderlands between life and death. The ulcers advanced down his throat. If they reached his tonsils, he would die. They halted at the base of his uvula. Axé. Through it all, the memory the drums and the clapping hands, the stamp and bell-jingle of the Sisters as they whirled in their ecstasy dances; the cheers and tears and praises to Our Lady, Our Wonderful Lady. Down, into the drums.

Crying. Soft and faltering, at the very end of tears, more gasp than sob. Edson slips from the thin foam mattress. The sound comes from the camarinha, the innermost, holiest sanctuary, the heart of axé. Fia sits in the middle of the floor, legs curled, fingers twined. Around her the statues of the saints on their poles lean against the walls, each draped in his or her sacramental color.

"Hey. It's only me. You know, we shouldn't really be in here. It's for the Sisters and the high initiates only."

It takes a long time for Fia's gasps to form words. Edson's cold and shivering after his sleep; the energy of the night has left him. He could hold Fia; his comfort, her warmth. But it's not *her*.

"Did you ever have a dream where you're at home and you know everyone and everything, but they don't know you, they've never known you, and no matter how much you try and tell them, they never will know you?"

"Everyone has that dream."

"But you know me, and I've never seen you before in my life. You say you are Edson Jesus . . ."

"Oliveira de Freitas."

"I think I need to know this now. Who was I?"

So among the shrouded saints Edson tells her about her father with his New Age columns and stable of accountancy bots and her mother with her urban farm and her brother away across the big planet on his gap-year chasing surf and surf-bunnies. . . .

"Sorry, what?"

"Yoshi, your brother. You have a brother, where you come from?"

"Of course I do, but he's in his first year at the São Paulo Seminary."

Edson blinks in astonishment.

Fia asks, "Edson, what was I like?"

"You. Not you. She liked bags, clothes, girlie things. Shoes. The last day I saw her, she went to a shop to get these shoes printed."

He sees the soles, the logos bobbing before him as the crash team slides the stretcher into the back of the ambulance.

"Shoes, printed?"

Edson explains the technology as he understands it. When Fia concentrates, she tilts her head to one side. Edson never saw the real Fia do that. It makes this Fia look even less true, like a dead doll.

"She never got on the back of my bike. She always took taxis. She hated getting dirty, even when we were up in Todos os Santos she was immaculate, always immaculate. She had quite a lot of girlfriends." *How little I know*, Edson realizes. A few details, a scoop of observations. "She was very direct. I don't think she was comfortable being too near to things. All those friends, but she was never really close to them. She liked being an outsider. She liked being the rebel, the quantumeira."

"I'm nowhere near as wild and romantic as that," Fia says. "Just a plain quantum-computing postgrad specializing in multiversal economic modeling. My world; it's less paranoid. We don't watch each other all the time. But it's more . . . broken. I'm broken, everyone's broken. We leave bits of ourselves all over the place: memories, diaries, names, experiences, knowledge, friends, personalities even, I suppose. I loaded everything I could, but there are still important parts of me back there: pictures, childhood memories, school friends. And the world is broken. It's not like this. This is . . . like heaven."

Edson tries to imagine the point at which Fia's world branched off from his. But that is a trap, Mr. Peach had taught. There is no heart reality from which everything else diverges. Every part of the multiverse exists, has existed, will exist, independently of every other. Edson shivers. How can you live with that sort of knowledge? But Fia notices him shiver.

"Here, you're freezing." She peels off her ripped hoodie. Beneath she wears a tight sleeveless T, dragged up to her breasts by the cling of the hoodie. Edson stares. Beneath the crop top is a tattoo like none he has ever seen before. Wheels, cogs, meshing; arcs, spirals, paisleys, fractal sprays, and mathematical blossoms. A silvery machine of slate-gray ink covers her torso from breastbone to the waistband of her leggings. Edson's hand stays Fia's as she moves to pull her top down.

"Oh my God, what is that?"

Fia stands up, pulls up her top again, and coyly wiggles her leggings down to the sweet tiny pink bow on the hip-band of her panties where the tattoo coils in to nestle like a snake against her pubis. Not taking her eyes off Edson, she hooks her red hair back behind her left ear. There is a cursive of gray ink over the top of ear and along her hairline, like one of Zezão's sinuous abstract pichações that now have preservation orders smacked all over them.

"You wear your computers," Fia says as she restores her clothing. "We're more . . . intimate . . . with ours."

Edson lifts a finger, whirls into a crouch.

"I hear something." He slides Mr. Peach's gun out of the waistband of his Jams and pushes it across the foot-polished wooden floor of the camarinha to Fia. She knows what to do with it. Edson moves cat-careful between the shrouded saints. The layout of the terreiro is as inviolable as its obrigacões. Beyond the sacred camarinha is the great public room of the barracão, then the hall with the ilê where the saints stand when they are awake. He checks the front door. The manioc-paste seals are intact, the coffins of the Good Dead laid out on the floor, dusted with white farofa. Nothing to be scared of there. Probably one of the abiás getting up for a piss. The quarters run around the back of the terreiro and open onto the barracão and the backyard where the chickens and Vietnamese pot-belly pigs are kept and the holy herbs are grown in fake-terracotta planters. The Sisters maintain private room upstairs. Edson opens the door from the corridor to the big kitchen, where the food for the gods, hungry as babies, is prepared.

A foot smashes into his breastbone, sends him sprawling, windless, across the barracão, scattering offerings. He sees a figure wheel out of the darkness in a capoeira meia lua de compasso into a poised ginga. A white woman, in sports top, Adidas baggies, and bare feet. She wears odd metal bracers on her forearms. Edson fights for words breath sanity power.

A shot. From the holy camarinha.

"Shit. He's already here," the woman hisses and flicks her right hand into a fist. A blade flashes from the bracer over her balled knuckles. Blue light flickers around its Planck-keen edges. She whirls through the door to the barracão in a one-handed dobrado cartwheel. Gasping for breath, Edson limps after her.

The camarinha is a martyrdom of slashed saints. Fia holds off a man armed with a Q-blade using a statue of Senhor de Bonfim on his pole, gold-tassled shroud flapping. Faint hope in the saint: the Q-blade cuts through it like smoke. Mr. Peach's beautiful silver gun is already in two pieces, cut through the firing chamber. The assassin's blur of blue light drives Fia back to the wall. By tradition this sacred room has only one door. The killer knows this tradition. The woman wheels into the camarinha and drops into the negativa fighting crouch. The assassin spins to face her. He is a young man, pale skinned, with floppy hair and a goatee. Blades blur past each other; the capoeira woman's foot wheels up to deliver a stun-blow to the side of the Q-blade man's head. But the killer ducks under it and rolls across the camarinha to put space between him and the woman. Fia hunts for a gap, feinting with her mutilated orixá, but the assassin is between her and the door. Frantic with fear, Edson looks for an opportunity. Voices, behind him. The terreiro is awake. Abiás in their underwear, shorts, jog pants, Sisters in their night-gowns. Their hands are raised in horror at the violation of the sanctuary.

"Get everyone out of here!" Edson shouts. The boys understand and herd the Sisters back to the kitchen and the safety of the garden, but Tia Marizete is paralyzed at the vision of her saints, her murdered saints, their desecration. Arms out, she rushes to comfort them. Edson grabs her by the waist, drags her away. The assassin's attention flickers to him. The capoeirista uses the moment to spin up into a great flying leap, blade-arm drawn back. With a roar, the assassin leaps to meet her. They clash, they pass in a flash of ionization in the middle of the air above the heart of the camarinha. Then they are both crouched like cats, glaring, panting. Their shattered blades spin on the wooden floor, flat sides, safe sides down.

"Yeah," says the woman. "But I've got another one. Have you?" She snaps her left hand into a fist, and a fresh Q-blade flicks out from the magnetic sheathing on her wrist-guard. The killer scores the possibilities in an eye-flash. He dives flat, arm outstretched, and with the tips of his fingers catches the flat side of the Q-blade and flicks it at the capoeirista. At any speed the quantum-sharp cutting edge is a sure kill. Then Edson's vision goes into martial arts–movie slow motion. The woman bends back from the hips, trying to roll away from the blade cutting toward her throat through a wake of burned blue air. Fia brings the Senhor do Bonfim sweeping up under the flying blade. An orixá-blessed hit. She catches the harmless flat of the shard. The fragment spins up into the air, but the flick is too feeble to carry it to safety. The Q-blade shard loops down and cuts sweetly, cleanly through the man's shoulder and upper right thigh before vanishing into the floor of the camarinha. He stares a moment at his arm, his severed leg, and then explodes in blood.

The capoeirista seizes Fia while she is still frozen and drags her out into the barracão.

"Shit shit shit shit shit," the woman swears. "That went wrong. I needed to know if he was Sesmaria or Order." She's in one place long enough now for Edson to see her properly. She's short, thin as a cat, loira skin and bubble-blonde hair. "They know where you are. Get out of here." The little Asian pigs are spooked, turning in their tiny pens, snorting in alarm. Sirens, Sisters, frantic initiates, and in a moment Fia is going to lose it. The entire bairro is awake. Alarm fireworks explode all across the sky. Police and drug lords alike have been blessed by the hands of the Sisters of the Good Death and will come to their aid.

Edson turns to call to the woman to help him with Fia, but she is gone. Vanished as she appeared. Tia Marizete is there, her arm now around Fia's shoulder. She stares at Fia's torso tattoo.

"I'm sorry," Edson whispers to his aunt. The gay boys are inconsolable, some weeping, most looking petty, vengeful. He cannot begin to imagine the desecration he has worked on the camarinha.

"Edson, what have gotten yourself into? These *Take Out the Trash* people, we have no argument with them, they have no argument with us. Why have they come here, why have they come for you?"

"It's not *Take Out the Trash*," Edson says. "It's . . ." What indeed, Edson Jesus Oliveira de Freitas? Quantum blades and quantum computers. Priests and orders. A gazillion universes next to each other. Capoeiristas and killers. And this Fia, this refugee with bad clothes and a computer tattooed on her belly. "I don't know, but I can't stay here."

But it won't be the Yam that takes him to safety. It lies bisected headlight to exhaust in a pool of alco and engine fluids. The insane energy, the stubborn refusal to believe what is happening to him that has kept Edson running for what feels like lifetimes gushes out of him. He feels old and scared and more tired than any human can be and there is still farther to run. He stares dumbly at the two fillets of his lovely, lovely motorbike.

"Come on, son," commands Tia Marizete, taking his hand now and drawing him after her with divine strength. "There's a ladeiro up here." Past the hysterical pigs, above the herb terraces, is a gate in a wall that leads to a steep, narrow staircase lurching between houses into a greater dank dark that smells of wet green growing. Edson stumbles after Tia Marizete, feet slipping on the slippery concrete steps. He glances back at Fia. Behind her upturned, dazed pale face, beyond the roof tiles of the Igreja, the street pulses blue and red from police beacons. Then they are out into cool and mold, above the build-line, on the hilltop in the forest. The old austral forests of north São Paulo have always been a refuge and highway for the hunted; índios to runaway slaves to drug runners. Now quantumeiros.

From her nightdress Tia Marizete finds a fist of reis—such is the axé of aunts and Sisterhood attorney generals—and presses them into Edson's hand. There's another object in there.

"Take care, be clever, be safe. This man will protect you."

More by touch than sight Edson identifies the object in his hand, a little cheap bronze statue cast from recycled wire, a malandro in a suit and porkpie hat: Exu, Lord of the Crossings.

The last place the light fills is the hollow where the water drops over the ledge into the shallow pool. The cold cold water strikes away the daze and dreams of the night. Edson gasps, paralyzed by the chill. An edge of light shines between the skinny boles of the trees, growing brighter with every moment, its dazzle burning away the silhouettes of the trunks until they dissolve into sun. Edson climbs up into the light. Fia sits as he left her, knees pulled to chest for warmth. Bronze sky, brass city. The sun pours into the bowl of São Paulo, touching first the flat roofs and sat-dishes of the favelas just beneath their feet where the people have been up for hours, on their long journeys to work in the endless city. It flows from the hilltops down the roads like spilled honey, catching on the mirrors and the chrome, turning the rodovias that curl along the hillsides to arcs of gold. Now it lights the smoke spires: the plumes from the industry and powerplant stacks, the more diffuse auras from the scattered bairros; then caught the tops of the high towers rising above of the dawn smog, towers marching farther and farther than Edson can imagine, city without end and expanding every moment as the swift-climbing sun draws lesser towers up out of the shadow. He watches an aircraft catch the light and kindle like a star, like some fantastic starship, as it banks on approach. A big plane, from another country, perhaps even another continent. *It has flown farther and yet never as far as this woman beside me*, Edson thinks.

"We lost the sun," Fia says, face filled with light. "We gave it away, we killed it. It's gray all the time; we had to fix the sky to beat the warming. Constant clouds, constant overcast. It's gray all the time. It's a gray world. I think everyone should be made to come up here and watch it so no one can take it for granted." She gives a small, choked laugh. "I'm sitting here looking at the light, but I'm thinking, Sunburn Fia, sunburn. I used to be in this university bike club, and there was this crazy thing we used to do every year: the nude bike run. Everyone would cycle this loop from Liberdade through the Praça de Sé and back wearing nothing but body paint. We used to paint each other in the wildest designs. But I'd never have burned." She bows her head to her bent knees. "I've just thought; they'll be wondering what happened to me. I just disappeared. Gone. Walked away and never came back. Oh yeah, that Fia Kishida, I wonder what happened to her? I couldn't even say good-bye to any of them. That's a cruel thing for me to do. That's one of the cruelest things anyone can do, walk away and never look back. But I could go to their houses, knock on their doors—I know where they live—and they wouldn't know me."

Edson says, "The way you're talking, it's like you'll never see them again."

Fia looks up into the holy sun.

"The crossing only works one way, there to here."

Edson thinks, *There is a smart brilliant creative Edson answer to this problem.* But there is nothing but morning out there. Everyone hits that wall at the end of his competence. Impresarios cannot solve problems in quantum computing. But a good impresario, like any man of business, knows someone who can.

"Come on." He offers a hand. "Let's go. We're going to see someone."

Five hillsides over the sound of voices drives Edson down into the undergrowth, creeping forward under cover. From behind a fallen log he and Fia watch a gang of eight favela boys camp around an old dam from the coffee age. Empty Antarctica cans and roach ends are scattered around a stone-ringed fire burned down to white ash. Three of the teenagers splash ass-naked in the pool; the others loll around on the bubble-mats, stripped down to their Jams, talking futebol and fucking. They're good-looking, beautiful-bodied, laughing boys; sex gods caught at play. Like gods, they are creatures of pure caprice.

"They're cute," Fia whisper. "Why are we hiding?"

"Look." One of the men rolls onto his side. No one could miss the skeleton gun butt in his waistband. "Malandros come up here all the time to lie low from the police. The cops have no chance of catching them; they all learn jungle skills on national service."

"Even you?"

"A businessman can't afford to give two years to the army. I worked myself a medical discharge after two months. But they would rob us, and they would have no reason not to kill us too. We're going, but move very slowly and don't make any noise."

They make no noise; they move slowly; the boys' voices recede into the forest buzz. The sun climbs high, pouring heat and dazzle through the leaf canopy. Minutes' walk on either side of this ridge trail are rodovias, lanchonetes, coffee, and gossip; the morning news is a touch away on the I-shades, but Edson feels like an old, bold Paulista bandeirante, pushing into strange new worlds.

"If I am going to help you, there's stuff I need to know," Edson says. "Like priests, and the Order, and that guy with the Q-blade, and who was that capoeirista?"

"How do I say this without it sounding like the most insane thing you've ever heard? There's an organization—more a society really—that controls quantum communication between universes."

"Like a police, government?"

"No, it's much bigger than that. It covers many universes. Governments can't touch it. It works on two levels. There's the local level—each universe has its agents—they're known as Sesmarias. Sesmarias tend to run in families: the same people occupy the same roles in other universes."

"How can it run in families?"

"I told you it would sound crazy. Some of them are very old and respectable families. But the Sesmarias are just part of a bigger thing, and that's the Order. "

"I've head that word twice in one day. You, then that capoeirista woman. So the man who attacked us at the Igreja, he was from the Order, right?"

"No, he would have been just a Sesmaria. They aren't terribly good, really. Sesmarias are allowed to contact each other but not cross. I'd hoped the Sesmaria back where I come from hadn't been able to track where I was going. Wrong there. But the Order can go wherever it wants across the multiverse. They have agents: admonitories. When they send one through, they have to tell everyone from the president of the United States to the pope."

Edson presses his hands to either side of his skull, as if he might squeeze madness out or reality in. "So capoeira woman, who is she?"

"I've never seen or heard of her before in my life. But I do know one thing."

"What?"

"I think she's on our side."

We could do with that, Edson thinks, but then a sound, a rushing sound, makes him look up, the dread back his heart. But it is not police drones moving carefully between the branches. Edson smiles and grins: high above the treetops wind turbines are turning.

"Stay as long as you need."

"You don't understand. . . ."

"I do understand. Stay as long as you need."

The moment Mr. Peach saw Edson on his security camera, and the girl behind him, he knew nothing would ever be simple again. Beneath the cherubic ceiling of the baroque living room, Sextinho and the girl are sprawled unconscious on the Chesterfield, innocently draped around each other like sibling cats. Sextinho—no, he can't call him that now. The young woman on his sofa is a refugee from another part of the polyverse. Swallow that intellectual wad and everything else follows. Of course they are caught between the ritual assassins of a transdimensional conspiracy and mysterious saviors. Of course refuge must be offered, though it marks him irrevocably as a player.

Something has fallen from Edson's fist. Mr. Peach lifts it. An ugly, mass-manufactured icon of Exu. Crossings, gateways. He smiles as he balances it on the arm of the sofa. *Watch him well, small lord.* The girl sleeps on her back, arms flung back, crop top ridden up. Mr. Peach bends close to study the tattoo. Liquid protein polymer circuitry. Infinitely malleable and morphable. There must be self-organizing nanostructures. Quasi-life. Extraordinary technology. Direct neural interface; no need for the clumsy, plasticy tech of I-shades and smart-fabrics. What was the sum of the histories of her part of the polyverse that gave rise to so similar a society, so radically different a technology? But they're all out there. There is a universe for every possible quantum state in the big bang; some as similar as this girl's, some so different that life is physically impossible.

Edson is awake, one eye open, watching.

"Hey."

"Hey. I've made you breakfast."

October 1–2, 1732

"Such fine design and so ingenious; yes yes, I can immediately see applications for this device in my own work." Father Diego Gonçalves turned the crank on the Governing Engine and watched the click and flop of the card chain through the mill and the rise and fall of the harnesses. "Drudgery abolished, mere mechanical labor transformed. Men liberated from the wheel."

"Or a subtler slavery." Through the delicately worked wooden grille Luis Quinn looked out at the river. Father Gonçalves's private apartment was at the rear of the basilica-ship, high to catch what few cooling breaths the river granted. None this day—only a heat of oppression and distant growls of thunder. Quinn pressed his head to the screen. "Someone must put his back to that wheel, someone must press the holes in the cards, and someone there must be who writes the sequence of those holes." Quinn watched a small boy squatting in the stern steering his leaf-light craft in and out of the larger canoes in Father Diego Gonçalves's entourage. The boy's younger sister, a tiny round-faced thing with her hand in her mouth, sat dumpily in the waist. For three days Quinn had watched the boy paddle from the black of the Rio Negro into the white of the Rio Branco, feeding the infant manioc cakes that he carefully unwrapped from parcels of broad forest leaves. Again, the soft rattle of Falcon's infernal machine.

"Oh, that is simplicity itself, Father Quinn: an industrial engine would be harnessed to a water sluice, or even a windmill. And the very first engine you build is the one that copies the pattern of holes for all its successors. But your third point raises an intriguing philosophical question: is it possible to construct an engine that writes the sequence for any other, and therefore logically itself?"

Thunder boomed, closer now, as if summoned by the clack of the Governing Engine. A universe ruled by number, running like punched cards through the loom of God. Luis Quinn had thought to destroy it privately, cast it into the huge waters: he had delivered it into the hands of his enemy.

Nossa Senhora da Várzea, Our Lady of the Floodplain: that was the name of the green saint on the banner and of this construct of which she was patron, a saint alien to Luis Quinn's hagiography. It had not been until he saw the short, thin figure in black descend the basilica steps that Luis Quinn realized that with every oar-sweep and paddle-stroke upstream he had been mentally drawing a picture of Father Diego Gonçalves, one sketched, like Dr. Falcon's intelligence maps, from the crude charcoal of supposition. Now as they shared the fraternal kiss of Christ, he had found those lines erased completely, beyond even this phenomenal recall, save that the Diego Gonçalves he had envisioned bore no resemblance to this bounding, energetic, almost boyish man. *This is the brother I must return to the discipline of the Order*, Luis Quinn had thought. *Open your eyes, your ears, all your senses as you did in Salvador, see what is to be seen.*

"You know what I am?"

Father Diego Gonçalves had smiled. "You are the admonitory of provincial de Magalhães of the Colégio of Salvador in Bahia."

So it was to be a duel, then.

"Would that news traveled as swiftly downriver as it travels up. Kindly have your men stop that immediately."

Índio sailors, naked but for geometrical patterns of black genipapo juice on their faces, torsos, and thighs, with feather bands plaited around upper arms and calves, were unloading Quinn's bales and sacks from the pirogue. Zemba watched suspiciously, paddle gripped two-handed, an attitude of defense.

"Forgive me, I presumed you would accept my hospitality, Brother." Father Diego's Portuguese was flawless, but Quinn heard old Vascongadas in the long vowels.

"If you are aware of my task, then you must surely be aware that I cannot compromise myself. I shall sleep in the pirogue with my people."

"As you wish." Father Diego gave orders. Quinn identified a handful of Tupi loan words. "But may we at least share the Sacrament?"

"I should at the least be interested to see if the interior of your . . . mission . . . matches its exterior."

"You will find Nossa Senhora da Várzea a complete testimony to the glory of God in every aspect." Gonçalves hesitated an instant on the steps. "Father Quinn, I trust it would not offend you if I said that word has also preceded you that you enjoy a reputation with the sword."

"I trained under Jésus y Portugal of Léon." Quinn was in no humor for false humility.

"Montoya of Toledo was my master," Father Diego said with the smallest smile, the shallowest dip of the head. "Now that would be fine exercise."

Passing beneath the watchword of his order into the basilica, Luis Quinn was at once brought up by profound darkness. Shafts fell from the high clerestory, broken into leaf-dapple by the intricate grille-work, revealing glimpses of extravagant painted bas-reliefs. An altar light glowed in the indeterminate distance; ruddy Mars to the scattered constellations of the votives. This was the dimension of a more intimate organ than the fickle eye. Luis Quinn breathed deep and extended his sense of smell. Sun-warmed wood, the rancid reek of smoking palm oil, incenses familiar and alien; green scents, herbs and foliages. Quinn started, caught by a sudden overpowering scent of verdure: green rot and dark growing. Now his sense of space and geometry came into focus; he felt great masses of heavy wood above him, decorated buttresses and bosses, a web of vaulting like the tendrils of the strangling fig, galleries and lofts. Figures looked down upon him. Last of all his eyes followed his other senses into comprehension. The exuberance the craftsmen had displayed on the basilica's exterior had within been let run into religious ecstasy. The nave was a vast depiction of the Last Judgment. Christ the Judge formed the entire rood screen; a starveling, crucified Messiah, his bones the ribs of the screen, his head thrown back in an agony of thorns each the length of Quinn's arm. His outflung arms judged the quick and the dead, his fingertips breaking into coils and twines of flowering vines that ran the length of the side panels. On his right, the rejoicing redeemed, innocent and naked índios. Hands pressed together in thanksgiving, they sported and rolled in the petals that blossomed from Christ's fingers. On the left hand of Jesus, the damned writhed within coils of thorned liana, faces upturned, begging impossible surcease. Demons herded the lost along the vines: Quinn recognized forest monsters; the deceiving curupira; the boar-riding Tupi lord of the hunt; a one-legged black homunculus in a red Phrygian cap who seemed to be smoking a pipe. Father Gonçalves waited at Quinn's side, awaiting response. When none came, he said mildly, "What does Salvador believe of me?"

"That you have transgressed the bounds of your vows and faith and brought the Society into perilous disrepute."

"You are not the first to have come here bearing that charge."

"I know that, but I believe I am the first with the authority to intervene."
Gonçalves bowed his head meekly.

"I regret that Salvador considers intervention necessary."

"My predecessors, none of them returned; what befell them?"

"I would ask you to believe me when I tell you that they departed from
me hale in will and wind and convinced of the value of my mission. We are
far from Salvador here; there are many perils to body and soul. Fierce forest
tigers, terrible snakes, bats that feed on man's blood, toothed fish that can
strip the flesh from his bones in instants, let alone any number of diseases and
sicknesses." Father Gonçalves gestured for Quinn to precede him to the choir.
The screen gate was in the shape of the heart of Christ; Gonçalves pushed it
open and bade Quinn enter.

The altar was the conventional wooden table, worked in the fever-dream
fashion of Gonçalves's craftmasters to resemble twined branches, the crucifix
its only adornment, an índio Christ, exquisitely worked, sufferings incomprehensible to the Old World borne on his face and scourged, pierced body. But
the crucifix had not taken Father Quinn's breath, powerful and alien though
it was; it was so monumentally overshadowed by the altarpiece behind it that
it seemed an apostrophe. The east end of the church, where lights and lady-
chapel would have been in a basilica of stone and glass, was fashioned into
one towering reredos. A woman, the green woman, the Saint of the Flood,
wreathed in life and glory. Nude she was, Eve-innocent, but never naked. The
saint was clothed in the forest: jewel-bright parrots and toucans, some decorated with real plumage, were her diadem; from her full breasts and milk-
proud nipples burst flowers, fruit, and tobacco; while from her navel, the
divine omphalos, sprouted vines and lianas that clothed her torso and thighs.
The beasts of the várzea dropped from her womb to crouch in adoration at
the one foot that touched the ground and struck roots across the floor into the
rear of the altar: capybara, paca, peccary, and tapir, the green sloth and the
crouching jaguar. Her other leg was bent, sole pressed to thigh, a dancer's
pose; an anaconda circled it, its head pressed to her pubis. Her right hand
held the manioc bush, her left the recurved hunting bow of the flood forest;
and fish attended her, a star-swarm like the milky band of the galaxy reflected
in black water, swimming through the woven tracery of tree boles and vines

against which Nossa Senhora danced. But true stars also attended her, the Lady twinkled with glowing points of soft radiance: glowworms pinned to the altarpiece with thorns. Again Luis Quinn caught the noble rot of vegetation; as his eyes grew accustomed to the deeper gloom around the altar and the monstrous scale of the work revealed itself to him, he saw that where rays of light struck down through the tracery of the clerestory, precious orchids and bromeliads had been planted in niches in the screen of trees: a living forest. Our Lady of the Floods was beautiful and terrible, commanding awe and reverence. Luis Quinn could feel her forcing him to his knees and by that same token knew that to genuflect before her would be true blasphemy.

"I cannot receive Mass from you, Father Gonçalves."

Again, the coy dip of the head that Quinn understood now concealed fury.

"Does not your soul crave the solace of the Sacrament?"

"It surely does, and yet I cannot."

"Is it because of the Lady, or because of the hand that gives it?"

"Father Gonçalves, did you attack and raze a Carmelite mission and take its people into slavery?"

"Yes." Quinn had expected no worming denial from Father Diego, yet the flatness of the acknowledgment shocked Quinn as if a pistol had suddenly been discharged.

"You did this contrary to the act of 1570 prohibiting enslavement of the indigenous peoples and the rule and example of our Order?"

"Come, Father, each to his role; you the admonitory, I the examiner. You are aware what that means?"

"You are empowered to judge and declare Just War against those who scorn the salvation of Christ's Church. I saw the house of God burned to the waterline, our brothers and sisters in Christ put to the sword. I spoke with a postulant, a survivor, dreadfully burned. Before she died she told me she had seen angels walking on the treetops, the angels that adorn the masts of this self-consecrated basilica."

Gonçalves shook his head sorrowfully, as at a woodenly obtuse schoolboy.

"You speak of enslavement; I see liberation. When you have seen what I have worked for Christ in this place, then presume to judge me."

Quinn strode from the choir. Day was a plane of blinding white beyond the door.

"I shall call upon you this evening to begin the examination of your soul."

But Father Gonçalves's words, thrown after him, hung in Luis Quinn's memory.

"They were animals, Father. They had no souls, and I gave them mine."

A flicker of lightning momentarily lit the receiving room. By its brief illumination Quinn saw Father Gonçalves's face as he took apart the Governing Engine; the delight and energy, the pride and intelligence. It had not been the soul of Diego Gonçalves that had been examined in this hot, high airless room; it was his own, and it had been found light. *I am of so little consequence that you prefer to study a machine.* Now came the thunder. The cloud line was almost upon them; Luis Quinn felt warm wind buffet his face. Hands ran to the rigging, reefing sails. A tap at the door; a lay brother in a white shift.

"Fathers, we have raised the City of God."

Gonçalves looked up from his study, face bright and beaming.

"Now this you must see, Father Quinn. I said you could not presume to judge me until you had seen my work; there is no better introduction."

As admonitory and pai climbed by ladders to the balcony above the portico, the basilica was simultaneously lit by lightning and beaten by thunder, a rolling constant roar that defeated very word or thought. Luis Quinn emerged into deluge; the threatened storm had broken. Such was the weight of the rain Quinn could hardly see the shore through wet gray, but it was evident that Nossa Senhora da Várzea was preparing for landfall. The greater body of the canoe fleet had fallen back, and now only two remained, big dugouts, thirty men apiece, each hauling a thigh-thick rope from its bowser beneath the narthex. Combing otter-wet hair out of his eyes, Quinn could now discern piers running far into the river; mooring posts, each the entire trunk of some forest titan sunk hip-deep in mud rapidly reverting to its proper elemental state. A cross, three times the height of a man, stood at the highest point of the bank.

The double doors opened, men and women in feather and genipapo bearing drums, rattles, maracas, reed instruments, and clay ocarinas. They stood impassive on the steps, the teeming rain running from their bodies. Father Gonçalves raised a hand. Bells pealed from the tower, an insane thunder audible even over the punishing rain. In the same instant, the assembly burst into song. Lightning backlit the monstrous cross; when his eyes had recovered their acuity, Quinn saw two streams of people pouring over the top of the bank, slipping and sliding on the mud and rain-wash, summoned by the beating bells. Again Gonçalves lifted his hand. Nossa Senhora da Várzea shook from narthex to sanctuary as she shipped oars. Now the shore folk stood waist deep in the water, fighting to seize hold of the mooring lines. More joined every moment, men and women, children alike, jamming together on the jetties. The ropes were handed up to them; the men pulled themselves out of the blood-warm water to join the effort. Hand over hand, arm by arm, Nossa Senhora da Várzea was hauled in to dock.

"Come come," Father Diego commanded, darting lightly down the perilous rain-slick companionway. Quinn could refuse neither his childlike delight nor his galvanic authority. Gonçalves raised a hand in blessing. The jetties, the piers and canoes, the haulers in the water and all across the hillside, went down on their knees in the hammering rain and crossed themselves. Then Gonçalves threw up his arms, and choir, tolling bells, thunder, and rain were drowned out by the roar of the assembled people. The choir fell in behind him, a crucifix on a pole at their head, a dripping, feather-work banner of Our Lady of the Várzea at the rear. Quinn hung on Gonçalves's shoulder as they slogged across the slopping red mud, canoes running up onto the bank on every side. Bodies were still pouring over the hill; the steep bank was solid with people.

"Citizens of heaven, subjects of Christ the King," Gonçalves shouted to Quinn. "They come to me as animals, deceptions in the shape of men. I offer them the choice Christ offers all: Accept his standard and have life in all its fullness, become men, become souls. Or choose the second standard and accept the inevitable lot of the animal, to be yoked and bound to a wheel."

Quinn wiped away the streaming water from his face. He stood with Gonçalves on a rise at the lip of the bank; before him palm-thatched longhouses ranged in concentric circles across a bare plain to the distant, rain-smudged tree-line. Remnant palms, cajus, and casuarinas gave shade, otherwise the city—no mere aldeia this—was as stark as a sleeping army. At the vacant center rose a statue of Christ risen, arms outstretched to show the stigmata of his passion, ten, ten times the height of a man. The smoke of ten thousand fires rose from the plain. And still people came, mothers with infants slung from brow straps, children, the old women with drooping flat breasts, pouring from the malocas into the muddy lanes between, their feet and shins spattered red. Striped peccaries rooted in the foot-puddled morass; dogs skipped and quarreled. Parrots bobbed on bamboo perches.

"There must be forty thousand souls here," Quinn said.

The leaping rain was easing, following the storm front into the north, set to flight by bells. To the south, beyond the masts and crowning angels of the floating basilica, shafts of yellow light broke through curdling clouds and moved across the white water.

"Souls, yes. Guabirú, Capueni, Surara nations—all one in the Cidade de Deus."

Luis Quinn grimaced at the bitter liquor. The Guabirú boy who had offered him the gourd cringed away. The storm had passed entirely, and sun rays piercing as psalms swept the plantation. Leaves dripped and steamed; a bug kicked on its back in the puddle, spasming, dying. What Luis Quinn had thought from the purview of the bank was the edge of the great and intractable forest was the gateway to a series of orchards and plantations so extensive that Quinn could see no end to them. Manioc, cane, palm and caju, cotton and tobacco, and these shady trees that Gonçalves had been so insistent he see: Jesuit's Bark, he called them.

"The key that unlocks the Amazon."

"I assume from its bitterness it is a most effective simple against some affliction."

"Against the ague, yes, yes; very good, Father. What is it holds us back from taking full stewardship of this land, as Our Lord grants us? Not the vile snakes or the heat, not even the animosity of the índios, though many of them display a childlike enthusiasm for violence. Sickness, disease, and especially the ague of the bad air, the shivering ague. A simple preparation from the bark of this tree affords complete cure and immunity, if taken as a regular draft. Can you imagine such a boon to the development and exploitation of this God-granted land? A thousand cities like my City of God; the Amazon shall be the cornucopia of the Americas. The Spanish have souls only for gold and so dismissed it as desert, wilderness; they could not see the riches that grew on every branch and leaf, under their very steel boots! As well as my Jesuit's Bark there are simples against many of the sicknesses that afflict us; I have potent analgesics against all aches and pains, herbal preparations that can treat the sepsis and even the gangrene if caught early enough; I can even cure disorders of the mind and spirit. We need not cast out with superstitious exorcism when a tincture, carefully administered, can take away the melancholy or the rage and quiet the demons."

Luis Quinn could still taste the bitter desiccation of the almost-luminous juice on his tongue and lips. A chew of cane would cleanse it; a good cigar better. He had smelled the curing leaf from the drying barns, and his heart had beat sharp in want. Now he felt a fresh cool on his still-wet back; glancing round he saw the sun halo the giant Christ, its shadow long over him. The mass bell of Nossa Senhora da Várzea intoned the Angelus; in maloca, field, and orchard the people went to their knees.

As they returned along the foot-hardened walkways, the field workers bowing in deference to their Father, Quinn let himself slip down the march to fall in with Zemba. The swift night was running down the sky; the shifting layers of air around the river pressed the smoke of the cook-fires to the ground, dense as fog.

"So friend, is this the City of God you have been looking for?" Quinn spoke in Imbangala. In the weeks chasing legends up to the confluence of the Rio Branco, Luis had been fascinated by, and learned a conversational facility with, Zemba's language. Learn the tongue, learn the man. Zemba was not so much a name as a title, a quasi-military rank, a minor princeling betrayed to Portuguese slavers by a rival royal faction of the N'gola. His letters of manumission, sealed by the royal judge of São Luis, were forgeries; Zemba, he was an escapee from a small lavrador de cana in Pernambuco who had lived five

years in a quilombo before it was destroyed, as all the colonies of escaped
slaves were destroyed, and ever since had searched for the true City of God,
the city of liberty, the quilombo that would never be overthrown.

"The City of God is paved with gold and needs neither sun nor moon, for
Christ is her light," Zemba said. "Nor soldiers, for the Lord himself is her
spear and shield."

The two-man patrols were ubiquitous; skins patterned in what Quinn
now recognized as the tribal identity of the Guabirú and armed with skillfully fashioned wooden crossbows, cunningly hinged in the middle with a
magazine atop the action. Quinn recognized the Chinese repeating crossbow
he had encountered in his researches into that greatest of empires, when he
had thought his wished-for task most difficult might lead him there, rather
than to this private empire on the Rio Branco. Quinn did not doubt that the
light wooden bolts derived much of their lethality from poisons. He murmured phrases in Irish.

"Your pardon, Father?"

"A poem in my own language, the Irish.

To go to Rome,
Great the effort, little the gain,
You will not find there the king you seek
Unless you bring him with you.

"There is truth in that." Zemba moved close to Luis Quinn. "I took my
own diversion while the Spanish father showed you the fields. I looked into
one of the huts. You should do that, Father. And the church, look in the
church; down below."

"Father!" Gonçalves called brightly. "Confidence in Our Lord is surely
the mark of a Christian; having seen what I have shown you, are you with
me? Will you help me in my great work?"

Zemba dropped his head and stepped back, but Luis Quinn had caught
the final flash of his eyes.

"What is your work, Father?"

Gonçalves halted, smiling at the ignorance of a lumbering adult, his
hands held out in unconscious mimicry of the great Christ-idol that domi-
nated his city.

"I take beasts of the field and I give souls to those that will receive them; what other work is there?"

You seek me to provoke me, Luis Quinn thought. *You desire me to react to what I see as arrogance and self-aggrandizement.* Luis Quinn folded his hands into the still-damp sleeves of his habit.

"I am nearing a judgment, Father Gonçalves. Soon, very soon, I promise you."

That night he came to the maloca that Diego Gonçalves kept as his private quarters. Pacas fled from Luis Quinn's feet; Father Diego knelt at a writing desk, penning by the yellow, odorous glow of a palm-oil lamp in a book of rag-paper. Luis Quinn watched the concentration cross Gonçalves's face as his pen creaked over the writing surface. Ruled lines, ticks, and copperplate, an account of some kind. Quinn's approach was unseen, unheard; he had always been quiet, furtive even, for a man of his size.

"Father Diego."

The man did not even start. Had he been aware all the time? Gonçalves set down the nubbin of quill.

"A judgment by night?"

The prie-dieu was the only solid furniture in this long, palm-fragrant building. Quinn settled his large frame to kneel on elaborately appliquéd cushions.

"Father Diego, who are those men and women beneath the deck of the ship?"

"They are the damned, Father. The ones who have rejected Christ and His City and so condemn themselves to animal slavery. In time they will all be sold."

"Men and women; children, Father Diego."

"They have brought it on themselves; do not pity them, they neither deserve nor understand it."

"And the sick, Father Diego?"

Gonçalves's boyish face was bland innocence.

"I am not quite certain what you mean."

"I looked into one of the malocas. I could not believe what I saw, so I looked into another, and then another and another. This is not the City of God; this is the City of Death."

"Overtheatrical, Father."

"I see no play, no amusement in whole households dead from disease. The smallpox and the measles rend entire malocas and leave not one alive. Your ledger there, so neatly ruled and inscribed—have you records there for the numbers who have died since being liberated into your City of God?"

Gonçalves sighed.

"The índio is a race under discipline. They have been given over to us by God to be tried, tested, and, yes, admonished, Father. Through discipline, through exercise, comes spiritual perfection. God requires no less than the best of us as men and as a nation sacred to Him. These diseases are the refiner's fire. God has a great plan for this land; with His grace, I will build a people worthy of it."

"Silence." Luis Quinn's accent cut like a spade. "I have seen all you have wrought here, but I take none of that into account into my judgment, which is, that you are guilty of preaching false doctrine: namely, that the people to whom you have been sent to minister are born without souls and that it has been granted you the power to bestow them. That is a deadly error, and with it, I find you also guilty of the sin of hubris, which is the fatal sin of our Enemy himself. In the name of Christ and for the love you bear Him, I require you to place yourself under my authority and return with me to São José Tarumás, and then to Salvador."

Gonçalves's lips moved as if telling beads or chewing sins.

"Buffoon."

Rage burned up in Quinn's heart, hot and sickening and adorable. *That is what he wants.* Quinn continued in the same flat, emotionless voice, "We will leave at dawn in my canoe. Instruct your headmen and morbichas in whatever they require to maintain the aldeia until your replacement has been sent from Salvador."

"I truly had expected more." Gonçalves's hands were folded piously in his lap. Palm-oil lamps cast unreadable shadows on his face. "A man of languages, from Coimbra indeed; not one of those local péons who can barely even read their own names, let alone the missal, and hear devils in every thunderstorm and várzea frog, a man of learning and perception. Refinement. Have you any idea how I long for a brother with whom I could discuss ideas and speculations as far beyond the comprehension of these dear, simple people as the firmament? I am disappointed, Quinn. I am sadly disappointed."

"You refuse my authority?"

"Authority without power is empty, Father. Brazil has no place for empty authority."

"You have seen my commission; you are aware of the license Father Magalhães has given me."

"Really? Do you really imagine you could? Against me? Almost, almost I might try it. But no, it would be a waste." An index finger lifted a fraction, and directly a dozen crossbows were trained on Luis Quinn. Quinn let his hands fall meekly open: *See, like Christ I offer no resistance.* How soon he had forgotten the guile and skill of the people of the rain forest.

"'I ask for a task most difficult,'—you said that once." Was there no limit to this man's information? "I have such a task for you. I had hoped you might embrace it willingly, even gladly; recall. Now it seems I must compel you."

"I do not fear martyrdom at your hands," Luis Quinn said.

"Of course not, nor do I imagine I could coerce you by threat to your life. Merely consider that for every bow pointed at you, three are trained on Dr. Robert Falcon as he sleeps in his hammock at the meeting of the White and Black rivers."

The two men knelt unspeaking. The compline of the forest spoke around them: insects, frogs, shrieking birds of night passage. Luis Quinn gave the barest of nods. Father Diego's finger scarcely flickered, but the bowmen disappeared like thoughts.

"Your task most difficult."

"There is a tribe beyond the Iguapará River, a vagrant people, the Iguapá, forced from their traditional terrains as other peoples flee the bandeirantes and lesser orders. You will be interested to note that their language is neither a Tupi derivative nor an Aruak/Carib variant. Among all the people of the Rio Catrimani and Rio Branco, they are known as a race of prophets. They seem to believe in a form of dream-time, akin to real time, inverted. All tribes and nations consult them, and they are always right. Their legend has bought them immunity: the Iguapá have never been involved in any of the endemic warfare that so delights these people. It is my burden to bring the Iguapá the love of Christ and his Salvation, but they are a fugitive, elusive nation. The tribes protect them, even those assimilated into my City of God, and my missionaries have so far been unsuccessful."

"My predecessors," Luis Quinn said. "The ones you said departed from you hale in will and wind. You sent them to martyrdom."

Gonçalves pursed his lips in contemplation.

"Why, I had not considered it in that fashion, but you are right, yes, yes, martyrdom I suppose it is. Certainly none survived."

"They returned to you?"

"Burning with visions and ravings, insanities and impossibilities. Their minds were quite destroyed; some were babbling and incoherent; a few even had lost the power of speech or were completely insensate." Gonçalves pressed his hands into unconscious prayer, touched them to his lips in wonder and devotion. "Most succumbed after a few days. One individual, a stout German, endured two weeks. Father Kaltenbacher led me to speculate that an individual with even more highly developed mental faculties might survive, even with the mind intact to communicate what they had seen among the Iguapá."

"Your overweening pride leads you to madness if you believe that my coming was anything other than at the order of Provincial-General de Magalhães."

"Is that what you believe?" Gonçalves asked. "Truly?" Again he touched his praying hands to his lips. "Tomorrow you will leave with your native slave and a crew of my Guabirús and travel up the Catrimani and the Iguapará. The peoples who make use of the Iguapás' talents know how to find them when they need them. You will understand if I do not take you upon your honor to travel unescorted."

"Manoel is not my slave. Neither is Zemba; he has papers of manumission, he is a free man."

"No longer; he will become a member of my personal entourage. Now I bid you a good night, Father; you have a long and arduous journey tomorrow, and you would do well to refresh yourself. Eat, rest, and devote yourself to prayer and contemplation. Rejoice, Father, you will behold glories none have ever seen and lived."

Again, the merest twitch of a finger and crossbows emerged silently from the darkness. Luis Quinn, a giant among his painted captors, glanced back. Gonçalves knelt at his desk, the quill again moving steadily over the paper. Sensible of Quinn's regard, he looked and smiled in pure, broad pleasure.

"I envy you, Father. Truly, I envy you."

OUR
LADY
OF
THE
TELENOVELAS

O Dia had it on the front page. It was relegated to page two in *Jornal do Brasil*, pushed off the cover by a photograph of the wife of the head of CBF in just a pair of soccer socks and a strategically held ball. *O Correio Brasilense* likewise carried the scoop on page two, with a recap in the entertainment pages and a three-page analysis in the sports section, concluding that maybe it was time to look objectively at the Maracanaço and that it had swept away a swaggering complacency and so led to the mighty Seleçãos of 1958 and 1970 and that Carlos Alberto Parreira might well heed the lesson of 1950. Even *Folha de São Paulo*, which deigned anything carioca as beneath serious regard, carried the story in the bottom of the front page: RIO REALITY SHOW

TO PUBLICLY TORTURE MARACANAÇO VICTIM. *Jornal Copacabana*'s Sunday Special splashed a full front page of "Professional Carioca" Raimundo Soares, arms folded, a look of righteous disgust on his face with the Sugar Loaf behind him and the lead-line SHE MADE ME BETRAY A FRIEND. *O Globo* opted for the full nuclear. Its cross-media network was ten times the size of Canal Quatro, yet it saw the upstart, adolescent independent channel as a grave threat to its key demographic and never wasted an opportunity to shit on it. A sixty-point screaming banner headline declared WELCOME BACK TO HELL. Beneath it was the lead photo of Barbosa, kneeling as if in prayer in the mouth of the Brazil goal, the ball sweetly in the back of the net. In the bottom left column was a picture of Adriano in surf shorts taken at the Intersul Television Conference in Florianopolis. *Adriano Russo, responsible for bad-taste youth-oriented shows as* Gay Jungle, Jailbait Superstar, *and* Filthy Pigs, *said that the show was in the early stages of development among a raft of World Cup Season programming and that it had not yet been green-lit. When asked if the program intended to drag the eighty-five-year-old disgraced former goalkeeper out of retirement and subject him to "trial by television" and public humiliation, Canal Quatro's director of programming said that the channel would maintain its position as the leading producers of edgy, noisy, and controversial popular television but that it was not, nor ever had been, its policy to hold older or weaker members of society up to shame.*

They had called Adriano at dinner with his wife and guests in Satyricon, made him talk in front of the diners and all the waiting staff.

Page two ran a picture of the headquarters on Rua Muniz Barreto under the headline THRONE OF LIES. Beneath, the LIST OF SHAME ran down a chart of Canal Quatro's sleaziest shows, from *Nude Big Brother* to *Queen for a Day: I'm Coming Out!* And there she was on page three, a grainy cellular snap of her at the commissioning party in Café Barbosa (a sign, a sign it had been, but against all she had assumed it to be) up on the table shaking it with her liter of Skol in its plastic cool jacket in her hand and Celso rolling his eyes as he pretended to lick her ass.

Queen of Sleaze

This is the Canal Quatro producer responsible for the Barbosa outrage, snapped during a drink-, drug-, and sex-fueled media party. Marcelina Hoffman is one of Canal Quatro's most controversial program makers: her Jailbait Superstar, *a talent show for inmates of a women's prison, created a record number of complaints when it was revealed that the winner would be released, no matter what she had done. Ironically, it was Senhora Hoffman herself who gave the game away by accidentally sending an e-mail revealing the true purpose of the program to crusading journalist Raimundo Soares, after she lied to the King of the Cariocas in return for his help in finding Barbosa. Senhora Hoffman is a well-known Zona Sul party girl, infamous for her drinking and consumption of cocaine, and is described by work colleagues as a "borderline plastic surgery addict." Her name has recently been linked with Heitor Serra, Canal Quatro's respected newsreader. . . .*

The paper fell from Marcelina's fingers. With a keening, animal cry she lay back among the tabloids and broadsheets scattered across Heitor's floor, haloed in shouting headlines. HELP US FIND BARBOSA FIRST! RS 50,000 REWARD! SAVE BARBOSA. FIFTY YEARS IS ENOUGH.

Footsteps. Marcelina opened her eyes. Heitor stood over her like a Colossus, like the anticipation of water-sport sex, bizarrely foreshortened.

"I'm dead."

Heitor kicked the papers across the room.

"How long have you been here?"

"Forever. I couldn't sleep, and when I could I dreamed I was awake. Do you have to get all the papers delivered?"

"It's my job."

Heitor had dropped back from the studio after the eleven thirty news update expecting Furaçao Marcelina to have blown through his apartment, strewing books, upturning tables, shattering glasses and fine china, shredding suits slashing paintings smashing the religious statues and images he had so adoringly collected over two decades of spiritual seeking. He had found something much more frightening: Marcelina seated in the middle of the floor, naked but for tanga, one knee pulled up to her breasts, the other folded around its ankle. She clutched her shin with both arms. Television cast the only light. When she looked up, Heitor saw a face so ghost-eaten, so alien that he had almost cried out, home invaded.

"Look."

Marcelina had uncurled a fist holding the DVD remote, beeped it at the screen.

"What is it?"

"Don't you see?" Marcelina had howled, and in her voice the hurricane broke. "It's me."

Heitor prised the remote out of her fingers, vanished the apparition paused in the act of looking up into the camera.

"In the morning."

"No, not in the morning."

"Get that down you."

He had filled a glass from the refrigerator.

"What is it?"

"Just water." Plus a capsule from his kitchen pharmacopoeia. "You need to rehydrate."

"She wants rid of me," Marcelina had said, sipping the water.

"Who?"

"The me."

The pill kicked in before she had finished the glass. Heitor lifted her into his bed. She was as small and light as a street dog. Heitor felt ashamed of all the times he had pinned her under his broad body; her thin, angular bones bending, her wiry thighs wrapped around his wide hairy back.

Ninety percent of Heitor's cabinet of cures was out of date. Marcelina had come up out of the sleeping pill like a sea-launched missile. He snored; she padded into the living room to look again at the thing she could not comprehend. Again and again she watched the figure in the sweet black suit enter through the revolving door, go up to Lampião, and finally turn to look up into the camera for some clue, some truth. She had slowed the DVD down to a click through the individual frames. That was how she had found the tiny hint of a smile on her face, as if she—her—had intended that Marcelina see her grand imposture. Again and again and again, until the engine drone and brake-creak of the delivery boy's LiteAce, the sound of feet on steps, and the thud of bundled papers against the back door.

Across the room Marcelina's cellular sang "Don'cha Wish Your Girlfriend Was Hot Like Me," Brasiliero remix.

"Aren't you going to get that?" A bone-deep media-ista, Heitor could be driven to high anxiety by an unanswered telephone.

"It'll be the Black Plumed Bird."

"I'll get it for you."

"No!" Then, gently, "I don't want her to know you're here. The papers . . ."

"I can see the papers. You have to talk to her sometime."

The SMS alert jabbered, a recording of a very high travesti raving at the Copa carnaval party about his upcoming surgery.

"Give me a sweatshirt or something, then."

On the balcony Marcelina strode up and down in panties and a holey old hoodie. Across the lagoon the apartment blocks were a holy city of silver and gold; the last rags of early mist burned off the green hills, and fit girls were running on the lakeside loop. Heitor tried to read Marcelina's hands.

"So?"

Marcelina dropped onto the leather sofa.

"Bad enough. She told me to take some unofficial leave; basically, I'm suspended on full pay."

"They could have fired you on the spot."

"She talked Adriano down from that. She's giving me the benefit of the doubt that I didn't send the e-mail, that it was some kind of industrial espionage or someone hacked my computer. I think I may have got it wrong about the Black Plumed Bird."

"And the show?"

"Adriano thinks it may have done us some good. APRIGPR."

"We don't get his text speak down in News and Current Affairs."

"All PR Is Good PR. He'll wait until he sees if there's a ratings backlash against *Rede Globo*. I may get it yet."

"There's another call you need to make." Heitor's espresso machine filled the kitchen zone with shriekings and roarings.

"I know. Oh, I know." Her mother would be drunk, would have been drinking slowly, steadily all night, one slow little vodka at a time, watching the mesh of headlights along the rainy avenues of Leblon. Frank Sinatra had turned away. It had always been nothing more than reflections from a glitterball. Your self shattered into a thousand spangles and mirrored back to you. "And I will make it. But I can't stay here, Heitor."

"Oswaldo has hinted that it might not be the best thing for my professional objectivity. Stay as long as you need. I'm not Jesus."

"It's not about you. Can you understand that? It's not about you. It's just that, while she's still out there, I need you to be able to trust me, and that can only happen if you know that if I call or e-mail or drop round, it won't be me. It'll be her and whatever she says will be a lie."

"I'd know her. I interviewed a policeman once who worked with forged banknotes. I asked him how he learned to spot the fakes and he said, by looking at the originals. I'd know you anywhere."

"Did Raimundo Soares know? Did any of the people she sambaed past at Canal Quatro know? Did my sisters and my own mother know? No, it's safer this way."

"And how will I know when it's over?"

"I haven't worked that out yet!" Marcelina snapped. "Why are you making this harder for me? I don't know how any of this is going to work, but I do know that I am a very, very good researcher and it's time for me to stop being the hunted and turn it all around and become the hunter. What am I hunting? Myself. That's all I can say about it. Something that looks like me, sounds like me, thinks like me, knows what I'm going to do before I do it, and is absolutely dedicated to destroying me. Why, I don't know. I'll find that out. But I do know that if it looks like me and thinks like me and talks like me, then it is me. How, I don't know either. You tell me—you've shelf-fuls of books out there on everything under the sun. You've got a theory for everything: give me one, any one that makes any sense."

"Nothing does make any sense." Heitor sat heavily on the opposing creaking leather minimalist sofa-cube across the glass coffee table.

"That doesn't matter. Do you want to see the DVD again and tell me that isn't real?"

"Some error of timing?"

"Ask my entire development team. They were smoking my blow at the time."

"Well, if your evil twin is barefaced enough to get deliberately caught on camera at Canal Quatro, why did she disguise herself at terreiro?"

"I don't know. Maybe it wasn't her. Maybe there's another player. I'll find out." Marcelina fiddled with her coffee cup. "Do you think I have an evil twin? Do you think my mother . . . ? She had her glittering career—she was Queen of Beija-Flor—and I always felt I was inconvenient. Could she have . . . no. Not even her at her most fucked up. . . ."

But it seduced, a great archetype: the twins separated at birth, one spun into the neon and sequins of the Copacabana; the other to obscurity hungry, and now she had returned to claim her birthright. Had she seen this in a telenovela once?

"Ask her," Heitor said.

Perhaps the coffee, perhaps the psychotherapeutic arrangement of the sofas, perhaps just the bell-like clarity of a friend listening and asking the one question that made it fall apart into brilliant facets. Suddenly the face in the freeze-frame, the papers scattered across the floor, were clear and simple. Of course there was no spirit-Marcelina woven out of stress and wisps of axé blowing between the morros. There was no magic in the hills or in the city: Heitor's bleak philosophy allowed no magic into the world at all. No ghosts no Saci Pererés no doppelgängers no parallel universes. Just an old family secret come to take her due. But you don't know Marcelina Hoffman. She is the capoeirista; she takes down the smart boys with jeito and malicia: she is the malandra.

She had dried her clothes at midnight in Heitor's tumble dryer—his cleaner believed in laundry on a Monday and it was no use asking Heitor; white goods hated him. He could not even properly operate his microwave and certainly his oven had never been used. Her jeans were tight and stiff as she forced her way into them, the top shrunken to overclinginess and her shoes still damp, the insoles stained. She swung her bag over her shoulder.

"Where will you go?"

"I'll find somewhere. Not home."

"How will you let me know when you've done whatever it is you need to do?"

"You'll know, newsboy." She stood up on tiptoes to kiss Heitor, old big growly bear-man. So easy to stay among the books and the minimalist leather, the picture glass and the slinky little playsuits, so easy to drop everything onto him and burrow down into his mass and depth. So dangerous. No one was safe until she had the mystery under her foot in the roda. "How exactly do you go about asking you mother, 'Mum, do I have a secret twin sister you gave away at birth?'"

Heitor's Blackberry chirruped. It was not the first time sex had been interrupted by his RSS headline feed. She felt him tighten against her, muscle armoring.

"What is it, big bear?"

"That guy you went to see at the terreiro."

"Bença Bento?"

"He's been found dead. Murdered. Cut to pieces in the night." Heitor hugged her to him, that strong-gentle crush-fearful delicacy of big men. "You be careful, oh so careful."

The hat was shaped like an enormous upturned shoe, the sole brimming low over the kiss-curl, the heel—solid, chunky, Cubano even—a brave crest. Marcelina lifted it with the reverence of the host.

"Go on, try it," Vitor urged, his face silver-screen brilliant.

Marcelina almost laughed at her reflection in the long mirror, put her hands on her hips and struck vampish, Carmen Mirandaesque poses, pout pout. Mwah. Then the light shifted, as it did dramatically in this old dream-theater, and in the sudden chiaroscuro she saw the Marcelina Hoffman her mother had dreamed: a silvery, powered night-moth, the toast of the Copacabana stepping out of the deep dark of the mirror. Marcelina shivered and snatched off the hat, but the sun grew strong again through the glass roof and she saw in the flaking silvering a pair of silver wings, and silver muscle-armor—pecced and abbed and burnished—and there a bloated, chinoiserie horror-baby mask.

"It's . . . ," she said, wondering.

"The wrong Brazil," Vitor said. "They were striking set after the shoot, and it was all a dreadful kerfuffle and someone thought it was the shipping destination."

Vitor was of a generation whose duties and obligations went beyond those of alt dot families and honored still the carioca tradition of providing a bed and a beer for a night or a year and asking no questions. He had flung open his little shop of kitscheries to Marcelina, blown up the air mattress for her in

the box room cluttered with boxes of old movie magazines and soccer programs, and when she had asked if there was a place where she could see her
apartment without being seen, had without a word unlocked the door at the
end of kitchen and ushered her through into the only true magic that Rio still
knew. Marcelina had always wondered where Vitor had found the art deco
treasures that had so perfectly topped off the interiors in *Kitsch and Bitch*. His
apartment, odd-proportioned, impractical rooms, strange staircases, and interior balconies, was the converted foyer of a lost cinema, a jewel box of the
1940s smothered in cheap, shoving blocks like a forest tree within a strangler
fig. Beneath the vaulted ceiling all the old movies had come to die. Props, sets,
flats, lighting rigs, and costumes, entire World War Two fighter aircraft,
pieces of ocean liner, cafés, and casas were jammed and piled together.

"They put everything in here, just in case they ever needed it again," Vitor
said as he led Marcelina up to the top gallery. "And then someone locked the
door and walked away and everyone forgot about it until I did a bit of dig-
ging into the *Jornal* records. Mind your step there, the damp's got in."

There's a program idea in here somewhere, Marcelina had thought; and it was
grounding, it was sanity, it was the ineluctable truth of the trivial. There was
a sun still in the sky and Jesus on a mountain. Now, even as she laid down
the surreal shoe-hat, she gave a little cry: perched on a polystyrene head, all
waxen pineapples and bananas be-dusted, was the original tutti-frutti hat.

"Here's a good place." Heitor opened a door into blinking, blinding
light; a small room one side of which was a great circular window, leaded as if
with vines. He patted a wicker chair. "You can see everything from up here, and
no one will see you because no ever looks up. I'll bring you tea by and by."

It was a fine belvedere, part of a former bar, Marcelina theorized, commanding a sweep of street life: the convenience store, the two bars, the kilo-
metric restaurant and the dry cleaners, the video store and the Chinese restaurant, and the lobbies of thirty apartment blocks, her own among them. So
near, so secret. How many times, she wondered, might Vitor have watched
her comings and goings? A freeze of fear: might her enemy have watched
from this very seat and noted down her routines? Vitor would not have
known; Vitor had met her already, when she snubbed him on the street, and
had not known the difference. Paranoia. Paranoia was understandable.

Once, twice, three times Marcelina jerked herself awake, nodding into a doze in the comfortable, dusty warmth of the cupola. Investigative work, surveillance, had never been her thing. Running around with cameras and sound booms, PDAs and release forms; that was the game. Vitor brought tea, twice. He never asked what she was doing there, watching the silver door of her apartment, never once mentioned her brief notoriety in the Sundays—a proper World Cup scandal had swept her into the center pages on all but the Globo papers. The old men and women came back from the beach. The street vendors worked the intersection. The bars put out tables and lit up televisions, a steady line of home-shifting workers went into the 7-Eleven and came out with bottled water and beer and beans. She learned the timetables of the metro trains arriving at Copacabana Station by the pulses of pedestrians down the streets. She saw Vitor take his accustomed seat by the street, order his tea, and open his paper. Friends and acquaintances stopped to chat for a moment, a minute, an hour. *That looks a good life*, Marcelina thought. Uncomplicated, investing in relations, humane and civilized. Then she thought, *You'd be bored bored bored within half an hour. Give me* Supermodel Sex Secrets *and* How to Make Love Like a Porn Star.

She could procrastinate no longer. Marcelina called her mother.

"Hi. It's me. Don't hang up. Are you all right? Are you okay? Have you been, you know? Don't hang up."

"Iracema's very hurt. I can't even begin to say how hurt she is; Gloria too, and me, well I'm more disappointed than anything. Disappointed and surprised; it's not like you, why did you do a thing like that?" An edge of rasp in the voice, a three-day vodka hangover simmering off.

Ask her, ask her now; you have your opening. All the shadow-lengthening afternoon she had toyed with tactics, openings and moves, feints and concessions, the edged tools from her box of professional instruments but ultimately hinging around the one strategic problem: to apologize and call later with the Hard Question, or to say it once and for all.

Marcelina decided.

"I know you won't believe me if I say it wasn't me—and I know I should just have apologized there and then. I don't know why I started that argument, but I did and I'm sorry." *This much is true.* Pleading guilty to a lesser charge. Another sharp little tool of the information trade. "You've probably seen the stuff in the paper by now."

"Are you all right? Is everything okay?"

Are you a liar and a hypocrite? Marcelina asked herself. *So long and so old and so tired it's become truth?*

"Mum, this is going to sound strange—maybe even the strangest thing I've ever said—but, am I the only one?"

Dead air.

"What, love? I don't understand. What are you talking about?"

"I mean, is there . . ." The sentence hung unfinished. Marcelina heard her mother's voice squawking, "What what what?" Standing in the open doorway of the apartment block applying lippy, closing a little Coco bag, the door swinging softly, heavily shut behind her. Her. The one. The evil twin. "Got to go Mum bye I love you."

Marcelina dashed through the dark loom of the gallery knocking over dummies, sending costumes rocking on their rails. She jumped over the rotten woodwork, took the stairs two at a time. Lilac evening had poured into the streets; lights burned; people stared as she ran past them. Where where where? There. Marcelina ran the intersection; cars jolted to a halt, aggressively sounded horns.

"Darling . . . ," Vitor called after her.

Good suit. Good heels, confident heels—she can see them snapping at the sidewalk twenty, nineteen, eighteen people ahead of her. *She walks like me. She is me.* Left turn. *Where are you going? Do you live within a spit of my home; have you lived here for years without my knowing, our paths and lives always that step out of synchronization; the two Marcelinas?* Fifteen, fourteen people. Marcelina shouldered through the evening strollers, the dog-walkers, the power walkers. She could see her now. A little heavier? Hands a little broader, nails unsophisticated. Ten, nine, eight people. *I'm behind you now, right behind you, if you looked around right now you would see me. Me.* And Marcelina found that she wasn't afraid. No fear at all. It was the game, the burn, the car lifted on the Rua Sacopã, the pictures coming together in the edit, the pitch when they get it, see it, when it all opens up in front of them; the moment when idea becomes incarnate as program.

I am behind you now.

Marcelina reached out to touch her twin's shoulder.

"Excuse me."

The woman turned. Marcelina reeled back. This was no twin. A twin she would have known for its differences, its imperfections, the subtle variations spun out of the DNA. This was herself, precise to the moles, to the hair, to the slight scar on the upper lip, to the lines around the eyes.

"Ah," Marcelina said. "Oh."

She heard the blade before she saw it, a shriek of energy, an arc of blue. And the malicia kicked: before sense, long before conscious thought, Marcelina dropped back to the ground in a negativa angola. The blade whistled over her face. Screams, shouts. People fled. Cars stopped, horns blared. Marcelina rolled out of the defensive drop with a kick. The blade cut down again. Marcelina flipped into a dobrado, then wheeled for a crippling kick. Two hands seized her pants and ankles and pulled her away. The knife slashed again, seeming to cut the air itself; the A-frame sign for the Teresina pay-by-weight restaurant fell into two ringing halves. The woman turned and ran. Marcelina struggled, but the hands held her.

"Leave it," a man's voice ordered. "This is beyond you. Leave it."

Now she was quite quite mad, for the voice, the hands, the face belonged to Mestre Ginga.

FEBRUARY 2–10, 2033

Mr. Peach adores her.

"First halfway-stimulating conversation I've had in months," he says to Edson in the privacy of breakfast moments while Fia is in the shower. She is a bathroom girl; the sound of her happy splashing carries far up and down the fazenda's cool tiled corridors.

"Never mind that," says Edson. "Is all the gear stowed away?"

Mr. Peach holds up a big old iron key. Fia comes in patting the ends of her hair dry with a towel. She knows Mr. Peach as Carlinhos; a kind of uncle in Edson's far-flung family, scattered like stars linked in a constellation. They're going to talk science again.

Edson hates it when they do that. He bangs aluminum things in the kitchen while they argue quantum information theory.

The best Edson understands it is this: Fia had been part of a research team using her University of São Paulo quantum mainframe to explore multiversal economic modeling, entangling so many qubits—that, Edson understands, is the word—across so many universes that it has the same number of pieces as a real economy. And, Mr. Peach says, if the model is as complex as the things it models, is there any meaningful difference? In Fia's São Paulo—in Fia's world—it seems to Edson that tech-stuff took a different turn sometime in the late teens, early twenties. Where Edson's world solved the problem of processors and circuit boards so small that quantum effects became key elements, Fia's world learned to use proteins and viruses as processors. Semiliving computers you can tattoo on your ass as opposed to cool I-shades and the need to reel out ever-more-complex security codes to satisfy a paranoid, omniscient city. But Fia's people killed their world. They couldn't break the oil addiction, and it burned their forests and turned their sky hot sunless gray.

They were on about superpositions again. That's where a single atom is in two contradictory states at the same time. But a physical object cannot be two things at once. What you measure is that atom and its exact corresponding atom in another universe. And the most likely way for both to be in a state of superposition is for them each to be in quantum computers in their own universes. So in a sense (big brain itch here, right at the back of Edson's head where he can't reach it) there are not many many quantum computers across millions of universes. There is just one, spread across all of them. That's what Fia's economic model proved; what they're calling the multiversal quantum computer. Then she created a quantum model of herself and found that it was more than a dumb image. It was Mr. Peach's storm blowing between worlds. It was a window to all those other Fia Kishidas with whom it was entangled. The ghost Fias Edson had glimpsed in the workshop in

Cook/Chill Meal Solutions were counterparts in other worlds spellbound by entanglement.

Edson bangs down the pot and cups.

"Carlinhos. I need to borrow your car." Edson's going shopping. Out on the streets of his big dirty city with his hands on the wheel and one of the many backup identities he's stashed all across northwest Sampa, I-shades feeding him police maps, Edson feels his mojo returning. Careful. Overconfidence would be easy and dangerous. For this kind of operation he would normally have picked up an alibi, but that's not safe after that poor bastard Petty Cash. The Sesmarias may be out of the game, but there are those other bastards: the Order, who ever they are; and then the cops, always the cops. No, a malandro can't be too careful. He takes camera-free local roads and backstreets to the mall. Among the racks and hangers is bliss. It is good to buy, but he dare not use his debit account. If the stores don't give him a discount for cash—and many will not even accept notes—he moves on to another one.

"Hey, got you something to make you look less like a freak." From the glee with which she throws herself on the bright bags, Edson concludes there are other things than physics that light up Fia Kishida.

"Did you choose for me or for you?" she asks, holding up little scraps of stretchy sequined fabric.

"You want to look Paulistana?" Edson says.

"I want not to look like a hooker," Fia says, hooking down at the bottom of her cheek-clinging shorts. "But I love these boots." They are mock-jacaré, elasticated with good heels, and Edson knew she would coo and purr at first try-on. The crop top shows off the minute detail of her tattoo-computer; in the low light slanting across the fields of oil-soy it burns like gold. Edson imagines the wheels and spirals turning, a number mill.

"Where I come from, it's rude to stare."

"Where I come from, people don't have things like that tattooed on them."

"Do you ever actually apologize for anything?"

"Why should I do that? Come and eat. Carlinhos is making his moqueça. You need to eat more."

In the cool of the evening, Edson finds Mr. Peach leaning against his balcony rail with a big spliff in his hand. The burbs glow like sand beneath him; the stars cannot match them. Even the light-dance of the Angels of Perpetual Surveillance, like attenuated bioluminous Amazon insects, up on the edge of space, is muted and astrological. The night air brings with it the slur of wind turbines up on the old coffee plantations, a sound Edson has always found comforting and stimulating. Endless energy.

"Hey, Sextinho." Mr. Peach offers Edson the big sweet spliff.

"I've told you not to call me that," Edson says, but takes a good toke anyway and lets it swirl up into the dome of his skull. Mr. Peach leans toward him. He takes another toke from Edson, slips an arm comfortably around his back. He holds the spliff up, contemplates it like holy sinsemilla.

"This the only thing keeping me from running right out that gate and getting on the first plane to Miami," Mr. Peach says, looking at the coil of maconha smoke

"Miami?"

"We've all got our boltholes. Our Shangri-las. When it's abstract, when it's more universes than there are stars in the sky, than there are atoms in the universe, I can handle it. Numbers, theories; comfortable intellectual games. Like arithmetic with infinities: terrifying concepts, but ultimately abstract. Head games. She didn't know me, Sextinho."

Edson lets the name pass.

"She didn't recognize me. She would have known me, same as . . . the other one. Jesus and Mary, the word games this makes us play. Quantum theory, quantum computing, quantum schmauntum; at that postgrad level you work across disciplines. But she didn't recognize me. I wasn't there. Maybe I was dead, maybe I was in jail, maybe I never was a physicist, maybe there never was a Carlinhos Farah Baroso de Alvaranga. But I know: I'm in Miami. I could have gone. Twenty years ago I could have gone. Open arms, they'd have had me. Lovely doe-eyed Cuban boys with nasty Mafia connections. But Dad would have had to go into a home, and I couldn't do that. Leave him. Leave him with strangers. So I turned the offer down, and he lived three years and I think he was happy right up to the end. By then I was too old, too entangled. Too scared. But he went. He's leading the life I could have led. I should have led."

Mr. Peach quickly wipes any tears gone before they gather gravity.

Edson says gently, "I remember you told me once that it was all fixed, from beginning to end; like the universe is one thing made out of space and time and we only dream we have free will."

"You're not reassuring me."

"I'm just trying to say, there was nothing you could have done."

The spliff has burned down to a sour roach. Edson grinds it flat under the sole of his Havaiana.

"Sextinho . . . Edson. I think I really need to be with you tonight."

"I thought we'd agreed."

"I know but, well, why should it matter if it's not her?"

Edson loves the old bastard, and he could come for him, without games, without boots and costumes, without masks, pretend to be that nasty Cuban malandro, pretend to be whatever he needs to send him to Miami in his mind. But still, it does matter. And Mr. Peach can read that in Edson's body, and he says, "Well, looks like it's not fated in this universe either."

In retro Hello Kitty panties, Fia backstrokes laps of the pool. From verandah shadow Edson watches sunlit water dapple her flat boy-breasts. He checks for stirrings, urgings, dick-swellings. Curiosity, getting a look, like any male. Nothing more.

"Hey." She treads water, face shatter-lit by reflected sun-chop. "Give me a towel."

Fia hauls herself out, drapes the towel over the mahogany sun lounger and herself on the towel. Nipples and little pink panty-bow.

"This is the first time I've felt clean in weeks," Fia declares. "He's not your uncle, is he? I found your stuff. I couldn't sleep so I went poking around. I do that, poke around. I found these costumes and things. They're very . . . sleek."

"I told him to make sure they were locked up."

"Why? If you guys have something going on, I'm cool with it. You don't have to hide stuff from me. Did you think I would be bothered? Did she know? That's it, isn't it? She didn't know."

"You're not her, I know. But are you bothered?"

"Me. No. Maybe. I don't know. It bothers me you didn't tell her."

"But you said—"

"I know, I know. Don't expect me to be consistent about this. What did you do, anyway, with the gear and all that?"

"Superhero sex."

Her eyes open wide at that.

"Like, Batman and Robin slashy stuff? Cool. I mean, what do you actually do?"

"What's it to you?"

"I'm a nosy cow. It's got me into trouble already."

"We dress up. We play. Sometimes we pretend to fight, you know, have battles." Hearing it spoken, the secret spilled, Edson feels burningly embarrassed. "But a lot of the time we just talk."

"I'm trying to picture Carlinhos in one of those full suits. . . ."

"Don't laugh at him," Edson says. "And I call him Mr. Peach. The first time we met, he gave me peaches for minding his car because he didn't have any change. He watched me eat them. The juice ran down my chin. I was thirteen. You probably think that's a terrible thing; you probably have some clever educated middle-class judgment about that. Well, he was very shy and very good to me. He calls me Sextinho." There is an edge in his voice that makes Fia feel self-conscious, tit-naked in an alien universe. It's their first row. A motorbike passes the gate. Edson notes it, remembers fondly his murdered Yamaha scrambler. A few seconds later it passes the gate again in the opposite direction. Slow, very slow. Edson feels his eyes widen. He looks up. A surveillance drone completes it buzz over the shiny new gated estate, but does it linger that moment too long on the outward turn? He had been so careful in Mr. Peach's car, but there were always cameras he could have missed, a new one put up, an eye on a truck or a bus or in a T-shirt or even a pair of passing I-shades that later got into a robbery or an I-mugging or something that would have had the police running through the memory. Paranoia within paranoia. But everyone is paranoid in great São Paulo.

He says, "How long have you been here now?"

"Three days," Fia says. "Why are you asking?"

"You've been talking all that physics—"

"Information theory . . ."

"Whatever shit, but I want to ask, have you found a way back yet?"

"What do you mean?"

"You said it was a one-way trip, there was no going back."

"Well, a quantum mainframe the size of São Paulo U's would do. Why do you want to know?"

"Because I think they're looking for us." That gets her sitting upright. Hello Kitty. "In fact, I think they know where we are. We're not safe here. I can get you safe, but there's one problem. It's going to take a lot of money."

Bare-ass naked on the pseudo-Niemeyer wave mosaic by the green green pool Edson holds the towel in one hand and asks the soldados, "Where do I go?"

They grunt him to the landscaped sauna at the back of the spa. Both High and Low Cidades know The Man has a morbid fear of age and wreck and spends profanely on defeating it. No one in the two cities expects him to live so long, but he has resident Chinese medics and Zen hot springs for his hilltop pousada. Some sonic-electric field tech thing holds in the heat. The Man beckons Edson join him on the hardwood bench. Around him sit his soldados, as naked as he; stripped-down guns at easy reach on the hot wood: the Luz SurfTeam, they call themselves. They have surfers' muscles and scrolls of proud dotted weals across their chests and bellies where they pierce themselves and carefully rub in the ashes of scarification ritual. Edson sits carefully, conscious of his shaved genitals, unsure of the etiquette of being caught staring at your drug lord's dick.

"Son, do we find you well?" The Man is nested in as many names as his corporate structure. The lower city, where his writ runs partial, knows him as Senhor Amaral; in the upper city he is Euclides. Only the priest who baptized him knows his full name. Layers, pyramids: he is fleshy, rolls of fat tapering toward his hairless head, shaved as close as Edson's balls. "And the dona, how is she this weather?" When Anderson died, Euclides the Man sent flowers and condolences with a picture of Our Lady of Consolation. He claims to be as omniscient as the Angels of Perpetual Surveillance, but he does not know that Dona Hortense shredded the card and, by dark of moon, threw the flowers into the fetid, Guraná-bottle-and-dead-piglet-choked sewer that is Cidade de Luz's storm drain. "I hear you've been causing that good lady grief, Edson."

"Senhor, I would not put my own mother in any kind of danger, believe that." Edson hears the shake in his voice. "Could I show you something? I think you'll be impressed." Edson lifts his hand. The SurfTeam stirred toward their guns. The Man nods. Edson completes the gesture and out of the changing room bounds Milena in her monogrammed top and patriotic thong and socks, soccer ball skittering like a puppy before her, blithely chewing her gum before her audience of naked male meat. *Remember what I taught you*, Edson wills at her as she keeps the ball up up up. *Smiling smiling always smiling.*

"So, senhor, what do you think?" *After this*, Edson thinks, *one hundred thousand fans at Morumbi are easy.*

"I am impressed; the girl has a talent. Now, she will need some surgery up top, and I am sure you have that already planned, but her ass is good. She has a Brasilian ass. How long can she keep it up for?" The Man slaps the soldado beside him hard on the thigh. "Hey, you like that white ass? That getting you stiff, eh?" Slap slap. *I would remember that, if I were him*, Edson thinks. "Jigga jigga eh?" Slap slap slap. "Who's got boners, eh? Come on, show me, who's hard?" Everyone but The Man, Edson notices. And Edson. "So, son, I am rightly entertained, but you didn't come up here just to show me your Keepie-Uppie Queen."

"That's correct," Edson says. "I'm here because I'm planning an operation, and I need your permission."

Pena Pena Pena! The word up and down the ladeiros, running down the serpentine main street of Cidade de Luz like sheet-water, rumored through the diners and supermarkets, the ball courts and the lamp standards where carpimpers hard-wired their arc-welders and spray-guns. Black cock tail-feathers stuck into the verge mud, poked through the wire mesh of a front gate, tucked under windscreen wipers. Stencil-cut roosters sprayed onto shop shutters, curbstones, into the corners of bigger, bolder swaths of street art; the cheeky, ballsy little black cock. His crow sounded across the hillside from the rodovia to the bus station, from the Assembly of God to the Man high over all: call the boys, the good old boys, the gang is back.

They met in the back office of Emerson's gym among the broken exercise machines: Emerson himself; Big Steak—could do with patronizing his own gym; Turkey-Feet with his Q-blade; that fool Treats because if he had been left out he would have blown the whole thing; then the car boys Edimilson and Jack Chocolate from the garage; Waguinho and Furação the drivers; and, honorary Penas, Hamilcar and Mr. Smiles for stealth and security, looking simultaneously superior and scared.

"And me," Fia had said. "You used my money, I want to see what you're spending it on."

"It wasn't your money. Someone had to know how to place the bet. And some of the guys, they knew you from before."

Edson had to admit, it was a brilliant little scam. Fia had come banging on his door in the wee wee hours, a look of wide-eyed astonishment on her face. Edson had been out of his bed in an instant, bare-ass naked, reaching for Mr. Peach's gun thinking, *Killers Sesmarias pistoleiros.*

"I can't believe it, you've got *A World Somewhere!*"

O Globo 12 ran twenty-four-hour telenovelas, and in the insomniac hours Fia had channel surfed onto a quantum marvel. ("Everything happens somewhere in the multiverse," Mr. Peach had said at breakfast the next morning where they cracked the plan over the eggs and sausage.) Not just that Edson's universe too had *A World Somewhere*, but that it was identical to the one to which Fia had been secretly addicted: cast, characters, and plot. With one significant, big-money-making difference: the telenovela in Edson's universe was a week behind. Edson even remembered the cause: Fia—the other Fia—had explained that it was a strike by the technicians. It had gone to the wire, but they had walked out all the same. It had seemed important to her at the time. In Fia's universe, they had made the deal.

"The same, word for word?"

She nodded, dumbfounded.

"Are you sure?"

Big big eyes.

"Information is power," he had declared over breakfast eggs and sausage. "How can we make money out of this?"

"That's easy," Fia said. "Boy-love." Mr. Peach scrambled eggs, unperturbed. For two months now *A World Somewhere* had been working up to a culminating moment of passion and oral between Raimundo and Ronaldão. If Edson ever bothered to watch the television read mags follow the chat channels, he would have known that the most important question in Brasil was *will they/won't they?* The bookies' odds were dropping day by day as the Notorious Episode approached: it surely must happen: boy-love on prime time. As part of the buildup the writers had been holed up in a hotel under armed guard. Expectation was sky-high, advertising prices cosmological.

But Fia had already watched that ep.

It was a complicated bet; small amounts liquidated from antiques donated by Mr. Peach spread around backstreet bookies all over northern São Paulo, never enough to shift the odds, sufficiently far apart to break up a pattern. Edson, Fia, and Mr. Peach cruised the boulevards, swinging coolly into the back-alley rooms and slapping the reis down on the Formica table.

Edson was so engrossed sending the black feathers and the pichaçeiros with the cockerel stencils out into Cidade de Luz to summon the old team that he completely missed the Notorious Episode.

Old Gear summoned his safe out of the floor and fetched sufficient reis to bathe in.

"How did you know they'd chicken out at the last moment? Were you holding a scriptwriter's mother hostage or something?"

"Or something," Edson said.

And standing up in front of the old Penas in Emerson's gym, sports-bags full of reis under the desk, Edson had watched the years scatter like startled birds. He was twelve again, and with the rolling back of hope and achievement came the bitter realization that for all his ambition he had never been able to fly fast enough to escape Cidade de Luz's gravity. *You end as just another malandro with a gun and a gang.*

"Thank you all for coming. I have a plan, an operation. I can't achieve it myself; I need your help. It's not legal"—laughs here: *As if, Edson*—"and it's not safe. That's why I wouldn't ask you as friends, even as old Penas. Don't think I'm insulting anyone's honor when I offer to pay you, and I'll pay well. I had a bit of a windfall. A couple of bets came in. You know me; I will always be professional." He takes a breath and the room holds its breath with him. "It's a big ask, but this is what I want to do. . . ."

"I see no political objections to you planning an operation," says The Man, leaning into the heat so that the sweat drips from his nipples. "Edson, I respect your businesslike attitude, so I'm offering you fifteen percent off the standard license fee."

Edson realizes he's been holding his breath. He lets it out so slowly, so imperceptibly, that the sweat-beads on his thin chest do not even shiver.

"It's a generous offer, senhor, but at the moment, any monetary fee hits my cash flow hard."

The Man laughs. Every part of him jigs in sympathy.

"Let's hear your payment plan, then."

Edson nods at Milena, still keeping it up, still smiling at every bounce.

"You said she was impressive."

"I said she needed surgery."

"I've got her a try-out with Atletico Sorocaba." It's not quite a lie. He knows the first name of the man there; he's left an appointment with the secretary.

"Not exactly São Paulo."

"It's building a following. I've a career development plan."

"No one could ever accuse you of not being thorough," The Man says. "But . . ."

"I'll throw in my fut-volley crew."

The Man scowls. The SurfTeam copies his expression, amplified by *hard*.

"They're girls."

The Man rolls his head on his sloping, corrugated neck.

"They do it topless."

"Deal," says The Man, suddenly quivering with laughter, rocking back and forth, creasing his big hairy belly, slapping his thigh. "You kill me, you fucking cheeky ape. You have your license. Now, tell me, what do you want it for?"

"Very well, senhor, with your permission I am going to break into the military police vehicle pound at Guapirá and steal four quantum computers."

OCTOBER 29, 1732

Some Notes on the Hydrography of the
Rio Negro and Rio Branco

By

Dr. Robert Francois St. Honore Falcon:
Fellow of the Royal Academy of France

The Rio Negro, or "Black" River is one of the largest tributaries of the Amazon, joining with the Rio Solimões some two hundred and fifty leagues from the Amazon's mouth, three leagues beneath the settlement of São José Tarumás, named after the now-extinct tribal Tarumá, or São José do Rio Negro. The most striking characteristic of the Rio Negro is that from which it derives its name—its black waters. And this is no imaginative or fanciful appellation; forasmuch as the waters of the ocean are blue, those of this river are jet black. The Rio Branco, a tributary of the greater Negro, is, as its name suggests, a "white" river. Rivers in greater Amazonia are of these types, "black water" and "white water." Beneath the Rio Branco all the northern tributaries of the Rio Negro are black water—those to the south are cross-channels connecting with the Solimões.

From the Arquipelaga Anavilhanas I proceeded to this more promising camp at the confluence of Black and White Rivers where I have undertaken a series of tests of the waters and substrata of the two rivers. Both rivers are exceptionally deep and show a distinct stratification in the species of fish that live there. However lead-line soundings from the Rio Negro show a dark sediment, rich in vegetable matter, in its bed while the Rio Branco's is soft, inorganic silt. An immediate speculation is that both rivers rise over differing terrains: the Rio Branco being hydrologically similar to the Rio Solimões which rises in the Andes cordillera, it seems a reasonable conclusion to draw that it too rises in a highland region, as yet uncharted but in all likelihood situate in the vast extent of land between the Guianas and the viceroyalty of Venezuela. . . .

Dr. Robert Falcon set down his quill. The voice of the forest deceived; many times in river camps he had thought he heard his name called or a distant hallo, only, on closer listening that verged on a hunter's concentration, to perceive it as a phrase of birdsong or the rattle of some minute amphibian, its voice vastly greater than its bulk. Again: and this was no bird flute or frog chirp. A human voice calling in the lingua geral that his porters and paddlers, from many different tribes, used among themselves. A canoe in the stream. What should be so strange about that in these waters to set his men a-crying?

Falcon carefully sanded and blew dry his book. His gauze canopy, only partially successful against the plaguing insects, was set up just within the tree line. A dozen steps took him down onto the cracked, oozing shore, the river still falling despite the recent violent thunder squalls. Never had he known rain like it, but it was still a drop in the immense volume of the Amazon rivers.

His men were arrayed on the shore. The object of their attention was a solitary canoe, a big dugout for war or trade, drifting on the flow. Falcon slid on his green glasses for better discrimination, but the range was too great. He turned his pocket-glass on it; a moment to focus, then the canoe leaped clear. An immensely powerful black man sat in the stern, steering a course to shore. Falcon knew that form, that set of determination: Zemba, the freed slave Luis Quinn had taken into his mission up the Rio Branco.

"The camp!" Zemba cried in a huge voice. "Is this the camp of the Frenchman Falcon?"

"I am he," Falcon shouted.

"I require assistance; I have a sick man aboard."

Look for me by the mouth of the Rio Branco.

Falcon plunged into the river as Zemba steered the canoe in to shore. Luis Quinn lay supine in the bottom. His exposed skin was cracked and blistered by the sun; the seeps and sores already flyblown and crawling. But he was alive, alive barely; his eyelids flickered; rags of loose skin trembled on his lips to inhalations so shallow it did not seem possible they could sustain life.

"Help me, help me with him, get him up to the shelter," Falcon commanded as the canoe was run up on to the shore. "Careful with him now, careful you donkeys. Water; get me clean water to drink. Lint and soft cotton. Careful now. Yes, Luis Quinn, you have found me."

"What world is this?"

Dr. Robert Falcon set down his pen on his folding desk. The tent glowed with the light of clay oil lamps; fragrant bark smoldering in a burner repelled those insects that had infiltrated through flaps and vents. Those outside, drawn helpless to the light, beat mechanically, senselessly, against the stretched fabric, each impact a soft tick. On the long nights he had sat vigil by the hammock Falcon had imagined himself trapped inside a monstrous, moth-powered clock: a great Governing Engine.

"Might I say, Father Quinn, that is a most singular question. What day is it, where am I—that would not be unexpected. Even, who are you? But 'What world is this?' That I have never heard."

Luis Quinn laughed weakly, the laugh breaking into dry, heaving coughing. Falcon was at his side with the water sack. When he had half the bag down him, swigging immoderately, Quinn said, voice croaking, "You certainly sound like the learned Dr. Falcon I recall. How long?"

"You have been fever-racked for three days."

Quinn tried to sit up. Falcon's hand on his chest lightly but irresistibly ordered him down.

"They will be here, he is coming, he's very near."

"You are safe. Zemba has told me all. We are beyond the reach of your Nossa Senhora da Várzea, though I admit I should be intrigued to see such a prodigy."

A flash, like lightning in the skull. A moment of lucidity, Zemba running the canoe out into the dark water and lying in the bottom as the current carried it away from Nossa Senhora da Várzea. "I have you, Pai, you will be safe." Staring up into the starry dome, past exhaustion, past sanity, the black filling with stars, and then constellations appearing behind those constellations and ones beyond that, and beyond that, black night filling up with alien constellations until it blazed, more and still more stars until the night was white and he was not staring up into forever but falling facedown toward the ever-brightening light, infinite light. Quinn cried out. Falcon took his hand. It was yet fever-dry, thin as parchment.

Three days, working with Zemba to dress the burns with paste the Manaos prepared from forest leaves, removing blowflies one by one with botanical forceps, bathing sweating brows and shivering lips, forcing spastic jaws open to pour in thin, poor soup or herbal maté to see it moments later spewed up in a stream, hoping that some fragment of good had gone out from it. Water, always water, more water, he could not have enough water. Nights of fevered ravings, shrieking demons and hallucinations, prophecies and stammerings until Falcon thought he must stop his ears with wax like Odysseus or go mad.

"It has always been so," Zemba said as they bound Quinn's hands to the hammock ropes with strips of cotton to stop the priest putting out his own eyes. And then the roaring ceased, that silence the most terrifying, when Falcon crept to the hammock not knowing if sanity or death had claimed Quinn.

"Zemba . . ."

"Outside, waiting."

"He saved me. There are not thanks enough for him. . . . Listen Falcon, listen to me. I must tell you what I have seen."

"When you are rested and stronger." But Quinn's grip as he seized Falcon's arm was strong, insanely strong.

"No. Now. No one ever survived; this may not be the end of it. I may yet succumb, God between us and evil. This may be only a moment of lucidity. Oh Christ, help me!"

"Water, friend, have more water." Zemba entered with a fresh skin;

together the two men helped Quinn drink deep and long. He lay back in the hammock, drained.

"For a hundred leagues along the Rio Branco the emblem of the Green Lady is an object of dread, the Green Lady, and the Jesuit dress. My own black robe, Falcon. He has made a desert land, the villages empty, rotting; the plantations overgrown, the forest reclaiming all. All gone; dead, fled, or taken to the City of God, or the block in São José Tarumás. The friars at São José said nothing; that is their price. Plague is his herald, fire his vanguard: whole nations have retreated into the igapó and the terra firme only to be annihilated to the last child by the diseases of the white men. But he sees the hand of God; the red man must be tried by the white, must grow strong or perish utterly from the world.

"From the City of God to the Rio Catrimani is five days, and eight farther to the Iguapará. I had not thought there could be so much water in all the world. Endless, empty forest, with only the voices of the beasts for company. Manoel had passed into a silent, trancelike state of introspection; even the Guabirú guards were mute. I have heard that the índios may will themselves to stop living and very soon pass into a melancholic decline and die. Many have chosen to escape that way from slavery. I believe Manoel was on the edges of that state; such were the rumors of what the Iguapá would work upon us.

"The Iguapá are a nation of seers and prophets; pagés and caraíbas. They are consulted only on matters of the gravest import and they are never wrong. Thus they have lived a thousand years unmolested by war, famine, or disease. Their legend is that by Amazonian forest drugs they are able to see every possible answer to the supplicant's question and so select the true. But the price is terrible indeed. Very soon after the climax of the ritual trance the caraíba descends into confusion, then to full hallucination and a final collapse into insanity and death. They see too much. They try to understand, they overbalance, they fail, they fall . . . I outrun myself. At such a price, the Iguapá do not sacrifice their own. No, their prophets are prisoners of war, hostages, rivals, criminals, outcasts. And of course the black priests of an alien, ineffectual faith. What is our weak prayer, our unseen hope, our whimsical miracles, compared with their iron certainty of the truth, that there is an answer and they will always know it? We could ask them about the mysteries of our God and faith, and they would answer truly. Dare we ask that? Dare we let it darken our imaginations?

"For five days we camped at the designated shore, leaving the signs and markers, invisible to me but as obvious to a native of these forests as a church cross to a European. When you have need of them, they will come to you. On the sixth day they came. They were wary; they have always been jealous with their secrets, but in this time of dying and vast migrations through the várzea they have grown more cautious. Like spirits out of the forest, so silent they were among us, their arrow-points at our hearts, before we knew it. I did not think they were of this world, so uncanny was their appearance: their faces shone gold; they habitually apply the oil of a forest nut they call urocum, and their foreheads, which they shave almost to the crown, slope sharply backward to resemble the shape of a boat. They bind the skulls of their infants with boards and leather while they are still soft and malleable. Manoel and I were bound and led by the hand; the Guabirú guides blindfolded. Their interpreter, a man named Waitacá, told me this was a recent courtesy: the eyes of all but the questioner would have formerly been put out with splinters of bamboo. We of course were never expected to return capable of speech.

"I do not remember how long we stumbled through the forest—days, certainly. The Iguapá trap their forest trails with snares and pitfalls; they could hold at bay an entire colonial army. As we detoured around the strangling nooses, poison arrows, and beds of spines, one question vexed me, what did Gonçalves wish with them? So simple a thing as conquest? The triumph of the tyrant is not his aim. He styles himself a political philosopher, a social experimenter. Were there questions—questions like those I dared posit on faith and the nature of the world—to which he required infallible answers? He believes himself a true man of God: did he seek that prophetic power to destroy it? Or is his overweening vanity so great that he seeks that power for himself, to know without faith, to eat of the tree of the knowledge of good and evil?

"For all their cunning defenses, their village was poor and mean, foul with the filth of peccaries and dogs, huts sagging, thatch rotted and sprouting. There was not a child there that did not bear sores and boils or sties of the eye and lip on their golden faces. A special maloca was reserved for the caraíbas, as we sacrificial victims were known—a title of great honor, I was informed by Waitacá, though I had by now picked up the gist of their own, quite singular language. The hut was the vilest in the village, the thatch raining insects and spouting rain in a dozen places.

"In my wait I learned the basic tenets of Iguapá belief. They worship no God, have no story of creation or redemption, no sin nor heaven nor hell. Yet their belief system—it can never be a theology—is complex, thorough, and sophisticated. Their totemic creature is a frog—neither the loudest nor the most venomous nor the most colorful, though its skin has a beautiful golden sheen which they copy in their face-painting. This frog, which they call curupairá, was first of all creatures and saw the first light, the true light of the world—or should I say worlds, for they believe in a multiplicity of worlds that reflects every possible expression of human free will—whole and entire. It retains that memory of when reality was whole and undivided, like the pages in a book before they are cut. It still sees that true light, which is the light of all suns, and by the grace of the beings that inhabit those other worlds beside our own, can give that sight to humans. It is the extract of the curupairá, which is slowly boiled to death in a sealed clay pot with a spout, that induces the oracular vision.

"The ceremony seemed designed to lull both petitioners and victims alike into a near-ecstasy. Drumming, the piping of clay ocarinas, circle dancing, figures passing repeatedly in front of the light from the fire: all the old tricks. We were dragged from the hut, stripped, anointed with the golden oil—I bear traces of it still—and lashed to St. Andrew's crosses. I remember it raining, a punishing downpour, but the women and children danced on, shuffling around that smoking fire. Their pagé entered at the tail of the dance, the flask in his hand. He came to Manoel, then to me, forced our mouths open with a wooden screw, and poured a jet of the liquid into our gullets. I tried to spit it out but he kept pouring, like the old water ordeal."

Again Quinn seized Falcon's hand.

"It came so fast, brother, so fast. I had not time, no word of prayer, no moment even of recollection to prepare. One moment I was a golden idol crucified, the next I was swept away, across worlds, Robert, across worlds. My vision expanded and I saw myself, bound to the cross, as if I stood outside my own body. Yet this was not me, for in every direction I looked, I saw myself, bound to that cross, other Luis Quinns sharing my plight and my vision. A hundred mes, a thousand mes, receding like reflections of reflections in every direction, and the farther I looked, the less like me they were. Not physically, nor even I believe in will or intellect, but in the circumstances of their lives. Here were Luis Quinns who had failed in their mission, who had declined the burden of Father James in Coimbra, who had never joined the Society of Jesus. Here were Luis Quinns who had killed the slave in Porto without a backward look. Here were Luis Quinns who had never killed that slave at all. Luis Quinns leading lives of commerce and success, married, fathering children, captaining great ships or houses of trade. Here were Luis Quinns alive and dead a thousand different ways, a myriad different ways. All the lives I might have led. And Falcon, Falcon, this you must understand if nothing else: they were all as true as each other. My life was not the trunk from which all others branch at each juncture or decision. They were independent, complete, not other lives, but other worlds, separate from the very creating word of God to the final judgment. Worlds without end, Falcon. Naked I was sent out across them, my expanded mind racing down those lines of other Luis Quinns' other worlds, and I could see no end to them, no end at all. And the voices, Falcon, a million, a thousand million, a thousand times that, voices all speaking at once, all combining into a terrible wordless howl like the roaring of the damned in hell.

"Then I heard a word speak through the cacophony, one voice that was a thousand voices, the pagé saying over and over 'Ask! Ask! Ask!' He too was surrounded by a bright blinding halo of his other selves; everyone, everything, the whole mean shambles of the village, my brother in suffering Manoel; I saw them all across countless worlds.

"'Ask'? What could this mean? And then I heard Paguana the leader of the Guabirú speak in a voice like a whirlwind: 'When will the Guabirú achieve victory and rule over their enemies?' And they heard, Falcon, all those uncountable voices; they heard and asked it of themselves, and each spoke his answer. I knew that somewhere among them, in that vast array of possible answers, was the truth; simple, complete, incontestable. Beside me, Manoel, endless Manoels, more than blossoms on an apple tree, asked that same question of his other selves and would, I knew certainly, receive the same infallible answer.

"Once more I was spun forth among my other selves, across the worlds, faster, ever faster, outracing light and thought, even prayer. Godspeeded, I traversed a million worlds until an echo brought me up, to a room, a plain whitewashed room, furniture simply fashioned from heavy, valuable woods, a room in Ireland I knew from the taste of the air and the small square of green I could spy through the narrow window. There I saw myself, Luis Quinn, with a hound beneath my hand and an infant rolling at my feet. I looked myself in the eye and said, 'The Guabirú will never rule over their enemies, for their enemy rules them already and water will run red with their blood and then they will become nothing but a memory of a name.' And I knew this was true prophecy, because, Falcon, Falcon—it has happened. You wondered if the universe might be modeled by a simple machine: here is your answer. There is a world for every possible deed and act, but they are all written, preordained. The stack of cards runs through the machine. Free will is an illusion. We imagine we have choice, but the outcome is already decided, was written the moment the world was made, complete in time."

"I cannot believe that," Falcon said, the first words he had spoken since Quinn began his testimony. "I must believe that the world is shaped by our wills and actions."

"The Rio Branco will run with the blood of the Guabirú and they will vanish utterly from this world: it will happen, it has already happened. Manoel spoke it first, and Paguana in a fit of rage seized a spear and ran him through, again and again. He would have done the same to me had he not been restrained by the Iguapá, and in truth, what good would it have done? The words spoken cannot be taken back. The Guabirú will be destroyed whether the oracle is spoken or not. This is the true horror of the Iguapá gift: the foreknowledge of that which you are powerless to change.

"For that instant only the truth spoke clear out of all the possible answers; then the roar of voices resumed, doubled, redoubled in volume; a million million voices and I could hear each one of them, Robert. I was driven down and apart so that I forgot who I was, where I was. I fled between worlds, a ghost, a demon. I know now I was cut down from the cross and that the Guabirú, with little grace, bound me to a litter to take me back to the City of God. I believe the Iguapá only let me go because they knew I would certainly die. There are moments of sanity and surcease when I became aware of this world: lurching through the trees, carried by blindfolded bearers, and again, at the river, when the Iguapá seized Paguana and poured poison into his eyes, for he had committed sacrilege against the caraíba.

"I recall Nossa Senhora da Várzea at night, a thousand lights upon her, and Diego Gonçalves's face looking down upon me: I recall seeing my own face flecked with Iguapá gold in a mirror and my own breath misting my image. And all the while the one sane thought in my head was that he must not have it, that I must exert myself, discipline myself not to give voice to the truth I had learned in my madness and visions of other worlds. Deny him it, deny him it; I believe now it was that simple, potent need that drew me back from destruction. But I had no strength, my body was a traitor. Then among the worlds I heard my name spoken and it called me back, and there was Zemba, good Zemba. He it was who slipped me from my hammock and took a canoe and pushed us out into the stream, and then all the stars of all the universes opened upon me and I was lost in light.

"Water, Falcon, I beg you."

Hands trembling, Robert Falcon held the water skin up to Luis Quinn's lips. Again Quinn drank deeply, desperately. The tent fabric glowed with the promise of day: a night had been talked away, and all the birds of the forest joined in one whooping, shrilling, clattering chorus.

"My friend, my friend, I cannot believe what you are saying. If it is true . . . Rest, restore your strength. You are still very weak, and it is clear that some residue of the curupairá still affects your reason."

Marie-Jeanne had given Falcon the flask—a precious, pretty little thing, chased silver, easily slipped into the place next to the heart—at the reception in the Hotel Faurichard the night before his embarkation to Brest. *For when you are far from home, and wish to remember it, and me.* How he wished for a sip of its fine old Cognac. This monstrous river, this dreadful land, this terrifying endless silent forest that hid horrors at its heart but spoke never a word, gave never a sign. One sip of France, of Marie-Jeanne and her bright, birdlike laughter; but he had stowed it, restowed it, stowed it yet again, it was lost. Not one world but many worlds. A drug that enabled the human mind to see reality and to communicate with its counterparts, the implication being— given that the universe ran to explicable, physical laws and not a quixotic divine will or thaumaturgy—that all minds must therefore be aspects of the one, immense mind. Quinn's image returned to him, a stack of loom cards unfolding one at a time through the toothed mill of a Governing Engine.

Quinn had forced himself upright, gaunt face tight with energy and mania.

"Even now I see it, Falcon, though the vision fades—no mind can look on such things and survive. Gonçalves was correct in his supposition that my particular cast of mind—something in my facility for language, some innate ability to see pattern and meaning—allowed me to survive where those before me that he sent to seek out the oracle perished. But I am ridden by a terrible fear, that in my delirium I betrayed the Iguapá and even now that monstrous blasphemy of a basilica is casting off into the stream to enslave them. Falcon, I must go back. I have betrayed my order and my vows. I have left undone that which I ought to have done. There is no help in me. Doctor, I may have need again of your sword."

"That you shall not have," Falcon said, preparing manioc mush. "For I shall have need of it myself, at your side."

The signs are set, the markers laid down; yet the Iguapá do not come. This is our fourth night upon this strand, and the fear haunts me that they have already been knocked down at the block in São José Tarumás. On the third night of our journey up the Catrimani and the Rio Iguapará we stole past Nossa Senhora de Várzea, the monstrous carbuncle, but was it ascending, or descending with its holds full of red gold? Falcon paused to swipe at a troubling insect, then bent to his journal again. *Diligently I log this journey, leagues traveled, rivers mapped, though the purpose of my expedition is utterly lost. I record villages and missions, navigation hazards and defensible positions; but increasingly I ask myself, to what end? Too readily I convince myself no one will ever read these reports and dispatches. Quinn would tell me that desperation is a sin, but I dread that I shall never leave this green hell, that my bones*

*will lie down in the heat and the rot and the pestilence and be covered over with veg-
etation and every trace of me will be lost. And yet, I write . . .*

A twitch at the tent flap. Zemba entered the scriptorium.

"The Mair wishes me to inform you, they are here."

Mair: the hero, the supernatural leader, the extraordinary man. The
legend was beginning. Falcon's own Manaos now used it among themselves;
he soon expected to hear it addressed to Quinn directly in place of the com-
monplace *Pai*. Zemba had appointed himself Quinn's lieutenant, but what
else besides? Falcon realized that his opinions of Zemba were prejudices
drawn from his physical size and the color of his skin. Here was a man rich
in skills and insight, taken from his home and people in the sure knowledge
that he would never see any of them again, that to him they were the dead,
that any life he must make would be here, rootless, reduced to an insect, a
speck in the vastnesses of Brazil.

"I am coming."

Falcon stepped from the tent into a ring of blowpipes. The unworldly
golden faces, the elongated, sloping foreheads of the Iguapá reminded Falcon
strikingly, terrifyingly, of an altar screen by some maniacal Flemish painter,
judgments and dark deliverers and strange, sharp instruments of inquiry.
Twenty weapons drew on Falcon. Quinn sat at his ease propped on a barrel of
salt pork, merry almost, though one of the Iguapá, a speaker of the lingua
geral, stood before him in clear accusation. It was like a dance between them:
the Iguapá striding forward to stab with his blowpipe, bark a question, then
step back into the company. Quinn would answer in the same tongue, slowly,
patiently, at his ease.

"The índio asks if the Mair is man or spirit. The Mair answers, 'Touch
my hands, my face,'" Zemba translated for Falcon.

Quinn held out his arms, a black crucifix. Waitacá composed himself
before his hunting brothers, then stepped boldly forward and pressed the fingers of his hands into Quinn's palms.

"The índio begs forgiveness, but it has never happened in the memory of
the Iguapá that a caraíba's soul has returned to his body from the worlds of
the curupairá," Zemba whispered. Quinn spoke, and the circle of hunters
gave a low rumble of astonishment and anger. Falcon noted that some of the

golden-faced warriors were still uncircumcised boys. *Oh for my sketchbook!* he thought. *Such singular crania; they must be achieved in infancy by binding the head, as was the custom of many of the extinct peoples of the Andes.*

"What did the father say there?"

"The Mair said, 'Ask me a question, any question.'"

The Iguapá called to each other in their own language. The Manaos waited at the edge of the firelight, suspicious, ready for fight. Falcon caught the eye of Juripari, his Manao translator. One word and the Manaos would strike. One word and it would be more bloody anonymous death on the river sand, unseen, unheard, unmourned.

Waitacá jabbed his blowpipe at Quinn with a simultaneously stabbing question.

"He says, 'And where was your God, O priest?'"

For too many heartbeats Falcon felt every poison dart trained on him. Then Quinn snatched the blowpipe from Waitacá's and smartly, impertinently, rapped him on his sloping forehead. Waitacá's hand flew to the serrated wooden dagger slung across his chest, eyes bulging in rage. Quinn held his gaze; then his face gently creased and folded into a smile, into helpless laughter. The infection of the ridiculous: Waitacá's wounded pride evaporated like a morning mist; shaking with barely contained mirth, he took the blowpipe back from Quinn and, with deadly pomp, tapped the Jesuit on the crown of the head. Quinn exploded into guffaws; released, every Iguapá let free their repressed laughter. Waitacá managed to bellow out a choking sentence before he doubled up. Against will, reason, and sanity, Falcon felt the clench of laughter beneath his ribs.

"What did he, what did the índio say?"

"He said, 'Of course, where else?'"

The laughter was slow spent, the madness of fear transfigured.

"But my friends, my friends," Quinn said, wiping his eyes with the sleeve of his filthy black robe, "I must warn you, the other father, the Black Pai, is coming. His great church is less than a day from you, and all his thought is turned upon you." In a breath all laughter ceased. "He intends the reduction of the Iguapá, and all your concealments and traps will not avail you, for he has as many warriors as there are stars in the sky and he would sell every one of their lives to assimilate you into his City of God. Your gods and ancestors will wander lost; your name will be forgotten."

A warrior called out a question. Waitacá translated.

"How does the Black Pai know this?"

"Because in my madness I told him," Quinn said.

A susurrus of dismay passed from warrior to warrior. A youth, a still-fat boy, asked, "Will the Black Pai take us?"

Quinn sat back on his barrel, turned his gaze upward to the band of stars.

You know the answer to that, Falcon thought. *You see them still; I think you see them always, those stars of the other skies. All the worlds you told me are open to you.*

"Bring your women and your children," Quinn said. "Your beasts and your weapons, your tools and your cooking pots. Sling your hammocks upon your backs and gather up your urocum and the bones of your ancestors. Make cages for your curupaira, as many as you can carry, male and female both. When you have done all this, burn your village to the earth and follow me. There is a place for you. I have seen it, a hidden place, a safe place, not just for the Iguapá but also for everyone who flees the slave coffle and the block. There will be no slaves. This place will be rich in fish and hunting, manioc and fruits; it will be strong and defended." Quinn inclined his head to Zemba. "No one will be able to take this place, not the bandeirantes, not the Black Pai and his Guabirú fighters. The name of it will be Cidade Maravilhosa, the Marvelous City. Falcon, gather your supplies and what equipment you deem necessary. Burn your canoes and whatever you do not require on the journey. We leave this instant. I shall lead you."

"Quinn, Quinn, this is insanity, what madness . . . ?" Falcon cried, but Luis Quinn had already disappeared into the dark of the forest. One by one the golden bodies of the Iguapá followed him and vanished.

OUR
LADY
OF
THE
GOLDEN
FROG

JUNE 10–11, 2006

The book fitted the palm of the hand like a loved, kissed breviary; small, dense, bound in soft, mottled-gold leather that felt strangely warm and silky to Marcelina's touch, as if it were still alive. Hand-sewn header tapes, a bookmark made from that same brass-and-gold leather, edged with new bright gold leaf; this was a volume that had been bound and rebound any times. The hand-painted endpapers were original watercolor sketches of a river journey, both banks represented, right at the top, left at the bottom, landmark trees, missions, churches all marked. Índios adorned with fantastical feathered headdresses and capes stood in canoes or on bamboo rafts; pink river dolphins leaped from the water. In the top of a dead tree red howler monkeys had been depicted in the oversize but minute detail of a dedicated chronicler. All was annotated with legends Marcelina could not decipher.

Mestre Ginga signaled for her to set the little book down. The cover bore only the outline of a frog, embossed in gold leaf. With gloved hands he moved it reverently to the end of the folding camp table before setting the coffee in front of Marcelina. She too wore gloves, and had been instructed under no circumstances to get the book wet. She sipped her coffee. Good, smoky, from a Flamengo mug. The walls of the little kitchen at the back of the fundação were painted yellow, the handmade cupboards and work surfaces blue and green. A patriotic kitchen. A lizard sprang from stone motionlessness to skim up the wall between the framed photographs of the great mestres and capoeiristas of the forties and fifties, before the joga became legal, let alone fashionable; men playing in Panama hats down in rodas down by the dock, stripped down to the singlets, pleat-top pants rolled up to the knees. The classic kicks and movement but with cigarettes in their mouths. That was true malandragem.

"So," Mestre Ginga said. "What did you notice about the book?"

The car had taken off like a jet from the side of the street, and in the daze and confusion and the shock but above all the single, searing icon of her face, her face, her own face behind the knife, all Marcelina could think to say was, "I didn't know you owned a car."

"I don't," said Mestre Ginga, crashing gears. "I stole it." It soon became clear that he didn't drive either, blazing a course of grace and havoc between the taxis on Rua Barata Ribeiro, scraping paint-thin to the walls of the Tunel Nóvo, leaping out in a blare of horns into the lilac twilight of Botafogo. "I mean, how hard can driving be if taxi drivers do it?"

Marcelina saw the glowing blue free-form sculpture that crowned Canal Quatro appear above the build-line. It was a reassurance and a sorrowing psalm, a promised land from which she was exiled. She breathed deep, hard, the calming, powering intake of air that gave her such burning strength in the roda or the pitching room.

"I need a few things explained to me."

Into Laranjeiras now, under the knees of the mountain.

"Yes, you do," said Mestre Ginga, leaning back in his seat and steering one-handed. "It's knowing where to start. We'd hoped that you wouldn't get involved, that we could handle the admonitory before you learned anything, but when the bença was murdered, we couldn't hold off."

"That was you at the terreiro."

"You always were too clever to be really smart," Mestre Ginga said. Familiar streets around Marcelina, they were heading up to the fundação. *And you still have a Yoda complex.* "I've been keeping an eye on you ever since that clown Raimundo Soares sent you to Feijão. If he'd kept his mouth shut . . . But after the split with the bença he felt aggrieved. It should have been him got cut up; then we wouldn't have been in this mess."

"Wait wait, what is this mess anyway?"

Onto the corkscrew road, scraping the ochre and yellow-painted walls of the compounds.

"You want to be down a gear," Marcelina said, troubled by the knocking, laboring engine. "You're taking it too low."

"And since when have you been Rubens Barrichello?"

"I watch my taxi drivers. So; that woman with the knife, who was she?"

"Who did it look like she was?"

"Me."

"Then that's who she was. There's a way to explaining this that makes sense. Otherwise, trust me, in this game nothing is coincidence."

Then the stolen Ford drew up before the graffitied walls of the fundação with its brightly colored, tumbling, happy capoeiristas; and Mestre Ginga, with a haste and tension Marcelina had never seen in him before, unlocked the gates and showed her round the back into the patriotic kitchen.

"The book's some kind of expedition journal by an eighteenth-century French explorer on the Amazon. I didn't read very much of it; I find that old stuff kind of hard to read."

"I didn't ask what it was. I asked you, what did you notice?"

"Well, it's been rebound several times, and the contents are handwritten but they're not original, I suspect; the illustrations inside the cover had coded writing on them, and knowing the way Brazil was in the eighteenth century, I reckon it's a good guess that it was originally written in code as well."

"Good guess. Anything else."

"Like I said, I didn't read much of it. Now, I'm sure this old eighteenth-century book has something to do with my evil double trying to kill me, but it might be a whole lot simpler if you just got to the point."

"Anything else."

Marcelina shrugged; then a realization of strange, a sense of cold wonder, shivered through her. In the blossom-perfumed heat of Mestre Ginga's kitchen, she saw the gooseflesh lift the fine, blonde hairs on her forearm.

"There was a plague, a plague of horses." She knew the look on Mestre Ginga's face; so many times she had seen it in the roda as he squatted in the ring, leaning on his stick. *Go on, my daughter, go on.* "All the horses, the donkeys, even the oxen, they were wiped out by the plague. That never happened. It's fiction, it's a story."

"No, it's true. It's a history. It's just not our history."

"This is insane."

"Lick the book," Mestre Ginga ordered. "Pick it up and just touch the tip of your tongue to it."

Sense of cold wonder became vertiginous fear. Favors and privileges had flowed around the Organ Queen of the Beija-Flor, one of them free and unlimited access to the private pool and beach of the Ilha Grande Hotel at Arpoador, the rocky point between the golden curves of Copacabana and Ipanema. Dalliances and liaisons blew through the airy corridors and cloisters, but the children who splashed round the rocks were as oblivious to this as they were to satellites. The big thrill was the Leaping Point, a five-meter rock that overhung a Yemanja-blue plunge pool: a hold of the nose, a quick cross, and down like a harpoon into the clear cold water. Marcelina—age eight—had always envied the bigger girls who filled their swimsuits and the gawky boys who could make the leap. For hot holiday weeks she had tried to call up the courage to go up on to the Leaping Point, and then at the last day of summer before school resumed she had worked up sufficient force of soul to climb up the rock. Her mother and sisters, racked out on the wooden sun loungers, waved and cheered, *Go on go on go on!* She crossed herself. She looked down. The deep blue water looked back up into her soul. And she couldn't do it. There was swallowing madness down there. The climb back down the rock-cut steps, backward, feeling her way one hand, one foot at a time, was the longest walk of her life.

Marcelina looked into the book. The golden eye of the frog held her. Where would the walk back down from this painted sanctuary take her? Not back to any life she could recognize. The old capoeiristas, the great mestres and corda vermelhas, taunted her with their jeito. *Our Lady of Production Values, who is our Lady of Jeito, aid me.*

Marcelina lifted the book to her face and touched the eye of the golden frog with the tip of her tongue. And the book opened the room opened the city opened the world opened.

Marcelina lifted a hand. A thousand hands bled off that, like the feedback echo of visual dub. The table was a Church of All Tables, the green and blue cabinets a Picasso of unfolding cubes. And Mestre Ginga was a host of ghosts, an Indian god of moving limbs and heads. The book in her hand unfolded into pages upon pages within pages, endless origami. Voices, a choir of voices, a million voices, a million cities roaring and singing and jabbering at once. Marcelina reached for the table—which table, which hands—and rose to her feet through a blur of images. Then Mestre Ginga was at her side, prising open her mouth, pouring strong, hot, startling black coffee down her throat. Marcelina coughed, retched up bile black cafezinho and was herself again, lone, isolate, entire. She dropped into the aluminum kitchen chair.

"What did you do to me?"

Mestre Ginga ducked his head apologetically.

"I showed you the order of the universe."

Marcelina slung the book across the table. Mestre Ginga caught it, squared it neat to the end of the galvanised tin top.

"You drugged me!" She accused him with a finger.

"Yes. No. You know my methods. Your body teaches." Mestre Ginga sat back in his chair and laughed. "And you accuse me?"

"There's a difference. That was a spiked book."

"The book is bound in the skin of the curupairá, the sacred golden frog."

Marcelina had been to the Amazon to research *Twenty Secret Ways to Kill Someone* and had seen the murderous power of brightly colored forest frogs.

"You could have killed me."

"Why should I do that? Marcelina, I know what you think of me—you don't have anywhere near as much malicia as you think, but believe me when

I say, what you do have, you are going to need. Every last drop of it. So stop thinking stupid and start acting like a malandro, because stupid is going to get not just you killed but everyone else around you."

The room shivered around Marcelina, spraying off multiple realities like a dog shaking water from its coat.

"So it's some kind of hallucinogen, like ayahuasca."

"No, nothing like ayahuasca. The iâos of the bença believe that the Daime stimulates those parts of the brain that generate the sensations of spirituality. Curupairá shows the literal truth. The eye of the frog is so sensitive that it can perceive a single photon of light, a single quantum event. The frog sees the fundamental quantum nature of reality."

The snap was on Marcelina's lip: *And what does a capoeira Mestre know about quantum theory?* In surliness was security; she was in a place as familiar and comfortable as home, yet the step from the yard where she played the great game into the green, blue, and yellow kitchen was the step from one world to another. Rio had always been a city of shifting realities, hill and sea, the apartment buildings that grew out of the sheer rock of the morros, the jarring abutments of million-réal houses with favela newlywed blocks, piled one on top of another. And where the realities overlap, violence spills through. Heitor, whose private life you entered through books, had so many times tried to explain quantum theory to Marcelina, usually when she just wanted him to tell her how hot her ass looked in the latest little mesh number. All she understood of it was that her career depended on it and that there were three interpretations (as she tried to get him to take a line from the glass-top table), only one of which could be true; but whichever one was, it meant that reality was completely different from what common sense told us. So shut up the mouth and listen to Mestre Yoda.

"Whatever's in the frog skin allows our minds to perceive on the quantum level."

"What did you see?"

"Like everything had a halo, had other selves. . ." She hesitated over the two words that would turn her world upside down, shatter it into glittering dust. "Many worlds."

There are three main interpretations of quantum theory, Heitor had said. It had been three days after carnaval, when all the marvelous city still had huge stashes of recreational drugs to use up before the feathers and the sequins and the skin glitter were put away and the world of work reaffirmed its dull authority. Marcelina had been reeling around the apartment blessed on Iguaçu white, practicing her booty shake before it was put away until the New Year Yemanja festival. *The Copenhagen interpretation is considered a purely probabilistic interpretation in that in physical terms it gives undue prominence to observation, information, and mind. The Bohm carrier-wave theory is essentially nonlocal, in that every particle in the universe is connected across space and time to every other, which has been seized on by various New Age charlatans as supporting mysticism. The Everett many-world theorem reconciles the paradoxes in quantum theory by positing a huge, maybe even infinite, number of parallel universes that contain every possible quantum state.*

Why are you telling me this why is this important what does it mean come and have some coke, Marcelina had jabbered. She had never forgotten Heitor's answer.

What it means is, any way you cut it, it's a mad world.

Again the room, the fundação, Jesus on his mountain spasmed around Marcelina. *I am seeing across multiple universes, parallel Rios, other Marcelinas. What of the ones I can't see, the ones who were that hair too slow on Rua Rabata Ribeiro and were cut open under that knife?* She took a sip of her strong, now-cold coffee.

"I think you're going to have to explain this to me."

Mestre Ginga sat back in his chair.

"Very well then. You won't believe it, but every word is true."

"There is not one world. There are many worlds. There is not one you; there are many yous. There is no universe; there is the multiverse, and all possible quantum states are contained within it. Write down ninety-nine point nine and as many nines after that until you get bored with it. That many universes are empty, sterile, exercises in abstract geometry and topology; two-dimensional, gravityless, impossible. Out of that chain-of-zeroes point one that remain, the greater part are universes where the constants of physics vary by a tiny degree, a decimal here or there, but even that minuscule variation means that the universe immediately collapses after the big bang into a black hole that expands infinitely in a fraction of a second so that every particle ends up so far from its neighbor that it is effectively in a universe of its own, where stars do not form, or burn out in a three-score and ten. And in the same fraction of those universes as they are to the multiverse, the fine-tuning of constants allows the ultimate unlikelihood of life to exist, to exist intelligently, to found empires and build beautiful Rios, to learn martial arts and make television programs and quest into the nature of the universe in which it finds itself so improbably. We have penetrated to ten to the three hundred thousand universes and still we are not a thumbnail's thickness into the rind of the multiverse, let alone begun to exhaust the universes where we exist in some form recognizable to ourselves.

"Everyone's got a theory. Ask any Rio taxi driver and he'll give you his free. Taxi drivers know how to make a better country and a perfect Seleção as well as all the best places to eat. What matters is, how useful is your theory? Does it explain the everyday as well as the weird and spooky? Physics is no different. We've had Newton and we've had Einstein and we've had Bohr and Heisenberg, and each time the theory gets a little better at explaining what's real; but we're still a long long way from a final Theory of Everything, the ultimate taxi driver theory that you plug a value in and it gives you everything from the reason there is something rather than nothing to the soccer results. Physics is now a roda: all the malandros standing round clapping and singing while two theories go in and try to out-jeito each other. There are two big strong boys who think they have the malandragem to be the theory of everything. One of them is String theory, or M-theory as it's also called. Facing it in the ring is Loop Quantum Gravity. They're calling names at each other, taking each other's measure, trying to trick the other into a simple mistake they can use to make him look stupid, like you made Jair look stupid with that boca de calça. The LQG boys, they're shouting at the String theorists that it's not even wrong. The Stringeiros, they shout back that it's just dreadlocks in space. Which is right? I'm just a guy who runs a capoeira school and who needs some theory to explain what a little book with a frog on the cover has shown him, and that's a hell of a lot of parallel universes.

"Me, I go for dreadlocks in space. Loop Quantum Gravity's main theory is that everything is made from space and time woven into itself. Everything can be made from loops of space and time pulled through themselves. Yeah, it's not dreadlocks, it's knitting. But I was reading on online forums—I read the physics forums, why shouldn't I?—and there's a guy in the terreiro at Rio U who says that maybe what we think of as space is just connections between pieces of information. Everything is connected information in time, and we have a word for that: it's *computer*. The universe is one huge quantum computer; all matter, all energy, everything we are, are programs running on this computer. Now, stick with me here. What I know about quantum computers, they can exist in two contradictory states at the same time, and this allows them to do things no other computer could. But I know, because I've seen them, that reality is a multiverse, so those computations are being done in many universes at once, so in fact all the multiverse is one vast quantum computer. Everything is information. Everything is . . . thought. Our minds are part of it. Our minds run across many universes—maybe all of them. That's what the curupairá does, reduces our perceptions to the level where we become aware that we are part of the multiverse quantum computer. And listen, listen well, if it's all information, if it's all thought and computation, then that information can be rewritten and edited. You can write yourself into any part of the multiverse, any place, any time. And another you has written herself into this universe, and will run you down and kill you. Think of her as a kind of policeman. A militár. She is part of an organization that polices the multiverse, that seeks to keep the true nature of reality secret, controlled only by a small, elite group. She will take your place, and then she hoped to use that to infiltrate us, and eliminate us all.

"I told you you wouldn't believe it. But it's the truest thing there is."

Marcelina rocked back in her chair.

"Have you got, could you get me, I really need something to drink."

Mestre Ginga went to the refrigerator. Full dark had fallen; the blue light from the cool cabinet was painful as he hunted for a Skol. Marcelina started at the sound of car tires squealing on the greasy road. Every twitch, every fidget and rustle was an enemy. Marcelina drank the beer. It was stupidly cold and gloriously real and it slid through her like rain through a ghost, touching nothing. The Mestre's cellular rang; a slow ladainha for solo voice and berimbau. As he talked—low, short phrases—realization passed through Marcelina in the shadow of the beer.

"I'm a fucking cop out there. Somewhere."

Mestre Ginga clammed shut his phone. Dew ran down the sides of the cans.

"In a sense, yes. The term we use is an *admonitory*; it's an old religious expression. There is an organization; call it an *order*. It's old—it's a lot older than you think, it all goes back to that book I gave you. The Order's purpose is to suppress knowledge about the multiverse; that it is possible to cross it, that it exists at all. I can understand why: all our beliefs about who and what we are challenged; the great religions just comfortable stories. Humankind cannot stand too much reality. The Order suffered a partial defeat when quantum theory itself developed the many-worlds interpretation, but they still have a firm grip on their central mission, to control communication and travel across the multiverse; and deep down, that is the ability to rewrite the programs of the universal quantum computer. They are the reality cops. Locally the Order is hereditary; it runs in certain old families who have access to the highest level of government, business, and the military. When Lula got elected, the first thing they did was shake his hand and say 'Congratulations, Mr. President.' The second thing they did was take him into a back room and introduce him to our Brazilian Sesmaria. The Sesmarias move slowly; the last thing they want is to attract attention. They have to live here; they're not allowed to cross between worlds. But sometimes the opportunity arrives to strike a blow, and that's when they call in an admonitory."

"Me, when I started looking for Barbosa, that was their opportunity."

"You were doing all their work for them. First they discredit you; then they replace you. And when they're finished, they walk away into the multiverse again."

"It's nothing to do with me, is it? I'm just convenient, a way for the Order to get to you."

"In the multiverse, you are everything you can be. Villain, mother, assassin, saint. Maybe even hero."

A crunch of tires. A horn blew twice. Mestre Ginga looked up. He left the small kitchen with its lingering tang of dende. Doors opening, doors closing; voices on the edge of audibility. Marcelina felt Mestre Ginga's bright kitchen expand around her until it became a universe, her trapped in it, alone, isolate. Heitor used to say that when God is dead all we have left is conspiracy. This cold illusion, this book of ghosts would have satisfied his hard, gloomy worldview: the whirling noise and color and life of the city a dance of dolls knitted from time and words. Mestre Ginga's cellular lay on the table. Cellular, beer, a coffee mug for a futebol team, a book from another universe. A Brazilian Last Supper. She could pick up that phone. She could call Heitor. He alone remained. Career, friends, family had been stripped away from her like a skin peel, deeper and deeper, rawer and rawer. She should call Heitor, warn him. Pick up the phone. Press out the number. But she had said that the next voice he heard would not be hers. He would not believe her. But she might have gotten to him already. Her: the other Marcelina. She knows you; she knows everything about you because she is you. Your thoughts are her thoughts, your strengths her strengths. You are your own worst enemy.

Your weaknesses her weaknesses.

The creak of the wrought-iron gate, footsteps on the floor tiles. The kitchen door opened. An old man, hair gone grizzle-gray but his skin still bright and black and his bearing upright and glowing with energy, entered. He wore a light linen suit, pants taper-cuffed, high-waisted, and an open-necked silk shirt. Mestre Ginga followed. It was evident in every motion and muscle that he held the visitor in the greatest reverence. Marcelina felt compelled to rise. The old man shook her hand and settled himself heavily on a kitchen chair. "Good evening to you, Senhora Hoffman. I am very pleased to see you well. I am the man who made all Brazil cry."

February 12, 2033

Two by cab. Two on the Metro Linea 4, on separate trains. Two in the van, the biggest risk; two already out and running in the rig. Edson by moto-taxi. Last of all, Fia. In one hour she will take a minibus cab to the rendezvous at the dead mall. *No different from a show*, Edson thinks. *It's all choreography.* Each player is equipped with a one-shot cloned identity and has been rigorously de-arfided. Hamilcar and Mr. Smiles's bill had taken the jaguar's share of the *A World Somewhere* prize money; even so, Edson, clinging to the moto boy as he accelerates between two lines of traffic, imagines the talons of the Angels of Perpetual Surveillance reaching for his kidneys.

Efrim checked the restaurant thirty-six hours before go-day. Long tables, clean tiled floors, good food, and no one put their thumbs on the scales. Now in his Edson persona, he picks the big table by the window. The car pound runs from front to back on the block opposite; they'll make their entrance from the rear.

Emerson and Big Steak first. Shake hands, a little high-carb, low-protein dinner. Then Edimilson and Jack Chocolate, that's the garage team on-site. First real risk here: their gear is in a false-registration van parked out on the street. No one should get curious, but Edson taps his long, tapered fingers together in anxiety.

"Here, eat something." Edson passes a roll of reis to the mechanics. He's not eating, himself; he took a little corajoso when he paid the moto-boy, and it kicks in with an accompanying swooping nausea. His stomach lurches as he watches the mechanics load up on meat from the churrascaria. *Keep it down, Edson.* Waguinho and Furação in the rig will arrive on target at the designated time. Where are Turkey-Feet and Treats? He flicks the time up in the corner of his I-shades. Fia will already have set off from the fazenda. Mr. Peach will drop her by the rodoviaria in Itaparacá; there is something headed into town every two minutes. He picked the old mall because it is enclosed and free from the eyes of cameras, but it's big and out of the way and full of weirds and he doesn't love the idea of her hanging around among them too long.

Where are Turkey-Feet and Treats?

Then Edson's corajoso flickers and is snuffed out. Six cops have just come in, sat down at a table, big guns at their thighs, and are studying the menu.

Two good-byes.

"Hey, my mama."

The custom in Cidade de Luz is that every sunset the women come out of their houses to walk. Singly or in pairs, by three or fours, feet encased in sports shoes worn only for this social occasion, elbows pumping to maintain aerobic capacity, they pace a time-hallowed route: the winding main road, the old High Road that runs parallel to the rodovia, the long slow ascent of Rua Paulo Manendes where by some economic gravitation only car-part factors and veterinarian supply stores have taken root. Men too walk the walk. They set out half an hour after the women and always walk widdershins, to meet the women face-to-face. They are invariably younger men, or fresh divorcees.

In the fast German car, Edson caught up with Dona Hortense and her walking friends outside the Happy Cats Veterinarian Supply Company and cruised in to the curb beside her. Dona Hortense peered under the brim of the white pimp's hat.

"Edson? That you? Kind of you to come over and see me rather than sending that uneducated Treats round to my door to collect your laundry."

"Come on, Mama, you know the trouble I'm in."

"I don't know, that's the thing." The girlfriends are looking at him as they might a cop or a debt collector.

"Mama, this is not the place." Edson opened the door; Dona Hortense slid into the car, ran her hand over the leather upholstery.

"This is nice. Is it yours? Where did you get it?"

"A man. Mama, I have to go away."

"I thought you might."

"A long way, a very long way. I don't know how long I'll be away, but it will be a long time."

"Oh Edson, oh my love. But call me, pick up the phone, let me know you're all right."

"I can't do that, Mama." The light was fast fading, and in the dark of the car, behind polarized windows by Cidade's de Luz's happenstance street lighting, Edson thought his mother might be crying silently.

"What, they've no phones this place you're going? A letter, something."

"Mama . . ."

"Edson what is this? You're scaring me."

"I'll be all right, and I'll be back. I promise you, I'll find a way back. Don't put me in the Book just yet."

"Is there anything I can say?"

"No. Not a thing. Now, kiss me and I'll drop you back at the house, or do you want me to leave you back with the girls?"

"Oh, in a big flash car like this, drop me back at the house," said Dona Hortense.

And again, good-bye.

"This is probably the most romantic notion I have heard in my entire life," said Mr. Peach. Geography is not always a subject of the vast and slow, of eons and crustal plates. It can spring up in a night; the new green space opened one afternoon by the next morning is crisscrossed by footpaths, always mystically following the shortest routes to the shops or the bus stop. In the days that Fia has been a refugee at Fazenda Alvaranga, the old drying shed where the sun loungers are stored in winter has been Sextinho and Mr. Peach's Place.

"It's the last place they would think we'd go; back to where she came from."

"And you, Sextinho? It sounds like a hard world, hers. Gray skies, pollution, wrecked climates."

Fia's world was strange and challenging, but in those differences lie opportunities a man of business and wit can exploit to make money. As long as there was still an Ilhabela, and an ocean to wash the feet of the house, he would make it there. His dreams had moved sideways.

"But no Angels of Perpetual Surveillance."

"No angels. You going to get one of those computers tattooed on your belly?" It was a joke. Mr. Peach knows well Edson's abhorrence of anything violating the sanctity of his skin. "But one thing: you will be there."

"Of course I'll be there."

"No, I mean, there will be an Edson Jesus Oliveira de Freitas somewhere in that city."

It was one of the first things that Edson had thought when he made the decision to flee with Fia back to her São Paulo. He never could resist a mirror: how would it reflect him? Richer, more successful, a man of big business, married, dead? Worst, just some dust-poor favelado? He could not bear that. It could not be any kind of good luck to meet your ghost-self, but how could he fail to intervene in a life like that? Closer than any twin or freaky clone-thing but further than the farthest star. Him, in every atom. He owed it to himself.

"It won't be the first time I've had to get a new identity," Edson said flippantly, but he was spooked, iced in the vein. "Maybe I'll even become Sextinho."

"Do you know what's so silly, and so impossible? I want to go too. All my life I've been teaching the multiverse. I know the theory, I know the math; they prove it more accurately and beautifully than any gross human sense, but I want to see it with my eyes. I want to experience it, and then I'll truly know. If I taught you one thing about physics, Sextinho, it's passion. Physics is love. Why would anyone do this thing, beat their lives against truths we can barely understand, if not for love? Fia says that when you enter superposition, you experience all the other universes at once. So many questions answered. But you, you little bastard, you won't even appreciate what you're seeing. Go on, hero, do well."

Among the moldering showerheads and aluminum nets and scoops for fishing leaves out of the pool, by the cleaning robot's little hutch, Mr. Peach hugged Edson to him. The kid was so small, so thin and frail-looking, but strong beneath, all sinews and wires. Hard to embrace.

"Just one question," Edson said. "When you cross over, do you think it hurts?"

Treats and Turkey-Feet bowl in eighteen minutes late, laughing and swaggering and acting cool cool cool. Edson is ice with them; they make to laugh at his anger but then see that none of the others are smiling.

"Why are you late?"

"We were starving, so we got something to eat and a couple of Chopps."

"You've been drinking?"

"Oh, come on Edson . . ."

"You're drawing attention to yourselves and to me. We are friends meeting up for a meal after work. Now, whether you've eaten or not, go up and get something from the buffet. No beer. This is an alcohol-free operation."

All the while he watches the policemen go up to the counter for seconds. They're fat, ordinary cops, civils; they're just out like Edson and his team for a bite with friends after work. Edimilson and Jack Chocolate the mechanics tell track-side tales from Interlagos. Edson hardly hears them; every second that ticks away on the countdown in the corner of his I-shades is slower than the one before until they freeze like drips in an icebox.

I can't do it. I can't do it. It's all just something I made up.

Then he sees himself pushing his plate away from him, standing up, straightening his cuffs, spiking up his hair, and hears his voice say, "Are we all done? Then let's go."

Tremendous stuff, that corajoso.

The lift hits as he pulls the bandana up over his face. His heart kicks; his breath is shallow and fast and fills him with fire. It's not the corajoso; it's old hot liquid adrenaline, molten in his skull. It's hitting the best deal; it's that Number One Business plan clicking into place.

Turkey-Feet has the Q-blade out. Two searing passes and the rear gate is free from its hinges. Emerson and Big Steak lower it lightly to the ground. The guys are already moving as the lasers try to get retina lock. No luck there, militars: everyone's I-shades are stacked with stolen eye-scans. As the alarms kick off *woo woo woo*, the drone goes in so low over Edson's head he can feel its downdraft muss up his careful gel-spikes. It's an old Radio Sampa traffic-report drone that Hamilcar and Mr. Smiles got in a jeitinho deal and reconditioned to their own gray purposes. It circles like a little spook from a kids' cartoon, pumping out enough variant DNA to bust the budget of any forensics company that tries to profile the crime scene. Lovely boys, clever boys.

It might only be graveyard shift at the car pound, but the militars are quick—nothing on Globo Futebol tonight, then—and tooled for general assault. Firing from cover, Big Steak and Emerson Taser the first two out of the trap. Unlike his kid-times-six brother, Emerson enjoyed his army service. Even as the cops hit the ground twitching, Treats and Turkey-Feet are on top of them. Turkey Feet has his Q-blade at the dazed, dazzled policeman's throat. The guy can't move, can't speak, can only follow the dancing blade with his eyes. Blue on blue. Edson smells piss: the Tasers do that, he's heard. So does fear. It's a hostage situation now: the remaining four nightwatch throw down their weapons and up their hands. They can read the time and geography as well as Edson: twenty seconds, maybe thirty if they've had a big dinner, for the regional headquarters to assess the threat. Another thirty to establish level of response, another twenty to alert units. They won't tender out to seguranças. The military police enjoy a good firefight too much. Surveillance drones will be over the target within two minutes of the general alert. Surface units will converge within five minutes. But Edson has it timed to the tick, and the garage van is bowling in over the felled gate, pulling up beside the maimed Cook/Chill Meal Solutions trailer. Edimilson has already run the hydraulic jack in and is easing up the left side like he is a superhero: Captain Pitstop. Jack Chocolate takes a wheel off in fifteen seconds with the power wrench. Emerson and Big Steak drag the slashed, hemi-tires away and roll the new ones out of the back of the van. The militars boggle at the skill and speed.

"You should see them at Interlagos," says Treats, gun trained on his close knot of hostages.

"Fuck up," says Turkey-Feet.

The first wheel is on. The second. Edson glances at the timer: the truck should be arriving *now*. And there it is, rounding the intersection with two fragrant biodiesel belches from its chromed exhausts. Waguinho swings it through the gap in the fence, wheels round and backs up close as a kiss to the trailer. Last wheel is on; the Interlagos brothers throw their gear in the back of the van; Emerson and Big Steak jump in behind it. Edson hauls himself up into the truck cab beside Waguinho and Furação. The trailer locks, Waguinho engages, and Cook/Chill Meal Solutions rolls. As they sweep out through the gate Edson sees Treats and Turkey-Feet back toward the open rear of the van. At the last minute Emerson and Big Steak scramble them in. The militars at

once go for their guns, but Edimilson spins the wheels and roars out of the
pound onto the street. In the wing-mirror Edson watches the van turn in the
opposite direction. They'll burn it and scatter on foot from the drop-point.
Edson sees the DNA-drone skip over the cab roof, climb vertically, and vanish
among the rooftop water tanks. He pulls off his bandana, leans back into the
seat. The butt of the gun is hard and unexpected against his belly muscles as
an erection. He never drew it. He kept that honor; he never showed the gun.
Edson pushes his head back into the seat-rest, stares at the rosary and the icon
of St. Martin dangling from the interior light fitting. Joy beyond utterance
cracks through him; he can barely hold himself still from the huge, shaking
energy. He did it. He did it. He stole four quantum computers from the São
Paulo Zona Norte Military Police car pound. He wants Fia. He wants her
waiting for him at the pickup point with nothing but him in her manga eyes;
he wants her spread and begging on the hood of Waguinho and Furação's
truck saying, *You're The Man, Edson, malandro of malandros, you are Lord of the
Crossings. What you did will be talked up and down the ladeiras for years; that Edson
Jesus Oliveira de Freitas, that was wit, that was malicia.*

That Edson Jesus Oliveira de Freitas, Dona Hortense's crazy son; whatever happened to him? That is what they will say. Where did he go?

Edson pulls one knee up onto the seat, hugs his knee to him. The in-cab
display shows police cars converging on the car pound. They may not have an
arfid lock, but they have a description of the trailer and an idea where it
might be headed. Can he hear sirens? *Woo woo all you like, militars. In a moment
I will pull my last, best trick.* On the far side of the city, parked up behind a
bakery that does good pão de queijo, Hamilcar and Mr. Smiles glance at an
icon on their I-shades and scatter Cook/Chill Meal Solutions's cloned arfid ID
around fifty vehicles in the truck's immediate vicinity. A smart trick and an
expensive one, but there had been enough change from Hamilcar and Mr.
Smiles to convert into six cut Amazonian emeralds. They nestle in lubricated,
folded latex in Edson's colon. When he gets to the other side, he's going to
require some convertibility.

And there she is, sitting on the wall where the light from the soccer
ground next door falls brightest. She registers the truck swinging in across
the stream of taillights; she jumps up and down in un-self-conscious joy. Her

little pack bounces on her back. Edson cannot rid himself of the image of her Hello Kitty panties. The truck bowls across the parking lot past the decaying glass and steel hulk of the food court, draws up under the lights and stops in a gasm of airbrakes.

"Great choice of location, Edson," Fia says. "Between soccer jocks over there whistling at me and alcos and junkies." Then she runs and kisses him hard full right then right there where he's dropped to the hardtop, standing on her tiptoes. Maybe it's relief, maybe it's the blaze of success, maybe it's his corajoso leaving him, but Edson feels as if the soccer ground floods have broken into a shower of light raining down on him; photons, actual and ghost, pounding him cleaning him, bouncing softly from the stained concrete, entangled as kitten-wool with other lives, other histories. The city and its ten thousand towers spin around him: he is the axis of Sampa, of all Brasil, of the whole wide planet and all its manifestations across the multiverse in this instant in the parking lot of a dead mall.

Fia runs her finger along the flank of the trailer, stops at the great circular hole cut out of the side. She leans carefully in to stare up into the trailer interior. Edson knows she is thinking, *I died in there.*

"The back's open," he says.

Memory is such a little Judas. So many times Edson has recalled the interior of Cook/Chill Meal Solutions, and now, as Fia finds the light switches and illuminates the décor, the sofa isn't where he remembered and it's bigger and a different color, and the coffee machine is on the other side of the counter, and the footstools are zebra skin not jaguar, and the spiral staircase is more Kung-fu Kitsch than Guangzhou-Cybercool. Yet Edson feels as if he's on a first date: this is his place and he's invited her back. She walks around the furnishings, touching, stroking, deeply fascinated by the trails her fingers leave in the dust that has accumulated on the plastic surfaces.

"This is weird, weird. I feel her here much much more." She glances up at the plastic cube over her head, gives a small gasp of wonder and climbs the spiral staircase. Edson watches her move around the studio, awakening the quantum cores one by one. The blue glow of quantum dots skeined across universes underlights her cheekbones in sharp relief, Japans her. He had seen a ghost then, a presence in the empty studio: a quantum echo.

Edson joins Fia in the glowing blue cube.

"The guys want to move the trailer inside. It's not secure out here."

Fia waves her hand: *Whatever.* Her tongue protrudes slightly between her teeth, caught in concentration. Edson steadies himself on a stanchion as Cook/Chill Meal Solutions lurches into motion; Fia moves unconsciously with the flow.

"This should be in an art gallery." She sounds love-dazed, incoherent with ecstasy. "Four quantum-dot Q-cores. And she built them from . . . junk? Where I come from, the São Paulo U Q-frame . . . this is decades ahead of anything we have. It's like it's come from the future. Every part of this is beautiful."

"Can you get it to work?"

"Your language and protocols are different, but I can recode."

"But can you make it work?"

"Let's see."

She slips off her long coat. The tattoo on her exposed belly glows with reflected quantum-light. The wheels within wheels on her stomach start to turn. Fia feels Edson's stare.

"It's just an effect thing, really." She taps keys, leans forward into the blue light. She frowns; her lips move as she reads from the screens. Edson has never seen her so beautiful. "It's finding a common communication channel. Ooh!" Fia starts, smiles as if to some intimate delight. "We're in." She rattles keys; her skin crawls with gears in motion. "Yah! Yah! Come on, you puta!" She slaps the desk. As if it has heard and obeyed, the truck lurches to a stop. Fia throws her hands up. "What did I do?"

Voices, echoing from the naked rolled steel girders of the rotting mall. Voices Edson doesn't recognize. He rattles down the spiral stair, cautiously pokes his head out the Q-blade-cut hole. The glinting sin-black visor of a HUD visor looks up into his face. Beneath it, a grin. Beneath the grin, the muzzle of an assault gun. Visor, visors. The truck is ringed by armed and armored seguranças. The rear doors of the trailer slam open: twenty more seguranças with assault weaponry. The grinning face waves its gun toward the rear of the truck.

"Get your ass out here, favelado."

AUGUST 6–15, 1733

A crowd always gathered for the pendulum. Falcon nodded to his audience as he adjusted the telescope housing and wound the clocks. Children's voices, underscored with the deeper notes of men for whom this was a famous novelty, chanted greeting. Falcon sighted along his nocturnal on Jupiter rising above the tree line and noted the ascension on his wooden shingle. Tomorrow he would have words with Zemba about getting some more paper. The observatory, which was also Falcon's library and home, stood five minutes' walk along forest paths from the quilombo. The canopy had been felled to afford open access to the night sky, and the clearing was popular with couples who wished to take in the moon or the soft ribbon of the Milky Way. With a flick of the stylus Falcon picked three spectators to open the porch roof and operate the clocks; the telescope required protection from the daily downpour, daily oiling to keep the molds from clogging its hair-fine mechanisms. Falcon jabbed again with his stylus at a girl in the front row, breasts budding on her child's torso.

"What is the name of this celestial body and why is it important?" Falcon's command of the lingua geral had developed to where he could play the curmudgeon, a role he found he enjoyed very much. The girl shot to her feet.

"Aîuba, that is the world Jupiter, and it has moons around it as we have a moon, and the moons are a clock."

Aîuba. Falcon had thought the word an honorific in keeping with his fourfold status as geographer and city architect; doctor of physic; archivist of the Cidade Maravilhosa and professor of the University of Rio do Ouro: teacher, wise one, stargazer. He had been gravely discommoded to learn that it was Tupi for his pale, shaven head. He had long ago fixed his longitude by Cassini's tables and calibrated his three Huygens' clocks; hundreds of observations, inked in genipapo on the walls of his house, had proved his theory. What Falcon performed was a Mass of science, a memoriam that the proofs of physics were as true in the forests of the Rio do Ouro as the Paris salons. He demonstrated the validity of empiricism to himself as much as to his audience of Iguapás, Manaos, Caibaxés, and runaway slaves. He thought rarely of La Condamine now; his rival's pamphlet might be under the keenest discussion among the Academicians while his would likely remain trapped in this forest, but it would be held to scorn because it was not empirically true. In his bamboo-and-thatch observatory, Robert Falcon set up his great experiment and declared, *See, this is how your world is.*

"I shall now observe the satellites of Jupiter." Greatest of spheres, visibly flattened at its poles even in this traveling telescope. On Earth as it is in heaven. "Bring me the journal." A Caibaxé girl, keeper of the book, knelt beside Falcon with journal and carved wooden inkwell on a leather pillow. Falcon noted time, date, conditions. So little paper left. And in truth, why make these marks when the truth they represented was partial and lesser? A Jesuit crazed on sacramental forest drugs had hinted at a deeper order, that this oblate world was merely one of a prodigious—perhaps infinite—array of worlds, all differing in greater or lesser degrees. But how would one ever objectively prove such an order of the universe? Yet if it was physical, it must be capable of mathematical description. That would be a challenge for a geographer growing old and alone far from the rememberings of his peers. Such a notation would take up what remained of the house's wall and floor space. Caixa would complain and throw small things at him; she was clean and house-proud and intolerant of his slovenly habits.

"The time in Paris is precisely twenty-seven minutes past eleven o'clock," Falcon intoned. "I shall operate the pendulum. On my mark, start the timing-clocks."

Falcon drew back the bob of the surveying pendulum until the wire matched the inscribed line on the goniometer. He let it fall and lifted his handkerchief, which Caixa kept virtue-white for this purpose. Three hands came down on the starting levers of the chronometers. The pendulum swung, counting out time and space and reality.

"I cannot allow you any more paper."

The cannon blast dashed any protest from Falcon. Zemba leaned out over the parapet and clapped the pocket-glass—Falcon's former pocket-glass—to his eye.

"Barrel and breeching are intact," he declared. "I think we might now try it under full charge. And a ball also." Since declaring himself protector of the Cidade Maravilhosa, Zemba had increasingly taken the trappings and manners of an N'golan Imbangala princeling. Falcon climbed up on to the revetment to watch the Iguapá gunners charge the huge cannon, clean-bored from a single trunk of an adamantine mahogany, out on the proving range. He watched the paper-wrapped charge—his paper, as his glass had been requisitioned—vanish into the barrel of the monster.

"I appreciate the necessity for dry powder in this humid miasma, but we apply ourselves so wholly to our defense that we neglect what we are defending," he commented mildly as the crew loaded the ball. Each wooden shot took a full day for a carpenter to turn and lathe to the necessary smoothness. Zemba had sneered at the Aîuba's suggestion: a wooden cannon, such a thing would fly into a million splinters the first time it was touched, more deadly than any fusee of the enemy. But Falcon's calculations had withstood scorn and gunpowder. Yet it irked that to this great man—a dazzling general and terrible warrior—his learning was respected only insofar as it served military ends. *Techne, the whore of Sophos*, Falcon muttered to himself.

Zemba had drawn his defenses deep and strong on Falcon's looted drawing books. The Iguapá traps and snares formed the tripwire to a monstrous system. A gargantuan *cheval de frise* of poisoned stakes embedded in ranks twenty deep directed attackers into murderous crossfire fields between heavy repeating-crossbow bunkers. An inner ring of earthworks modeled on European star-emplacements next poured ballista-fire and buckets of hot stones from trebuchets on the wretched survivors. The inmost line was zigzag trenches three deep from which a sea of quilombistas would charge, armored in padded leather *escaupil* and targes, armed with hardwood spears. Foot-archers gave killing support over hideous distances. Cidade Maravilhosa's classical defenses would have dismayed a Roman legion, but Zemba desired the destroying power of modern artillery. A bylaw pressed through the city aîuri made compulsory the use of public latrines that might be scraped for saltpeter: Falcon's half-remembered chymistry had produced black powder, but in the Rio do Ouro's steamy climate it fizzed and puffed in the touch-hole until Falcon, twisting little paper bangers to terrify the children, lit on paper cartridges. The charges, in varying weights, hung from the rafters of the drying huts like albino bats.

The gunners unwound a long fuse; Zemba lit it with the slow-match. Falcon felt the ground heave beneath him, and a detonation that must have been audible in São José Tarumás drove the wind from his lungs and the sense from his head. In a trice Zemba was at his overlook, glass to eye, Falcon a blink behind him. The cannon had been blasted back a dozen toises into the bush but stood intact on its sledge.

"We have it, by Our Lady, we have artillery."

Falcon did not need the proffered glass to see the tree branches, in a rising arc along the trajectory of the ball, waver, then one by one split, splinter, and crash down.

Even at his measuring station by the river he could still hear the booms as Zemba refined his artillery. "River" was generous to a lazy stream barely eight paces wide that eased into the Rio do Ouro carpeted velvet green with jaguar-ear. Pistol cocked over his knee against the jacaré, Falcon watched Caixa wade out, now thigh deep, now belly deep, the soft, dew-teared jaguar-ears brushing against her small breasts, to the farther measuring post. Gold on green, she enchanted him. He had taught her to letter, to number, to read the sky and recite in French. This little tongue of sand, where the forest opened unexpectedly onto the river was his by word of the Mair. Often he made love to her in this place, roused and repelled in equal measure by the soft spicy full-ness of her flesh and the golden, alien contours of her skull. She was a generous and appreciative lover, if unimaginative, and by the lights of her people, faithful. But most he loved this place by night when each jaguar-ear and dark-blooming water lily held the spark of a glowworm, a carpet of light, the far bank glimmering with fireflies and high over all, the scattered stars.

Caixa called back the reading. Rising still. But this was not the flood season. Smiling, she plowed through the water toward him, the carpet of green parting around the smooth, plucked triangle of her sex. He recalled his first sight of her, shy and smiling, prodded forward by her girlfriends to walk

beside the white man with the uncanny eyes. He had offered to bear for a
while the basket she wore from a brow strap; angrily she had stepped away
and had not come near him again until the evening when the Iguapá nation
straggled into its first camp.

So soon had the sense of the pilgrim nation given way to silent stoicism
and that determination that set foot before the other, day in, week in, to helpless anger. The Iguapá nation straggled over half a day through the varzea of
the Rio Iguapará and the Rio do Ouro. The last, the oldest, the youngest, the
weakest stumbled into the camp many hours after the Mair and his guard of
pagés struck for the night. Some never arrived.

The Iguapá nation knew hunger. The varzea, so rich in botany, was
meager in forage. Food hooted and whistled in the high branches of the
ucuuba and envira; on the ground, in the damp shadows, it was guarded with
barbarous spines; fruits and vines sickened or poisoned or drove mad with
visions. Falcon's manioc war flour and beans fed a people; Caixa sharing out
the thin rations, making sure the old and sick were not bullied out of their
portion. The Manaos gravely reported the state of the supplies; Falcon noted
them down and did dismal mathematics. Even then, Zemba had set himself
between Falcon and Quinn. It was only with the greatest persistence and the
muscular weight of his Manaos that Falcon had been permitted through the
circle of pagés to the Mair.

"You must give them time to rest and hunt and regather their strength."

"We cannot, we must go on, I have seen."

In the end the people walked from insane desperation. There was no
other choice than to swing up the hammock-pack, slip the strap over the blistered brow, and push the children before. Caixa freely permitted Falcon to
share her load. The chests of war flour were emptied and cast aside. Falcon
cut up instrument cases, bookbindings, shoes and laces, and satchels to boil
soft enough to chew out a little sustenance. The people starved, but the frogs
were fed; the sacred curupairás in their pierced ceramic jars. Old men sat
down with a sudden sigh at the side of the track, unable to move or be
moved, left behind, the green closing around them and the look on their faces
relief, only relief. Falcon pushed one foot in front of the other, scourging himself in intellectual guilt: his tools, his instruments, the brass and the ebony

and the glass; the iron and the lead shot, the books half gone to mold without their covers, the clothes and keepsakes—he must set them down and forget them. Each time he returned the same thunderous denial. No he would not, never, for when all else was reduced to the animal, to the mechanical, they were the dumb witnesses to this indifferent vegetable empire that this was more than a march of ants.

Then Quinn—a haggard, bearded, Deuteronomical patriarch leaning on his stick—declared, *This is the place.*

Falcon had barely been able to frame the question.

"What have you seen?"

"Enough, my friend." Then he had turned to his people as they filed into the small, sunlit shard where a tree had fallen, revealing the sky. "This is the Marvelous City. We shall build a church and raise crops and live in peace and plenty. No one who comes to this place shall be turned away. Now, let's burn."

That night, in the smoke and the embers, Caixa came to Dr. Robert Falcon and never again left.

The Mass was ended. Women, men, children with their heads bound in the wood and leather casings that forced their still-soft skulls splashed barefoot from the church through the silver twilight rain, through the narrow lanes between the malocas shin-deep in liquid mud, touching their foreheads in salutation to the Aîuba as he passed. Falcon ducked under the dripping thatch. The iâos, the brides of the saints, still danced in the foot-polished clay ring, each bearing the emblem of his or her saint: the three-bladed sword; the hunting bow; the peccary's tusks; masks of the tinamu, the catfish, the frog. The musicians on their raised dais had worked themselves into trance; drums, clay ocarinas. They would play for the rest of the night, the iâos swirling before them, until they fell over their drums and the blood started from their palms. The great pillared hall of Nossa Senhora de Todos os Mundos reeked of incense and sweat and forest drugs. Falcon passed through the dancers like a specter, pausing to cross himself and kiss his knuckle before the crucified Christ, at his feet a woman, face upturned in marvelment, orbs in each hand

and upon her brow, her own feet resting upon a golden frog: Our Lady of All Worlds. Out again into the rain and across the fenced compound to the vestibule. Pagés waited on the verandah, golden faces naked in their suspicion of Falcon, jealous of his privileges.

"I did not see you at the Mass, brother." Quinn removed his stole, kissed it, hung it on the peg.

"You know my opinion. I see little of Christ there." At the climax of the Mass, after hours of drum and dance, Quinn was carried around the throng of worshipers, passed overhead hand-to-hand, spewing prophecies. Not even in the grimmest privations of the Long March had Falcon seen him so drained.

"It is like there are no lids to my eyes. I see everything, everywhere. It consumes me, Falcon. The apostles were sterner men than I; the gifts of the Paraclete burn those who bear them."

"It takes more every time, does it not? Give it up. It will destroy you, if not in body, certainly in the seat of reason," Falcon said in French.

"I cannot," Quinn whispered. "I must not. I must take more, and greater, if I am to be able to turn passive observation into action and join the others who walk between the worlds."

"You talk arrant nonsense; you are deranged already. Already the quilombo suffers from want of a guiding hand on the tiller."

"I am not the only traveler—how could I be, when on countless worlds similar to this one, Father Luis Quinn, SJ, has taken the curupairá and held in his hands the warp and weft of reality? Throughout history there have been—and will be—ones who travel between worlds and times."

"Now this is nonsense, Luis. Travel across the ages as if stepping from one room into the next? I give you an immediate paradox: the simple effect of treading on a forest butterfly in the past might set in motion a chain of events that make it impossible for Luis Quinn, Society of Jesus, to even exist, let along gavotte merrily through time."

Quinn pressed his hands together before his face as if in prayer.

"Of course. And where would I walk, but to the singular moment in my life that shaped it beyond all other? I have stepped through and in an instant returned to that lodge in Porto. I have looked on my own face, and seen the look on that face to find itself confronted with a spectral visitor beyond horror: his own gaunt, aged form dressed in priestly black; the *'Mene, Mene, Tekel, Upharsin'* that having written, moves on. It takes little more to stay the hand, to set the death-dealing mug down on the table, to reel away from friends and comfort and warmth into the street. I have seen myself go on my knees and beg my forgiveness, yet each time, when I flip back to that page that is my own time, this time, I find nothing changed. There is a law here; we may step back through time, but never to the history of our own world. We always walk backward to another world, that world where I appear to myself like a visitation and then vanish never to return, for to do so would violate that great Censor who requires that we may write the stories of others but never our own."

"Now you offend me," Falcon flared. "Now this is indeed madness. If I had a piece I would pistol you so that your insanity should not infect others. Airily you claim to breeze between worlds and histories, by whim, by thought, by will-o'-the-wisp or fiery chariot, and with a wave of your hand my world is abolished; rationality, scientific inquiry, the knowability and pre-dictability of the physical world merely a tissue of illusion over a void of . . . magic. Divine fiat, the power of word and thought over mundane reality."

"But, Falcon, Falcon, what if that is what the world is made from? Word and thought?"

Falcon slapped the center pole of the hut. "This is real, Quinn. This is reality."

Quinn smiled weakly. "If the simulacrum were detailed enough, how would we ever know?"

"Oh, for the love of God!" Falcon leaped to his feet. Golden faces looked in at the door, withdrew at Falcon's hostile glare. "The water is up again. That is what I came to tell you. I want to take a canoe and a party of my Manaos away from the cidade."

"Talk to Zemba. He is protector of the cidade."

"I desire to talk to you. I desire you to ask me why I want a canoe and a party, why I want to investigate the rising water. You have become remote, distant, aloof, Quinn. You have set colonels and counselors between yourself and me, Luis; between yourself and your people."

The bark curtain over the door twitched. Zemba entered, his skin glossy wet from the rain.

"Is all well here?"

"Nothing has occurred here," Falcon said. "I was merely telling Father Quinn that I am taking a reconnaissance party onto the river to investigate the rising water."

"All such applications must be made to me as chief of security."

Falcon bristled.

"I am not your slave. Good evening, sir."

Robert Francois St. Honore Falcon: Expedition Log 8th August 1733

Often I feel that the only important feature of my journal is the date in the heading. Too easily the days slip into an eternal present; without past, facing a future indistinguishable from now, disconnected from human history. But surely the first duty of a chronicler is to establish his own history within the greater flow of time. So I write 8th August 1733 and rejoin common humanity.

How good it is to be abroad on the river, in a ten-man canoe with Juripari before me, Caixa at my back, and all the vegetable riches of the Rio do Ouro arrayed before me. Cidade Maravilhosa had become oppressive and hostile; not in the physical sense— that would not be tolerated, not even from Zemba and his military claque—but to my qualities, my profession, my beliefs. The City of Marvels is a City of Blind Faith. I had believed in the aîuri, that wise body of índio morbichas and ebomis from the escaped black community, to steer the community sanely and sagely, but it has been filled with pagés and young warriors under Zemba's sway. A council where older and more careful heads—I count myself among them—are shouted down by the zeal of young males is not beneficial to the community.

This is the fifth day of the expedition, and we are now running downstream. At good speed and in good heart we set off from the cidade and made twenty leagues a day upriver, taking us into the high Rio do Ouro beyond the exploration of any Paulista bandeira. Here are índio nations that have never seen a white face before, yet the canoe parties we encountered—Juripari found a simplified Waika could effect basic communication—knew of the Marvelous City and the great caraiba who walked between worlds.

I was initially nonplussed to find the levels on the Alta Rio do Ouro to be lower that at Cidade Maravilhosa, the precise reverse of what one would expect for a flood descending from the headwaters. But the scientist, in the face of conflicting facts and theory, always modifies theory to reality. A set of measurements taken below the cidade will confirm if the river is filling from the lower courses. I have one set of measurements now, from a point some three leagues beneath the quilombo as drawn on my rudimentary chart of the Rio do Ouro fluvial system—some fifteen as the river wends—and they seem to support my general hypothesis. A second set taken at tonight's camp will put the seal on it. . . .

"Aîuba!"

Over floods and centuries the Rio do Ouro, rounding a prominent ridge, had eroded a wide bow, almost a bay. Falcon's canoe cut close to the bluff, doubled the point, and found itself bow to bow with a fleet. Falcon saw paddles, bright brass, the glint of sun from steel, plumed hats.

"Scarlet and buff!" he cried. "Portuguese soldiers!"

The Manaos swiftly, sweetly reversed their seating in the canoe, dug at the water with their paddles. Falcon's smaller, lighter craft could outpace the heavily laden war canoes, but there was headway to be lost; and as he came about and seized his own paddle to lend his speed to the craft, the pursuers bent to their blades. The chase was on. A dull pop, little louder than a musket, and a plume of water flew up some paddle-lengths to the left of the canoe. Another, and Falcon saw the ball pass with fluttering howl and bounce three times from the water before vanishing.

"Paddle for your lives!" Falcon shouted. He slipped the glass out of his pocket. Six swivel guns bow-mounted in heavy, thirty-man war canoes. As he glassed the soldiery—a dozen colonial infantry in each of the lead boats, dress coats patched and mold-stained after weeks on the river—the swivel gun spoke again. The ball bounced from the river in a splash of spray that soaked Falcon and cleared the canoe between Juripari and a Manao deserter called Ucalayí. A narrow target and the flat trajectory over which the Portuguese were firing had served thus far, but soon the gunners would load shot rather than ball and make murder of them.

"Caixa! The muskets."

She was already rodding the first of the two pieces that Falcon had kept sacrosanct from Zemba's requisitioners. *A woman of skills is a pearl beyond price.* Falcon drew on the red-and-gold division flag in the stern of the center war canoe. Before it sat an officer in dress uniform, his tricorn hat edged with feathers, grimly gripping the sides of the canoe. Falcon recognized Capitan de Araujo of the Barro do São José do Rio Negro. A simple shot, but Falcon lets his sight slide forward to the buff-coated gunner bent over his piece in the bow.

"Steady, hold her steady!" It was a delicate calculus; the cease-paddling made the shot surer but necessarily brought them into the range to the muskets of the colonial infantry. At his earliest clear shot Falcon discharged in a crack and cloud of smoke. Zemba's cartridges answered truly. The gunner jerked and went down into the floor of the war canoe, shot clean through the crown of the head. A roaring jeer went up from the pursuers; the body was rolled without let or ceremony into the river. Full five swivel guns replied, their shots falling all around the canoe, some so close water slopped into the dugout. The paddlers bent to their task; dark river water peeled away from the bow. Caixa handed Falcon the second musket and reloaded the discharged piece. The musketeers in the índio canoes were risking longer shots now, at extreme range and wildly inaccurate but sufficient to keep Falcon off his aim. And it was as he had feared: rounds of canister shot were being handed down the length of the gunboats.

"Steady, I have him I have him. . . ."

"Aîuba, we cannot yield any more headway," Juripari said.

"Steady, steady . . ."

The capitan was clear in his sight. *Cut the command off at the head.* Falcon squeezed the trigger. The lock closed; the flint flared. Falcon saw the hat fly from the officer's head into the stream; then glowing slow-matches met touch-holes.

"Down! All down!"

The river flew up around Falcon as if shattered like glass; splinters flew up from the raked gunwales, but the hull held, by Jesus and Mary; the shot bounced from that adamant forest trunk. A sigh; Juripari, endlessly surprised to find the side of his head shot away, slid gently into the river.

"Lighten, lighten!" Caixa commanded in lingua geral. Supplies, water, the second musket, all cartridge and shot but for a sniper's handful, followed Juripari. Falcon watched with leaden heart the black water close over his beautiful, precise, civilized instruments. He rolled his journal into a tight cylinder and pushed it into the bamboo tube he had designed for just such a pass: so closely capped as to be watertight, *in extremis* it might be thrown into the river in the vain hope that it might someday, some year be found and returned to the French Academy of Sciences. The canoe surged forward. Pirogues broke through the drifting bank of powder-smoke and gave chase. Falcon lay prone in the stern, sighting over the gunwale, dissuading the musketeers from incautious fire. Alone in the canoe Caixa's head was up as she read the varzea for a landmark.

"Cover me!" Caixa shouted. Falcon wiped the spray from his green glasses and let crack at the lead musketeer. The weapon flew from the soldier's hands, shattered in the lock. Caixa touched a fuse from Falcon's smoldering pan; with a shriek and rush the signal rocket went up beside his head and burst in brief bright raining stars. Its detonation rolled across the roof of the forest; startled hoatzins plunged clumsily from their roost. The soldiers exchanged hand signals; the two hindmost canoes backed water and turned.

Then two gleaming bolts stabbed out like lightning from either bank and pierced the disengaging canoes through and again. A wavering shriek rose from the canoe on the left bank; a ballista bolt had run an índio paddler through the thigh, a terrible, mortal wound. The water rippled and parted, lines appeared from beneath the surface. Invisible defenders hauled the hapless canoes in to shore. The soldiers tried to hack the lines with bayonets, but they were already within the short range of the repeating crossbows. A storm of bolts annihilated the crews; those who leaped into the river to save their souls were run down by bowmen loping along the shore. The soldiers' thighboots filled with water and dragged them under the black water.

The chase had become a rout, the entrapped canoes circling, firing into the varzea as they tried to withdraw. Twice again Zemba's ballistas struck, once capsizing an entire canoe. Soldiers and índios alike cried pitifully as the Iguapá hunters waded thigh-deep into the water, shooting them like fish with their poisoned darts. Falcon found his body trembling from the excitement and the pure, dispassionate efficiency with which Cidade Maravilhosa's defenders set about destroying their enemies to the last man. Yet Falcon's exultation was partial, and brief. Even as Zemba's defenders had repulsed the attack by water, raiding parties of índios and caboclo mercenaries had attacked and set torch to the manioc plantations.

The boy poled the pirogue through the trees. An oil lamp, a wick in a clay pot set on the prow, struck reflections from the night-black water. Cayman eyes shone red then sank beneath the surface. Father Luis Quinn stood in the center of the frail skiff; black on darkness, an occlusion. To the boy he seemed to float over the drowned forest. Fragments of voice carried across the water, heated and impatient; the lights of the observatory passed in and out of view as the boy steered among the root buttresses and strangler figs. A fish leaped, splashed, its belly pale.

"Here," Luis Quinn said softly. The pirogue halted without a ripple. Quinn stepped into the knee-deep water and waded toward the light and the voices. The observatory had been built on a high point to give an uninterrupted window onto the sky; now it was the only building of any consequence above water in Cidade Maravilhosa and therefore the natural conclave for the aîuri. Worlds flickered across Quinn's vision as he slogged from the water, leaves clinging to his black robe; worlds so close he could touch them, worlds of water. The voices were clear now.

"The revetments will be overtopped by morning," he heard Zemba's musical voice say as he entered the observatory.

"God and Mary be with all here." The aîuri of Cidade Maravilhosa were seated in a democratic circle on the floor of the great room, Falcon's calculations and theorems crawling around them like regiments of ants. Quinn kicked off his saturated leather slippers and took his place among them. The hem of his black robe dripped on to the foot-polished wood. The aldermen crossed themselves.

"This is clearly an artificial phenomenon," Falcon said in his halting lingua geral. Even in the half-light of palm-oil lamps he wore his glasses. Quinn noticed Caixa squatting on her hams in the deeper shadow at the edge of the hut. The waiting woman. "If my expedition had been permitted to continue its planned course, I am in no doubt that we would have encountered a . . . a . . . ." He gave the word in French.

"A dam," Quinn said in the lingua.

"Yes, a dam. It is clear that the Rio do Ouro has been dammed with the intention of flooding the quilombo and rendering us helpless," Falcon said. "To construct such an artifact—I have made some calculations as to the size and strength required—requires an army of labor. There is only one person in this vicinity who can set whole populations to work."

"And set whole populations to war," Zemba said. He turned to Luis Quinn "Did you see, Mair? Were you there when the Portuguese maggots burned our crops? I had thought we might see you, leading us to battle with the high cross. But I did not see you. Did anyone see the Mair? Anyone here?" Zemba's young cocks crowed behind him. Quinn hung his head. He had expected the admonition; it was meet and right, but his pride, his damnable, Satanic pride wanted to crow back. He saw a pewter mug in his hand as he had seen it in so many worlds, in those worlds stopped himself from murder and yet in this world nothing could be changed.

"I was . . . away." He caught Falcon's look of surprise. Murmurs sped from mouth to mouth; the aîuri rolled and swayed on their thin kapok-stuffed cushions. Oil flames bent on their wicks as a sudden warm gust possessed the observatory. "You must trust me when I tell you that our troubles here are only part of a greater conflict, a war waged across all worlds and times, so vast that I cannot encompass it."

"Troubles. Ah, that explains it, then."

Flames flickered across worlds.

"I cannot explain it to you; I barely apprehend it myself. Nothing is as it seems. Our existence is a veil of illusion, and yet in a thousand worlds, I see the quilombo between fire and water, the torch and the flood."

Consternation among the old men, muttered aggressions among the young.

"And among these thousand worlds, did you find an answer?" For all his feathers and finery Zemba seemed diminished, dismissed, desperate to regain some degree of stature before his men. *This is when we are our most dangerous,* thought Luis Quinn the swordsman, *when our pride is broken before our friends.* "For if I understand this rightly, the Portuguese capitan's great guns and Father Diego Gonçalves's men can sail right over our defenses and annihilate us to the last infant."

"I do not need to go out among the worlds to find the answer to that," Quinn said. "Dr. Falcon."

The Frenchman pushed his glasses up his nose.

"It is very simple. The dam must be destroyed."

The young, aggressive men all started to bellow questions.

"Silence," Zemba shouted. "How may this be achieved?"

"This also is quite simple. A sufficient charge of powder, placed in proximity to that part of the dam under greatest hydrostatic pressure, would effect a breach that would swiftly carry all away."

Zemba squatted on his hams, supporting himself with his stick.

"How much powder would be required?"

"I have done calculations on this as well. It is a simple linear analysis; every hour the pressure on the dam increases, thus decreasing the amount of explosive we require. However, every hour we wait makes an attack more likely; if we attack within the next day, I believe our magazine of powder would suffice to breach the dam."

"All our powder."

"That is what I have calculated."

"Our artillery, our musketry . . ." Falcon had helped the quilombistas haul the massive mahogany cannon up the greasy, mud-slick hill called Hope of the Saints. Now he was telling Zemba they were useless, worse than useless; they squatted on valuable strategic positions. "And if it is not sufficient, we would be defenseless."

"That is not my calculation to make."

Zemba laughed, a deep, house-shaking chuckle. "Aîuba, you offer me some chance and no chance, which is better than damnation by a hair. How would this charge be delivered?"

"Our magazine could be transported in six large war canoes."

"You shall have the best navigators," Zemba said, gesturing to his lieutenant, who at once loped from the observatory.

"They would of necessity travel by night—without doubt, our enemy has moved his basilica and war-fleet upstream. At the dam . . ." Falcon shook his head. "Once I see it I believe I could quickly calculate the weakest point of the structure."

"Of course, Father Gonçalves would not fail to have posted guards against just such an eventuality," Luis Quinn said. "There will be a fight while you make your calculations, Doctor. No, what is needed is someone who can in an instant know where to set the explosive."

Cries of dismay and protest rang out around the circle of the aîuri.

"Silence!" Zemba roared again. He beat the heel of his staff of office on the floor planks. "The Mair is correct."

"I will know where best to site the powder; I will know where Gonçalves should set his guards. And, though I have forsworn the way of the sword, there must be a time for the setting aside of oaths. Would God hold me in greater contempt if I renounced my word or failed to protect His people?" Then he murmured in Irish, "*I should wish for a task most difficult.*"

"It's decided," Zemba said. "The Mair will lead the attack on the dam. The powder will be ready with canoes and good fighting men, with what steel we can spare. I will prepare for the defense of the Kingdom of God. Christ and Our Lady bless us."

The aîuri broke up, old men stiff from the floor.

"Luis." Falcon held out a short, thick bamboo tube with a plaited lanyard to Quinn. "Take this for me, would you?"

"What is it?"

"The history of the quilombo of Cidade Maravilhosa; partial and poorly styled, overly emotional and lacking in any academic objectivity, yet true nonetheless. If the dam cannot be breached; if the charge is insufficient; if you, God between us and evil, should fail, surrender this to the waters downstream and pray to whatever God is left to us that it will find a safe landfall."

The glow of early light leaked through the woven walls. Quinn lit a cigar. "The last I shall enjoy for some time," he quipped. Falcon felt a touch on his arm; Caixa, her golden face telling him he had done right for her and that was all this woman wanted. He wondered if she might be with child. A distant cry, like a bird but no bird of the varzea, came across the lightening sky. A second voice picked it up, a third until the canopy rang as if to the roars of the howler monkeys. Zemba rushed to the railing, snapped out his glass, but Falcon had already swiveled the great observatory telescope in its mount and was scanning the skyline beyond the eyries of the Cidade Maravilhosa's lookouts. He let out a cry. In the objective, distant yet kindling in the rising sun, angels—vast angels in red and green and heaven's blue, the instruments of divine warfare in their hands—advanced over the distant treetops.

OUR
LADY
OF
ALL
WORLDS

June 11, 2006

The burned skeletons of construction machines still smoked, the orange paint blackened and bleached down to bare metal. The pichaçeiros had already been at work with their busy little rollers. Me me me. A shout out to the world from Rocinha. The slab concrete of the wall resisted fire, resisted even sledgehammers, chipped down to the reinforcing rods but still adamant. So it had been colonized. Every dozen paces the black tag of the ADA, Amigos dos Amigos, laid claim to the territory within. The red CV stamp of the Comando Vermelho challenged it: graffitis struggled to overtag each other. Lord wars: the great favela was one of the last surviving medieval city-states. One hundred and twenty-five thousand people lived draped over this saddle between the two great morros; the apartment blocks rose eleven floors high, balconies flying with laundry, looking down from their mountainside on the lesser towers of comfortable São Conrado and Gávea. The alleys and ladeiras were busy as rats with white plastic waterpipes, the black power cables festooning the sagging poles dipped so low children in their smart school T-shirts and track-suit bottoms ducked under them.

The police barely glanced at Marcelina Hoffman as she joined the throng moving up toward the street market. White was no less rare within the new favela wall than without. Anyone could go in—the São Conradeiros had to buy their cheap meat and cocaine somewhere. The walls were only there to protect passing drivers from ricochets and stray bullets. No other reason but the gunplay, the stray bullets. Anyone could leave, any time, during working hours. Surf boys with great muscles strolled, boards under arms, down to the beach at the Barra da Tijuca. Their Havaianas crunched broken glass and empty cartridge cases. The police looked them over more in envy then enmity. The sun was hot the sky was blue the surf was up and there was peace, of its Rocinha kind.

Ten reggaes bounced from as many windows and verandahs; rain had fallen again that morning and pooled water on the plastic stall roofs turned into treacherous rivers, pouring over the edges of the weather-sheets on to startled, laughing shoppers. Marcelina pressed up against a trestle across which two lambs lay in absolute dismemberment as a tour passed, whey-faced gringos in two olive-drab open-top Humvees, armored for the Baghdad green line. Devil-incisored teeth grimaced in the stripped sheep-skulls, eye-balls glared, loira. They were right; she had been around the green globe and even across the Tijuca Bridge but this was the first time she had set Manolo in a favela. Marcelina had grown up at the foot of great Rocinha, but she was as much as tourist as the ianques in their armored tour-buses. And she thought, *Why are we ashamed? We decry those tourists in their roll-bar Jeeps bouncing down through the market as if they're on safari; Brasilia rails against the unstoppable wave of favelization; we tear down shacks and put up walls and declare bairro status like tattooing over the scars from a terrible childhood illness, one the ianques eradicated decades ago. Don't visit them, don't look at them, don't talk about them, like idiot siblings taped to the bed in the back room; but they are not stumbling*

*blocks on Brazil's march to the future. They are the future. They are our solution to
this fearful, uncertain century.*

A cellular shop. A man making manioc bread on a little glass-fronted
barrow. This was the place. Marcelina leaned against the storefront and
watched Rocinha's busy past. All our worlds, separate yet intersecting. She
felt pretty damn pleased with her philosophizing. Worthy of Heitor himself.

The moto-taxi passed once, turned, returned. The rider, a lanky morena-
fechada in Rocinha uniform of Bermudas, basketball vest, and Havaianas,
drew up beside her.

"You're the Físico," Marcelina said.

"Show me," the boy ordered.

Marcelina took out the little frog she had bought from the expensive
Centro chocolatier. Moto-boy waited. She unwrapped the gold foil and
popped it in her mouth. The sweat-heat chocolate left a little print like the
spoor of something hunted in her palm. The boy nodded for Marcelina to slip
onto the pillion. She locked her arms around his waist, and he hooted his way
out into the throng of market-goers. Across the cracked blacktop serpentine
of Estrada de Gávea the moto-taxi took to its native element like a monkey,
the steep ladeiras zigzagging up between the rough, gray, graffiti-slashed
apartment blocks. Amigos dos Amigos. It was half a year since Bem-Te-Vi
had been cut down by the police, the ultimate arbiters in the wars between
the drug kings, but the CV's takeover had hardly reached out from the main
arterials. Medieval private armies fighting for feudal lords to rule a renais-
sance hill town, with walls, even. And cellulares. And a functioning sewerage
system and water supply.

Dogs skipped and barked; women toiling uphill with plastic shopping
bags moved aside to the shelter of apartment steps; girls smoked in front
rooms, tipping ash through window grilles. And everywhere children, children children. Marcelina shouted over the shriek of the laboring engine, "Are
you really a physicist?"

"Why shouldn't I be?" the boy said, turning onto an even steeper ladeira.
The moto jolted up shallow, foot-worn steps. Marcelina's toes scraped the
rain-wet concrete.

"Nothing. It just seems, well . . ." Whatever she said would show her

Zona-Sul-girl prejudice. Why should Loop Quantum Gravity physicists not live in Rocinha?

They were high now, the tree line visible between the tenements that clung to the almost vertical hillside. Marcelina looked down on the sweep of flat roofs with their blue water tanks and satellite dishes and lines of laundry. But the favela was fecund, uncontrollable; beyond the build-line new houses went up; cubes of brick and concrete, pallets of blocks and mortars sent up by the hoist-load to bare-chested bricklayers. Físico stopped outside a corner lanchonete so new Marcelina could smell the fresh paint. Yet the Comando Vermehlo had laid claim to its tithe on the shape of a red CV on the ocher brick wall. The owner nodded; a barefoot boy trotted out to mind the bike.

"We walk from here."

A dark archway led between doorways and windows. Televisions blared behind metal grilles; not one tuned to edgy, noisy Canal Quatro, Marcelina noted. Sudden steps led down into a small court; apartments piled unsteadily on top of each other leaned inquisitively over the open space. Two parrots perched on the web of electricity cables that held the whole assemblage in constructive tension. Down another flight of steps into a lightless passage, past a tiny neon-lit cubby of a bar, the seat built into the wall across the alleyway from the tin counter. A bridge crossed a stream buried beneath the concrete underpinnings of the favela, dashing and foaming down from the green, moist morro into a culvert. Up and out into the light at the foot of the narrowest, sheerest ladeira yet. Físico held up his hand. Marcelina felt the mass and life of the favela beneath her; but here, high on the upper ranges of Rocinha, they seemed the only two lives. The empty, blank tenement blocks were eerie in their silence. Higher and higher, like Raimundo Soares's Beckham story. Then Marcelina heard a ringing, slapping sound, a rhythm that made her gooseflesh stir. A soccer ball bounced into the stop of the ladeira from a higher flight, struck the wall, and zigzagged down the steep steps. Físico stepped under the bounce and caught the ball. He beckoned Marcelina up. She rounded the turn in the ladeira. At the top of the steep flights, dark against the bluest sky, was Moaçir Barbosa.

The Man Who Made All Brazil Cry.

Over the ten years she had worked her way up the Canal Quatro hierarchy from production runner to development executive, Marcelina's life had necessarily been woven with an eclectic warp of celebrity: Cristina Aguilera, Shakira, Paris Hilton, even Gisele Bundchen, Ronaldo, Ronaldinho, all of CSS, Bob Burnquist, Iruan Ergui Wu, and more wannabe popsters and tele- novela actors than she could remember. Star-sickness she got over the first time she had to run to fix a rider for a spoiled celeb—that brand of water at that temperature and shrimp for the doggie. Many had impressed, but none had ever awed, until Moaçir Barbosa had stepped out of legend and sat down at the table in the Fundação Mestre Ginga. Swallow in throat, push back the tears. She had been brought from her childhood bed to look upon the face of Frank Sinatra, but those blue eyes had never moved her the way Barbosa set- tled heavily, painfully onto the aluminum chair. This was death and resurrec- tion; this man in his pale suit had harrowed hell and returned. It was like the risen Jesus had climbed down from his hill high above this cool cool house.

"Have you read it?" He rested a finger on the book.

"Some. Not all. A little." She was stammering. She was Day Three on the job, pop-eyed at Mariah Carey.

"It'll have to do." Barbosa slipped the little book into his jacket. "I only came for this, really. Well, you've found me; and a world of trouble you've made for everyone, but most of all yourself. I suppose there's nothing for it. Ginga will bring you up tomorrow and we will sort it out."

"I don't know what you mean."

"You made the mess; you're going to have to clean it up." Barbosa rose as stiffly as he had sat down, yet, like all former athletes, a fit ghost inhab- ited him, the lithe and limber orixá of a cat-agile goalkeeper. He threw back a parting question from the door.

"Would you have done it?"

"What?"

"Put me on trial, like Soares said in the papers."

For the first time Marcelina's power of professional mendacity fails her.

"Yes. That was always the idea."

Barbosa laughed, a single, deep chuckle.

"I think you would have found it was I who put Brazil on trial. Tomorrow. Don't eat too much, and no alcohol."

"Senhor Barbosa."

The old man had lingered in the doorframe.

"Is it true for you? About the goalposts?"

A smile.

"You don't want to believe everything Soares says, but that doesn't mean that it's all lies."

High Rocinha opened itself to Barbosa the goalkeeper. The suspicious streets opened shutters, doors, gratings, and grilles. Electrically thin teen mothers with children on their hips greeted the old man; young, haughty males with soldado tattoos at the bases of their spines bid respectful good mornings. Barbosa tipped his hat, smiled, took a pão do quijo from a lanchonete, a cafezinho from a stall. Físico dawdled behind.

"I don't want to have to move on from here. It's a good place, people have time, people look out for each other. I'm too old, I've moved on enough, I deserve a little peace at last. I've had five good years; I suppose you can't ask for much more. I should have told Feijão I was dead."

Marcelina asked, "What do you have to move on for?"

Barbosa stopped. "What do you think?" He tossed his empty plastic cup into a small brazier tended by two small boys. "You should be at school, learn something useful like my friend here," he said to the boys. "Well, at least you understand now."

"The curupairá, the Order? I don't—"

"Shut up. We don't talk about that in front of the gentiles. And that wasn't what I meant. What it's like to have everything, to be King of the Sugar Loaf, and have it all taken away from you so that not even your best friends will talk to you."

They didn't take your family away, Marcelina thought. *They left you that.* It was a ramshackle conspiracy: a disgraced World Cup goalkeeper, a favela physicist, a middle-aged capoeira mestre, and now a wrecked television producer. The flimsiest of girder-works over the deepest of abysses, that this world, these streets, the skirt of rooftops spread out beneath like a first Communion frock, the blue sea and the blue sky and the green forest of the hills, even the soccer ball Físico carried with the clumsiness of a geek-boy, were a weave of words and numbers. Solipsism seemed so unnecessary under a blue sky. But it was the world in which Marcelina found herself, and the conspiracy suitably dazed and uncertain, as if both white hats and black hats could not quite believe it. Heroes and villains barely competent for their roles—that was the way a real world would work. An improvised, found-source favela solution.

Físico unlocked a small green door in a fresh brick wall and flicked on a bare bulb.

"You wait in here."

"It's kind of little," Marcelina said.

"It won't be long."

"We have things to get ready," Barbosa said. Marcelina heard a padlock snap on the hasp.

"Hey! Hey."

The room was concrete floor, roughly pointed brick, a couple of plastic patio chairs, and a beer-fridge filled with bottled water plugged into the side of the light fitting. The door was badly painted planks nailed across a rudimentary Z-frame, but they banished the sounds of the streets as utterly as deafness. Spills of light shone through the boards. *Alone with your dreads*, Marcelina thought. That's the purpose. Descanso: chilling the head. A place between, the dark in the skull. Half an hour passed. It was a test. She would pass it, but not in the way they wanted. She pulled out her PDA and drew the stylus.

Dear Heitor.

Scratch it out.

Heitor.

Too abrupt, like calling a dog.

Querida. No. *Hey.* Teenage. *Hi Heitor.* E-mail-ese. Like Adriano's acronym-speak.

I said I wouldn't get in contact so that's how you'll know it really is me. That sounded like Marcelina Hoffman. *I'm writing this because it's possible I may not see you again. Ever.* Overly melodramatic, going for the first-line grab, like one of her pitches? The stylus hovered over the highlight toggle. This is supposed to be . . . What is it supposed to be. A confessional?

A love letter.

Let it stand.

That makes this easy because it's the coward's way out; I'll never have to live up to anything I've written here. Glib but true: he'd read that and say, "That is Marcelina." *It's silly, I'm sitting here trying to write this to you and I can think of all the things I want to say—that's so easy—but for once the hand won't let me believe them. Funny, isn't it, I can pitch any number of ideas I don't really, deep down love, but when it comes to writing about something important, something real, I freeze.*

The treacherous hand hovered again, the stylus ready to delete. What could it not believe? This big, bluff, old-fashioned, glum, romantic, pessimistic, hopeful, catastrophically uncool square-headed newsreader-man. His books. His cookery. His wine his time his listening. His big gentle hands. His love of rain. His always availability, states of Brazil and world permitting. His too too many suits and shirts and always-respectable underwear. His sexiness that was never anything so modern or obvious as raunch, but something older, cleverer, dirtier, and more romantic; burlesque, louche, decadent.

She saw her stylus had written, *You make me feel like a woman.* Almost she consigned it to nothingness. But he did. *You do.* So long she had burned with acid envy at her sisters and their men and their security, and she had not realized that she had her man, she had her security; a modern relationship, not something off the shelf marked *21st Century Bride* or *Hot Teenz.* A grown-up thing that had evolved from a meshing of work schedules and body parts but in the end it was a man, a relationship, a love.

Her hand shook. She wrote slowly, *You know I've gotten myself into something bad—if I told you I would just scare you and there still wouldn't be a thing you could do about it. It's all up to me now. I am very very scared. I can't help it. I find I have to play the hero, and that's not a role I know anything about. Give me Jerry Springer trailer trash and Z-list scandal. And I find there are no scripts for this; I'm making it up as I go along. But I've been doing that all my life. It's the thing I know best. I can pitch it. But I honestly don't know how this is going to end. I don't want to think. Barbosa: it would have made the program of the century, but not in the way anyone thought. A show I would have been proud of.*

Not much of a love letter. Or maybe it was, a Marcelina love letter where she bitches and moans about herself for two pages and then at the end drops in the line, *Oh, by the way, I love you. I think I've loved you for a long time. Can you do that, love someone without knowing? It would be so much better if you could, clean and quick and none of the mad, embarrassing stuff, none of the phone-bombing and SMS-assaults. And then of course I start to think, is it me? And I'm not sure which is the more difficult answer because one way I'm stupid and I've hung my heart out and the other I didn't know and you didn't say. Agh! I have to go. I love you. Wish me well. I'm not a very good hero, I'm afraid.*

Her thumb waited over the e-mail key. It deserved better. He deserved better. The Lisandras dated by e-mail, dumped by SMS. Show some malicia.

A scrape, a painful wedge of light opening into a parallelogram of day. Físico stood in the brightness. Marcelina thumbed save and slid the PDA into her bag.

"Okay then," she said. "Let's go."

The bateria had been playing for two hours now, a steady two-tone tick of an agogô begun before sunset and sent out over the cellular network, the call to prayer. The barracão of the Igréja of the Holy Curupairá was a large living room on the first floor of a new-build apartment block. Cheap vinyl was rolled up, the furniture piled against a wall. A folding kitchen table was the altar, pushed against the big window with its breathtaking view down across the glowing carpet of Rocinha to the towers of São Conrado. A fair gold cloth dressed the table and was scattered with assentamento: cubes of cake, cones of yellow farofa, saucers of beer, little oranges stuck with joss-sticks. Holy medals, soccer stickers, animal-game lottery cards, centavos, and cigarettes. The air was sickly and headachy from incense trickling from church-stolen burners and Yankee Colonial scented candles in glass jars. Squat saints and orixás guarded the altar; most had índio features and carried Amazonian plants and animals in their hands, snakes and jacarés beneath their feet, like the vehicles and attributes of Hindu gods. The only one unfamiliar to Marcelina was a near-life-size wood carving depicting an índio woman, naked but her skin painted gold, balancing on one foot and entwined, like a dollar sign, in an S of snake-headed vine. She juggled planets. Marcelina recognized Saturn by its rings, Jupiter by its satellites on projecting sticks. Our Lady of All Worlds. The serpent's head was pressed to the woman's pubis. The statue was old; the wood cracked with age, pocked with the flight-holes of wood-worm, but the craft and care spoke of an age of faith made manifest. Sweepers worked the floor, two street boys with twig besoms. The susurrus of sacred amaci purification soothed Marcelina.

The bateria occupied the left window corner of the room, and the drummers were already far into their improvisation, trading tempos and breaks. On the opposing wall the kitchen door led to the improvised camarinha. As initiate zemba Marcelina was permitted into the fundamentos, which seemed to consist of Barbosa sitting at a worktop with a cup of coffee reading the soccer results off his WAP cellular. A brass cage stood beside the bottle-gas cooker; within, a golden frog, stupid eyes wide, throat throbbing. A grasshopper skewered on a pin and wired to the bars offered temptation. An antique brass kettle on the gas hob spelled its fate.

Summoned by drums, the egbé had been arriving since twilight; mostly men, some few women, pausing to purify themselves with a splash of holy water from the stoups by the front door. All wore white, though watches and jewelry showed they came from outside Rocinha. Many had painted a single stripe of gold down the center of their faces, brow to chin. Marcelina was dressed in a high-neck racer-back top and capoeira pants—all white—Físico had sourced down in the town. The pants were a little chafing in the crotch; otherwise Físico had read her size right. Full dark now, the great favela a fog of light spilling down from the green mountaintops to the sea. The bateria unleashed its full force. The terreiro shook, cups rattled on hooks, the refrigerator door was shaken open. Glancing out into the barracão Marcelina saw the space before the altar was as crowded with white-clad, dancing bodies as any Lapa 4 AM club, and yet more piled in behind. Some wore full bridal dress, gleamingly white and virginal; they pushed up to the very front of the barracão and whirled, already ridden by the orixás. She saw Mestre Ginga arrive, hastily bless himself, and work his way along the wall to the camarinha. He kissed Barbosa on each cheek and set a long flat object wrapped in banana leaves on the table.

"Awo," he said to Marcelina's puzzled look. *Secret.*

Now the alabé was calling, the egbé and the bateria responding, and Marcelina felt the music kick open an inner door so that fear and apprehension flowed into excitement and anticipation. The drums caught her, lifted her. Even the glorious abandoned insanity of the réveillon and its two million souls had not thrilled her so, called the deep axé and sent tears down her cheeks, shaken her to the ovaries. Barbosa touched her gently on the hand, rose from his seat. Marcelina fell in behind him, Mestre Ginga at the rear. Before quitting the camarinha he lit the gas under the kettle.

A wall of sound greeted Marcelina. She lifted her fists: Mick walking onto the stage on the Copacabana Beach before half of Rio. The egbé went wild. Over the physical hammer of drums, so hard it hurt, came a shout from the golden faces. Zemba! Zemba! The iâos in their bridal dress whirled in bolar, the deep possession of the saint. The Daime at Recreio dos Bandeirantes had been a security-guarded, middle-class madness: the terreiro of the Curupairá was the true spirit: axé burned along the concrete floor, from light fitting to light fitting. Marcelina was whirled time out of mind; space stretched; time shrank; she may have danced, she may have been lost for a time among the white-clad bodies; then she was back at the altar. Barbosa raised his white cane. Drums, voices, feet fell silent and still. He spoke in a language Marcelina did not understand, part índio, part church Latin, but its meaning was clear to her, the calls, the shouted responses: she was the zemba, the warrior, the protector of the egbé. Barbosa guided her to the front of the altar. The people murmured greeting. Mestre Ginga brought the copper kettle from the kitchen, dancing a fidgety, malandragem little tap-step as he worked around the assentamento past the drummers. The alabé started a rattle on his agogô; the bateria took it up, whisper of skin on skin. Mestre Ginga lifted the kettle before the congregation, who again murmured, like the sea. Barbosa took the kettle, quick as only a corda vermelha could be; Mestre Ginga caught Marcelina, pinned her arms. Excitement burst inside her. Barbosa brought the kettle up to her lips. She opened her mouth eagerly. This was the sexiest thing she had ever ever done. Pae do Santo Barbosa poured three drops of liquid onto the tip of her tongue. The curupairá was rank, bitter, Marcelina grimaced, tried to spit it out. On the third spit, the multiverse blossomed around her.

The barracão was a dazing blur, room upon room superimposed within, next, above each other, yet each accessible from every other. The eyes perceived; the comprehension reeled. More people, more people, the population of an entire city, and the entire planet, crammed into this one room. Blinded by the white: Marcelina lifted her hand to shield her eyes and saw a thousand hands halo it. Edit. Everything is edit, cutting down those endless tapes of footage to meaning. Peering through the white barracãos she caught glimpses of other rooms, families coming together, televisions, meals on battered sofas. Car engines on carpets. And beyond them all, the dark forest. She whirled, throwing off a firework spray of alternatives to the window. Rocinha was a universe of stars; galaxies beyond galaxies of lights. Marcelina cried out, her ghosts and echoes called around her. The gravity was irresistible; she might fall forward forever into those clouds of lights. Beyond them, other skylines, other Rios, other entire geographies. She saw unbounded ocean; she saw archipelagos of light; she saw green cordilleras and great pampas.

Marcelina turned to Barbosa. She saw him alive, she saw him dead, she saw him gone, she saw him glorious, a hero, the greatest goalkeeper Brazil ever knew, a government minister, a UN goodwill ambassador. She saw him hounded and humiliated on prime-time television; she saw an old man take off his hat and his jacket and walk into the waves off Ipanema; she saw twenty million fingers poised over the TV remote red button to vote: innocent or guilty?

Next the curupairá touched the auditory centers and opened them up. One voice, ten voices, a choir, a cacophony. The reverential silence of the barracão became an ocean of soft breathing, became a hurricane. Marcelina clapped her hands over her ears, cried out. The cry rang out from a million universes, each clear and distinct. Beyond the edges of the cry were voices, her own voice. Eyes squeezed shut against the shatter of the multiverse, Marcelina forced her understanding toward the distant voices, tried to pick them out one by one. There was a way to navigate the multiverse, she discovered; what you sensed depended on what you focused upon. Focus on the terreiro, on the favela light, and you saw geographically. Concentrate on a person, on Barbosa, on her own voice, and you steered from life to life, ignoring distance and time. Mind was the key. Top to bottom, beginning to end, it was all thought.

Marcelina gingerly opened her eyes. She stood at the center of a cloud of selves; a mirror-maze of Marcelina Hoffmans before, behind, to left to right, above, below but all connected to her and to each other. One mind, one life in all its fullness. She saw herself a star, commissioning editor, channel controller, telenovela director, pop producer. She saw herself a journalist, a fashion designer, a party gatinha. She saw herself married, pregnant, children around her; she saw herself divorced, alcoholic; she saw herself down; she saw herself dead more times than she wanted: in a fast German car, in a mugging, with a belt around her forearm, in a toilet, at the end of a blade that could cut through anything. There. Fast as a bat, moving away from her sight as she touched it, crossing from world to world to world. Herself. Her enemy. The anti-Marcelina, the hunter, the cop, the police.

I see you, she thought. In that revelation, she saw beyond, to the blur of quantum computations, to the fundamental stuff of reality, the woven fabric of time and calculation. And she saw, as she remembered sitting backstage with the hands watching the Astonishing Ganymede, the famously bad conjuror of the Beija-Flor, waiting for her mother to sweep up from the band pit on her mirrored Wurlitzer, how the trick was done. It was simple, so very simple. Everything was edit. Take a sample here, another there, put them together, smooth over the joins with a little cutaway. New reality. Innocent and shining with wonder, she reached out her hand to seize reality.

Mestre Ginga's arms were around her again; fingers forced open her mouth, a million open mouths, a billion fingers. Coffee. Marcelina choked, gagged, heaved in Mestre Ginga's wire-strong arms. The flocking universes flew away like a storm of butterflies.

"Coffee," she swore, retching dryly over the assentamentos.

"You're very much mistaken if you think it's just coffee," Mestre Ginga said, slowly releasing her. "Even those three drops can be too much."

"I saw everything," Marcelina said. She leaned on the edge of the altar, shaking, head bowed, sweat dripping from her lank hair. "I was . . . everything." Every muscle spasmed. No capoeira jogo had ever wrung her so dry. Slowly she became aware that there was a roomful of expectant devotees in white, waiting for the word from the multiverse. "I saw . . . her."

"And she saw you," Barbosa said. "She knows what you are now."

"The zemba."

"You are not the zemba yet," Barbosa said. *Tock-tock*, said the agogô, beginning a fresh rhythm. The iâos swayed and swirled, left to right, their dresses floating up around them. Físico entered from the camarinha carrying the leaf-wrapped object. He set it reverently on the altar. Shards of other worlds flickered around Marcelina. Would it always be this? She suspected so. On the edge of her vision, like a floater in the eye that, when looked at, perpetually flees the focus of attention, she was aware of the anti-Marcelina, and that she was aware of her. The curupairá, the gathering of the egbé, Barbosa revealing himself as Pae do Santo of the terreiro were to prepare her for the inevitable showdown. Marcelina stripped away the dry, dust-smelling banana leaves. The leather scabbard was the length of her forearm, worked with an image in ridged stitch work of the Lady of All Worlds. She took the handle.

"Careful," Barbosa warned.

The blade drew like silk over glass. It seemed to Marcelina that it did not actually touch the inside of the sheath but was suspended in some kind of invisible filmlike oil. The blade was long, curved, beautifully dangerous. She held it up before her eyes. The only sound in the barracão was the clock-tock of the agogô. Marcelina looked closely; the edge was blurred, she could not focus on it, it appeared to fizz and boil, a heat-haze on the edge of vision. Marcelina made a sudden cut. The egbé let out a great coo of wonder. She smelled electricity, saw blue burn across the line of her slash.

"I've seen one of these before."

"It's the standard-issue ritual weapon of the Order," Físico said. "It looks like a knife, but we think it's an information weapon. It cuts down to the quantum level. It undoes the braids of quantum loop gravity. This is technology beyond us, beyond any of the worlds of the multiverse. I think it may always be beyond us; it's part of the fabric of the universal quantum computer itself."

Marcelina spun with the knife in a wheeling capoeira armada. Did she hear the shriek of fundamental computations coming apart?

"Where did you get this?"

"It came with the book. The annexes say that Our Lady of All Worlds brought it up from the bottom of the Rio Negro."

Again the multiverse pulsed around Marcelina. Cut. Edit. You are not unarmed now. You are not a victim. She held the knife high over head. The egbé roared. The iâos whirled, petticoats held out. The bateria took up the argument of the agogô as Marcelina strutted around the altar, blade held high.

"Zemba!" Mestre Ginga roared, and the terreiro took it up.

"Zemba! Zemba! Zemba!"

The weather closed in as the Rocinha Taxi Company cab took Marcelina up over the top of the town and down toward the floodlit oval of the Jockey Club. Fingers of low cloud that joined together into a great palm of stratus blew in from the west and pressed down on the morros. By the time the taxi reached the lagoon it was raining steadily. Marcelina itched and fidgeted in the middle of the backseat, burning still with the brief vision of the curupairá. Every flash of passing headlights, every flicker of pink and yellow street neon cast shadows of other universes. With the quantum blade tucked into the top of her white Capri pants and her clingy top, Marcelina could have conned free entry to any club in Rio. She was death. She was the hunter. She was beyond cool. The driver had been instructed to take her to a safe house Mestre Ginga knew in Santa Teresa, but as he cruised the Avenida Borges de Medeiros, the lagoon dark, rain-pocked reflections, Marcelina leaned forward between the front seats and said, "Can you take me a detour?"

"I don't know. I mean the mestre said—"

"I just want to drop something in; it'll not take five minutes. It's just down on Rua Tabatingüera; it's not even really out of your way."

"I suppose I could, then."

Marcelina took the steep concrete steps that rose almost sheer up the face of the morro a reckless two at a time. Love does that. Rain punished her. Good rain. Sweet rain. She pressed the PDA close to her chest, protecting it from water. Pools were already forming on Heitor's gloomy garden patio, a lightless concrete rectangle between the rear of the apartment tower and the dripping raw rock. His light- and love-starved climbing plants shed rain like sweat. Marcelina knew the key code by heart. Her finger stopped a millimeter above the chrome button.

The door was open a crack.

Marcelina slipped back from the door and pressed herself against the wall. She called up the live Canal Quatro newsfeed on her cellular.

". . . and the police report that Maré and Parada de Lucas are quiet tonight, with armed incidents returning to normal levels," Fagner "Death-and-Destruction" Meirelles reported Live! from a militar cordon. Hissing through her teeth, Marcelina thumbed the volume down. "And back to the studio." And there was Heitor standing in front of the giant green-screen map of Brazil. *The only newsreader who has to worry about the color of his socks*, he always said.

Marcelina sent him into darkness. In one G3 call elation turned to dread, to more fear than she imagined anyone could know and live. Every part of her ached. It would be very very good to be sick, even if it was only hot bile, cold coffee, and terreiro drugs. She could feel the multiverse flickering around her, a cloud of orixás and angels. Now. This was the time. She drew the blade, crouched into a fighting ginga stance. Slowly slowly she pushed the door open. Cat-careful, Marcelina advanced through the lobby of books. Stiff, so stiff, and no time to warm up. She would have to go from cold into explosive action. This was no jogo, no game.

No lights, but squatting in cocorinha by the side of the living-room door Marcelina saw a silhouette cross the glittering panorama of the lagoa. The destruction was to be total: her career, her family, her friends, her lover. Then, one by one, Físico, Mestre Ginga, Barbosa the goalkeeper: the entire terreiro, any and all who knew the secret shape of the multiverse, and about the Order that protected it. And at some point, Marcelina Hoffman. That point was now. *Malandros mestres corda vermelhas all you great fighters and dancers, give me malícia.* She stood up, flicked on the main light, and cartwheeled into the room in a one-handed aú. Marcelina came up into ginga, blade ready.

She stood momentarily dazed in the light by the kitchen annex, black to Marcelina's white. Of course. This was elemental battle. Her. More than any twin could ever be. Curupairá vision flickered around Marcelina, and for an instant she saw herself through her enemy's eyes, loira angel, white capoeirista. *We are each other.* One mind shattered across a hundred billion universes. Then the anti-Marcelina came like a jaguar. Marcelina dropped under the blow in a simple resistencia, spun out in a wheeling S-dobrado kick. Her foot grazed her enemy's head; then Marcelina rolled into a waist-bend, one hand on the floor, the other gripping the quantum blade for all love, and came up into the dancing, defensive ginga.

The anti-Marcelina advanced on her in a blinding weave of cuts that struck small lightnings from the air in the apartment. Marcelina ducked, rolled, dived, flipped away from the burning blade. One thing, one edge in malicia. Her enemy did not play capoeira. She did not know jeito.

A scything blow left the glass coffee table in two capsized halves. Marcelina backflipped over one of the leather sofas into ginga.

"Say something, will you? Say my fucking name."

Her enemy smiled and in three strokes reduced the sofa to hide and spring and stuffing. Now Marcelina realized that she had underestimated the power of her enemy's weapon. She could run, she could dance, but the anti-Marcelina would cut, cut, keep cutting through anything and everything, keep cutting, keep coming until she was too exhausted to play capoeira anymore. *You have lost the initiative. Time to stop playing defensive. But I'm not a killer. Yes you are. Look.*

Marcelina aimed an asfixiante punch at her enemy's nose, then brought the blade in a scything sweep. The anti-Marcelina dodged the punch and brought her own blade cutting down onto the flat of Marcelina's. There was a flash of light, a cry of reality maimed. Marcelina saw the severed blade of her knife flash up into the air, fall point first into the floor and vanish. She imagined it dropping through the apartments below, level by level. Even solid concrete and rock could not resist it. She hoped there was no one directly beneath.

The anti-Marcelina smiled sweetly, held up her own intact blade. Then she beckoned. *Finish it.*

Marcelina Hoffman ran. Jeito. Street smart. The true malandro knows when and where to fight. A gashed sofa, a bisected coffee table—these Heitor could explain on an insurance claim. A corpse that looked like your lover and disgraced TV producer: that was a career killer.

Marcelina knocked off the lights (these silly tricks worked, but that was the essence of malandragem, the pant-pull boca de calça that had felled arrogant Jair—the stupid and obvious was the last-seen) and ducked out the elevator lobby door. The slam would betray her, but the few seconds it took for the anti-Marcelina to cut through the lock would give her time and space. Marcelina pelted up the emergency stairs. Two flights up she heard the door crash onto concrete. *I'm a dancer not a runner*, she shouted at herself. Footsteps slapping on bare concrete. *Up up up.* But Jesus and Mary the curupairá had taken it out of her. The curupairá and every other torment and mystery and threat and revelation of the past two weeks. From Blue Sky Friday to Fight-for-your Life Sunday. She fell through the door onto the roof. Room to move. Space to fight. Heitor had brought her up here with champagne and coke when she won the commission for *UFO Hunt: Live!* By night, in the rain, it was moltenly beautiful, strips and clouds of soft light, the flow of head- and taillights along the lagoon road, the soft shurr of tires in the wet, and beyond all, above all, the dark look of the morros.

The door crashed open. Her enemy was here. Marcelina rolled into a defensive stance. The anti-Marcelina hefted her blade to a killing grip. Back and forth they fought, strike and counterstrike, across the puddled rooftop, slipping on the loose gravel, tripping on the satellite cables and water pipes. Feint by feint Marcelina drew her assassin to the sheer face of the morro, pressing to within centimeters of the parapet. Above her concrete pillars rose like organ pipes, stabilizing the rock face. There were service ways up to those piers. She hopped on to the edge and leaped across the gap on to the hill itself. Her enemy followed but Marcelina was already up on to the service path, a precipitous ledge with only a chain for handrail. A sudden tug almost pulled her from the path; Marcelina reeled back hard against the wet rock. The chain that had almost dragged her down fell away into the dark between the flat roofs of the apartment blocks below. Her enemy looked up into her face. With the last of her strength Marcelina ran up the steps onto the top of the morro. Rio lay beneath her, the lagoon an oval of darkness, a jet jewel set in gold. Leblon, Gávea, the shining spill of Rocinha; Ipanema a line of light interrupted by dark hills, beyond it the glowing scimitar of the Barra da Tijuca. To her left the lights of the Copacabana were a golden necklace between the shouldering morros.

The anti-Marcelina appeared over the top of the steps, panting.

"Let's have it out," Marcelina said. "Here. No more running or clever stuff. Let's do it here."

The anti-Marcelina shook her head. Rain flew from her golden hair. Marcelina was shivering, wet to the bone, but it would end here, far from the eyes of the world, high above Rio de Janeiro. The enemy launched at her. She was good, but she had no jeito, no malandragem. Marcelina dropped into a banda, caught her enemy's legs between her own, and twisted. The anti-Marcelina went sprawling. Marcelina followed with a down-and-dirty kick to the side of the head. The anti-Marcelina howled but rolled into a knife-fighting crouch. She menaced, jabbing, feinting with the quantum-blade. *You picked the wrong martial art*, Marcelina thought, floating in ginga, coiled like a jaguarundi. *The true capoeirista will always appreciate a good dodge more than a good blow.*

"You know," she said, "that you don't give a damn about anything that gets in your way, the casual cruelty, I can understand. I've done that myself. But what I can never, ever ever forgive is that part of me that wants to be a fucking cop."

The anti-Marcelina struck. The tip of the Q-blade grazed the inside of Marcelina's forearm. There was no pain, no shock; then Marcelina saw blood well from the long, shallow line. The anti-Marcelina reversed her grip, came in again. Marcelina ducked into a defensive cocorinha and saw it. It was simple, it was beautiful, it was malandragem. She grabbed the cuffs of the anti-Marcelina's pants and pulled up. With a cry the anti-Marcelina went back over the edge of the morro.

Marcelina watched her own face, eyes wide, drop through the spears of rain. There was no cry, no scream, but the quantum-blade cut a line of blue light through the air. She watched her other self strike the edge of a rooftop and bounce, spinning into the greater darkness beneath.

Marcelina stood a long time in the hammering rain, counting breaths. Breathing was good, count them, slow the heart. *Count the breaths one two three. Don't think about what you did. Don't think about the look in your eyes as you fell down into the dark between the apartment blocks. You died there. You lost. You won; but in winning, you lost. The multiverse pulled a final malicioso move on you. That's your body down there.* Even now she could hear the police sirens, see the

flashing lights coming around the dark lagoon. *Marcelina Hoffman, the contro-*
versial Canal Quatro producer who recently gained national notoriety when she pro-
posed putting disgraced goalkeeper Moaçir Barbosa on trial, was found dead at the
foot of Morro dos Cabritos on Sunday night. Police are continuing their investigations,
but suicide has not been ruled out. Adriano Russo, director of programming at Canal
Quatro, said that Senhora Hoffman had been under a lot of strain recently, at work
and in her domestic life, and had been acting erratically. She imagined Heitor
looking into the autocue. He would be professional. He was always professional. He would mourn later. Her family would bury something. The police
would keep the quantum-blade and wonder among themselves for decades
just how a dead television producer came to be in possession of a knife that
could cut through anything.

Marcelina looked down into the darkness where her enemy lay. *She lost,*
but she beat you. You are dead too.

Footsteps on wet rock.

Marcelina spun into defense. A man in loose dark clothing, formless
against the night. A thumbnail of white at his throat; priest's vestments?

"If you want me you can have me, I'm dead anyway." She stood upright,
opened her arms.

"You can never win against yourself." A big man, white-skinned, dark
hair, hollow-cheeked; gaunt, she thought, with more than age. His Portuguese was strangely accented, stiffly archaic.

"So, who are you? Order or player?"

"I was an admonitory," the man said. "Now I am a visitor. A traveler. An
explorer. A recruiter, perhaps."

"Explorer of what?"

The man smiled. Marcelina could make out that he had the palest blue
eyes.

"You know that."

The sirens were close now.

"Recruiter?"

"What does one recruit for, if not a war?"

The sirens had shut down.

"Come with me," the priest said. "Here. Now. This is the one chance you'll get. It will mean leaving everything you've ever hoped for and loved behind, but you've lost those anyway, and there are ways back. There are always ways back. There is a war, but it's bigger than you ever thought. It's bigger than you can think. It's your chance to make a universe. You are a maker. Come and make reality."

Marcelina felt the multiverse open around her like wings, each feather a universe. The priest turned away; a billion doors opened before him.

"Who are you?" Marcelina shouted.

"Does it matter?"

What was there? *The Girl Who Came Back from the Dead* would be a hell of a program, but no producer should ever be the star of her own show. The husband, the beautiful children, the babies, the stellar career—they would never happen. One thing she could do.

"I'm not a cop."

"Oh no," the priest said. "Never that."

"That's all right, then," Marcelina Hoffman said, and stepped after him out among the universes.

APRIL 18, 2033

The ball hangs motionless at the top of its arc. Freeze-framed behind it, perfect sky perfect sunset perfect perfect sea. A hand reaches up and smashes it hard over the net. The girl in the red baseball cap and matching tanga dives, meets the ball with her two fists, a beautiful block. Her partner follows the volley, times her jump and is there to spike it down on to the enemy sand. Thigh muscles belly muscles upper arms are in perfect definition. Asses in mathematically curved precision. The breasts are high and firm and big, but they move like real flesh. Cheekbones knife-sharp. Noses flattened, kissy-kissy pert lippies.

They're stupidly fabulous, but Edson's not watching them. He follows the coconut boy sauntering over the sand with his machete and his wares slung around his shoulder. He's in good shape, swimmer's definition, muscles but not too many, natural not surgical. He sees Edson looking over as he drags past, catches his eye. A toss of the head. It's on for tonight. Edson turns and leaves the sunset beach for the strip. Behind him robots scurry from scrapes to rake smooth the sand, erasing all trace of his presence. The glory-girls do not even glance away from their game.

Beaches, Edson has ruefully decided, are very overrated. Before him rises the titanium-and-glass cliff of *Oceanus*. One hundred and fifty vertical meters of inverted social order. Penthouses fringe the beach-strip, then the restaurants, sea-view bars, clubs, casinos, the high-marque specialist shops that consider themselves too exclusive for the cavernous rain-forest ravine of the Jungle! Jungle! shopping mall. Next up the apartments and hotels; higher still the office units and businesses; higher again the medical centers and manufacturing zones; and over all the airport occupies most of the kilometer-and-a-half run of the top deck, apart from that sector at the prow reserved for the golf course.

The great ship cruises just outside Brasilian territorial waters two hundred kilometers off Pernambuco, shadowing the coast of Brasil southward. Three hundred and fifty thousand citizens speak thirty tongues; Portuguese, the only one Edson understands, among the least and quaintest. Her twelve-million-ton deadweight can punch through hurricanes, cyclones, taifuns. The nuclear reactor at her core propels her at a lax, unceasing eight knots: a circum-navigation of the world's continental shelves every three years; extraterritorial, beyond national jurisdictions, the ultimate free-trade port and corporate tax shelter. Category error. *Oceanus* is no ship: she's an oceangoing city-state.

When the seguranças made him kneel hands clasped behind neck, head bowed, Edson had been certain he had seconds to live. Assault guns had stood over the raiders of the lost car-pound while the mercenary crew buckled a tautliner cover over Cook/Chill Meal Solutions. Two men in black had dragged Edson out of line across the scabby concrete, scraping the polish off the toes of his good shoes, and thrown him into the back of a black quiet car that said *money* more effectively than any hood ornament. Fia was already belted in, fidgety with apprehension.

"I asked them to bring you," she whispered as car and truck accelerated out of the dead mall. "It's not the Order; they won't touch the guys, it's just us they're after. Me, I mean." Edson understood. The Order would have left nothing alive in the mall. There was a third player in the game.

By the third rodovia gantry Edson had worked out they were heading to the airport. The convoy swept past the militar guard to the air-freight terminal. Embraer bizjets stood on the apron with their variable-geometry wings folded like anhingas'. A woman in a very well-cut suit escorted Edson and Fia onto a bizjet. Her safety demonstration as the bizjet taxied was as much a declaration of her absolute power over her guests as instruction on what to do in the eventuality of landing on water. Edson barely noticed when the plane left the ground and he left the city of his birth and life for the first time. He was entranced by a single word on suit-woman's lapel badge: *Teixeira*.

Every man of business has his saints. Edson's are those who come from nothing: the favelado become futebol legend; the Minas Gerais boy who seduces the nation with his voice; the Paulistano who turns his kibe stand into a global franchise; Alcides Teixeira.

He was born one of the landless; that great Brasilian archetype, the drought-stricken peasant of the northeast sertão who, like so many before, embarked on the trek to the silver city. His legend began where all the others ended: at his first glimpse of the towers of Fortaleza, and the sprawling favelas around them like scabs. *My face to the boot, my wife to the streets*, he said, and he and his wife got straight back onto the bus. The driver didn't charge them. No one had ever done a return trip before. Alcides Teixeira had taken a development loan from the MST, the Landless League, and planted five hundred hectares of dust-poor sertão with gene-modified rape seed. Within three years he was power farming three thousand hectares. Within five years, he signed output deals with Petrobras and Ipiranga and became EMBRAÇA. Twenty-six years later Alcides Teixeira's land covered four continents with green soy and yellow rape and was stealthing down the cool cool hillsides upon the Fazenda Alvaranga. Such a man would be within that golden circle privy to the secret order of the multiverse. Such a man would dare use that information to his profit. Multiverse economic modeling had been Fia's specialty in her world. Where there is a differential, a boundary, there is money to be made across it.

His mind spinning with plans and potentialities, Edson saw the dawn through the cabin window, spilling light across the shadowed land so that it kindled and lit. He felt the breath catch in his throat. Roads were silver wires. Rivers were gold. Every instant the pattern of shadows across the land changed. Then Edson saw the blue curve of the ocean. He pressed his face to his window. Big sea, getting bigger. Whitecaps, white boats. Land gone now, nothing but open ocean, and the plane settling toward it. The wing was changing shape, unfolding its cruise sweepback. Edson felt the wheels slide out and lock. The whitecaps were growing closer; Edson gripped the armrests. There was nothing out there. How did that landing on water go again? Lower. Engines roared, the pilot put the nose up, and the Teixeira bizjet dropped sweet neat onto a pure white runway scuffed with grubby tire marks. There were Embraers at stands, a control tower, even a dinky terminal. Suit was out of her seat while the plane was still rolling. She stood in the aisle, arms braced on seatbacks.

"Welcome to *Oceanus.*"

The daughters of Alcides Teixeira were goddesses. They had been built that way. Krekamey and Olinda: tall and pale from surgery, languid hands and thighs of gold. Creatures like Edson Jesus Oliveira de Freitas were beneath their regard, but their elongated, almond eyes opened as far as surgery would permit at the sight of the cyber-wheels turning slowly on Fia's belly.

One thing you can't buy, putas.

Alcides Teixeira led the tour personally, pointing out the offices and company apartments. Heroes are usually shorter than you imagine; but Edson hadn't expected the bad skin. The sertão had engrained itself in acne pocks and sun-creased lines. Perhaps the thing about Alcides Teixeira's level of wealth was the power to say, *World, live with it.*

"And this is where you'll be working."

Cute muscly boys in EMBRAÇA high-visibility coveralls were already installing the Q-cores in the huge glass-walled room high above the sea: blue, blue glass. Fia berated them: *Not there; when the sun gets round this side of the ship, I won't be able to see a damn thing.*

"We had a hell of a job catching you," Alcides Teixeira said. "You just kept running."

"We thought you were the . . . Order," Edson said. Teixeira, Alcides Teixeira, Alcides Teixeira of EMBRAÇA was standing beside him, close enough to smell his aftershave, talking to him. The glorious daughters moved before him like visions. But he could not deny it was embarrassing, the realization that the pistoleiros at Liberdade from whom Edson had rescued Fia were in fact Teixeira private seguranças. They had been successfully running away from salvation.

"Son, if we know about Fia here, we know about the Order. We can take care of a bunch of old queen fidalgos."

Edson ventured, "Mr. Teixeira, if I could just say, you've always been a hero to me. I'm a businessman myself." Never be without a card. First rule of business. He pressed it on Alcides Teixeira.

"Talent and light entertainment. Good on you, son." He nodded at his glorious daughters. "See those two? Bloody spoiled bitches, the pair of them. Spend all their money on their tits and asses." Krekamey—taller, blonder, weirder—scowled. "There's a job for you here if you want it. We'll find you something to exercise your talents, son."

"Mr. Teixeira, if you don't mind, I'd rather exercise my talents for myself." In thirty minutes down from the landing strip Edson had seen enough of *Oceanus* to know it was a ship of death. Death to Edson, to all he hoped to be. A kept boy, he would grow lazy and fat and doped and boozed and sun-soaked and dissolve into nothing. Dead.

Alcides Teixeira balked momentarily, not a man accustomed to refusal; then he grinned hugely and slapped Edson on his bird-frail back.

"Of course of course, I'd say that myself. Paulistanos always had a great work ethic."

Edson rides the moveway along the central spine of the great ship. The perspectives of the central strip awe: they're designed to. A straight kay and half; fifty meters vertical. The walls are lined with baroque balcony walks and cupolas, restaurants hang like weaver bird nests from the roof. Airbridges, elevator shafts, escalator runs crisscross the airspace. Kinetic fabric sculptures flex and bow in the air-conditioning. The air is fresh with ozone and saltiness. Main Street opens up into the central atrium of Jungle! Jungle! the forested heart of *Oceanus*; the vast cathedral-windows of Dawn and Sunset on opposite sides of the ship flood the chirping, chittering, dripping, reeking mass of verdure with true photosynthesizable light. Macaws whoop, toucans swoop, and birds of paradise flutter. Stores are tiny jeweled nests set among the foliage. Behind the storefronts are labels Edson and Efrim alike would kill for, but his back would blister at the touch of unearned silk. But Efrim lately is a stranger, a woman with whom he once had a fine, elegant affair. Even Edson is numb among the retail opportunities.

It's a hell of a walk home from the beach, through the twilight ecologies of *Oceanus*, but Edson knows this world is killing Fia. He doesn't pretend to understand what she's doing up in the R&D levels—not even Mr. Peach could explain it, he suspects—but he knows what he sees dragging back from the office, piling into the sofa to sit curled up against the armrest silently sullenly flickering her eyes over *A World Somewhere* on her I-shades, fridge-feeding, putting on weight. And sex is completely out the window.

So Edson has this thing he does, because a man has to.

The security jockey on the desk at the residential level is a Maceio boy watching *Bang!Bang* on his transparent desktop. He despises Edson but must respect the Teixeira authority on his I-shades. Most of *Oceanus*'s labor has been shipped in from the northeast. *Is this what we aspire to?* Edson thinks. *Cheap offshore meat exports. Brasil, the nation of the future, and always will be.*

The apartment has luxuries Edson could never dream even for his fantasy Ilhabela beach house: an I-wall, a spa bath, massage chairs, a free-flow bed that learns its occupants' sleep patterns and molds itself to them. Edson has taken to the fold-down in the living room. *She's the worker, she needs the quality sleep*, he tells himself. The sun beaming through the glass wall wakes him every morning. He brings Fia morning coffee and takes his out onto the balcony to watch the light out of the sea. Not even a kiss. *This is it, Edson Jesus Oliveira de Freitas*, he tells himself as he sits at the deck table and feels the warmth on his face. *The one thing you wanted.*

"Hey."

The apartment is in darkness, but there is a moon and light from the sea: *Oceanus* is pushing through a huge current of phosphorescence. Edson lifts his hand to the lights.

A sigh.

"Leave it."

Fia is on the balcony, curled up on the decking against the partition wall in panties and vest-top. By ocean-light Edson can see she's been crying again. He knows her enduring fear: she's a postdoc researcher into quantum economic modeling who stumbled from one universe to another by luck and desperation, and she is expected to direct the sharpest theoreticians Teixeira money can hire. She fears they know that, that one day one of them will casually ask, *Who told you you could do this?* Edson has spent his life staying one answer ahead of that question.

"Are you all right?"

"No. Do you want to know, Ed?" She has taken to this nickname. Edson doesn't like it. It's not a self he's made. But he kicks off his shoes, slides out of his jacket. The air is soft and skin-warm, tanged with salt. He never imagined the sea would smell so strange: like it hates the land and all who come from it.

"Want to know what?"

"Do you want to know what the Order is keeping secret? We've found it. It's a doozy, Edson. Tell me this, why are we alone? Why are humans the only intelligence in the universe?"

"I know this argument. Mr. Peach used to talk about this; he had a name for it. Something's paradox."

"Fermi's paradox, that's what you're looking for. Keep that in your head while I ask you question two: why is mathematics so good at explaining physical reality? What is it about numbers and logic?"

"Well, that's the universal quantum computing thing. . . ."

"And Mr. Peach told you that too."

"Don't laugh at him. I told you before. Don't laugh at him."

Fia starts at the sure ferocity in Edson's voice.

"I'm sorry. Okay, let's just leave that as something I will never get. But why should computation be the root of reality? Why should reality be one huge system of rendering—no different from a very big, very complicated computer game? Why should it all look like a fake? Unless it is a fake. Or a repeat. Maybe there are no alien intelligences out there because what we think of as our universe is a massive quantum computation simulation. A rerun. All of them, reruns."

Edson slips his arm behind her back.

"Come on. You need to get to bed, you're tired."

"No Edson, listen. Before we killed the Amazon, in my world, there was a legend. In it the jaguar made the world, but not very well; and it ended on the third day and we—the world, everything we think is real—are just the dreams of the third night. It's true Edson, it's true. We're the dreams. We're all ghosts. Think about it: if a universal quantum computer could simulate reality exactly, any numbers of times, what are the odds of us being in the very first, original one, as opposed to any other? Do you want those numbers? I can give you those numbers. We've worked them out. They are so so so so small. . . . The real universe died long ago, and we're just ghosts, at the end of time, in the cold, the final cold. It's running slower and slower and slower, but it will never stop, over and over again, and we can't get off. None of us can ever get off. And that's what the Order is keeping from us. We are not humans. We're ghosts of humans running on a huge quantum simulation. All of us. All the worlds, all the universes."

"Fia, come on, you're not well, come on, I'll help you." He doesn't want her talking about the Order, their Sesmarias and killers. Edson fetches water from the kitchen zone. The water on this boat tastes sick; like sea that has been through too many bladders. He's added a couple of additions from the farmacia to it. She's been working too hard. Rantings, mad stuff. "Come on, sleep."

She's a solid girl, growing more massy on junk food, no exercise, and homesickness. Edson helps her to the bed.

"Ed, I'm scared."

"Ssh, sleep, you'll be all right." Her eyes close. She is out. Edson arranges the pillow under her head. He looks long at Fia swashing down into sleep like a coin through water. Then Edson pulls on his polished shoes and straightens his hip-ruffled shirt and goes out to meet his coconut boy. Fake it may be, lies and deceptions, but this is the world in which we find ourselves, and here we must make our little lives.

Coco-boy meets Edson at the back of the double-deck driving range stand. The nets are floodlit; stray light glints from the steel sea far below. A whistle.

"Oi."

"Oi."

"It's been delayed. There's something else coming in ahead of it."

It's a sweet little business arrangement. Coconut and guest workers come in on the night flights and with them Pernambuco's finest mood-shifters. It's not illegal—very little is illegal on extraterritorial *Oceanus*, where the corporacãos rule like colonial donatories. Neither is it particularly legal. *Oceanus* is a nuclear-powered gray economy, and Edson moves through the informal economy like a cat in a favela. Personality adjuncts are marketable: Edson has sent roots down into the club level, and his business plan predicts doubling the number of personalities on *Oceanus* in six months. God and his Mother; those blandroids need all the character they can get. And tonight tonight tonight eight kilos are coming in from the farma shops of Recife, and everyone knows the people of the nordeste are the best cooks in all Brasil.

Lights in the dark sky, fast approaching. Now engine noise. Growing up in a flight-path, Edson has noticed how aircraft engines are never on a sliding scale of audibility, from whisper to rush to roar, but go from silence instantly to audible. Quantum noise. The kind of thing you would find in Fia's fake universe.

"That's the other flight," Coco-boy says. He has the jeitinho with the airport staff.

"That doesn't sound like a plane," Edson says. A jet-black helicopter, visible only by the gleams of moonlight on its sleek, jaguar flanks, slides in over

Oceanus. Edson and Coco-boy both see the green and yellow Brasilian Air Force stars morph up on its fuselage. It settles but does not land, hovering a meter and half above the strip. A door opens. A figure drops out, landing lightly on the runway. In an instant he is up and away. In the same instant the helicopter climbs and peels away from *Oceanus.* It shivers against the sky and then fades into the night, stealth systems engaged.

"Fuck," says Coco-boy.

"Back," says Edson. "Hide." His balls are cold and tight. Wrong here. His balls have never lied to him. Even as Efrim. Lights come on in the control tower; seguranças run around not quite knowing what has happened or what they should do. The running figure pauses not five meters from Coco-boy and Edson's hiding place behind a plastic welcome banner. He turns. Backscatter from the driving range floodlights catches on an object slung across his back; at first Edson thinks its bone, a spine, something bizarre. Then he sees it is a bow, cast and shaped to an individual hand. And, as the man runs soft, swift, silent as light to the emergency stairwell, Edson sees another thing: an unforgettable blue glow, seemingly from the arrowheads in their quiver. Quantum-blades.

At age twelve Yanzon could shoot the eye from a monkey among the forks and leaves of the tallest, densest tree in the forest canopy. In those plague days monkeys were not good eating; Yanzon did this merely to display his supreme skill. After the fifth pandemic reduced the Iguapá nation to twenty souls, Yanzon made the long descent of the white and black waters to Manaus. His shooting eye earned money among the people who bet on the street-archery contests. When no one would bet on him anymore, he was taken up by a patron who groomed him to represent his nation in the Olympic games. In Luzon in 2028 he won gold in all his shooting disciplines. *The Robin Hood of Rio do Ouro*, the papers said, *the last Iguapá.* But Manaus's memory flows away like the river, and Yanzon would have slipped down through low-paid jobs into casual alcohol but for the aristocratic alva who arrived at his door one morning and offered him a job with travel prospects beyond his imagination. His old soul was unsurprised; the Iguapá had always known of the labyrinth of worlds and the caraibas who walked between them.

Now he runs lightly down the service stairs from *Oceanus*'s airport into the heart of the great ship. Yanzon touches the frame of his I-shades: a sunset-colored schematic is projected onto his retina. He can see through bulkheads, into sealed rooms, beyond walls and ceilings. Extraordinary technology; a world where everyone and everything may be located with a thought. A world with no room in which sin may hide. And music too; TV, movies everything. Not for the first time he wonders what his Brazyl might have achieved, but for the seven plagues.

His right hands hold the bow. It is an appallingly beautiful piece of killing gear. The compound limb is printed molecule by molecule from carbon nanofiber and molds to his grip like a prayer to a pain; the tip pivots are spun diamond. Pure titanium wheels give a hundred kilos of pull for an effortless, whip-fast draw. Gyros in the airspaces of the limb ensure exceptional stability and freedom from vibration; Yanzon can sight, aim, and have three arrows in the air and one on the nock before the first has punched home. Seeing it, you would say, *That is one beautiful evil bow*, but the words would not even leave your lips before Yanzon put an arrow clean through you. The real evil is not the bow, but the arrows.

Yanzon, last archer of the Iguapá, first hunter of the Order, arrives on Avenida Corporacão. The main business thoroughfare is cool, air-conditioned, cypress scented. A touch to the frame of Yanzon's I-shades blinds the security eyes, but the baroque double doors of EMBRAÇA resist his code. This is what comes from leaving things to a hereditary aristocracy. Amateurs. The Buenos Aires Sesmarias could have handled this, but they are scared the Zemba will appear again as she did at the church when she destroyed the São Paulo family. Let her come. Yanzon has long anticipated matching her fighting art against his Q-bow. Kill the researchers, destroy the Q-cores, and the helicopter will return him to the DOI quantum computer and the crossing back to his Florianopolis beachfront apartment. He should try and pick up something in Brasilia for Rosemeri's sixth birthday. A pair of these shades would be good, but they're probably incompatible. It is never clean eliminating someone as prominent as this man of business, but Yanzon has seen every great man as a beggar elsewhere.

The door is quantum coded. Amen. What quantum seals, quantum shall undo. He draws the Q-blade and with one economic gesture cuts the door free from its frames. The two halves hang a moment, then fall backward onto the woven grass carpet of the reception area. As Yanzon's boot soles crush the faces of carved baroque angels and demons, silent alarms detonate across his expanded vision.

Edson hammers on the elevator call button. Every street-sense, every gene of malandragem says never trust the elevator when your soul and love depends on it. But he's seen what's down the stairs. It's here: *bing.* Stupid stupid stupid elevator AI: I don't care about safety instruction. My girlfriend's down there with an admonitory of the Order and a Q-bow. *We can take care of a bunch of old queen fidalgos,* Alcides Teixeira had said. No you can't. They don't care for your money, they don't care for your empire, they don't care for your political patronage and your power. They are beyond mere economics.

The elevator bid Edson a good night. The door opened on chaos. The great baroque doors of the EMBRAÇA headquarters, appropriated from a church in Olinda, lie on the ground. Twenty alarm lights flash; a panicked sprinkler system douses the hardwood front desk. No one on that desk. Does he spy fingertips on the carpet? Running feet, voices cracking over com channels. Teixeira's seguranças will shoot whatever they see. Move out, Edson Jesus Oliveira de Freitas. But he takes a grain of reassurance from his eyeblink reconnaissance. The admonitory is working through the corporate levels first. He has still time to make the apartment.

Yanzon sees the running guards through two corridors. He will take one and the other will run away. His weapons are expensive, even for the Order, and should be reserved for the mandatory targets. His mission on this level is complete, all targets accounted for. His I-shades track the two figures through the wall: in one breathtaking, killing move he draws an arrow from the magnetic quiver, nocks, pulls. The bow's complex pulleys and levers slide with molecular precision. Fires. The Q-blade-tipped arrow cuts through wall, room, wall, running guard, out through the closed-down spaces of EMBRAÇA's corporate headquarters, out through the glass wall of *Oceanus*. A flash of blue light and a man is down, dead, pooling blood across the pimpled black rubber. Yanzon steps around the corner, a new arrow strung. The terrified survivor throws his hands up, his gun down and, as predicted, flees. Yanzon mouths a brief consignatory prayer for the dead man. The Lord will receive his own. If he does not know the Lord Jesus, then he must prepare for the Lake of Fire. Yanzon has yet to visit a universe that does not know the saving power of Christ. He has seen the true, the unimaginably true, extent of God's might. The glowing icons of Teixeira security move erratically: panicked, afraid. Slipping through their indecision, Yanzon takes the emergency stairs two at a time down to the residential levels.

Fia mutters in chemical sleep; soft babyish utterings.

"Theory of Computational Equivalence. If anything can be a computer everything can be a computer. Ah!"

Edson shakes her again.

"Get up!"

Her face creased into the pillow, she mutters, "What is go away let me sleep."

"The Order is here."

She sits up, eyes wide, electrified, a thousand percent awake.

"What?"

Edson claps his hand over Fia's mouth. The sound the smell the state of the air the prickle of electricity: all his favela-senses tell him *death is here*. He grabs I-shades; his, hers, and throws them on to the bed as he rolls Fia on to the floor. The oldest, best malandro trick: they trust too much in their arfids and their Angels of Perpetual Surveillance. As he claps his hand over Fia's mouth two flashes of ionized blue pierce the bed and it explodes in twin gouts of feathers and foam. Edson pushes his cidade senses to their most attenuated fringes to pick out nanoshifts of pressure, rustles on the edge of audibility, a quantum's difference in the slit of light under the door.

"He's gone. Now, with me. Don't say a word."

Hand in hand, he scuttles with Fia to the balcony. Stupid stupid stupid rich man's apartments with only one door. Edson peers over the balcony. Up: the black helicopter hovers, waiting to rendezvous with the admonitory. Down is a long long drop to an iron sea. Edson jerks a thumb toward the neighboring apartment.

"That way." High-waist flares and a ruffle-front shirt are not the best things in which to monkey across the face of a twelve-million-ton kilometer-and-a-half-long cruise ship. Edson springs up on the balcony rail, seizes the stanchion, and with a prayer to Exu swings round to the neighboring railing. "Piece of piss. Just don't look down."

Fia boggles at the drop, then in one ungainly movement makes the crossing.

"Hey! Look at me!"

Edson touches finger to lips. Apartments light up around them. Edson hears distant alarms, vehicles rushing overhead and far below. The great ship swarms like an ants' nest spiked with battery acid. The hunter is still in there.

Yanzon, admonitory of the Order, moves unopposed through the residential boulevards of the Teixeira corporacão, destroying the enemies of the Order. The alarms are irritating him now, and he has had to eliminate a few of the more bold segurancas; but he has established dread and awe across the EMBRAÇA headquarters. They showed him once the order the Order enforces. When he crosses and becomes superposed with all his alters, that is the truth. There is a universal mind, and all are notions of it. The prelates and the presidents, the pontiffs and prime ministers call it the Parousia, the end-time, but the eye of a simple man's faith can better know it as the kingdom of God. The Enemy says that is a lie, an endlessly repeated dream grinding ever slower as the multiverse wheels down, and they seek to break it, to wake the dreamers. They call this freedom and hope. To Yanzon it is pride, and annihilation, an endless drop into the final, eternal cold. A dream is not necessarily a lie.

He glances up. Through three floors he sees Alcides Teixeira trying to escape within a cadre of his bodyguards. They are heavily armed and equipped little sensor ghosts. Small avail against a hunter who can shoot through solid bulkheads. Yanzon sets arrow to his Q-bow, aims up through the ceiling. He whirls. Multiple contacts, closing fast. *Oceanus*'s marines have found him. Yanzon lowers his bow and breaks into a loping run. His mission now is to destroy the Q-cores and reach the extraction point. Or kill himself. The Order has always understood that its agents die with their secrets. One fast, easy pass with the Q-blade; almost accidental in its casualness. Yanzon has often imagined what it would feel like. He imagines his flesh parting down to the quantum as something silver and so subtle, so painless you would only suspect when the blood began to rush. No pain. No pain at all. And no sin, no sin at all.

Edson counts windows. Eleven, twelve.

"I feel sick," Fia says.

"Here."

Lights burn behind drapery. If he had a Q-blade, Edson could cut his way in neat as neat, a big circle of glass just falling away in front of him onto the bedroom pile. He doesn't, but he can trust that *Oceanus* builders did it as cheap and shoddy and minimum wage as every other piece of work done for rich people. He grabs the stanchion, swings up, and punch-kicks forward. The whole doorframe comes away from its track and swings inward.

"Ruuuunnnnn!" yells Edson at the naked twentyish man standing startled in the middle of the floor. Tech-boy gives a little scream and flees into the bathroom. By Edson's calculation they should be opposite a stairwell. Not even an admonitory could be fast enough to catch both of them on the short dash from door to stair. Surely. He flings the door open. The corridor is swarming with Oceanus marine security. Targeting lasers sweep walls, floors, ceiling. They catch Edson's heel as he pushes Fia up the stairs.

"This is the quantum computer level," Fia says.

"I know," says Edson grimly. "There's only one way off this ship. Can you work it? You have to work it."

They exit the stairwell the same instant as Yanzon comes around the corner. Only the fact that they should be dead saves them. In that instant of astonishment, Fia hits the security scanner, Edson pushes her through the door, and they both dive to the floor. The blue bolts sear through the air where their heads would have been, stab through the floor like lightning.

"Come on, he can cut his way through here like butter," says Edson.

The inner lock opens to Fia's blink. Inside, the four stolen Q-cores and more mess than tidy and precise Edson has ever seen in his life. Girlie mags makeup drinks cans food wrappers balled-up tissues pairs of socks pairs of shoes pens and coffee cups with crusts of mold in their bottoms.

"This is it?" Edson asks. The gateway to the multiverse. But Fia has pulled off her top, an action Edson always finds deeply deeply sexy, and coronas of gray light flicker around the cogs on her belly as the wheels begin to turn. The Q-cores answer with the ghost-light of other universes. *It is a terreiro*, Edson thinks. Junk magic. A loud crash tells Edson the hunter is now in the outer lab. Of course. They may be invisible to him, but he wants the cores, the Q-cores. The Order is Jesuitical in its thoroughness. And there is only one door to this windowless room. No, there are a million doors, a billion doors. And in that thought they open. Edson reels, blinking in the silver light. Figures in the light; he is lost in a mirror-maze; a thousand Edsons stretch away from him on every side, an infinite regress. Those closest are mirror images, but as they recede into the light differences of dress, style, stature appear until, tear-blind in the glare of the multiverse, they might be angels, radiant as orixás. And he feels them, he knows them, every detail of their lives is available to him, just by looking. Entangled. As he knows them, they know him and one by one turn toward him. Ghost-wind streams Fia's red hair back from her head: she is the Mae do Santo, and all her sisters attending her. Some of the doors are empty, Edson notices. And Edson also notices a squeal of plastic paneling coming apart at the quantum scale. He whirls as the Q-blade completes the circle. The wall panel crashes forward. The assassin's amber I-shades crawl with data and trajectories and killing curves, none of which he needs because he has them there, right here right now, at arrow point.

"Now Fia, now anywhere!" Edson yells as the hunter draws, fires. Then time gels, time goes solid as the arrow drifts from the bow, cutting a line of Cerenkov radiation through the air. Edson sees it bore toward his heart, and then there is a jump, a quantum jump, and the arrow is in another place, another doorway, flickering from universe to universe as the probability of it killing this Edson Jesus Oliveira de Freitas dwindles to zero, as he becomes superposed with everywhere at once. The hunter gives an incoherent, rageful cry, drops his astonishing bow, and pulls the Q-blade. And a fourth figure is in the place above universes with them; the blonde short loira woman, the miraculous capoeirista: a thousand, a million alters of her, charging across the multiverse. In one instant she is a universe away; the next she arrives, panting, beside Edson.

"Hello again," she says, and slaps half a handcuff around Edson's wrist. She ducks under the assassin's Q-blade strike; delivers a crunching kick to the solar plexus that sends him reeling, agonized, out of the sanctorum; and slaps the other half of the handcuffs around the astonished Fia's arm. "You'd just end up in two hundred kilometers of Atlantic," she says. "And you're no use to us there." She hauls on the chain linking Edson and Fia. The doors swing wide; they fall through every door at once into the silver light. A billion lives, a billion deaths flash through Edson. He needs to cry piss vomit laugh pray ejaculate praise roar in ecstasy. Then he is standing in light, sunlight, on rain-damp concrete, by a low curb surrounding a statue of a man in soccer kit holding boldly aloft the kind of torch that only appears in statuary and political party logos. The man is bronze, and on the sides of the plinth are plaques in the same ritual metal bearing names. Legendary names, galactic names. Jairzinho and Ronaldo Fenómeno. Socrates, and that other Edson: Arantes do Nascimento. Before him is a curved triumphal gateway in mold-stained white-and-blue-painted concrete and the words Stadio Mario Filho.

Edson is in a place he's never been before. The Maracanã Stadium.

"Rio?" Fia asks wearily, as if one more wonder or horror and she would lie down in the damp gutter and pull the trash over her.

"What's going on here?" Edson demands, frowning at the verdigrised plaques. "Where's the 2030 Seleção that won right here, and 2018 in Russia? When are we?"

"That's a slightly tricky question," the blonde woman says. "You see, we're not really any time at all. We're sort of outside time; it just happens to look like the Maracanã from my era. When I come from, we haven't won yet. We lost. That's the point. And it's not really Rio either. All you have to do is go as far as the edge of the dropoff zone and you'll see."

Edson almost hauls Fia off her feet. The cuffs the cuffs—he's forgotten they are chained together. Fia is still looking around her dazed, spun out on the chemical tail of two Teixeira corporação sleeping pills.

"Oh shit sorry about that," the woman says. She fiddles in a pants pockets for a key. "I didn't want you wandering off; if you'd got separated, we'd never have found you again." Two oiled clicks, then the woman stows the shiny chrome handcuffs in her belt. Edson rubs his wrist. He never ever wants to get any closer to things police than that.

"What are you, some kind of cop?" he throws back over his shoulder as he crosses the cobbles.

"Hey. I am not a cop," the woman snaps. But Edson's discovered a weird thing: as he stands between the flagpoles that line the curb and moves his head from side to side, the trees and office buildings across the road move with him.

"What is going on here?"

At the same time Fia says, "Where are all the people?"

"Coffee," the woman says. "This needs explaining over coffee." She places an order for three cafezinhos from an old black man with gray gray hair at a little tin stall in front of the colonnade Edson cannot remember seeing before. The coffee is dark and sweet and finger-searingly hot in the little translucent plastic cup, but these cariocas cannot make coffee. Paulistanos, now: they grow it, they know it.

"Think of it as a kind of movie set, only it's solid and real all the way through," the woman says. The old man leans his elbows on the counter of his little stand. "As real as anything really is. It's a safe haven. We have hundreds of them, probably billions of them. This one just happens to be the size and shape of the Maracanã Stadium circa 2006. I'm not actually much of a futebol fan, but the location has a kind of special significance to us. I've got places all over the place, but this is sort of our office. Corporate headquarters, so to speak. Fortress of Solitude."

Fia has been turning slowly around, manga-eyes wide.

"It's a pocket universe," she says. "That's so clever. You found a way into the multiversal quantum computer and hacked it out."

"It's a very small universe, like I said—just big enough to fit the stadium into. I'd've loved a beach, maybe the Corcovado, the Sugar Loaf, the Copa, but we daren't get overambitious. The Order knows we're there somewhere; they just haven't been able to find us yet."

Edson crumples his plastic cup and flings it away from him. A gust of wind rattles it across the cracked concrete.

"But that was real, and the coffee was hot and pretty bad. How can you make something out of nothing? I can feel it, I can touch it."

"It's not nothing," the old man on the coffee stand says. "It's time and information, the most real things there are."

"You can reprogram the multiversal quantum computer," Fia says with a light of revelation dawning in her eyes. The woman and the old man look at each other.

"You've got it," the woman says with a cheeky grin. "I knew we hadn't made a mistake with you. Okay, well I think you're about ready to go inside. It can be a bit . . . disorienting at first, but you do get used to it."

"Just one moment," Edson demands. Fia, capoeira woman, and bad coffee man are already at the blue-and-white colonnade. "Before I go anywhere, just who are you?"

The woman throws up her hands, shakes her head in self-exasperation.

"You know, I completely forgot. I just have so much on, I am completely ditzy." She offers a hand to Edson. "My name is Marcelina Hoffman, and I am what is known as a Zemba. I'm kind of like a superheroine; I turn up in the nick of time and rescue people. Now, come on, there's a lot more to show you." Edson briefly shakes the offered hand. Glancing back from the tiled lobby, he can no longer see the coffee stall, but the plaza flickers with more-guessed than glimpsed figures: ghosts of an old black man, a short white woman, a dekasegui and a cor-de-canela boy in a sharp white suit.

"So did Brasil really win in 2030?" The old man falls in beside Edson as he ascends the sloping entry tunnel. Edson drops his pace to match him. He whispers, "She really doesn't know anything about futebol. Television, that's her thing. Was her thing."

"Yeah, we won," Edson says. "Against the United States."

"The United States?" the old man says, then starts to laugh so painfully, so wheezily Edson thinks he is having a heart attack. "The ianques playing futebol? In the World Cup? What was the score?"

"Two one."

"Hah!" the old man says. "And Uruguay?"

"They haven't qualified since 2010."

The man punches fist into palm. "Heh heh. Son, you have made an old man so very, very happy. So so happy." Chuckles bubble up in him all the way along the curving corridor lined with photographs of the great and glorious. Edson stops; something in a photo of a goalkeeper making a spectacular save has caught his eye. And the date. July 16, 1950.

"That's you, isn't it?"

"It's not there in the original Maracanã. I mean the one where I come from. And it never was that photo."

Marcelina holds open the door to the presidential box. Edson steps into the blinding light. Two hundred thousand souls greet him. He reels, then draws himself upright and walks deliberately, gracefully down the red-carpeted steps to the rail where Fia stands, glowing in the attention. *Senhors, Senhoras, I present to you, Edson Jesus Oliveira de Freitas! Superstarrrrrrrrrr!*

"I told you it could be a bit overwhelming," Marcelina said. And in the moment after the tyranny of the eyes tells him, *Two hundred thousand fans*, the ears tell him different, and more strange. This thronged stadium is totally silent. Not a cheer, not an airhorn, not a thunder of a bateria or the chant of a supporters' samba. Not a firework. Not an announcer screaming *Goooooooooool do Brasil!* A stadium of ghosts. As his eyes catch up with his ears, Edson sees something very much like weather blowing across the stands and the high, almost vertical arquibancadas, like the huge silk team banners passed hand to hand around the huge circle, a change-wave rippling between worlds, between realities, between Fluminense and Flamengo, between decades. The fans of a million universes flicker through this Maracanã beyond time and space.

"I was finding I couldn't get anything done with the noise," Marcelina says.

Down in the sacred circle of green a match is in progress. Edson knows instinctively what game it is. No other game matters. But it is not one Fateful Final, it is thousands, flickering through each other, ghosts of players, crosses from other universes, goal kicks into the farthest reaches of the multiverse. Edson watches the cursed Barbosa ruefully pick the ball out of the back of the net; then reality shifts and he is rolling it out past the strikers coming in on the back of the save on a long throw to Juvenal.

"I'm used to it," says Moaçir Barbosa. "On average, we win. But hey, the USA two one? Oh, I cannot get used to that."

Edson lifts his hands from the rail.

"Okay, this is all very good and I'm prepared to believe I'm in some bubble outside space and time or some private little universe or whatever, but I have one question. What is it all about?"

Marcelina applauds. The sound rings around the eerily silent Maracanã.

"Correct question!"

"And the answer?"

"The universe—the original universe, the one in which we all lived our lives the first time—died long ago. Not died—it never dies, it just goes on expanding forever until every particle is so far from every other that it's effectively in a universe of its own. We haven't reached that stage yet; the universe is so old and cold there is no longer enough energy to sustain life, or any other process except quantum computation. But intelligence always tries to find a way out, a way not to die with the stars, and so it created a vast quantum simulation of its own history, and entered it. And we live it over and over and over again, ever more slowly as the universe cools toward absolute zero, until in the end-time it stops completely and we are frozen in the eternal present."

Edson, always thin, always undernourished, shivers in his sharp white malandro's suit.

"I'm alive," he says.

"Yes. No. An accurate-enough simulation is virtually indistinguishable from reality. It's only when you look up close that the cracks begin to appear."

"Quantum weirdness," Fia says.

"No way around it. The quantum nature of the simulation would always betray its true nature. That's what the Order was created to protect."

"Fia told me the Sesmarias are old fidalgo families. How long have we known about this?"

"I think there have always been individuals who understood the multiverse. But the Order has only existed since the middle of the eighteenth century, when a French explorer brought back an Amazonian drug that allowed the mind to operate on a quantum level."

Edson's head reels. *Stop this stop this. Give me sun and beer; give me a Keepie-Uppie Queen and a hot deal.*

"We're dead. We're ghosts, so what? We all die in the end."

He feels Fia's hand clutch his.

"It doesn't have to be that way," she says. "All available energy goes into running the multiversal quantum computer."

"The Order calls it the Parousia."

"But instead, all that energy could be put into something else. Something unpredictable. A random quantum event, like the one that inflated into this multiverse in the first place. A new creation. But you'd have to end the simulation first. You would have to turn off the Parousia."

"Wait wait wait wait," says Edson. "You turn it off, we all die."

"Maybe not," Fia says, overbiting her bottom lip in that way she doesn't know she does but Edson finds sweet-sexy. "'A black hole does have hair.' Information could be conserved through a singularity."

"I'm not a scientist, you know," Edson says.

"Me neither," says Marcelina. "But I have made some science shows. Mostly about plastic surgery."

"That's what you're fighting for," Fia says, and her eyes are bright, seeing to the end of the universe and beyond, reflecting that new light. "Death in the cold and dark, or the hope of rebirth in the fire."

"You should write scripts," Marcelina says. "That's very good. Very poetic. This is what the Order fears; that's why we are fighting it all across the multiverse, for a chance at something different, something magical. Places like this, they're a start, a tiny start. Edson, I need a word with your girlfriend, in private."

Edson turns again to the endless final. The bright watered green, the sky that only Rio makes so blue, the many colors of the crowd: ghosts, echoes. His own hand on the rail seems so thin and insubstantial he could see through it. He turns his face up to the sun and it is cold.

"Scared the hell out of me too, son," Barbosa says. He leans on the rail, decorously spits over the edge of the presidential box. "But whatever it is, this is the world we live in. We're men; we make our own way. Maybe it all begins anew; maybe we die and that's the end of it, no heaven, no hell, nothing. But I know I can't go on living what happened to me over and over and over, slower and slower until it all freezes. That's death. This . . . this is nothing." He looks around. "That was quick. I'll leave you young things" He climbs the steps, passes Fia on the red carpet.

"She offered you a job, didn't she?" Edson says.

"It's getting to be a habit."

"And did you take it?"

"What's the alternative? For someone like me, what's the alternative?"

"But nothing for Edson."

She can't look at him. Below them, in a million universes, Augusto lifts high the Jules Rimet trophy to a silent Maracanã.

"I can't make that decision for you."

"Did you even try?"

"It's too dangerous. You're not a player; I am, for better or worse. You can't come with me. Go back; we can send you back, it's easy. I can do it. The Order is looking for me now."

"But I wouldn't see you again, would I? Not if the Order is hunting you."

She shakes her head, chews her lip. There will be tears soon. *Good*, Edson thinks. *I deserve them.*

"Ed . . ."

"Don't call me that. I hate that. Call me my name. I'm Edson."

"Edson, you have a home to go to. You have all your family, and all those brothers and Dona Hortense and your Aunt Marizete and all those friends. You've got Carlinhos . . . Mr. Peach. He loves you. I don't know what he'll do without you."

"Maybe," Edson says, biting his lip because he can feel it coming and he does not want her to see it, not while he is hurt and full of rage, "maybe I love you."

She puts her hand up to her mouth, tries to push his words back into unspokenness.

"Don't say that, no, have you any idea how hard it is to hear you say that? How can I say this? This sounds the most callous thing. Edson, I died to you once already. I'm not her. I never was."

"Maybe," says Edson, "it's you I love."

"No!" Fia cries. "Stop saying this. I'm going, I have to go now, I have to do this quickly. You can't come with me. Don't look for me, don't try and get in touch with me. I won't look for you. Let me go back to being dead."

She turns and walks up the red carpet. Marcelina opens the door. Edson knows what lies beyond that door: all the worlds in the multiverse. Once she steps through, she will disappear between the worlds and he will never be able to find her again. He will go back to his office at the back of Dona Hortense's house in respectable hardworking Cidade de Luz. The fuss over the Q-cores will disappear as the police find easier meat to pick over. There will be other Keepie-Uppie Queens, other fut-volley teams, and there is the whole Habibi lanchonete business for De Freitas Global Talent. And on those rare clear nights in autumn and early spring he will look up beyond the Angels of Perpetual Surveillance to the stars themselves and the faint glow of the Milky Way, and see her out there, farther than any star, yet only a weave of the world away. The door is closing; Fia is already stepping through. One more step and he will lose her forever. And Edson finds he is running up those stairs, up that red carpet, toward that closing door. "No!" he shouts. "No!"

August 18–September 3, 1733

In the waxing light the quilombistas on Hope of the Saints Hill stood as one, silent, staring at the angels of God walking over the treetops toward them, haloed by the rising sun. Then Zemba beat his spear against his shield, ran up and down between the ranks, his iâos behind him, roaring and leaping, proud and furious.

"What pacas are you, that stand in awe of wooden puppets? For bauds and gauds you would put your wrists into the manacles? Fight, you pacas! This is the City of God. This!" The iâos in their bridal dresses joined their throats with his: a voice here, a voice there sounded; then of a sudden the whole hill shouted as one. Falcon felt the cry in his throat, the good cry of pride and defiance and laughter; then he too was roaring with the people: Hope of the Saints Hill red with bodies all shouting at the sun.

The hill was still resounding to the great cheer as Falcon took his Manaos down the slope into the flooded forest. There was treachery beneath the opaque, muddied surface: the old trench lines and pit traps remained; one step could leave an unwary warrior floundering in deep water, helpless under the enemy's blades. Falcon looked back but once, when he saw the angels come to a halt. Through the trees he glimpsed Caixa in her forward trench, passing out serrated wooden knives to the women and children of her command. Moments later the varzea shook to the crash of artillery and the whistle of mortar shells. The hilltop where Zemba had stationed his viable artillery exploded in smoke and red earth. Clods fell like rain, but from the clearing cloud of smoke Falcon heard the cheer of defiance renewed. Zemba's hasty earthworks had endured; the ballisteiros and trebuchistas danced on the parapet, waved their urocum-dyed manhoods at the hovering angels.

A bird-whistle; Tucuru held his left hand out at his side, fluttered it. Enemy within sight. Falcon peered into the gloom, but all he could see was a waterlogged sloth, lanky and lugubrious, rowing its way across the flood-waters like a debauched spider. Then in an epiphany of vision, the same as suddenly draws constellations upon scattered stars, he discerned the curved prows of war canoes pressing through the leaf-and-water dazzle. He held out his sword. His archers concealed themselves in the lush cove∴. They would fire twice, then withdraw to harry the enemy again. Close. Let them close. And closer yet.

"For the Marvelous City!" Falcon cried. Fifty archers fired, their second arrows in the air before the first had found their marks. All was silent. Then the forest exploded in a wall of cannon fire and the air turned to a shrieking, killing cloud of ball and splint. In that opening salvo half of Falcon's command was blown to red wreck.

"Second positions!" he shouted. Beyond the gunboats the waters were solid with canoes, more canoes than he had ever imagined. Crown and church had joined their forces not on a mission of enslavement but of annihilation. "Christ have mercy," he muttered. Against such odds all he could do, must do, was buy some little time. "Cover and fire!" he commanded. The line of gunboats fired again as it advanced through the trees. Trunks branches twigs flew to splinters and leaves, a deadly storm of splinters, ripped apart by canister shot. Sword beating at his side, Falcon splashed through the thigh-deep water. He glanced up at the whistle and crash of a salvo of iron-hard wooden balls stabbing through the canopy. The boy slingers on Hope of the Saints Hill were firing blind on ballistic trajectories. Cries in Portuguese; the paddlers raised their wooden shields over their heads. The Manao beside Falcon took the unguarded moment to turn and loose an arrow at a cannoneer. A musket spoke, the man spun on his heel, the arrow skied, he fell back into the leaf-covered water, chest shattered red. As the gunners reloaded their murderous pieces, Zemba's treetop snipers opened fire. Warm work they performed with their repeating crossbows, but each story ended the same: blasts of blunderbuss, clouds of smoke, bodies falling from the trees like red fruit. And still the boats came on. Falcon looked around him at the bodies hunched in the water, already prey to piranha. Less than a quarter of his archers remained. This was bloody slaughter.

"Retreat!" Falcon yelled. "To the trenches! *Sauve qui peut!*"

The canoes moved between the treetops. A biblical scene, Quinn thought: animals clinging desperately to the very tips of the submerged trees, each tree an island unto itself, the waters stinking with the bloated bodies of the drowned. A veritable city must have stood here to house and feed the workers, their huts the first to go under the rising water, all trace of the builders erased. Quinn tried to imagine the hundreds of great forest trees felled to form the pilings, the thousands of tons of earth moved by wooden tools and human muscles. A task beyond biblical; of Egyptian proportions.

In the deep under-dawn they had stolen away from the Cidade Maravilhosa into the tangle of the flood-canopy. Sensed before seen, like the wind from many worlds stirring the varzea, Quinn had become aware of a vast dark mass moving beyond the screening branches; oars rising and falling like the legs of a monstrous forest millipede. Nossa Senhora de Varzea, forthright in attack, confident in strategy. Satanic arrogance was yet Father Diego Gonçalves's abiding sin. Hunting shadows ran with Our Lady of the Flood Forest, dark as jaguars in the morning gloaming; a vast train of canoes, the City of God militant. Quinn pressed his finger to his lips; his lieutenants understood in a glance. Shipping noisy, betraying paddles they hauled themselves cautiously along boughs and lianas until the host of heaven was gone from sight.

Open water before their prow; the dam a dark line between the blue sky and the green-dotted deeper blue of the flood. The simplicity of the geometry deceived the senses: whatever the distance the dam seemed the same size to the canoes so that Quinn was unable to estimate its distance. The patrol maintained its position a quarter league to the south. Quinn had glassed the canoes at range as they darted out from the green tangle of the southern side of the lake, light three-man pirogues admirably suited to interception work, crewed by boys of no more than twelve years of age, painted and patterned like grown warriors; those grown warriors now assaulting the Cidade Maravilhosa. They signaled with bright metal. Flashes of light replied, and the world fell into perspective around Quinn: the dam was virtually within arrow-shot, the water very much higher than he had anticipated, almost to the top of the great log pilings. Figures ran from the palm-leaf shelters set up along the earthen walls; the first few arrows stabbed into the water around the canoes. Quinn turned the glass on them: old men, their hunting days past. He opened his sight to the other worlds, dam upon dam upon dam, all the water in the worlds mounted up behind them. *Show me, what is best, what is right, show me the cardinal flaw.* And then he saw it as clearly as if an angel stood upon the dome of the temple: a point slightly to the north of the center of the great, gentle bow of earth and wood where there was a slightly greater gap between the wooden pilings, the right answer plucked from the universe of all possible answers.

On Quinn's command the Iguapá archers laid down suppressing fire while a final croak of encouragement eked the last effort from the paddlers. The canoes collided with the massive wooden piers. With a roar Quinn swung up onto the dam and charged the sentries, sword grasped two-handed. Some of the braver old men hefted their war-clubs; then age and caution decided and they fled to the southern end of the dam.

"Let them go," Quinn ordered. "We do not make war on old men and boys."

While the Iguapá lashed the canoes into a tight raft between the piers, shifting barrels as close to the structure as possible, Quinn studied the construction of the dam. The upper surface was eight paces wide, of clay tamped on wicker hurdles. The earth rampart, already greening with fecund forest growth, sloped at an angle of forty-five degrees. The drop to the clay, trickling bed of the dead Rio do Ouro was ten times the height of man. Again he marveled at the energy and vision of his adversary. Could any amount of explosive blast away such massive soil and wood, such concentration of will and strength? A tiny crack was all that was needed. The water would accomplish the rest, the incalculable mass of flood penned league after league up the valley of the Rio do Ouro.

An arrow drove into the clay a span from Quinn's foot. Eight war canoes had emerged from the southern shore and were stroking fast for the dam, finding range for their archers.

"I would have been surprised had Father Gonçalves entrusted the protection of his dam to old men and boys alone," Quinn said. "Lay the fuse; there is not a moment to be lost."

The loading was complete. The Iguapá scrambled up onto the dam; Waitacá plugged the end of a fuse line into the barrel and reeled it out behind him as Quinn's archers laid down covering fire. The old men remembered their honor and picked up their war-clubs for a charge. Quinn and Waitacá ran for the northern shore: the reinforcements had given up their firing and were now stroking flat-out for the bomb.

"We must blow it now," Waitacá said.

"We're too close."

"Mair, now or never."

"Lord have mercy," Quinn whispered as he took the carefully guarded slow-match from the wooden pail and touched it to the end of the line. The fuse burned in a blink. A stupendous, stupefying blast knocked Quinn and the Iguapá to the ground. Winded, deafened, Quinn saw a great wave blow back from the dam and crash against it in the same instant as a pillar of water leapt up the same height that the dam stood above the dry riverbed. Dark objects turned and tumbled in its breaking white crown: war canoes, tossed up as light as leaves in a forest squall. "Christ have mercy."

Spray drenched Quinn; splinters of wood rained around him. His head rang from the explosion; his body ached. Slowly he rose to his feet. On the far side of the dam the old men halted their charge. The Guabirú boys stood up in their canoes, dumb with astonishment. Those reinforcements who had survived the blast stroked for their capsized canoes. The cloud of smoke and steam cleared away. The dam stood. The world hung; then the old men took up their charge again, the boys swung round to the aid of the stricken men in the water. The dam stood.

Dripping from every hem and seam, Falcon threw himself through the safe gap in the bamboo palisades into the foremost trench. Dry earth beneath his cheek. Leeches clung to the exposed flesh where his stockings had rolled down. An Iguapá pagé applied paste ground from forest bark. Stones, wooden shot, arrows flew overhead in a constant gale. Then Falcon heard a deeper report from the hilltop and, leeches to the devil, stood up to see five loads of hot stones arc over his head and burst in an impressive roar of steam where they struck among the gunboats. As trebuchets were recranked and fresh stones heated in the hilltop fires, the ballistas spoke, spears of fire stabbing out at the canoes. Falcon had devised the adhesive coating of resins and gums: a dreadful threat to gunboats heavy with shot and powder. Those so struck battled beneath a withering fire of slingshots and poison barbs to extinguish the clinging fire; when a gunboat blew up, a cheer rang around the hill, and a second when the swivel-guns retreated into the cover of the varzea, there to lay down a steady bombardment of Zemba's artillery.

Falcon worked his way uphill through the linked trench-lines, past battalions of grim-faced boys; gold-faced, strange-skulled Iguapá; Caibaxé with lip-plates, though they were too young to have undergone the formal rites of manhood, war makes any boy a man; the Manaos, their foreheads and crowns shaved into a singular tonsure. Each clutched a spear and wooden knife, waiting, waiting for the word from Zemba's Imbangala lieutenants. Falcon threw himself to the earth, hands clutched around his shaven head, as fresh bombard came screaming in. He felt the hilltop quake through his belly; blind, primal panic, what to clasp hold of when the earth itself shakes?

A dulled roar of voices from behind him; the war-rejoicing of the Guabirú. Pushing his green glasses up his nose, Falcon saw the hilltop in ruin; a trebuchet smashed, two ballistas burning. Yet Zemba's artillerists spoke again; hot stone plunged down through the leaf canopy, and now the heavy bowmen opened up, lying on their backs, bow braced against feet, bowstring hauled back with all the strength of two arms.

Zemba himself waited with his reserves and the cross of Our Lady of All Worlds in the trench-line beneath the battery. A constant chain of girl-runners darted in and out of his position, bearing reports, carrying his orders.

"Aîuba."

"General, the water is still rising. The foremost positions will be inundated within the hour."

"I am aware of it. You suggest that the Mair has failed?"

"I suggest only that we evacuate the women and children, the old, the sick and halt, while the way is still open."

"They will surely perish in that forest."

"They will surely perish here. This is no entrada. This is destruction."

Zemba hesitated but an instant.

"Evacuate the women and children."

His runners, crouching at his feet, bowed their heads to concentrate on his orders. Falcon zigzagged downslope to the trench to give the word to Caixa and her command.

"I will not desert you," she said fiercely. The women and smallest children quit the trench, the infants tear-streaked, wailing past all fear. "You need someone to watch over you."

A new mortar barrage punished the hill. The smoke and dust cleared, and there was silence from the battery. A great cry came from the hilltop. Zemba stood, spear raised, the cross of Nossa Senhora do Todos os Mundos lifted high behind him, burning in the sun. Falcon turned to see canoes push out from the deep forest. There was not clear water between the hulls, so many were they; Portuguese in buff and blood, the genipapo-stained skins of the Guabirú. The gunboats laid down a suppressing bombardment, but the cry sounded again and was taken up by the Imbangala captains and iâos, the morbichas and the pagés, by Caixa beside him, and then by Falcon himself as he drew his sword and went over the top of the trench, roaring down to meet the enemy.

Quinn stood senseless as a plaster saint. This was a world he had never traveled to before: the muted, desperate land beyond the battle song, beyond the glorious rage and the joy of the fight and of holding a life in his two hands, and the breaking of that life. This was defeat. This was failure; a quiet, ashen world. True humility and obedience, where the knee is bowed to the inevitable, the ring is kissed without pride or restraint. He gazed, thoughtless, heedless of the falling arrows, at the dam. Then there came a shriek like the teeth of the world being pulled. A tremor ran across the surface of the lake, another, a third, a fourth. Massive trunks of forest hardwood, adamant as iron, snapped with explosive force. Quinn felt the dam shake beneath his feet. Cracks opened in the clay roadway; the tops of the reinforcing piles leaned back toward the water.

"Mair, I think . . ." Waitacá did not need to complete the warning. Quinn, Iguapá, old men, boys in their little canoes fled as a twenty-pace section of the dam tilted into the lake and burst in a jetting plume of foaming water. Smashed tree trunks were tossed like twigs; with every second the rush of water tore away more earth and wood. The gap became a chasm as whole sections of dam broke free and slid into the fall.

"The men; mother of worlds, the men!" Waitacá cried. The capsized Guabirú tried to strike for the shore, for the upturned canoes, for the disintegrating dam itself, but the torrent was too strong. Their cries joined with the crash of rending timbers and the roar of water as they were swept under and sent spinning out in the crushing mill of wood and earth. Quinn whispered a prayer and kissed the cross of his rosary; then the earth beneath his feet cracked and fissured and he ran for the northern bank. Behind him the dam split loose, pivoted, and slid down the scarp face, breaking into great clods and piles of clay-clogged wicker. The dam was now one great waterfall, the lake a millrace of torn branches and dead creatures, the riverbed beneath a bounding cream-white torrent. Boles of wood burst from the surface like rockets only to tumble end for end and be dragged under again, the flood scouring bushes and trees from the shore. The Rio do Ouro was tearing a new channel from the varzea; now the very boulders were stripped from the soil to join the destroying wall of water and wood.

Quinn scrambled up the buttress of earth that joined the dam to the high terra firme. He felt Falcon's bamboo cylinder pressed next to his bosom. Quinn withdrew it, weighed it in his hand. He imagined it in the shatter of the great flood, that flood in time subsiding, the cylinder bobbing unregarded among the greater bulks of the forest trees, Rio do Ouro to Iguapará, Iguapará to Catrimani, to Rio Branco, to Rio Negro, to Amazonas. To the sea, on the currents to the shores of Ireland or the coast of Portugal, wavelets rolling it up a white strand. More to tell in this story. He slid the tube inside his black robe.

Canoes had been beached on this earthen ramp, run up above the floodline, light pirogues.

"Waitacá, would it be possible to make headway against the flood?"

Waitacá studied the river, the flow changing with every second as Father Gonçalves's dam was scoured away.

"It could be done through the varzea, with caution."

"I have need of speed."

"It could be done with both of those."

"Very good, then. Waitacá, I have need of your help at the paddle. I still have an admonishment to visit upon Father Diego Gonçalves."

Soldiers' boots, the bare feet of índios splashed into the water as the canoes ran through the flooded stake-lines onto the shore. Archers threw away their bows, took their knives in their hands to grapple hand to hand with the attackers. The hillside was a landslide of yelling, whooping índio bodies part running, part slipping, part falling in their charge; Zemba at their head, flinging light javelins as he charged, more airborne than earthbound as he leaped over bodies and half-filled trenches. And among them, Dr. Robert Falcon, sword held out ahead of him like a cuirassier's blade, screaming hate and obscenities never to be thought of a Fellow of the French Academy.

The two lines met with a shock that quailed Hope of the Saints Hill to its roots. Falcon found himself sword to bayonet with a charging Portuguese infantryman. He sidestepped and cut the man's legs from under him. Caixa finished the work with her spear. Falcon threw her the bladed musket, took the man's sword for himself. As he tested its weight and mettle, a Guabirú spearman lunged out of nowhere: Caixa caught him full on her bayonet, twisted the musket. The man gave a terrible wailing shriek and slid from her blade. She nodded in approval.

Two-bladed, Falcon did a demon's work along the front line, cutting halfway to the enemy's battle standard of a naked woman entwined in green, but for every man who fell three sprang up and more canoes packed in behind those run onto the shore, índio conscripts in half-uniform—a jacket, breeches, sometimes only a tricorn hat—running lightly from hull to hull to leap into the fight. And still the water rose.

Zemba led the nation like some relentless forest legend; the cross of Our Lady of All Worlds surged across the battlefront, a daring drive here, a feint and full-blooded attack there. But Our Lady of the Flood Forest commanded the waters, and the attackers were a red tide. The City of God drove the City of Marvels back across the first and second trenches. Beyond all thought, all reason, all language, Dr. Robert Falcon worked wrath and slaughter with his twin blades, and it was good. It was very good. He knew Luis Quinn's abiding sin in all its ecstasy and horror. To be so present within the moment and one's skin, the immediate and imperious liveliness of all the senses, the precipice of every second wherein one might kill or die, the luxury of such complete control over another. The Art of Defense, even the foot-boxing tricks he had learned from the waterfront men, were pale eunuchs of the ecstasy of battle.

Feathers waving upon the bloody hillside. Blood and buff and a shining sword.

"Araujo!" Falcon called through the clatter of war. "Now you shall have your contest."

The colonial officer ran to meet him as Falcon threw down his second, looted sword. Abruptly Araujo pulled up, whipped a pistol out of his sash of office. And Caixa was there between Falcon and the ball. A discharge, a gust of smoke, and Caixa went tumbling headlong. French, Portuguese, lingua geral, Iguapá—Falcon's shouts were incoherent. Caixa rose unsteadily to her feet, then grinned and opened her left hand to show her bloody stigmata where the ball had passed through.

"Kill him, husband!"

Araujo flung the useless pistol at Falcon, who deftly sidestepped. Falcon spread his hand in invitation, then dropped into the stance. Araujo saluted and returned the attitude. A new round of mortar fire howled down onto the hilltop, but nothing remained there but shattered flesh and wood. Falcon feinted, then attacked. Araujo, for all his European airs, was no practitioner of the Art of Defense. In five moves Falcon had sent his blade whirling away across the red earth and the Portuguese captain found a sword-point at his chest.

"Senhor, as a fidalgo to a fidalgo, I cast myself on your mercy."

"Senhor, alas, I am no fidalgo," Falcon said, and ran him cleanly through in one lunge.

A tumult from downslope; Falcon glanced up from cleaning his sword on Araujo's coat to see the great cross of Nossa Senhora de Todos os Mundos teetering madly in the center of a ring of Portuguese índio-conscripts. Zemba leaped and whirled, his spear and hide shield dashing and darting. Men fell, men reeled away bloody and ripped, but every moment more piled in. Falcon ran, sword ready. He could feel Caixa at his back, her wounded hand bound in Araujo's neckcloth, her spear held underhand to stab up into an enemy's bowels. Terrible, wondrous woman. The cross wavered, the cross went down, then Zemba snatched it up again, clutched against the back of his tattered shield.

Falcon threw himself into the circle of soldiers, cut and cut again. Zemba gave a cry, arched backward, and went down on his knees in the water, blood gouting from his severed hamstrings. His face wore a look of immeasurable sadness and wonder.

"Get them out of here, lead them, we are done for here," he gasped, and flung the cross on its pole like a javelin. Ribbon and streamers fluttered in the train of the Lady of All Worlds; then Caixa's bloody hand reached up and caught it.

Zemba smiled, eyes wet with tears. An auxiliary in a tanga and infantryman's jacket stabbed with his spear. The blade point burst from Zemba's throat and he fell forward into the flood, still smiling.

A pillar of smoke and fire stood over Cidade Maravilhosa, a sign for leagues up and down the Rio do Ouro. Again the great guns of the Nossa Senhora da Varzea fired. Quinn and Waitacá paddled steadily, stealthily, by root and branch. Quinn had glassed the basilica from the cover of a felled tree half a league downstream; Gonçalves thought the mortar crews—Portuguese gunners with Guabirú loaders—sufficient garrison. The east end of the basilica was undefended, and the flying buttresses and baroqueries afforded ample concealment. Waitacá and Quinn handed along the basilica's waterline to the cable eye they had agreed wordlessly from telescope-distance as the best entrance. Waitacá seized the mooring cable, slung his legs up, and climbed it like a golden sloth. Quinn's sword jammed momentarily on the narrow eyelet; a rattle and he was inside, in the reeking, oozy gloom of the stern bowser.

"Free the slaves before anything," Quinn said. "You will be able to easily overpower the mortar batteries."

Waitacá dipped his head and drew his steel knife. He knew the rest by heart. Cut the anchor lines, then take the galley slaves to attack the rear of Gonçalves's army.

I have given you the task most difficult, Quinn thought. *Mine is the task most necessary.* Boys' voices from the lavabo; chalice and paten were being cleansed for the celebratory Mass. Black on black, Quinn spirited past.

Quinn was prepared for the spiritual assault of Nossa Senhora da Varzea, yet his attuned, attenuated senses reeled as if from a physical blow. He walked down the center of the nave, heaven on his left hand, damnation on his right, judgment all around. Christ spread his arms wide across the titanic choir screen. His thorn-pierced heart stood open. Quinn freed his sword. Beyond the choir stalls a shaft of light fell on the altar, the crucified Amazonian Christ's head crowned with strange sufferings. Before the stellar glow of the Lady of the Flood Forest a figure in simple black knelt. The thunder of mortars beat the basilica like a drum. The Lady's dress of lights quivered; debris shook loose from the ceiling and fell in a snow of gold and Marian blue. Quinn strode up the choir, sword held low by his side.

"Would you murder me in my own cathedral, like St. Thomas à Becket?"

"I am the admonitory of Father de Magalhães, and I command you in the name of Christ to submit to my authority."

"I recall I refused you, as I refuse you again now."

"Silence. Enough of this. You will return with me to our Order in Salvador."

"The Order in Salvador. Yes. Some of us, however, are called to a higher service."

Gonçalves rose to his feet and turned to his admonisher. The Lady of the Flood Forest seemed to embrace him in her cope of verdure. "Still you persist in this, you ridiculous little man."

"Then I must compel you," Quinn said, and lifted his sword to let its blade catch the many lights of the reredos.

"You will not find me unprepared." Father Diego swept back his surplice to show the basket-hilted Spanish sword buckled at his side.

"In God's house," Quinn said, backing away from the treacheries of altar and choir stalls to the open nave.

"Come now, everywhere is God's house. If it is meet and right in that pigsty you call a city, that Capitan de Araujo is reducing to dust, then it is equally so here." Gonçalves cocked his head—that strange, infuriating bird-motion—at a sudden clamor of voices, shots, and steel from outside. His eyes widened with rage.

"Your former slaves, spiking your artillery," Quinn said. "Come now, no more delay. Let us try it here, your master against mine, Léon against Toledo."

He ran into the open nave. With a cry like a hunting bird, Gonçalves cast off his confining surplice and drew his sword. He flew at Quinn, blade dancing in a flickering flurry of cuts that caught the Mair off guard and drove him back across the floor, halfway to the narthex. Grunting with exertion Quinn formed a defense and beat Gonçalves back almost to the choir screen. The two men parted, saluted, circled each other, blinded with sweat in the stifling heat of the basilica.

And to it again. A crashing rally across the front of the roodscreen, Quinn driving, scoring a tear on Gonçalves's side, Gonçalves recovering and pressing Quinn back, trading the nick for a cut along Quinn's hairline—an unseen, unstoppable cut he had just managed to roll beneath, that would surely have taken the top of his skull. Quinn felt the floor move under him, saw the uncertainty reflected in Father Diego's thin, boyish face.

"The mooring lines are cut," he panted. "We are adrift." They both felt the basilica turn in the stream, captive of the ebbing waters. With a cry in Irish Quinn launched himself at Gonçalves; a *jetée* with mass and brute power behind it. Gonçalves slapped his spearing sword away; Quinn went sprawling and the Spaniard was on him, Quinn saving himself only by an instinctual block that struck sparks from both blades. He regained his feet but was at once driven hard against the base of the pulpit. Again Quinn rallied, and the two Jesuits dueled back and forth along the line of the side chapels. But it was clear to Quinn, with a chill clench in his testicles, that he had exerted himself too far on the destruction of the dam and the pursuit of Nossa Senhora da Varzea. His advantage in size and strength was used up, and in the pure way of the sword Diego Gonçalves was master.

The counterattack was immediate. Quinn retreated back through the open heart of Christ into the choir; his intention that the narrow files of box pews would constrain Gonçalves's balletic style. They battled up and down the choir stalls scattering psalteries and missals until Quinn was backed to the very altar. He could not get away. He could not escape. Fury swelled inside him; that he would die in this stupid vain place, this pagan altar, at the hands of this slight, effeminate Spaniard, that all he had wrought would be strewn to the winds and the waters in this desolate, wordless forest. He summoned the rage, his old demon, his old ally. It blazed hot and delicious inside him. And with a thought he pushed it down. Gonçalves knew of his old thorn; he would have tactics prepared for the rush of brute anger and unstoppable passion. Quinn opened his inner sight to the worlds. A blink, a flicker, but in that vision he saw all that Gonçalves would do. He saw the expression of anger and bafflement on Father Diego's face as he drove him back from the altar, his sword-point always ahead of the Spaniard's, back down the choir and through the gaping heart of Christ into the nave. Beneath the Christ of the Varzea, his outstretched hands blossoming into the twin apocalypses of the just and the lost, Quinn caught Gonçalves' sword and sent it across the floor.

"Kneel and submit," Quinn panted, sword-point at Gonçalves's eye. "Kneel and submit to the authority of the Society of Jesus."

Gonçalves went to his knees. Never once removing his eyes from Quinn, he reached into the open neck of his cassock; a rosary, to kiss and yield. Quinn saw a flash of light, and half his sword fell to the ground. Gonçalves held up the blade.

"Do you imagine they would have called us to defend the Kingdom without ensuring we are properly armed?" He came up in a sweeping blow that sheared Quinn's sword down to a useless stump and cut cleanly in two a stand of a tray of votives before the statue of Nossa Senhora Aparaçida. The lamps fell and rolled, spilling burning oil behind them. Tongues of fire licked toward the choir screen. Gonçalves leaned into a knife-fighter's crouch. Quinn hastily ripped the sleeve from his robe and opened it into a cape, which he held like a bullfighter's cloak.

"A cunning idea," Gonçalves said, with a lunging cut that left an arc of smoking blue in the air. "But quite ineffectual."

But Quinn had seen the fire leap up the open fretwork of the choir screen, a Christ wreathed in flame. He circled away from the blade, all the while keeping Gonçalves's back to the growing blaze.

"When did the Enemy seduce you?"

"You mistake. I am not the enemy. I am the Order. They have engines and energies beyond your imagining; did you think I built that dam unaided?"

Feint, slash, the tip of the blade cut a slit in the fabric. Quinn permitted himself a flicker of multiversal vision. In too many he saw himself kneel, gutted, on the floor, his entrails around his knees. Out there in the cornucopia of universes was the answer to Father Diego Gonçalves. The Spaniard lunged, the blade from beyond the world shrieking down to cut Quinn shoulder to waist. Quinn leaped back and saw the moment, the single true searing instant. He flung the cloth over Gonçalves's head, blinding him, seized the loose end and swung him around. Gonçalves reeled backward into the burning altar screen. The fragile screen swayed. Gonçalves ripped the cloth from his face, fled from the fire. Too slow, too late; the huge burning Christ, haloed in flames, heart ablaze, fire streaming from his outstretched fingers to turn both heaven and hell into purgatory, crashed down and drove Diego Gonçalves to the floor.

Quinn shielded his face and edged toward the inferno of blazing wood. Nothing could survive that pyre. Flames were leaping up the piers from angel to angel, licking across the clerestory screens, caressing the ceiling bosses. The choir stalls and screens were already ablaze; at the end of his strength, numb with awe, Luis Quinn watched the flames coil up and engulf Our Lady of the Varzea. The basilica was disintegrating, blazing timbers and embers raining from the ceiling, the smoke descending. Choking, Quinn rushed from the wooden hell. In a rending crash the roof fell and flames leaped up among the guardian angels, igniting the sails. Quinn marveled at the destruction. With every moment the current was taking the church farther from safety, closer to the falls at the destroyed dam. Quinn dived lightly into the water. Canoes pushed out from beneath the flood-canopy; a golden face glinted among the Guabirú. Quinn stroked toward Waitacá; then the fire reached the powder magazine. An apocalyptic explosion sent every bird flapping and screaming from the flood forest. Quinn saw the angels of Nossa Senhora da Varzea ascend, flung high into the air by the blast, and fall, tumbling end for end. Fragments of burning wood plunged hissing into the water around Quinn; as hands helped him into the canoe, he saw the blazing hulk of Nossa Senhora da Varzea spin slowly away on the current.

It was a rout now. The cross of Our Lady of All Worlds stood in the trench beneath the shattered hilltop, a sign and hope for the people. Portuguese snipers let fly with musket-fire; the Guabirú dispatched the wounded. Falcon leaned on his sword, the weight of the worlds suddenly upon him, a desire to lie down among the dead and be numbered with them. The floodwaters were thick with already-swelling bodies. He bowed his head and saw that the water was running away from around his sodden, cracked shoes. The water drained away from around his feet. The bodies were stirring, moving, drawn together into the recesses of the varzea. And the angels, the terrible visitants of wrath upon the mast tops of Nossa Senhora da Varzea, were moving. Very slowly, but with gathering impetus, moving downstream.

Falcon stood on firm land now.

I see the quilombo between fire and water, the torch and the flood, the Mair had said.

"But not here!" Falcon shouted. "Not this world!"

Now the army of Nossa Senhora da Varzea became aware of the water ebbing around their canoes and turned to stare as their patron angels vanished behind the treetops. Smoke rose, blacker, denser by the second. A great flash of light lit up the southern sky, momentarily outshining the sun. A plume of smoke in the shape of a mushroom climbed skyward; a few seconds later the explosion shook Hope of the Saints Hill. A grin formed on Falcon's face, broke into wonderful, insane laughter.

"At them!" he roared, circling his sword over his head. "One last charge for the honor of the Mair! At them!"

The canoe lightly rode the white water. A gray morning of low cloud after rain, scarves of mist clung to the trees. On such a dripping day they shouldered close to the river, dark and rich with rot and spurt. The canoe skipped among great boulders and the trunks of forest trees, smashed and splintered, wedged across rocks, half buried in the grit. The paddlers steered it down a channel that poured gray and white between two tumbled rocks each the size of a church. The golden cross set up in the prow wavered but did not fall. It shone like a beacon, as if by its own light.

The man on the shore raised his arm again, but the smoke from his fire was unmistakable now. *Heaven knows how he found anything combustible on such a day*, Robert Falcon thought. But his intent, he suspected, was always smoke, not heat.

The steersman ran the little pirogue in. Falcon splashed over the cobbles to shore. The strand was littered with leaves, twigs, whole branches and boles, drowned and bloating animals, reeking fish. He heard the grind of hull over stone. Caixa waded ashore and firmly planted the cross of Our Lady of All Worlds in the gritty sand.

"Dr. Falcon."

Luis Quinn sat on a boulder, a smoldering cigar clenched in his fist. A flaw of mist waved between the trees.

"Father Quinn."

The two men kissed briefly, formally.

"Well, we live," Falcon said.

On a plaited strap around his shoulder Quinn wore the bamboo tube that held the history of the Marvelous City.

"I am most glad, friend, that you ignored me and did not consign this to the waters," Falcon said. "The history of the Marvelous City may be finished, but that of the City of God has yet to be started."

"With your permission, that will be a new history from this," Quinn said. "This story has far to travel."

"Of course. You know they are already making legends of you. The Mair can foretell the future. The Mair has a knife that can cut through anything, even men's hearts and secrets to read their deepest desires. The Mair can walk between worlds and from one end of the arch of time to the other. The Mair will come again in the hour of his people's sorest need and lead them away from this world to a better one where the manioc grows in all seasons and the hunting is always rich and bountiful, a world the bandeirantes and the pais can never reach."

"I had expected tales, but not that last one."

The vanguard of the Cidade Maravilhosa's fleet appeared around the widely incised river bend, bobbing on the white water.

"What do you expect when you destroy the enemy's stronghold and then, the tide of battle turned and on the verge of victory, you disappear from the field of battle?"

Falcon had shouted his voice red raw, standing on that hill, sword in hand. Caixa waved the ragged cross of Our Lady of All Worlds, taking up Falcon's rallying cry in her own tongue. The destruction of Nossa Senhora da Varzea held the army of the City of God in thrall. Many Guabirú were on their knees in the bloody mud, rosaries folded in their hands. Some had already fled the field of battle. The Portuguese regulars faltered, conscious of how grossly they were outnumbered. And the water was running, away from the feet of the soldiers, eddying around the bodies of the dead, draining from the trenches in fast-running streams and little torrents, flowing out from under the beached canoes.

"At them!" A lone cry, then the last of the quilombo's men, red and black, came over the crest, arms beating, war-clubs, swords, captured bayonets waving, all roaring, all cheering. Caixa was swept up, Our Lady of All Worlds flying over their heads; then Falcon was caught up and carried away. The Portuguese formed defensive lines, but as the counterattack crashed into them a second wave of warriors broke from the varzea, brushed past the dazed Guabirú, and piled into their rear. Tribe won out; the vacillating Guabirú, seeing the charge of their liberated brothers, took up their weapons and joined the attack. Falcon glimpsed a figure in Jesuit black at the forest's edge. The Portuguese lines broke; the men fled for the gunboats. The Iguapá gave chase, slashing and clubbing at the soldiers as they tried to run their big canoes into deeper water. Now the women and children were coming down the hill, the women executing the wounded, the children picking the bodies clean. The flame of battle was snuffed out. Falcon rested on his sword, weary to the marrow, sickened by the slaughter under the dark eaves of the flood forest. None of those men would ever see São José Tarumás again. In that cold understanding was a colder one: Falcon would never see Paris again, never tease Marie-Jeanne in the Tuileries, never again climb the Fourvière with his brother Jean-Baptiste. His world would now be green and mold, water and heat and broken light, mists and vapors, and the flat, gray meanders of endless rivers. Canoes and bows and creatures heard but seen only in glimpses, a world without vistas, its horizon as distant as the next tree, the next vine, the next bend in the river. A vegetable world, vast and slow.

Luis Quinn prodded again at his smudge fire. "Have you thought what you will do at the City of God?"

"Destroy it." He saw surprise flicker on Quinn's face.

Then the Jesuit said, "Yes, of course. It is too big, too vulnerable. Break them up, send them off into the forest. How long do you think you can hold off the bandeirantes?"

"A generation with luck. It is the diseases that will destroy the red man before any slave-takers."

"All men are helpless before their legends, but do this for me if you can: disabuse that story that I will come again and take them to the New Jerusalem."

The main body of the fleet was passing now, families and groups of friends, nations and tribes, all riding the turbulent water through the rags of mist; children in tiny frail skins of bark, peccaries and pacas in bamboo cages loaded onto rafts, the sacred curupairá frogs in their terracotta pots, sacks filled with what manioc could be scavenged from the twice-ruined fields. The crazy yellow bill of a toucan tied to a perch in the prow of a family canoe was a splendid mote of color. It had taken many days to portage past the falls, the canoes slid on vines down slick clay slides, the terrified livestock lowered in cages or slings, the people winding down the paths, treacherous with spray, hacked from the stub of the dam, still an impressive barrage across the Rio do Ouro.

A raft of watercraft had now built up behind the flume, the gray river black with them as one by one they entered the white water and made the run between the two boulders. Some recognized the Mair on his rock and raised their paddles in salutation as they passed. Behind them the prison-rafts negotiated the run, the Guabirú guarded by the swivel-guns of the captured Portuguese war canoes. They might ransom their lives by negotiating a union of cities: *Cidade Maravilhosa* with war-weakened *Cidade de Déus*.

"As you rightly say, we are helpless before our legends," Falcon said, for he was no longer Aîuba, the yellow-head, the Frenchman, but protector of the City of Marvels, the zemba; and Caixa, war hero, the Senhora da Cruz, standard-bearer of the new nation.

"I will return as often as is safe," Quinn said. "I am still a novice in this; there are disciplines and arts of defense of which I know nothing. It is a war, but mine has always been a martial order."

Warm gray drizzle gusted in Falcon's face. He blinked and opened his eyes on a kaleidoscope. Each rock, each tree, each bird and wisp of mist, Luis Quinn and his stick and fire, were shattered into a thousand reflections that seemed to lie behind the objects they mirrored and at the same time beside, each adjacent to every other image, yet differing in greater or lesser detail. Even as he struggled to comprehend what he was seeing, the vision was lifted from him.

"It can be manipulated," Quinn said. "I am less than a novice in this compared to some walkers of the worlds; I possess enough skill to share my vision."

"This chaos, this uncertainty and clamor of the eyes, how can you ever know what is real and what is false? How can you ever find your way back to the true world?"

"They are all true worlds, that is the thing. We live in the last whispered syllable of time, dreams within dreams. Our lives, our worlds, have been lived a thousand, ten thousand times before. The Order believes that we must dream on, that all else is cold and death. But some believe that we must wake, for only then will we see a morning. For though our lives have been lived ten thousand times, our world reborn time after time after time, in every rebirth there is a flaw, an error, something copied imperfectly. A trick of the enemy, if you would have it. In our world, our times, that flaw is the curupairá, a window on the plethora of worlds and the reality that lies behind it, and thus our hope."

The greater party of the Cidade Maravilhosa had passed down the white-water gut; now the children, grinning and wet in their little skimming pirogues, took to the run. They waved to Caixa; she stood fast, the cross of Our Lady of All Worlds gripped in her wounded fist. Falcon shook his head.

"I cannot believe in such a world."

"The world persists whether you believe it or not." Quinn rose. "I must be getting on now. They are waiting for me." He dipped his head toward the forest edge, dark and dripping. Falcon imagined he saw two women standing there in the dim, one a white woman with a head of curling golden hair, the other of an Asiatic cast and complexion, her hair a dark red. A black man waited under the eaves of the forest. All wavered like mist on the edges of Falcon's perception; then he picked his way over the stones to the shore. When he looked back only the smoldering fire remained.

The Iguapá nation had passed, the children's boats melted into the mist. Caixa had returned the cross to its figurehead place in the canoe; the paddlers pushed out. Waitacá gave a cry; an object running the gut. For an instant Falcon thought it was a capsized canoe, a great war boat. It cleared the run into slack water. The paddlers hauled it in. An angel face, blank yet smiling, gazed up at the fast-running gray mist. Its hands held a three-bladed sword; an angel fallen from the pinnacles of Nossa Senhora da Varzea. Falcon pushed it out into the stream, and the rippling water running fast and chattering over the stones took it and carried it away.

GLOSSARY

Abiá: Uninitiated novice.

Agogô: Twin-horned metal percussion instrument used in candomblé and capoeira.

Aîuri: Tribal council.

Alabé: First drummer and song leader; male office in candomblé.

Aldeia: Missionary Indian village, usually Jesuit.

Alva: Skin-color descriptor: pure white, considered rare in Brazil.

Amaci: Herbal infusion used for purification.

Assentamento: Assemblage of objects, herbs, and water fed and venerated as the conjunction of a person and orixá.

Axé: Transformative power: magic, the force that makes things happen.

Baiana: From the state of Bahia, latterly come to mean the quasi-traditional costume of women from Salvador.

Baile: "Dance," used in Rio in the sense of an impromptu street sound-system party, giving rise to the popular carioca genre of "baile-funk." Constantly evolving.

Bairro: Official city district.

Barracão: Main ceremonial room of the terreiro.

Bateria: The percussion section of a samba school

Bauru: Paulistano hot ham-and-cheese sandwich, often in sweet bread.

Berimbau: Stringed instrument of African origins, a bow attacked to a resonator gourd, used in capoeira.

Bicha: Literally "bitch," but used as "queen."

Bolar: To "roll" in the saint—a spontaneous possession trance and common precursor to initiation as an iâo.

Branca-melada: Skin-color subtype. Honey-colored.

Caboclo: Mixed Indian/white, very much an Amazonian underclass. The term is mildly derogatory in contemporary Brazil. See also *mameluco*.

Cafezinho: "Small coffee," served strong, small, sweet, and on the go.

Caiçara: Riverside slave stockade.

Camarinha: Inmost, holiest chamber in a terreiro, reserved for the mae do santo and her consort. Also, in colonial Brazil, a town council.

Candomblé: Afro-Brazilian religion based around the veneration of orixás.

Captaincy: Division of Colonial Brazil; a segment of land bordered by two lines that ran parallel to the equator inland until they struck the Line of Tordesilhas, the demarcation between Portuguese and Spanish territories. Ruled by a donatory.

Catadores: Informal garbage collectors.

CBF: The Brazilian Soccer Confederation, the sport's governing body.

Chopperia: Bar selling draft beer.

Cidade Maravilhosa: "Marvelous City"; also, Rio's city "anthem."

Conselho Ultramarino: The crown council that ran colonial Brazil.

Corda vermelha: "Red cord"; the highest level of capoeira, analogous to a black belt in other martial arts disciplines.

Cor-de-canela: Cinnamon-colored: one of 134 skin types recognized and delineated in Brazil.

Crente: "Believer"—member of any one of Brazil's many evangelical Christian sects.

Dende: Palm tree whose fruit and oil are important in food offering to the orixás.

Descanso: "Chilling" on arrival at the terreiro—cooling the head.

Doces: Cakes, sweets. Cake is commonly served for breakfast in Brazil.

Donatory: Quasi-feudal fief holder of a colonial Brazilian captaincy.

Ebó: Offering of sacrifices to orixás.

Ebomi: Terreiro elder, initiated for more than seven years.

Egbé: Community based in a terreiro.

Ekedi: A usually female terreiro officer who does not trance but aids those ridden by the orixás.

Engenho: A sugar mill, including the land, buildings, slaves, and animals that worked it.

Entrada: Slave-taking expedition.

Enxofrada: Skin-color subtype of pallid yellow, jaundiced.

Escaupil: Kapok-padded leather or cloth armor worn by bandeirantes, considered impervious to shot.

Exu: Lord of the crossroads and entrances, messenger between gods and humans, dynamic principle. Often found at the entrance to the terreiro, and characterized as a typical Rio malandro.

Farofa: Manioc flour, often fried in butter for a nutty flavor.

Favela: Unofficial Brazilian shantytown.

Fazenda: Country estate for coffee or sugar, or a cattle ranch.

Feijoada: Great dish of Rio, a long-simmered cassoulet of pork bits with Brazilian sausage and other thrifty cuts. In Rio, always made with feijãos (black beans), though pinto beans are commonly used in the rest of Brazil.

Feitor: Trader or small industry owner; "factor."

Fidalgo: Portuguese knightly class.

Furação: Hurricane.

Furo: A cross-channel between two main river channels.

Futebol: the beautiful game, *real* football. Known in the United States as soccer.

Futsal: Five-a-side soccer played in a walled arena with a smaller, heavier, ground-hugging ball. Very fast, very popular, very good.

Gafieira: Dance hall/public dance. Paulistano equivalent of a carioca baile.

Gatinha: Young vivacious woman.

Gelosias: Wooden shutters on the upper windows of colonial houses.

Guaraná: Native Brazilian berry with high levels of caffeine, made into a series of stimulant products, including very popular, very sweet soft drinks.

Ianques: Literal transliteration of "Yankees."

Iâo: Initiate of a typical syncretist Afro-Brazilian religion.

Igapó: Terrain occasionally flooded by a river.

Jacaré: The cayman.

Jogo: "Game" or match of capoeira. Unlike other martial arts, one "plays" capoeira, emphasizing its street-smart, malandro aesthetic.

Kibe: Delicious deep-fried meatballs of Lebanese extraction, often found at breakfast.

Ladeira: Steep "ladder" like alley in a favela. Usually traversable only on foot or by moto-taxi.

Lanchonete: Lunch-stand/small café.

Lavrador de cana: Small-scale colonial cane-grower, owning at the most half a dozen slaves.

Lingua geral: "General language"; a simplified version of the languages of the Tupi peoples used as a universal tongue. In eighteenth-century Brazil it was more widely spoken than Portuguese.

Loira: White with blond hair.

Maconha: Marijuana.

Mae do santo: Candomblé priestess.

Malandragem: The entire capoeira philosophy of malicia and jeito (qv) as a theory of life.

Malicia: Capoeira term meaning "street cunning/warrior smarts"—the ability to see and take an unfair advantage if one is presented.

Maloca: Multigeneration Indian house.

Mameluco: Alternative expression for caboclo, usually in military service.

Moqueça: Bahian (usually seafood) dish based around coconut milk and dende.

Morbicha: Headman of a village.

Morena-fechada: Very dark, almost mulatta.

Morro: Steep hill characteristic of Rio.

Mulatinho: Lighter-skinned white-negro.

Orixá: A god, force of nature, divine ancestor, archetype—all of these and subtly much more; the expression of the divine in Bahian candomblé.

Pae do santo: Candomblé priest.

Pão de queijo: Cheese-bread. A Brazilian obsession.

Paulista: Inhabitant of São Paulo (state).

Paulistano/a: Inhabitant of São Paulo (city).

Patúa: Amulet worn to ward against evil spirits in capoeira.

PCC: Main Paulistano criminal gang. In Rio the favelas are divided between the ADA (Amigos dos Amigos) and the CV—Commando Vermelho, or Red Command.

Peças: Literally "pieces"; old colonial term for slaves.

Pelourinho: Slave whipping post, also that area of Salvador in which it was set up.

Pernambucano: From the state of Pernambuco in northeastern Brazil.

Pichação: Tag graffiti; in Brazil usually done with a paint roller.

Pistoleiro: Hired gunman.

Preto: Black—as in color or person. Racial terms are used more freely and with less political freight in Brazil than in the north.

Puta: Whore, most commonly used in the popular sense of "bitch."

Reconçavo: The early-settled area around the Bahia de Todos os Santos, the heart of colonial Brazil.

Reducione /reduction: A group of native villages or aldeias grouped into a working collective under Jesuit authority.

Réveillon: Mass beach ceremony in Rio at New Year when flowers are offered to Yemanja. Possibly even more popular than carnaval, certainly less commercialized.

Roda: The circle within which capoeira takes place.

Rodovia: Expressway.

Rodoviaria: Bus station.

Sampa: Paulistano name for their city.

Seleção: The Brazil international soccer team.

Sertão: The semiarid region in northeastern Brazil.

Soldado: Soldier—in the gangster sense.

Taipa: Brazilian mud adobe.

Tanga: Originally a triangle of fabric to cover the genitals of either sex, now a bikini style.

Telenovela: Insanely poplar, insanely badly made, and insanely trashy über-soap; the mainstay of Brazilian television.

Terra firme: High forest almost never flooded.

Terreiro: "Church" or temple of candomblé and umbanda—usually a converted urban or suburban house within a sacred enclosure.

Travesti: Transvestite.

Uakti: Legendary Amazonian forest monster.

Umbanda: Rio/São Paulo remix of Bahian candomblé, usually practiced by whites.

Vaqueiro: Cattle rancher.

Varzea: Flood-plain zone of a river, regularly flooded.

Yemanja: Yoruban deity; "Mother whose children are like fishes," absorbed into candomblé as a sea-goddess, who is venerated in a (recent) Mass celebration on the beaches of Rio at New Year.

THANKS

Daniela Prodohl, Paulo Prodohl, and Cleusa Nascimento for help with the Portuguese and rowdy arguments over doces on fine points of idiom. Any egregious errors are entirely my own.

Zack Appleton for assistance with biofuels.

Heidi Hopeametsa and Syksy Rasanen for lunch, capoeira, and physics.

SELECTED READING

The intellectual godfather of this book is David Deutsch's *The Fabric of Reality*. A few years old, but one of the most intellectually thrilling books I have read.

Books in English about Brazil are surprisingly hard to find: there are ten times as many about Cuba, a country you could lose in the Itaipu Dam, as there are about Brazil. Nevertheless, here are a few volumes I found special.

John Hemming: *Red Gold.* Peerless, beautiful, and grim, this is the definitive history of the Brazilian Indians.

David G. Campbell: *A Land of Ghosts.* A beautifully written, humane account of the ecology and peoples of western Amazonia.

Robert M. Levine and John J. Crocitti: *The Brazil Reader.* Invaluable for the 134 types of skin color alone.

Euclides da Cunha: *Rebellion in the Backlands* (*Os Sertões*). Classic, stunning story of the nineteenth-century Canudos uprising and its brutal suppression.

Alex Bellos: *Futebol.* The *Guardian*'s Brazil correspondent has produced the best book about the beautiful game in Brazil and the essential guide about how to be Brazilian. I freely admit sampling his definitive account of the Fateful Final. Not a dull page in it.

Peter Robb: *A Death in Brazil.* Fascinating journalistic study of political corruption in the northeast, but also a history, a travel book, and a cookbook as well.

THE PLAYLIST FOR *BRASYL* CONTAINS

Siri: "No Tranco"

Suba: "Tantos Desejos" (Nicola Conte remix)

Samba de Coco Raizes de Arcoverde: "Godê Pavão"

Acid X: "Uma Geral"

Bebel Gilberto: "Tanto Tempo"

Suba: "Na Neblina"

Fala: "Propozuda R'n'Roll"

Salomé de Bahia: "Taj Mahal" (Club Mix)

Céu (feat. Pyroman): "Malemôlencia"

Milton Nascimento: "Travessia"

Carlinhos Brown/Mestre Pintodo do Bongo: "Ai"

Bebel Gilberto: "Sem Contenção" (Truby Trio remix)

Mylene: "Nela Lagoa"

Tijuana: Pula

Carlinhos Brown: "Água Mineral"

Pagode Jazz: "Sardinha's Club"

Suba: "Você Gosta"

Bonde Das Bad Girls: "Montagem Skollboll"

Suba: "Abraço"

Milton Nascimento: "Cio da terra"

ABOUT THE AUTHOR

IAN MCDONALD is the author of many science fiction novels, including *Desolation Road*; *King of Morning, Queen of Day*; *Out on Blue Six*; *Chaga*; *Kirinya*; and *River of Gods*. He has won the Philip K. Dick Award, the Theodore Sturgeon Award, and the BSFA Award, been nominated for a Nebula Award and a World Fantasy Award, and has several nominations for both the Hugo Award and the Arthur C. Clarke Award. The *Washington Post* called him "one of the best SF novelists of our time." He lives in Belfast, Northern Ireland.

"Brazil
is not a
serious country"
Charles de Gaulle